forever FLAMES

KAYLENE WINTER

Sensitivity Statement

Forever Flames explores both the light and dark sides of family and love. Within its pages are depictions of difficult themes, including addiction, homophobia, and the lasting impact of growing up in a volatile household. These elements are not included for shock value. They are woven carefully into the narrative to reflect the challenges the characters face and to shape the choices they make.

The story follows characters who must confront painful pasts, generational wounds, and deep personal struggles. Through these moments, they grow, heal, and redefine what family, trust, and love mean to them. Every difficult subject is handled with care and respect, always in service of their journey.

At its core, *Forever Flames* is about resilience, the enduring power of love, and the hope of creating something brighter than what was inherited.

PADRAIG

Prologue - Present Day

I CAN'T GET THERE fast enough.

Every red light. Each turtle-speed driver feels like the universe testing my patience. Daring me to slam my foot on the accelerator and tear through the streets until this restless fire burns itself out.

More than a decade of wrong turns, missed chances, swallowed words.

Watching her life unfold from a distance. Sometimes with pride. Mostly with regret so sharp it's split me open.

Now she's in reach again.

Close enough I can almost smell her skin.

I let her slip through my fingers once. Stood there and watched the only woman I've ever loved walk away without a fight. Drifted, while she built something solid without me. A family and children whose faces I've mostly seen from the edges of photographs and stories. I tried to fill the hollow she left with anything else. Women. Music. Noise.

Nothing came close.

Until Rafferty. Becoming his father carved me open. Changed me in ways I never knew possible.

I've poured everything into being a man my son can be proud of. A safe place in a world that almost stole him before he took his first breath. I've found strength I didn't know I had, and I'm never putting my own life on hold again.

It's time to fight for what truly matters.

Every turn brings me closer.

The dark Pacific Northwest night sky bleeds into the windshield, bruised black and blue against the road unspooling in front of me. Trees, buildings, streetlights, none of it matters except my final destination. Every mile drags me deeper into the pull of her.

A war drum pounds in my chest, each beat locking in with the relentless thrum of tires on asphalt. The steering wheel bites into my palms, knuckles bone-white.

She's everywhere.

In the curve of every turn. Haunting the air between heartbeats. Burned into the backs of my eyes.

Every version of us hits in ragged bursts. Our first kiss. The last fight. The night we lost our virginity on her living room couch as we fumbled and clutched and couldn't stop.

The years we mapped each other's bodies like scripture written in sweat and breath. Worshipping and committing every sin.

I remember the taste of salt on her skin and the sweetness on my tongue when I'd bury my face between her thighs. Hear her gasps turn to raw, desperate cries when I fucked her deep and hard. Feel the molten silk of her pussy gripping me as her nails carve my back.

We tore ourselves apart to stitch our souls together, again and again, until the rest of the world ceased to exist and until there was nothing left but us.

Stevie and Padraig.

Forever flames.

Until we weren't.

Holy fuck, the weight of what's about to happen presses harder. I've tried to bury it. All of it.

Failed.

Fear rips through me, sharp and unrelenting. What if the man I've become isn't someone she could love again? The thought is like a fist closing around my heart, but I keep pressing on the gas.

I won't back off. I can't. Not when the thought of losing her twice is like a slow, cruel death.

I take the last corner too fast. Gravel spits under my tires as I pull into her driveway, killing the engine before I've fully stopped. I'm out before the thought's even finished, boots hitting the path in quick, sure strides. I don't know this house, but I know she's here.

I can feel her. Same as I always have.

Wide steps carry me to the porch. My fist hovers. I'm here to close the space between us and seal it shut forever. No matter what it takes.

I knock, sharp and quick, and before I can draw my next breath the door flies open and she's in my arms before I can say her name. Her mouth crashes into mine, wet and fierce, tasting of everything I've been starving for.

We manage to make it inside, the door thudding shut behind us. Her fingers claw at my shirt, shoving it up and over my head. My hands are under her skirt, dragging it up, fisting the fabric around her hips.

She's already got me unzipped, her hand wrapping around my cock like she's claiming it. A broken sound rips from my throat as she strokes me, slow for a heartbeat, then urgent, desperate.

"Now," she gasps against my mouth, and I lift her off her feet, securing my arms under her thighs. Her legs lock around my waist, heat pressed to me through one too many layers.

I shove her panties aside and feel the satiny heat of her pussy against my length. One thrust and I'm buried in her, raw and deep, her back slamming against the wall. She cries out, head thrown back, hands holding on to my shoulders for dear life.

Our eyes lock in utter deja-vu surprise. It's graduation day, all over again.

Like lightning, we move as if we're trying to erase the years apart. Fast, hard, unforgiving. Every roll of her hips drags me deeper, every cry from her lips pulls me closer to the edge.

Her teeth catch my chin. "Don't stop."

I couldn't if I wanted to.

I fuck her like she's mine, like she's always been mine, until there's nothing left between us but heat and breath and the pounding of both our hearts.

A sharp cry rips from her throat as I drive into her, finding the exact spot to make her tremble around me.

"Padraig—" My name breaks apart on her lips, half moan, half plea.

Unrelenting, I drive harder until my pubic bone grinds against her clit, my hands fused to her ass making sure she feels every single inch of me. Her heels dig into my lower back, urging me on, eyes locked on mine like she needs proof I'm real.

This is real.

Our fucking sounds fill the foyer. The slap of skin. My ragged grunts. Her breathy moans. The wet slide of my cock inside her.

Her pussy grips me tight like she's trying to suck me inside her body and never let me go.

"God, you're perfect." I kiss her hard enough to bruise her lips.

She winces, emitting harsh squeaks as she chases the edge. I match her pace, slamming into her until she's gasping, shuddering, and falling apart for me. Her core pulses around my cock when she comes, taking me back to every other time we've done this like it was yesterday.

The memory rips control away.

I lose myself in her, in the years of wanting and the truth that nothing and no one will ever fit me the way she does. With a battle cry of ten thousand warriors, everything I have to give erupts. I hold her against me until she milks every last drop from my body.

After, I brace her trembling body against the wall with my cock buried to the hilt. One hand cradles the back of her head, the other is locked around her hip, keeping her in place.

"This isn't over," I tell her with certainty. "Not now. Not ever. You're mine, Stevie. Always have been. Always will be."

She shakes against me, not from weakness but from everything she's carried this past year. Grief. Fear. Rage. Love.

It pours out in sobs and gasps, her lips desperate against mine. I take it all. Absorb every ounce until it's fused with me and part of the man I am from this moment forward.

"You're strong," I murmur against her chin. "Capable. The most incredible woman I've ever known. I'm going to be worthy of you. I'll fight for you every damn day. I will never let you go again."

Her fingers fist in my shirt like she's trying to anchor herself as her body clenches around me with every ragged breath. I smash my mouth against hers again, driving my vow deeper with every cant of my hips. Locking it in place.

She's home.
And so am I.

One

Fifteen Years Prior

SUNLIGHT CUTS ACROSS THE scarred lockers in long strips, exposing scratches and old tape marks like battle wounds.

Down by the library, somebody blasts Lil' Wayne from their phone. A pack of pimply freshmen argue over some bullshit at the stairwell. A couple of cheerleaders giggle conspiratorially when they emerge from the restroom.

Everything is familiar. It should feel like every other Friday. Except it isn't and never will be again.

As I contemplate how the hell my life has been completely upended, I lean against Stevie Hayes' locker with my arms crossed. I tap my toe to a rhythm I don't recognize at first until I realize it's one of our songs.

One Connor, Liam, and I wrote a few months ago before the accident.

My phone pings. Liam.

Dar, move your arse.

Fuck it. He can wait a goddamn minute.

Stevie's late again. *Always* late. Probably rescuing a freshman who's lost. Or charming the debate teacher into thinking it's his idea to let her drop the class.

She's the kind of girl people sense when she walks into a room. Striking without trying to be. Honey-blonde hair touches her shoulders in messy waves. Her expressive brown eyes always seem like they're holding something back. Her beauty's effortless, grounded in raw creativity and emotional depth.

Without her, I'd never have survived these past couple months. I'll admit it, my longtime crush has turned into something...more.

My phone buzzes again. I don't bother looking because the doors at the end of the hallway bang open and Stevie barrels toward me. A tiny tornado of torn jeans and stubborn light. Her t-shirt's knotted at the waist. She sees me and smiles like I'm the only person in the hallway.

Something knocks sideways inside my chest.

She slips between the couples making out next to me and stops in front of her open locker, breathless and grinning. "Seriously, McGloughlin?"

I push off the metal. "Apparently, you need a lesson in security clearance."

"Security clearance?" She jabs me in the ribs with her books. "You suddenly running some underground locker mafia?"

"Might be a good way to earn a few bucks." I grab her stuff before she drops it, flipping open her notebook. Her notes are chaos but organized in some random highlighted way. "You crack me up with your color-coding."

"Fuck you. It helps me think." Stevie shrugs as she reaches around me to grab her jacket. "Don't mock the process."

I hand the notebook back together with my sketchbook she safeguards for me. Her fingers brush mine.

Static. Electricity. *Something.*

No. Everything.

She's been my—*our*—best friend since we were all seven years old. I haven't told her my feelings have changed but I'm pretty sure she feels the same way.

Liam knows, of course. I don't need to say a word. We're telepathic in a way.

I'm not sure he's happy about this turn of events, though.

"Dar. Let's fuckin' go." Liam's hoodie is half-zipped. His backpack is slung over one shoulder. His hair's a mess. Dark mood on full display.

People always say we look exactly alike. We're twins, so it's true, but also not so much.

Liam's a storm. I'm the calm before.

"Nice of you to show up," Liam mutters, kicking his heel off the bottom of her locker.

Stevie flashes him a too-bright smile. Swings the door shut with her hip like she owns the place. "Aww, you missed me grump-a-lumps."

"We were supposed to peace out last period," he directs his comment toward me.

I glance up at him. "I had chemistry."

"You were going to ditch me?" Stevie rolls her eyes, reaches into her back pocket and pulls out a crinkled letter. "Oh, and by the way. I applied to Wazzu. You're not getting rid of me yet, Liam."

His face doesn't change. Other than the tiniest twitch at the edge of his mouth. He's not mad at her. He's mad at the world and how fucked up everything is.

"Congrats," he sneers.

Undaunted, she turns to me and tugs on my sleeve, eyes shining. "Well?"

"Fuck yeah." Unlike Liam, my heart fills to the brim. Full of a thousand possibilities I can't name. "Let's keep the party going."

"Can we get outta here?" Liam growls.

Stevie flips him off, loops her arm through mine and drags me toward the doors. He follows, slowly. A shadow trailing at the edge.

Outside, Da's original McGloughlin Construction truck with the dented fender sits crooked across the white line. This morning, we were pathetically late so it was more of an abandonment than a parking job.

Stevie yanks open the passenger door and climbs in without hesitation. Middle seat. Liam slides into the driver's seat, slamming the door hard enough to shake the frame. I take my place on the passenger side.

Stevie wiggles to get comfortable, settling back against the seat with my sketchbook jammed between her knees, causing her leg to press against mine. I don't move. Don't breathe. When we turn on to our street, she leans forward to adjust the vent. Her vanilla scent surrounds me.

"Mom made spaghetti." Stevie glances between us. "And brownies. You should come over. Bring the boys."

"Nah, I've got a thing," Liam scoffs as the truck creaks to a stop in front of our house which is next door to Stevie's. "Get the fuck out, kids. I'm taking the truck."

He doesn't wait for approval. The second our feet hit the ground, Liam peels out, gravel pinging the curb.

Stevie stands beside me, arms around my sketchbook like a shield. She's not looking at her house. She's looking at me.

"Dinner?" Her voice tilts. Hopes. "You can draw a bit in peace."

I'm not letting an opportunity to hang out with her slip by. "Aye. First, I should eat with the lads. I'll come over after they're settled."

"Makes sense." Stevie abruptly turns toward the steps to her house.

Shit. Three steps and I'm beside her again. "Wait."

She freezes. Doesn't speak. Doesn't run, either.

I catch her wrist. Light. Careful.

She turns halfway and her brown eyes peer up at me. Before I can stop myself, my lips graze hers. Not soft. Or gentle. Every ounce of pent-up sexual frustration I've kept at bay is unleashed.

Screw the friend-zone. I want Stevie in the fuck-zone.

My tongue twines with hers. My sketchbook hits the porch with a slap when she wraps her arms around my neck. My hands find her waist, then her back, then up into her hair. Every part of her burns into me.

After a moment, I pull away, barely enough to check in on her. "You good with this?"

"Wow. Padraig. Are you sure?" she pants, pink-cheeked, eyes wide.

"Fuck, yeah I'm sure, Stevie. I've been waiting to kiss you forever." I press my forehead against hers. "Since the day you wore the American flag bikini at the Fourth of July barbecue."

She laughs. "Four years ago? We were twelve."

"Well, I'm a slow burner." I kiss her again. Then I step back. "The faster I check on them, the faster I get back."

"Okay." I feel her watching me as I dash up the steps to my house.

Our kiss is buzzing on my lips when I push through the front door. The smell of Ma's beef and barley stew wafts through the air. Shocking. It's been weeks since she's cooked. I didn't expect her to be home. My stomach growls.

Connor's on the couch with the remote, one ankle balanced on his knee, eyes flicking between the match on screen. My oldest brother nods when he sees me.

"You good here for a bit?" I keep my voice low. "I was thinking I'd head to Stevie's. I'll keep my phone on me. If you need—"

Connor shakes his head, quick. "Nah. Go ahead, take the night off. Ma wanted to cook for the wee ones. Da's obviously at the hospital."

"You sure? I'm happy to stay and help out."

"Aye." His tired eyes find mine. "Check in later."

I nod, then head into the kitchen.

Ma's stew is cooling on the stove, dark and rich. Not able to resist, I ladle out a full bowl, tear off a thick slice of soda bread and wolf it down standing by the sink. It's perfect. Filling. Familiar.

I rinse the bowl, set it in the drying rack, and grab my hoodie from the back of the chair. When I pass through the living room again, Connor's fast asleep so I slip out the door to my destination.

The Hayes' porch light glows soft as a candle against the dark. Stevie opens the door before I can knock. Like she was waiting.

She's changed into pajama shorts and an oversized navy sweatshirt I'm almost sure used to be mine. Her hair's up in a messy floof of blonde. Bare feet. No makeup.

The most beautiful girl I've ever seen.

"Hey." She steps aside to let me in.

I walk through like I've done a hundred times, pretending my entire world didn't tilt sideways the second I kissed her.

Her house smells like laundry and brownies and whatever candle her mom always lights after dinner. The TV is on in the living room. I recognize the voices from some British teen show she makes me and Liam watch with her.

We sit close on the couch. Stevie tucks her legs under her, arms looped around her knees. The hem of my sweatshirt falls low on her thighs. I shift beside her. Try not to stare.

Fail.

I know every inch of this room from the crooked family photos to the chipped corner of the coffee table. How her dad's slippers always end up under the recliner. I know every inch of Stevie too. She bites the inside of her cheek when she's nervous, like now. Always hums along with the credits, even when she doesn't realize it.

What I don't know is how to pretend tonight is the same as any other night.

How can I when the air crackles between us?

"The brothers good?" She leans against me.

"Aye." My eyes are fixed on the screen. I have no idea what to do next. "Seamus was reading in his bed. Cillian and Brennan were fighting over the Xbox. Nothing new."

Her hand finds mine. "They're lucky. Having you."

"Bollocks. They need my ma. I'm the stand-in until Da gets home from the hospital." I squeeze her fingers.

"You're more than that." Her head tilts up to mine. "You take care of everyone."

I shift to face her. "I haven't stopped thinking about earlier."

"Me either." She leans forward as her fingers curl into the hem of my shirt.

It starts slow. A kiss meant to ease us into this new skin we're trying on. Then her hands are in my hair, and my arms are around her waist, pulling her into my lap like she belongs there.

"You kiss like you drum." She presses her cheek to mine. "Sexy. Fast, loud, a little chaotic."

Jesus God. My dick fills to capacity.

"I can slow down." I hover my lips against hers.

Her pussy presses against the hard line of my cock through my jeans, and I have to squeeze my eyes shut not to lose it. Her hands slide under my shirt, fingertips gliding up my ribs. My skin tightens, every nerve lit. "I don't want you to. Joni's in her room. Ziggy's playing video games. My parents are already in bed. They won't bother to check on us."

Stevie yanks the sweatshirt over her head, tossing it to the floor without a second thought. Holy fucking shit. I can see the outline of her dusky nipples through her sheer bra.

Good God, man. *Do. Not. Come. In. Your. Pants.*

"Padraig." She unhooks her bra behind her back, letting the straps fall from her shoulders. When it drops to the couch, I forget how to breathe.

Her tits are full and high and perfect with those pink buds puckered tightly into little bullets. Unable to stop myself, I cup her breast and drag my thumb across the peak, then duck my head and close my mouth around it. She gasps and grinds her hips against mine, fisting in my hair.

"I've wanted this forever," she mewls. "Haven't you?"

"Aye." I crash my mouth to hers.

We're a mess after that, fumbling with zippers and buttons. Quietly laughing through our clumsiness until things turn desperate again. She shoves her pajama bottoms down, catching her panties halfway around her thighs, then kicks them off completely.

"Holy fuck." My eyes lock in on her glistening pussy covered by only a wisp of blonde hair.

With only porn to guide me, I kneel between Stevie's legs and drag my tongue through her folds. She's delicious. Sweet. Tangy. My tongue explores everywhere, slow and deep until I find her little clit. Experimenting, I suck on it then flick it with the tip of my tongue until she's panting and shaking. Her thighs clamp around my ears and she moans into the cushion.

"Shhhh—" Her parents might be cool but I don't want to risk them interrupting the single greatest night of my life.

I manage to shove my jeans and boxers down, grabbing the condom I've carried for years. My cock springs free, thick and already leaking. She watches as I tear the wrapper open with shaking fingers and roll it over my length.

Settling between her legs, I guide the tip of my cock to her entrance, pressing in slow and steady.

Her breath catches sharp and I freeze. "Stevie, are you okay? We can stop…"

"No. Go slow. You know it's my first time." She grips my shoulders and urges me on.

"Shit. I'm sorry. It's mine too." I hesitate for a second before I push in again.

Gradually. Inch by inch. Her body takes me, tight and trembling. I have to grit my teeth against the need to rut into her. When I'm buried to the hilt, I cage her upper body with my forearms. "You feel…fuck. Stevie, you feel unbelievable."

"I'm so full. Should you move?" Her nails rake down my back as she shifts her hips, testing the stretch.

Yes. Yes, I should. Careful at first until her quiet moans turn needy. Then faster as her legs hook around me. Her pussy grips my cock on every thrust, wet and hot and fucking perfect.

She comes first, mouth falling open, body arching hard. She says my name like it's the only word that matters. I follow a second later, hips jerking, cock pulsing deep inside the condom.

We stay tangled together, skin slick, hearts thudding.

No fear.

No holding back anymore.

No pretending we were ever meant for anyone else.

Two

One Year Later

AN ENTIRE YEAR OF nonstop practice and we're experts at fucking.

I'm warm. Sticky. Wrecked. His breath is slow and heavy in the curve of my neck. The smell of sweat, old amps, and fresh sex hangs in the air like smoke. My skirt's up around my waist, panties...somewhere. His jeans are halfway down, and my tits jiggle every time his cock hits the magical place deep inside me.

The couch under us groans with every thrust. Padraig roars as he comes, his face contorting in ecstasy.

His chest is pressed to mine when the basement door creaks open.

"Jesus Fucking Christ," Liam snaps, his annoyance slicing into the haze. "Can you two *not* fuck on every surface in the practice room?"

Padraig barely lifts his head from the crook of my neck.

I don't bother with embarrassment. This isn't the first time Liam's caught us and it won't be the last. I tilt my head toward him. "You ever heard of knocking?"

"Uh, I fucking *live* here," he shoots back, marching into the room like we're the problem. "You're corrupting the wee ones. If I can hear everything through the ceiling and through the goddamn floorboards, so can they."

Liam's guitar is slung over one shoulder, dark hair damp from the shower. His t-shirt clings to him half-askew like he got dressed in a rush. He averts his eyes out of respect.

Padraig pulls out and tosses me his flannel. His fingers trail down my thigh as he shifts off me, breath ragged. He grabs his jeans and tugs them on, turning to give me some minute semblance of privacy as I try to cover myself.

"You're early, Dar." Padraig coughs roughly.

"Fuck off. I'm on time. If I didn't know better, I'd think you want me to see your pale, bare ass." Liam waves him off.

"Okay, I'm decent." I get up and sit cross-legged on Liam's amp like a queen reclaiming her throne. "Ready for rehearsal?"

Liam drops his bag with a thud and pretends to focus on tuning his guitar. Padraig locates his drumsticks under a pile of setlists. Takes his place behind the drums, rolls his shoulders and taps the snare like his brother didn't walk in on us.

Again.

"You two are a health violation," Liam grumbles.

I look down at my nails. "Then maybe stop barging in on us. I swear you do it on purpose."

Liam snorts. "The couch is a cesspool of come."

"Worth it." Padraig winks at me. Gives me the *look*. Makes my stomach flip even after the hundreds of times we've fucked. His gaze is hot and steady, like I'm the only thing in the room worth noticing.

It's shocking how perfect we are together. Well, maybe not, considering how long we've been best friends. I'm a safe place for him to escape everything going on in his family and all our other stresses. We mostly hang out. He draws. I read. Fuck when we can.

Graduation is in a couple weeks. College is looming. Real life is coming at us like a freight train.

"Are we actually rehearsing today?" Liam spins one of the tuning pegs with too much force.

Padraig clicks his sticks together. "Aye. Let's run through our set list."

They fall into place. Liam sings and shreds on guitar, Padraig hammers a beat so tight it shakes the ceiling dust loose and adds backing vocals. I sing along out of habit, not thinking, not planning. Muscle memory.

I've been here since the beginning, which was three or four years ago. Nothing's cohesive, but they both enjoy playing even if the wind's out of their sails without Connor.

Four songs in, as if he reads my mind, Liam cuts the song off. "He's never coming back, is he?"

Not a question. A statement. Aimed at no one.

Padraig and I look at each other, not sure what to say.

After a few minutes, Padraig sets his sticks on the snare. "He's working fifteen-hour days. Handling the paperwork for Da. He doesn't have time."

"Aye." Liam toes the ground. "I know. I guess I hoped Da would be back runnin' it by now."

He doesn't look at us when he says it. Doesn't have to.

We all know the truth.

Connor didn't take over because he wanted to. He sacrificed his own dreams so all of us wouldn't have to disrupt our own lives. Playing music is always a reminder for the twins of the unfairness of it all.

"I think you need to embrace the opportunity he's giving you. Have a more positive outlook," I say half under my breath. "Get a manager. Take it seriously."

Padraig perks up immediately. "So you're volunteering?"

"Absolutely not." I shake my head vigorously.

Liam looks up, interest piqued. "Except, you already do everything."

"Yeah, because I'm a sucker who's in love with the drummer. Not the same thing." I pull Padraig's flannel tighter around my body.

Padraig grins. "Ah, she says she loves me."

I throw a pick at him. He dodges, cheesing.

"You two are so fucking annoying." Liam rolls his eyes. "Look. Stevie. You're organized. Bossy. Controlling. Good with people. It's how every great manager starts out."

"Don't use up all your charm at once, dumb ass," I snort.

Padraig sits next to me and wraps his arm around my shoulder. "He's right, you know. You write all our set lists. Give good advice. All you need to do is book more shows like the garage party we played last month."

"My cousin owed me a favor." I throw my hands up in the air.

"It counts." Liam raises an eyebrow. "C'mon. Do us a solid. We can't trust anyone else."

I stare at them both. Their messy black waves. The scratches on Padraig's knuckles from hitting the rim too hard. The way Liam's shoelace is half-untied and he hasn't noticed. They're both brilliant and reckless and a little bit hopeless.

I love them both. Obviously differently. I'm not planning on fucking Liam—ever.

"Fine. I'll help," I acquiesce. "Only until you figure out what the hell you're doing. But, don't call me your manager."

Padraig kisses my cheek. "Sure. If you say so."

"I'm serious, guys. I don't want to spend my life on the road chasing gigs and counting Spotify streams. I have my own plans," I answer honestly.

"You have a great voice, though." Padraig nudges me with his shoulder. "You could sing."

I shake my head. "Stop. I don't want to be on stage. I have no desire to perform."

"When you have a gift," Liam stands in front of me, "you should share it."

"Don't pressure me." I push him away. "Singing's fun. I don't want it to be my job."

"Well, we need to do something. We're flailing." Liam slumps next to us.

I reach for Padraig's sketchbook on the coffee table. Flip to a page covered in messy half lyrics and sketches of potential band logos. "Try focusing on something. Maybe start with where you come from."

They blink in simultaneous confusion.

"You're Irish," I explain. "Not in a touristy 'Kiss Me I'm Drunk' kind of way. From your ma's stories, your entire extended family has generations of grief and grit to draw from. Use it."

Liam frowns like I've grown two heads. "Like what, trad music?"

"Exactly. Except flip it inside out." I lean back on my hands. "Drag it through distortion pedals. Make it burn. Recreate it."

Padraig is stunned. "You think?"

I nod. "I do. It's unexpected, which makes it cool."

The twins look at each other and do their stealth telepathic speaking thing.

Without another word, Padraig returns to his kit and spins his sticks. Liam adjusts his tuning, then tweaks it again. The air changes. Grows sharper.

They start to play again. Sloppier now, but louder. Padraig's tempo pushes too fast, Liam's chords turn sharp at the edges. The whole vibe is more punch than polish.

I don't interrupt. I watch because whatever they're doing isn't perfect by a long shot, but you can *feel* it in your bones.

Padraig throws himself into the rhythm like he's in a cathartic frenzy. Liam's movements are tighter. His shoulders are hunched, teeth clenched. They don't look at each other because they don't need to. They're twins. Tethered. Even when everything in their family is slipping.

As they play, they seem to be exorcising themselves of McGloughlin family secrets. Liam's secrets. Every ounce of sorrow and despair they've been through since Rory got hurt. Chasing. Searching. Reaching.

For what, I'm not sure.

Finally, an hour later, Padraig drops his sticks onto the snare and exhales so hard it turns into a roar. "Fuck, that felt good."

"It was a goddamn mess." Liam grabs a towel from the back of the chair. "A grueling disaster."

Padraig sneers, "You were playing on hyper speed."

"I was following your rhythm." Liam launches the towel at his brother. "You're the goddamn timekeeper."

Padraig tosses it back. "I try to be, when you let me."

I stay where I am, ping-ponging my head between them as they banter. "Neither of you were listening to each other. It felt like you were each trying to outrun feelings you're suppressing."

Padraig wipes his face, eyes narrowing. "What are you talking about?"

"Neither of you want to admit you're scared to leave for school." I look him in the eye. "Not when everything's already changing and neither of you know what to do."

"I'm not scared of shit," Liam snarls.

I hold his stare. "Don't bullshit me. You're scared of *something*."

He doesn't answer. Doesn't deny it, either.

"I'm psyched to go to college." Padraig rubs his hand through his thick waves, breathing hard. "I wonder if we should wait a year, though."

Liam sets his guitar down. "Wait for what? Da to sober up? For Ma to stop pretending she can fix him? For Cillian to suddenly become old enough to run the company so Connor can stop playing the martyr and play with us again?"

"No." Padraig looks at his feet. "I mean... I don't know what I mean."

Liam puts his hand on Padraig's shoulder. "You feel as bad as I do about leaving Connor with this mess."

His words land like a hammer. I glance at Padraig. The guilt in his eyes says it all. I flick my eyes to Liam. He hides it better, but it's there.

Sighing, I stay out of this one. Their family dynamic isn't something I can fix. What I can do is give the twins some relief. I get off my ass and gather their crumpled setlists. Put them in order. Stack the cords. Reset the amp levels.

Liam watches me, confused. "What are you doing?"

"Helping." I fluff the pillows on the couch. "Temporarily."

"Thought you didn't want to manage us." Padraig takes my hand.

I kiss his cheek. "I don't."

"Really?" Liam cocks a brow. "Could've fooled me."

I shoot him a look. "You two are chaos incarnate. At this point, I'm ensuring your survival."

"So what? You're our babysitter now?" Liam chuckles.

"No. I'm the fire extinguisher." I pretend to spray them and grab a marker for the dry erase board.

I erase the drawing of a giant peen with the sleeve of Padraig's flannel and start writing:

<u>SUMMER GOALS</u>
   1. 5 rehearsals/week

   2. Record demo in the practice room (no sex allowed)

   3. Learn three sets of traditional Irish tunes

Padraig and Liam flank me.

"Seriously?" they say in tandem, then look at each other and grin.

I cap the marker. "Yes. Unless you'd rather keep ripping off early 2000s pop-punk and pretend it's edgy."

"I don't hate it." Liam lets the idea sink into his skin.

"Learn some Irish songs and you'll be able to earn money for college by playing in pubs." I tap the whiteboard with the pen. "Meanwhile, start writing. Eventually you'll have your own set of updated original Irish music. Loud. Dirty. Yours."

The brothers don't answer. They stare at the board like it's got answers they didn't know they were looking for. While they stare, slack-jawed, I grab my bra from behind the speaker and head upstairs.

"I thought you weren't managing us," Liam calls after me.

"I said I'd help you until you *get* a manager," I say without turning. "Don't get used to it."

Padraig trails behind me. "Hey," he says once we reach the stairs. I pause. He pulls me toward him and envelops me with his entire body. "You're the only person he trusts besides me right now."

"I know." I settle into his embrace. "You're welcome."

Maureen's frustrated voice rings out from the back bedroom. Low. Tired. We can't hear the conversation, but Rory sounds angry.

Drunk.

Padraig stiffens behind me. The air is stagnant until the door closes again.

"Go," he whispers.

I escape out the back door unspotted.

Immediately feel guilty.

Padraig's stuck there and I'm unable to help the person I love most in the world.

Three

PADRAIG

Graduation Day

LIAM'S ALREADY IN THE passenger seat of the truck when I climb in.

His hair's wet from the shower, an ever-present pout decorates his face. My twin doesn't give a shit about graduation. Case in point: his gown's balled up in the back seat like he ironed it with a punch.

He's doing this for me. And Stevie. Well, and for our mother, who didn't get to see her oldest son graduate last year because of the accident. When I get settled, he lifts his chin in my direction and cranks down the window, letting the morning air cut through the truck's familiar smell—gas, rust, and old fast food.

I start the engine. The truck gives its usual shudder like it might die today, or maybe tomorrow, or maybe never. Our house behind us is motionless. So is Stevie's, she left with her parents over an hour ago to have breakfast with extended family prior to the ceremony.

Ma's wearing a blue wrap dress she saves for weddings and fancy dinners. She'll follow us with the wee lads later. When I left, she was pinning Seamus's tie and refereeing some argument between Cillian and Brennan. Waiting on Connor who had to swing by a job site before the ceremony.

No one mentioned Da. Or if he's coming.

Spoiler: he won't.

Fifteen minutes later, I park in the student lot and we head for the gym.

"Still time to make a run for it," Liam grouses as we pass through the double doors.

I elbow him in the ribs. "Shut up."

"Could be halfway to Portland by now." He shoves me in the other direction.

I throw my arm around his shoulder. "We did it. Ma is so proud of us."

He shrugs. Smiles for real for half a second. Then it's gone. Replaced by the ever-present glower.

Our classmates mill around the gymnasium entrance. When we check in, the freshman volunteer barely glances at us. "McGloughlin, Lime and McGloughlin, Pad-rag? You're in Row M, left side, second group to be called."

Rolling our eyes at the blatant mispronunciations, we follow the crowd into the gym to take our places. Three hundred seniors fidget with caps and cords, hug each other too tight and pretend this doesn't all feel fake.

My attention, of course, is elsewhere. I spot her instantly.

Stevie's across the aisle in the "H" rows, chewing gum and chattering to everyone around her. She has such a quiet confidence. One of the many things I love about her is, unlike me, she knows exactly who she is and makes no apologies.

Like a moth drawn to a flame, she catches me staring and grins. She mouths, "I love you" and blows me a kiss.

My whole body responds. Like it always does.

Stevie may be a wildfire in spirit and harbor a lot of ambition. Underneath it, she's all heart and home. Her dream is to have a noisy kitchen and ten kids underfoot. A big, loud, messy family. Full of love.

It used to be my dream too, to have the kind of life we used to have in my family. Before the accident, our house felt whole. Sunday dinners. Music from every room. Ma humming while she cooked. Da teaching us boys how to wrestle.

The McGloughlin's were unbreakable.

A year and a half ago, it all went to shit when Da got in a terrible car accident. It shattered our foundation and it's hard not to be bitter.

I guess my glasses aren't as rose-colored as Stevie's are.

Though, being in her presence gives me hope I can get back what I've lost. With her. With us.

Eventually...

The ceremony starts, snapping me out of my thoughts. Our principal says something about grit. The valedictorian quotes Rumi. The mic cuts out three times and nobody fixes it. By the time they start calling our names, Liam's dozing and I'm halfway there myself. Until...

"Stevie Hayes."

Her name rings out and my eyes fly open. I sit up taller without meaning to as I watch Stevie stand and throw both arms in the air. She struts toward the stage like it's a runway. The whole gym claps louder, probably because everyone loves her.

Me, most of all.

When she takes her diploma, she turns to wink at me before she disappears behind the curtain. My heart's thudding and I'm grinning like a goddamn love-sick fool.

Liam elbows me and rolls his eyes. "*Jesus.* Do you ever stop eye-fucking her?"

I ignore him and resume my nap. After a million years, we finally hear, "*Liam McGloughlin.*"

My brother stands slowly. Doesn't smile. Doesn't wave. Walks to the stage to a chorus of whoops from the bleachers and winces, as though today is a punishment and not a cause for celebration. He takes the diploma, nods at the principal, then disappears behind the stage curtain.

I turn to see where my family ended up in the stands. Connor's at the edge of the row, in his work clothes. Seamus is practically bouncing in his seat, whispering something to Cillian who looks like he's about to slug him. Brennan is focused on his phone. There's an empty seat beside Ma.

"*Padraig McGloughlin.*"

Stevie's voice cuts through the gym again. "*WOOOOOOOO PADRAIG!*"

I swear I see the principal flinch. Managing to keep steady, I cross the stage. Shake his hand. Take the diploma. Smile for the camera. When I turn, I see Ma with her hands over her mouth, in tears. Seamus and Brennan wave like I won a Grammy. Cillian pretends not to care. Connor nods once, tightly.

No Da. What a fuckin' prick.

Afterward, the entire graduating class explodes onto the football field.

Photos. Shouts. Throwing caps. Horns honking. Parents crying.

Stevie sprints through the chaos, tassel flying behind her like a ribbon. She jumps straight into my arms.

"We're officially done!" She kisses me once, twice. Her mouth's warm and sweet. My heaven.

I don't know how I got this lucky.

Lucinda, Stevie's mom, materializes in full modern-hippie glory. She wears a long, silk caftan in swirls of coral and green, huge sunglasses that probably cost more than my drum kit, and exudes a warm, grounding energy.

"My boys," she coos, hugging both Liam and me at once like we belong to her too. "We're so proud."

Liam shifts under her arms but doesn't pull away.

Stevie's psychologist dad, Hank walks up in shorts, a Hawaiian shirt and Birkenstocks over ankle socks. "Tacos are going to be epic. Cakes are in the fridge. We've got both chocolate and lemon, because someone," he nods at Stevie, "threw a fit about it."

"It was *not* a fit. I was communicating a respectful request." She smiles at her dad affectionately.

"Is the whole clan coming?" Hank asks. "Liam you'll be there, right?"

My twin doesn't answer, just raises an eyebrow.

Hank nods and looks away. He knows all about my da. They used to be best friends, and now...

Liam turns and walks away. Heads to the truck.

"I'll make sure he shows up," I assure Stevie's dad.

She squeezes my hand. "Don't sweat it. He'll come if he wants to."

The second I open the door to the Hayes' house, I'm hit with an overwhelming feeling of comfort.

Warmth. Color. Music that's somehow both too loud and exactly right. The Hayes' house has the same bones as ours—massive wood beams, built-in cabinets, stained-glass transoms. The similarities end there. Our homes feel like different planets. Unlike the gloom hovering over our place, over here it's as if someone left the doors unlocked and the sun moved in.

Stevie swirls through the open-plan living room with a champagne flute in one hand and a basket of rolled-up horoscopes in the other. A giant cut-glass bowl of limeade sits on the entry table, flanked by plates of edible flower cookies, like it's a damn fairy tale picnic.

Her little sister, Joni, is crouched on the arm of the couch, braiding neon thread into someone's hair. Their younger brother Ziggy streaks through the hallway in a Bowie tee and no shoes, holding a glitter wand and yelling something about stardusting the graduates for good luck.

I blink. Take it all in.

In the dining room, Ma and Lucinda arrange platters of food. They move like the old friends they are, lining up Hank's slow-roasted pork tacos in neat rows. Liam's crouched near the windowsill with our wee brothers and a plate full of food. All of them heads down, chewing like they haven't eaten in days.

I load up my own plate and barely breathe between bites.

Stevie materializes beside me and nods toward Liam who's helping Cillian with his taco. "See? He can't stay away. I'm glad."

"Yeah, me too." I pop the last bite into my mouth.

For the next half hour, we move through the party side by side, fielding congratulations and hugs from her extended family and a bunch of neighborhood friends.

Connor shows up after sunset, showered and clean-shaven with his shirt actually tucked in. He hands me a box, already wrapped, no explanation. Inside are studio sticks. Weighted. Perfectly balanced. The kind pros use.

"This is part of it." He claps my shoulder. "Your new kit's already set up in the practice room. I got Liam the Strat he's been coveting."

My throat locks. As thoughtful as his gift is, it feels like a concession. He's throwing in the towel on his musical dream when I thought he'd play with us always. It was supposed to be the three of us and now he's giving up.

I pull him into a fast, quiet hug and feel the weight of his expectation. Support. Of being believed in. Stevie slips her arm around my waist and leans her head against my shoulder. Looks up at me and gives me the eyebrow waggle.

Fuck yeah. We need to disappear for a while and have our own *private* celebration.

Stealthily, we slip out the back door toward the thick ivy hedge dividing our property. A shortcut between our houses we've used a million times. Never for this purpose, though, come to think of it.

Once through, we're behind our garden shed. Stevie's already lifting her dress.

"Oh shit—" I groan.

She's completely bare.

Winking, she grabs my shirt and yanks me toward her, mouth crashing against mine. No pretense.

"You trying to kill me?" I gasp when she unzips my slacks.

Her fingers wrap around my cock. "No, stupid. Obviously, I'm trying to fuck you."

I hiss through my teeth, bracing one hand on the fence as she strokes me and drags my crown against her slit. She's soaked. Warm. Ready. I grip her hips and lift her, line myself up and push inside in one slow, deep thrust.

Stevie arches back, hands clinging to my shoulders. She moans low in her throat, tipping her head up to the sky. "God, Padraig. I can feel every inch of you."

I start to move. Sharp, rhythmic, urgent. Her dress is bunched around her waist and she grinds against me, matching every thrust, every ragged breath.

"You're mine," she pants.

"Aye." My voice catches. "Since the second I met you."

Her hips jolt when I reach between us to rub her clit and her thighs tense around my waist. Within seconds her whole body pulls tight, pulsing around me as she comes hard, mouth open in a silent cry.

I thrust deep, heat rushing through me as I spill inside her.

Our chests are heaving with exertion, so I lean her back against the shed, my hands gripping her ass. Eventually I lower her down. She's gorgeous. Lips plump from our kisses. Sex hair. Eyes bright with mischief and love.

"Padraig, I know things are rough at home." Stevie caresses my cheeks between her soft palms. "I hope you remember the love we have is special. It never flickers or fades. It'll always burn steady, even when everything else goes dark. You're my forever flame." She kisses my cheek. "I'm heading back over. Follow me in a couple minutes."

Touched, I fight back tears as she ducks back through the hedge. A few minutes later, after I'm tucked and zipped, I follow. Join her at the drinks table like nothing happened and pour myself a limeade. Take a long sip.

Stevie snuggles up against me and lowers her voice. "My favorite memory of tonight will be right now. Standing here in the middle of our friends and family with your come running down my thigh."

"Jesus." I shove my hands in my pockets to hide the renewed bulge in my slacks. "You gave me another woody."

She bites her straw. "Don't tempt me to blow you in front of our friends and family."

I lean in and drop my voice to match hers. "If you're gonna say sexy-ass shit don't be surprised if I take you for round two in the garage. Bend you over the truck and christen your ass."

"Promise?" She licks her lips.

I kiss her temple. "You're killin' me."

We manage to blend back into the party. As far as I know, nobody missed us.

Until I notice—too late—the truck's not out front.

Liam's gone.

"Are you worried?" Stevie threads her fingers through mine.

I pull her into my side. "About Liam?"

"Well...yeah. But also, college. Leaving. Growing up."

I glance at her. "I'm scared of all of it," I admit. "Except one thing."

She lifts her brow.

"You."

She leans up and kisses me. Slow, aching and gentle as the moonlight. Then pulls back, searching my face. "Say it again,"

"You," I repeat. "You're the one thing I'm never scared of."

She melts against me. Nods. "Same. So, he left?"

"Didn't say a word."

She frowns. "He okay?"

"No." I pause. "Maybe."

Stevie leans her head on my shoulder. "He'll come around."

I want to believe her.

He's always searching, like there's a part of him missing.

All I can hope is for him to have what we have now.

If he'll let himself.

Four

STEVIE

A Few Months Later

LIAM PACES. AGAIN.

Bare feet on the scuffed dorm floor. Arms crossed. Fists flexing like there's a ticking clock he can't tune out.

I'm sitting cross-legged on Padraig's unmade bed, trying to finish my anthropology reading. Padraig is sprawled sideways in his desk chair, one socked foot braced against the bedframe. He's watching his brother with affection and amusement.

This scene has played out a million times since we started college. Every day is about the same. Padraig and I wake up and fuck. Get ready and go to class. Meet up with Liam for lunch then head back here to study or blow off studying.

Liam's usually prowling for a hookup by the time Padraig and I go to bed. Either way, we fuck until we pass out.

Repeat.

An idyllic freshman year, I won't lie.

It's exactly like it's always been with the three of us—only better. We're free. No parents. No rules. I've essentially moved into the boys' dorm room here in Rogers Hall. Padraig even cleared out his dresser and closet for my clothes.

My actual roommate, Bailey, seems grateful to have our room to herself. She's cool. Sharp and focused on her studies. Every so often she hangs out with the three of us and, fortunately, seems to be immune to Liam's devastating charm.

She's in the minority.

Halfway through our freshman year and Liam's already achieving legendary fuck-boy status on campus. He oozes sexuality and has zero shame. He doesn't hide the way he looks at anyone. Guys. Girls. Any combination thereof. It's all on the table now.

College cracked something open in him and, for once, he's not pretending. Not running. Not afraid of who he is.

It's kind of beautiful, actually.

Suffice it to say, nothing happened on the music front last semester unless you count two half-assed jam sessions. It's all gonna change though. Connor's parting words when we drove off were prolific.

"Make it count."

I don't think Connor meant it as pressure but, on the other hand, he's the one paying for all of this. Tuition. Food. Housing. Gas. Not to mention the brand new instruments the twins received as graduation presents.

His parting words kickstarted something. Suddenly, both of them are committed. Last year's procrastination has been left behind in Seattle.

I'll never say this out loud, but I can't help but wonder whether it's *their* dream. Or, at least, Padraig's dream.

Or, if it's a debt.

Padraig loves his brothers so much I worry about him going with the flow. From how much he's been loving his art classes, I'm pretty sure his passion lies elsewhere, but he can make his own decisions. I'm sure he'll work it out in his own time.

"What's the plan, Stevie?" Liam snaps, turning toward me. "You said this gig has a real setup. Mics? Amps? Or is it some guy with a set of bongos and a dream?"

Padraig shoots him a look. "Dar, fuckin' chill for five seconds. She hasn't had a chance to give us the details."

"Meh. I'm used to his snarky ass." I lift a shoulder. "To answer your question, it's a *real* party house with decent bands. If you guys want to get into the mix, we need to start showing up. Meet people. Mingle. Find a singer."

"I'm out all the fucking time. I already *know* what's out there." Liam massages his temple. "Shite."

"You're exhausting." I drag a highlighter through a passage in my textbook. "You're gonna scare off every singer before you even hear them."

Liam flops onto his back dramatically. "We wouldn't have to find one if *someone* joined us."

He doesn't look at me, but the jab lands right between my ribs.

"Liam, for the last fucking time, I'm *not* front-woman material." I bite my pen. "You need someone with *way* more ego. Someone who wants to live on the road. I don't want that life."

Padraig tosses a drumstick at Liam's shin. "Stevie's helping us get our shit together. We have to do our part."

"Yeah, right." Liam snorts. "Says the guy who'd rather spend all his free time fucking her instead of practicing."

I raise a brow. "Disrespectful. I'm right here."

"You want to talk disrespectful? I'm in the next fucking bed." Liam lewdly cants his hips. "Oh, oh, oh, yes. Right there."

"So wear headphones. Or, fuck one of your fan-club members." I stick my tongue out at him.

"Where do you think I am every night?" Liam grumbles.

Padraig's mouth twitches like he wants to smirk but doesn't quite get there. It's one of the many things I love about him. He lets me fight my own battles. Even with his twin.

"Maybe you should choose more wisely." Padraig palms my thigh.

"Oh, I'm picky." Liam stands in front of the mirror, fussing with his hair.

"Yeah, right. For someone so picky, is there anyone you *haven't* fucked on campus?" I roll my eyes.

He throws a sock at me. "You wound me, Hayes."

"You'll live." I pull on one of Padraig's sweatshirts and hop off the bed. "I'm only pointing out your reputation's practically mythic at this point."

Liam shrugs into a denim jacket. "It's college. I'm exploring. Maybe the two of you should try it sometime."

"Don't be an ass." Padraig laces up his boots. "Let's go. You might actually enjoy yourself."

"Doubt it," Liam drones, sliding on a black beanie.

I take point, leading them down the narrow stairwell of the dorm. The party's ten blocks off-campus, in a rickety rental. It probably used to be a frat house before it got excommunicated.

Padraig grips my hand as we approach the house. "Thanks for arranging this."

"No worries. Rumor has it, the lead guitarist once opened for Modest Mouse," I offer helpfully.

It's enough to get Liam's interest, even if he pretends otherwise, as evidenced by how quickly he bounds up the steps to the front door.

The porch sags under the weight of us. Inside it's like a dive bar. Sticky floors. Thrift-store couches shoved against the walls. Strands of dying Christmas lights cast everything in a weirdly colorful haze. Someone set up the amps in the corner and cables snake along the ground through half-crushed beer cans and a piles of discarded pizza boxes.

Bass pulses through the floorboards like a second heartbeat. Bodies cram into every corner. Dudes wearing thrifted leather and scuffed boots. Women in low-cut tops and glitter eyeshadow. It smells horrible. Like weed mixed with sour beer and body odor.

A beach ball bounces off Liam's shoulder. He doesn't flinch.

Padraig grins and slings his arm casually around my back. His fingers brush my waist. "You sure this isn't a rave?"

"Wrong kind of bassline." I lean up for a kiss.

He cups my face and plants one on me in the middle of a room full of strangers. I melt against his chest, content and happy.

It's funny. Even in a new environment, I'm always comfortable when I'm with the two people I'm closest to in the world. Bailey once asked me how I ever chose Padraig over Liam. Which is funny to me. Obviously, I love them both deeply. Liam burns hot and fast. Even as a kid, he was sharp edges and swagger. Dangerous. Unpredictable.

Padraig, on the other hand, has *always* been mine, Quieter. Steadier. Persistent. Safe. Our friendship morphed slowly from childhood playmates to best friends.

"For someone who didn't want to come, he's diving right in." Padraig gestures to Liam, who's in front of the makeshift stage where a girl with ink-black hair is yowling into a mic.

Her voice is scratchy in a way people mistake for edgy. It works, though. The guitarist's decent. Drummer's loud and showy, all biceps. Padraig and I hover at the edge of the room. He analyzes the band with the same hyper-focused intensity he uses to ace his exams. Or, figure out song structures.

"They're decent." Padraig rubs his chin.

I nod. "They've got a look."

"A lot of style over substance." He scrunches up his nose. "I'm not a fan of the arrogance."

"They're tight. And confident enough to fill a room like this," I counter.

"Okay, fair." Padraig nods, soaking it in.

Liam looks like he wants to be on stage more than he wants to breathe. He takes it all in, scanning the room like it's a battlefield. Sizing up the soundboard. Calculating what he'd do different.

He wants this. To have his own moment.

Padraig leans down, his breath warm against my ear. "I love to see him inspired. It makes me happy."

He'd never say it, but I feel it. Something's cracked open in him too. Pure enthusiasm. Radiating off him like static. He's not watching, he's wanting.

Maybe I was wrong earlier. This could be his calling.

God, I'm glad I dragged them here. This party surely isn't about impressing anyone. It's about giving them a kick in the arse to show up. Get seen. They're two guys with real talent who were dealt a shitty card, but have a wonderful big brother who's given them a second chance.

The least they can do is try to build something.

I have no problem helping them out for now. At least until they get their shit together. Or, until it stops making sense.

"Maybe I'll talk to their merch girl." I spot a makeshift table with a couple of t-shirts hanging from nails in the wall. "Figure out who booked this gig."

Padraig glances at me. His mouth doesn't move, but his eyes say it all. This is what he looks like when he's grateful

Go for it.

I'm about to make a move when Padraig's hand slides over mine. I look back at him. "Glad we came?"

He nods. "Yeah. Feels like the start."

He's right.

It is.

This is the beginning of everything.

Five

PADRAIG

Six Months Later

IT'S HARD TO BELIEVE Stevie, Liam, and I are home for the summer.

Three days back have felt like a year.

Our house is fucking suffocating.

Compared to our last semester, when the three of us immersed ourselves in the Pullman music scene, it's a hard dose of reality. With Stevie's help, we were out every night. Eventually, playing a couple basement gigs. A few open mic nights. One acoustic show in an Irish pub.

For now, we're playing mostly Irish trad songs. We took Stevie's advice though and wrote half a set of originals.

Irish-rooted. Loud as hell. Sharp enough to cut through anything.

If we stick to the plan, by fall, we'll have two sets ready.

For now, I'm flipping pancakes to give Connor and Ma a break. The syrup bottle is already warm from the heat coming off the stove. The fan overhead whirs a lazy rhythm, blades wobbling with each turn.

It's too hot for June.

Too quiet for comfort.

Seamus reads at the counter. Brennan and Cillian are sprawled on the floor, low-key arguing about a comic book. The least I can do is step up and feed them a few meals now and then.

Connor's already on a job site. Ma's at the office trying to balance the books. Liam is upstairs, waiting for me to distract the kids so he can sneak his latest hookup out without detection. The guy showed up sometime after midnight. Shaved head. Vintage band tee. Tattoo on his neck. Liam is likely itching to get the dude gone before Da gets up.

I should worry about him more, but I've learned it's a wasted emotion. Liam does what he wants without regret. He doesn't drink. Or do drugs. Or, as far as I know, put himself in danger. His vice is sex. Men. Women. Multiple partners. I'm the only one who knows the half of it. He hides this part of himself from the rest of the family.

Hopefully not forever. For now, it's probably best to lay low and stay off Da's radar.

Speaking of the devil, my phone pings.

WTF? Can you cover for me?

I type back: *All good. Coast's clear if you take the front stairs.*

I shut the burner off and start plating the pancakes to keep the boys busy here in the kitchen for a few minutes. The ceiling creaks overhead. His bedroom door slams. Hard. Two sets of heavy boots clomp above us toward the stairwell.

"Who the fuck's are youse?" Da's phlegmy voice rages from upstairs, already thick with drink at eight a.m.

Liam roars, "Leave it, Da. It's my business."

I freeze.

Seamus drops his fork. Brennan and Cillian stiffen. We all look up the back staircase, even though we can't see anything from this vantage point.

"This is my feckin' house, you wee bastard," Da yells followed by a loud thud. "Your business is my business. Who is he?"

"Stay here." I hold up my palm toward my younger brothers before slipping out to the living room.

Liam stands at the landing. Shirt half-buttoned. The dude stands behind him, silent, startled. The guy's trying to zip up a hoodie, shrinking backward at the unfolding scene.

"Jesus, Mary, and feckin' Joseph, my son's a feckin' poof." Da stumbles toward them, bare-chested. His hair is wild, eyes bloodshot and yellowed from whiskey. A knee brace hangs loose around one leg. The McGloughlin Construction T-shirt is tied around the other leg like a bandage.

Even from here, he reeks. Alcohol. Stale sweat. Something sour I can't name.

"Leave him be. Let's go." Liam turns to the guy and motions to the stairwell.

Hookup Guy bounds down the stairs. "Jesus, is your dad *homophobic*?"

Da grabs Liam from behind before he has a chance to follow.

"You dirty wee pansy," he slurs, spitting words like bile. "Is this what you are now, a faggot? Bringin' men into my house? Under your ma's roof? Corrupting your wee brothers?"

Liam doesn't flinch. "Go back to your room and pass out, you useless cunt."

His voice is low. Cold. *Dangerous.*

Da takes a step forward.

The house shifts.

"You fuckin' shame me," he growls. "I break my back for this family, and you're in my house suckin' cock like it's a badge of pride?"

"Stop." I move fast, bounding up the stairs and planting myself between them. "Let him leave. You're drunk. You don't mean it."

Da's eyes land on me. Bloodshot. Glazed. "Don't you feckin' defend him."

"I'm not—"

The slap comes from nowhere. Back of his hand across my cheek. Bone-to-bone. White-hot.

The sound echoes.

My head snaps sideways. Vision blurs. Knees buckle. I'm on the floor.

"Padraig!" Seamus screams from the bottom of the stairs.

Fuck.

Brennan pulls him back into the living room. Cillian stares at us with wide eyes.

Da isn't finished. He shoves me backward and goes after my twin.

Liam doesn't back down. Not an inch.

"You gonna hit me too, Da?" he taunts. "Try it."

Da snarls, *"You're not my son."*

Then he swings without warning. It's the concerted effort of a former boxer. Survivor of the Troubles in Northern Ireland. Not a father and husband who took pride in building a legacy for his family in America.

I hear it before I see it. His knuckles hit Liam like concrete. A sickening thud. Flesh hitting plaster. Bone cracking against something harder.

Followed by a sound I'll never forget: Liam tumbling down the stairs. One brutal collision after another. His boots. His elbow. His head.

By the time I turn around, he's already at the bottom. Twisted. Motionless. Blood blooms at his temple. His eyes flutter, unfocused.

Seamus screams. Sharp and animal-like. Brennan grips the table like he can absorb all of our shock with two hands. Cillian drops to his knees beside Liam, already chanting his name like it'll heal him.

Although I'm reeling, I manage to get on my feet and bound down the stairs. I hit the floor hard, jarring my knees. My hands tremble in the air above Liam's body, unsure where to land.

He's breathing. Barely. Shallow and wet.

"Liam," I croak. "Hey. Look at me."

Nothing.

Behind us, Rory lumbers back into his room like nothing happened. Muttering curses. Rifling through his drawers for a bottle. Doesn't look back. Doesn't pause.

Doesn't give two shits he might've killed his son.

"Cillian, help me." I motion to my brother.

"Don't move him!" Seamus blurts in a panic. "You're not supposed to if he hit his head. It could mess up his spine."

I stop cold, crouched beside my twin. "Liam." I hover over him. "Can you hear me?"

Nothing.

"Come on." I grip his hand but don't lift it. "Say something."

A grunt rattles from deep in his throat. His eyelids twitch. Then flutter. Then open, glassy and dazed.

"There." Cillian exhales, like he's been holding it in since Liam hit the floor. "He's okay, right?"

"I don't know." My voice cracks. "Dar. Can you move your arms? Legs?"

He doesn't answer right away. Then slowly, stubbornly, he wiggles his fingers. Flexes his wrists. Twists his booted foot straight out in front of him.

"Fuck," he croaks.

I sigh with relief. "You scared the shit out of us."

"I feel like I got tackled by a truck." Liam winces when he tries to sit up. "Help me up."

Seamus protests again. "Not yet! You're not supposed to—"

"I'm fine," Liam snaps, but softer than usual.

I look at Seamus. His lower lip quivers. Not convinced.

"Careful." I slip one arm behind Liam's back for support. "Tell me if it hurts too much."

He groans again as Cillian and I lift him together. Slow. Cautious. Shaky. His weight sags against me, one arm looped over my shoulder.

I'm holding it together. If he hadn't woken up...

"Let's get downstairs, lads."

We move as fast as we can. Brennan grabs Seamus and tugs him down to the basement ahead of us. One step at a time, I help my twin into the only space we trust. Our practice room.

Cillian and I ease Liam onto the busted couch. He lets out a hiss. Doesn't open his eyes. Brennan bounds upstairs and comes back with an ice pack and a wet towel. Hands them over without a word.

I press the towel to Liam's temple.

"Fuck." He flinches. "Hurts."

Seamus curls against the wall, arms locked tight around his knees. Brennan buries himself in his laptop like it's a shield. Cillian slumps in the corner and stares into space.

I look deep into Liam's eyes. *I'm sorry.*

He scrunches his nose. *For what?*

Not getting there sooner.

You tried.

My twin. Same face as mine. Same build. Same mouth. I can't stand to see him hurt. Physically. Emotionally. None of it.

"He looked at me like I was filth," he grits out. "I knew he'd fucking hate me for being fluid..."

I shake my head. "You're not filth."

"He thinks I am." Liam's face crumples. "Part of me understands. I want to be with women. I want to be with men. How am I supposed to choose? How will I ever have what you and Stevie…"

My chest splinters. He's never admitted this out loud. Maybe not even to himself.

"He's doesn't get to have an opinion about you." I grip his shoulder. "Never again. You're allowed to be yourself without worrying about him."

Liam closes his eyes. The ice slips a little. I hold it steady.

The five of us stay put for a while. A long while. Each contemplating what occurred in the cool, quiet of the basement. Brennan and Cillian doze off. Seamus keeps a close watch on the two of us. I want to text Stevie, but I don't dare retrieve my phone. She'll understand once I'm able to tell her what happened.

After a while, Liam shifts and sits up, wincing. Crosses his arms over his chest. "Fuck this woebegone bullshit. I wanna play."

"No. You're concussed." Seamus is at his side in an instant.

"Ah, I'm grand, wee one." Liam musses up Seamus' hair and rises to his feet. "I'll take it easy."

He moves across the room and plugs in his guitar. The amp crackles. He strums a chord. Rough. Broken. It mirrors his mood. I ease onto the stool behind the kit. Count us in with the click of my sticks.

Liam's face is a mess. Black eye. Split lip. Purpling cheekbone. Crusted blood clings to the cut above his eyebrow. We make music because we need a release to survive what happened today. He's immersed. Guitar slung low. Head down like he's praying to the strings.

He plays like he's possessed.

I manage to keep up. Every cymbal crash is like a jolt straight through my soul, but I don't stop. Not for two solid hours. If he needs this, I'm gonna give it to him.

Finally, Liam lets the guitar fall against his thigh. I set the sticks down.

"Let's head back up." I gesture. "We need to feed the lads."

Nobody speaks as we trudge upstairs. It's quiet on the top floor, Da's no doubt passed out cold by now.

Liam turns on the TV and curls around Seamus, who snuggles into his side. Brennan sits at the dining room table muttering to himself, lost in some coding loop. Cillian barely moves. He studies the ceiling like it might collapse on top of him.

All of us jump a little when we hear a key in the door and voices outside. It's Ma and Connor, of course, home from a long day at work. Oblivious, for the moment, at what went down a few hours ago.

Liam pulls his hoodie up to hide his face. I shake my head and reach for him. He shouldn't hide what happened. Otherwise, how are we going to get Da help?

"No!" Cillian begs. "She's gonna see."

"She needs to know." I tug the fabric off his face.

Liam doesn't stop me but warns, "Dar, she won't be able to unsee it."

"You shouldn't protect him by hiding what he did to you." I cup his shoulder.

Connor enters first, eyes scanning the surroundings instinctively like he's on a job site. His jeans are crusted in dried mud. A high-vis vest is slung over one shoulder. Ma's right behind him, mail clutched in her hand, keys dangling from her fingers.

She sees Liam before Connor notices. Her purse hits the floor.

"Holy God above." She rushes forward. "What happened to you?"

Liam doesn't answer. He sits. Back ramrod straight.

"Liam, answer her." Connor's voice is lethal. "Who did this? Did you lads have a go at each other?"

For all my bravado, I can only utter, "Da."

Connor's face contorts. Rage, disbelief, guilt. All of it.

Ma turns to me. Her eyes sweep over the welt on my cheek. "Padraig." Her voice cracks. "What—?"

"We're okay," I lie.

Ma's already across the room. She reaches for Liam's cheek, fingertips trembling.

He flinches. "It's fine. I can handle it."

"You shouldn't have to," Connor seethes, slamming his phone down hard enough to make Seamus stir. "Was it really Da?"

Nobody answers.

"Stupid fucker." Connor grits his teeth and looks upstairs.

"Language," Ma snaps, automatic. Then she sags down next to Liam. "Where is he?"

"Where do you think? Drunk." I gesture upstairs. "Locked in his room. Passed out. We haven't heard anything since—"

"I'll kill him myself." Connor starts toward the stairs.

"You won't." Ma grabs his wrist. "You'll go to jail."

"We need to do something," he roars.

"We will." She shuts her eyes, defeated. "Right now, I'm cleaning my son up and then making dinner. The kids need to eat. Then the four of us will talk." She turns back to Liam. "Sit at the table. I'll get the first-aid kit."

Liam hesitates.

"Go." She motions across the room.

Twenty minutes later, we eat microwaved shepherd's pie in silence. No one says what we're all thinking.

We didn't think it could get worse.

Now we know better.

Six

One Year Later

Family weekend at Wazzu.

It's been a long-ass time sleeping apart.

Three whole nights.

Padraig locks the door behind him and I'm already pulling off my sweatshirt.

Sleeping without him shouldn't feel so dire, but it sucked. As much as I loved having my family here, we're alone. Finally. He doesn't speak as he scans me from head to toe. Lashes low over heavy-lidded eyes.

He crosses the room in four steps and I'm in his arms.

His momentum propels us backward. My legs hit the edge of the bed as he grabs my face and his mouth crushes mine. There's nothing careful here. His tongue pushes deep. Tasting. Claiming. Drinking from me like I'm the only thing to quench his thirst.

I unzip his jeans and tug his cock free. It's thick and flushed when I wrap my fingers around the base and lick its head—slow and filthy—and Padraig's breath hitches.

"Did you miss this?" I lick along his shaft.

He doesn't answer. He can't.

I suck him deep. Take him down to where my throat tightens. His fingers tangle in my hair. I twist my wrist and slide my lips over him again and again. He tastes like salt and sweat and every aching second of the weekend we spent apart.

"Fuck, Stevie," he groans. "You're gonna make me come too fast."

I moan around him. Hollow my cheeks. He pulls out of my mouth with a hiss. His cock, covered in my saliva, bobs against his stomach.

"Get up," he rasps.

Before I can move, Padraig lifts me like I weigh nothing. I squeal, laughing and breathless as he tosses me on my back. His thumbs hook the waistband of my leggings and he strips them down my legs, taking my panties along for the ride.

Leaving me bare. Open. Dripping wet for him.

Padraig doesn't waste time. He kisses down my stomach and kneels at the edge of the bed. Something catches his eye—a navy-blue satin belt from my bathrobe which I tossed on the desk earlier.

He reaches for it and his eyes meet mine when he loops it around my wrists. "Okay?"

"Yes." My nod is fast and definitive.

With a wicked grin, he binds me and loops the ends around the metal bar jutting from the wall. My arms stretch taut above my head, making my spine arch. The cool air whisps across my nipples. With a dark, hungry look, he swipes his tongue across the peaks. My thighs fall open for him, exposing my swollen, needy pussy. He watches with a dark, hungry look I'll never get tired of.

Padraig's mouth finds the inside of my thigh. Then higher. Higher. Higher.

Tempered with control, his tongue traces through my soaked slit, pausing to circle and tease. He flicks upward, tracing a hot line to my clit, then sucks it deep into his mouth. His lips seal tight, relentless. I'm writhing—hips jerking, thighs clenching, my body begging for more without a single word.

"Stay still." He looks up from between my legs. "Let me savor you."

"I'm trying," I gasp, grabbing two fistfuls of his long hair. "Shut up and keep going."

I shove his face back where it belongs. He groans, then dives in, tongue plundering my pussy, slow, greedy, deliberately. His nose nudges my clit with every pass, sending sparks ricocheting through my core.

Then he shifts. The ties pull tight against my wrists as he lifts me by the hips. Steady. Controlled. My back presses to the wall, knees bent and hooked over his shoulders. My breath catches as Padraig goes back to work. He sucks on my clit, then licks lower, tilting his head until his tongue circles my pucker. Slow, wet, and utterly depraved.

"God," I gasp, as my spine arches off the wall, legs twitching against his shoulders.

Every nerve fires. I can't think. Can't speak. All I can do is take it. My whole body clenches. My entire being spasms with pleasure unlike anything I've ever experienced and I come with a strangled sound.

Padraig devours me through the aftershocks, drawing out my orgasm until I gasp for air, unable to endure any more. With a satisfied smirk, he lowers me, unties my wrists and lets me fall into his chest.

I collapse against him. Boneless.

"More," I whisper.

"You got it." He flips me, face down, across the bed. I hear him kick his jeans off and feel him rub the head of his cock against my soaked entrance.

Padraig fists my hair. Not to control. To anchor. The other grips my hip. He thrusts in. All the way. One stroke.

My mouth falls open. "*Jesus…*"

My words are cut off by another thrust. Hard, fast, deep. I claw at the blanket, sliding my knees forward. He pulls me back, adjusting the angle so his cock hits everything inside me that matters.

He leans forward, lips brushing my spine, then pulls out. "Up."

I turn my head in confusion.

Suddenly, Padraig lifts me like he owns me. His arms lock beneath my thighs and he slams up and in until his cock is buried to the hilt. No wall. No support. It's all him. Holding me suspended, fucking me reverse cowgirl style, midair.

Brutal. Primal. Perfection.

He tilts my hips precisely right, shifting my weight until I'm spread completely open for him. His cock slides even deeper. I scream and clench around his girth.

"Ah, fuck. *Yeah,*" he growls. "Do you feel my cock?"

"Every goddamn inch."

I cling to his forearms, panting, raw. The sound of our slick, obscene slaps echo off the dorm room walls as Padraig bounces me up and down. Grinding and rooting until I'm shaking. Hard. Ruthless. Fucking up into me with punishing force.

"Say it," he pants. "Tell me you're mine forever."

I'm holding on for dear life, in more ways than one. "God, yes. I'm yours. Fuck. I'm *always* yours."

My orgasm tears through me so fast it knocks the air from my lungs. I convulse in his arms, body bowing, pussy fluttering around his cock as he growls into my neck.

He keeps going. Keeps taking. Keeps using my body like it was made for him. Because it was.

I crane my neck and our mouths smash together. I come again, hard. He bites my shoulder, keeps going.

"Don't stop," I beg. I *never* want this to end.

He turns, buried inside me, and carefully sets me down on the desk. Then sweeps it clean. His sketchbooks tumble to the ground. A water bottle bounces along the floor. Nothing's going to deter him from sliding his hand between us to circle my swollen clit.

"Lie back," he pants, lifting my hips so one knee hangs over his shoulder. Then the other.

Now it's his turn. The desk creaks as he drives his cock deep. The stimulation is so intense, my scream slices through the air and I black out for a second when I come again.

By the time I blink back to consciousness, Padraig's fucking me senseless. Rough. Hungry. Chasing his own pleasure. He freezes. Every muscle pulls taut. A shudder rolls through him and he groans, long and raw, spilling inside me in thick, pulsing waves.

His weight sinks over mine and neither of us moves. We're breathless. Sweaty. Glued together. The truth is, we don't fuck like teenagers anymore. We're pros. Feral. Seasoned.

"Hey." Padraig's breath fans my collarbone, his lips brush the hollow of my neck. "You okay?"

Everything feels warm and floaty. I could stay like this forever.

I nod, smiling. My eyes still closed. *"Yeah."*

"You sure?" He nuzzles my cheek.

"Uh..." I grin. "I came so many times I've forgotten my name."

"Good." He chuckles and pulls out, reaching for his towel hanging on the hook by his bed. "C'mere."

I let Padraig clean me, because I'm too blissed out to move. He's careful, wiping my pussy like it's something sacred. Then he uses it on himself and chucks it into the laundry pile before picking me up and carrying me back to bed.

He shuts off the light and slides in, pulling me close until we're chest to chest. Forehead to forehead. I could drown in the way he holds me.

"I hate sleeping without you." I stroke the stubble on his cheek.

"Same." His fingers trace lazy circles on my lower back. "Worst three nights ever."

"C'mon. It was good to see everyone. It's been a few months." I nestle against him.

Padraig's eye twitches. "I guess. Connor's aged ten years. He looks so tired."

"He's carrying a lot." I hesitate. "Any updates on your da?"

Padraig's body tenses. Then softens. "Well...he pulled me and Liam aside."

"Yeah?" I lean back to look at him. "What'd he say?"

He shuts his eyes, lashes brush his cheek. "He told us not to come home this summer."

"What?"

"He said it's good we're away." Padraig rolls onto his back. "Ma threatened to leave Da if he ever gets violent again. Liam triggers him in the worst way. It's fucking embarrassing to realize my da is a prejudiced old cunt. Anyway, Connor doesn't want us to be hindered in our college experience worrying about the family."

My chest stiffens. "Babe..."

"I dunno." His jaw tics. "He told us we need to live our lives. Be free. It's fucking bullshit. I don't want to bury my head in the sand."

I tuck myself closer. "He's trying to do his best. He's not much older than you, give him a break. The last thing Connor needs is to worry about your da taking out his frustrations on the two of you."

"It doesn't feel right." He turns his head to look at me.

I brush the hair from his face. "Oh? Tell me this. Would you do the same thing for Seamus? Brennan? Cillian?"

Padraig goes quiet. His hand slips into my hair. "I think what happened last summer broke him a little."

"It broke Liam, too."

He nods.

We lie there for a while. The room is quiet save the slight hum of the mini-fridge.

I press a kiss to his chest, right above his heart. "You and Liam sounded tight last weekend, we could all spend the summer doing some gigs up and down the coast. Could be fun."

"You'd be up for that?" Padraig's mood shifts. "We've settled on a name. Connor-approved."

"Wait, really? You picked one without me?"

He arches a brow. "You vetoed Tin Bastards, remember?"

"*Obviously.*"

"We're going with Fireball."

I roar with laughter. "Because of your temper or his?"

"Because Liam thinks the name is cool and will inspire us to live up to it." Padraig chortles.

I roll my eyes. "Tracks."

He leans in and kisses me slow. Deep. When he pulls back, his expression shifts. "I know being on the road isn't your thing. It means a lot you'd want to hang all summer. The time with Connor makes me realize something. I'm dedicated to making the band work."

My heart swells and sinks at the same time. "How so?"

His hand cups my cheek. "I want to make Connor proud. Play music with Liam as my job. I do want to tour and it might be selfish, but I want you to be with me. I can't imagine not waking up next to you every morning."

I stifle a cough.

"Once we get it out of our system..." he continues. "I want a house of our own filled with our kids and maybe a dog who hates the mailman. I want to eat dinner with your parents on Sundays. I want you to yell at me for leaving socks everywhere."

"*Padraig.*"

"I want you." He swallows. "*Forever.*"

My pulse hammers.

His eyes are wide open. Scared. Brave. "When we graduate, I'm gonna marry you, Stevie."

Emotion claws up my throat.

"Don't say anything, this isn't your proposal," he clarifies. "I want this. All of it. You and me. Every day."

I kiss him because I don't have the words. Actually, no words will do.

Lying in his arms, I think of Connor and how love made him give up everything so his brothers could survive. How he's trying to do the right thing, but might be oblivious to the men Liam and Padraig are growing into. How much they can handle.

More troubling is, somewhere deep inside, I know no matter how I love him, I'm not cut out to live on the road. What happens if they become famous and he won't be able to take a step back?

Padraig may not crave the spotlight.

Liam does.

As much as he's committed to me, one thing's for sure.

He'll never walk away from the twin who can't live without him.

Seven

A Few Weeks Later

THE SKY OVER THE highway bleeds from tangerine to violet.

Grain silos blur past. A few cows. Golden fields.

We're heading north on the 195 with the windows cracked open. Warm wind slaps against my temple.

Liam glances over. His hair is as long as mine, wild and unbrushed. Blowing in the breeze. We're halfway to Spokane before I realize how quiet we've been.

Liam's foot taps the floorboard in rhythm with whatever beat's looping through his head. I feel a certain emptiness. Something's missing. My soft, steady touchstone.

Stevie.

"She texted yet?" Liam reads my mind, as he does.

"Yeah." I nod, though I keep my eyes on the road. "Said her mom nearly cried when she walked in. She'll check on Ma and the wee lads tomorrow."

"How long's she staying?"

"A couple weeks, I think."

He lets out a low breath. "So it's just us for a while."

"Yeah."

We lock eyes. Then he turns back to the road.

"I'm glad we have some time for the two of us. It's been years, you realize."

I glance over.

"There isn't any part of us she isn't there for anymore." His comment lands sharp between my ribs.

I shift in my seat uncomfortably. "You're not being fair," I fire back defensively.

"Why exactly are we checking this singer out? You know you're gonna choose her in the long run over me."

"What the fuck?" I turn toward him, utterly confused. "Do you have something you need to say?"

"She's not into the band stuff for the long haul. Do you not listen to her?" He shrugs.

My chest constricts. Not with guilt. With truth. Because I know he's right.

"I don't wanna do this with anyone else, Dar." Liam reaches over and grips my wrist. "But, I'm gonna do it no matter what. With or without you."

"What's gotten into you?" I'm struggling to understand. Have I not been showing up every goddamn day?

He cracks his knuckles. "You don't even notice I haven't been around much. At least you haven't said anything."

Huh. Is it true? Guilt overwhelms me.

"See." He juts out his chin. "You're so into your relationship, like it's the most important thing."

I stare out the window as we approach Spokane. City lights blur like static against the glass.

"She doesn't take me from you," I retort. "She fills something else."

"No, you fill *her*. Ten times a day. It's all you think about." Liam rolls his eyes.

"Don't be a dick. She's one of your best friends. She's the woman I love. I won't continue this conversation if you disrespect my relationship." I swallow hard, unable to process his harsh words.

"Fer fuck's sake. I didn't mean it as a shot. I'm not pissed. I'm realistic." Liam folds his arms across his chest and I know he's telling the truth. He's worried. Thinks I'm slipping away.

"I promise, you've got me."

"Not all of you." He sucks his lips over his teeth. "I'm not tryin' to get up in your grill, Dar. But, don't you think you're too serious? I heard you and her whispering about fucking marriage. You're twenty, for God's sake."

"Not for a few years, *Jesus*," I protest.

He turns, eyes sharp, hurting. "Don't feckin' lie to me or yourself."

I don't. I can't. The lie wouldn't land anyway. The truth is, I'd put a ring on her finger tomorrow if I thought she'd say yes and he knows it. I'm trying to be two things at once. His twin and bandmate. Her forever man.

Liam turns back to the road. Flicks on the headlights. "Would you choose her if she gave you an ultimatum? I deserve to know."

"I don't want to choose,' I answer honestly.

He nods once, hollow as if to say, *you already have.*

"Fireball is my priority. *You're* my priority." I wish I could punch the shit out of this situation. Crack it open and rearrange it.

His fingers drum the wheel. "Well, I guess we'll see."

The neon sign blinks ahead.

The Big Dipper. Spokane's premier live music club.

Liam slows the truck. Pulls up to the curb like it's no big deal even though we both know this night means something. It's supposed to be the start of something for the both of us. If we're gonna add a new voice to the band, I guess it makes sense he wants to know where my head is at before we go forward.

He stretches, arms behind his head. "Look, don't sweat it. I'm not trying to put pressure on you. All I'm saying is I'm looking forward to the next couple of weeks. It hasn't been just us since you started fucking her in high school."

"Dar—"

"What?" He shrugs. "You're tied to her like a feckin' balloon."

I reach for the handle. "I'm hopelessly in love with her."

"I know." He winces like the idea of love is a curse. "Don't get me wrong, I love her too—you don't get what being tied down means for us."

"I'm gonna call bullshit. You make her out to be some ball and chain. She's all-in on Fireball. Hell, she came up with the concept," I remind him and slump back against the seat.

This conversation has obviously been brewing for a while, but I'm not backing down. Stevie is nonnegotiable.

"What the fuck do you mean? We've got a name, a couple good songs, and no singer. We've been dicking around for months while you guys play house in our dorm room." Liam slams his palm against the steering wheel.

"We're here now." I remain calm. It's the only way when Liam gets agitated.

He doesn't stop. "You think you can tour with a wife?"

"She's not my wife."

"Not yet."

I roll my eyes. "As you said, I'm twenty. Not stupid."

"No?" He laughs, bitter. "Your priority is her while we're living on borrowed time."

Silence stretches out like wire between us.

"You wanna talk life choices? How many people have you fucked this month?" I turn it back on him.

He doesn't flinch. "Who keeps count? Are you?"

"No. I'm watching you spiral. Men, women, whoever looks at you twice." I soften my tone because I'm generally worried about my brother's inability to maintain a relationship. He seems so lost.

"I'm allowed to have fun, why discriminate?"

"Are you?" I place my hand on his shoulder. "Having fun?"

Liam looks out the window. His reflection in the glass doesn't smile. "I don't know what the fuck I am. Hell, maybe I'm jealous because it seems like I'm never gonna have a Stevie."

"You will." I assure him.

He shakes his head. "Name one person who'd be down to be in an open relationship forever. It doesn't exist, and probably shouldn't."

"You're in bum-fuck Pullman. You haven't even explored the possibility. You aren't the only person in the world who's bisexual." I try to give him something steadier to hold on to, though I know this nontraditional road isn't going to be easy.

"I already know the answer. Casual sex is the only way I can satisfy my cravings."

Fuck. I reach over, knock my knuckles against his leg. "You're the coolest, most talented guy in the family. Not bad looking, if I do say so myself. Have some patience."

"Says the gentle soul who found his perfect goddamn future at eight years old." Liam smiles almost apologetically.

"Fuck off. It was seven."

He grins, but his eyes are now glassy. "Connor's the hero. You're the heart. I'm the freak."

I stare at him, stunned.

He swallows hard. "You don't know what it's like. It's bad enough watching Da morph from a great man into a zombie. He'd rather be drunk than have a fag for a son."

I go still. The memory of what happened that afternoon vivid in my mind. I didn't realize how it felt for Liam to be shamed in front of our entire family.

"Liam..."

"I saw it in his eyes before he..." he whispers. "Like I ruined something sacred. Like I'm the one who made everything collapse."

I breathe slow. Careful. "You didn't."

"He hates me."

"No," I say, voice thick. "He hates himself."

We sit in that truth.

"I need this to feel like I'm worth something." He curls his lips around his teeth to stop himself from crying.

"I know. We're doing this. I promise—"

"We've got one shot," he interrupts. "Connor is putting us through school, he gave us the gear, our freedom. We owe it to him..."

"I get it." I nod vigorously. "I live with the weight of it every goddamn day."

"It shouldn't be a fucking weight. It's a privilege," he snarls.

His words scrape. Not because they're wrong. Because they hit too close.

Liam and I were born to walk beside each other. Stevie and I were born to be soulmates. How could I ever choose?

We fall quiet and our surroundings come back into focus. The parking lot next to The Big Dipper buzzes with a kind of static energy I didn't know Spokane had. Neon bleeds out the door every time someone stumbles through it.

"Let's go see if this chick's our singer and take it from there." I gesture to the building.

The place reeks of stale beer and overripe perfume. The floors are tacky underfoot. Colored lights pulse overhead. Dollar bills hang from the ceiling like jungle vines. A pack of girls in plastic tiaras screech-laugh by the bar.

Then a voice slices through the noise. The room hushes like it's been slapped.

Low. Smoky. The kind of tone that leaks into your bloodstream and takes its time. Like Ella Fitzgerald soaked in red wine with a little dose of Amy Winehouse and a sprinkling of Adele.

I don't breathe. Liam doesn't move.

The woman's dress clings to her like a dare. Midnight-blue satin, dipped low in the back. Long enough to brush her calves. Her hair's jet-black and wild, tumbling in loose coils down to her waist. Her lips are painted dark purple, like bruised plums. Sea-glass green eyes catch the overhead light and fracture it.

She hits the chorus and lifts into another register entirely. Clear, bell-pure, like she ripped a hole in the ceiling and dragged heaven down with her.

We've found her. If she'll have us.

Liam turns to me slowly. The look on his face says it all.

After the song is over, the crowd explodes into cheers. She introduces herself.

Felicity Clark.

Our future?

"She's a vibe." I nudge him. "Would she even *want* to join a Celtic rock band?"

"Don't know." He grins. "But we're gonna find out."

The lingering crunchiness of our previous conversation evaporates. This is Liam at his best. Fueled by a feeling. A spark. A whim. The most magnetic person I've ever known. I spend half my life reassuring him and the other half trying to catch up.

The next song isn't one I expect. She slows it way down. The piano drops into a lazy, minor-key intro, then slips into the first line of *You Don't Own Me*. Not the bubblegum version. This one's molasses and velvet. Full of broken glass and long stares. She doesn't wink. Doesn't flirt. Doesn't perform for anyone.

She's in her own world. Even the way she delivers the chorus—fragile, restrained, then suddenly soaring—is perfection. She makes every man in the place sit up straighter. Liam goes still beside me, frozen. Like he's afraid to miss a note.

The drummer watches her intently like he might miss a cue. The upright bassist closes his eyes, swaying like the strings are leading him instead of the other way around.

She launches into *Bennie and the Jets* next, completely reworked in a strange, lilting jazz rhythm, her phrasing twisted and playful, like she's rewriting the song as she sings it. The band keeps up, barely. They're good, but she's better.

"She's not merely singing," Liam murmurs. "She's bending sound."

He's right. Her voice changes with every bar. Growls into the lower registers, floats up into a falsetto so clear it rings in my teeth. Her vibrato is tight and controlled. The mic barely picks her up in the softest places, so the crowd leans in.

She has them—and us—by the balls.

When she starts *Here Comes the Sun*, I think of Stevie. The way she sings the song every morning while she brushes her hair without even realizing it. I wish she could be with us now to experience this magic, but she needed to spend time with her own family.

I text her a video. *We've found our singer*.

Felicity hits the final note with her arms raised and body arched like she's pulling the sound down from somewhere divine. Then she lowers the mic, gives the tiniest nod to the band, and finally smiles.

The room erupts. It's a bar in Spokane, Washington, not Carnegie Hall. The crowd treats this show like it's both.

Felicity doesn't say goodnight. She steps back and leaves the mic swinging.

Like two eager puppies, we edge past a line of drunk college guys and slip down a narrow corridor behind the stage. The green room's small and overheated. She's propped against the far wall, head tilted back, throat working as she drains a bottle of water. The confidence she wore on stage peels off her shoulders like smoke. Up close, she looks like she's barely out of high school. Certainly not old enough to carry that kind of voice.

She lowers the bottle, eyes locking on us.

Stills when she sees Liam.

Up close, her eyes hit harder. They're laced with gold. Her dark hair's now slicked into a ponytail, loose strands clinging to her neck. There's sweat at her collarbone. A flush across her chest. She's buzzing from the stage.

"Hey," I say as we approach.

She watches us, unreadable.

"I'm Padraig," I offer. "This is Liam. We're in a band called Fireball and we need a singer and were wondering if you'd be interested in talking about it."

Her gaze flicks between us. Lingers on Liam.

Something shifts.

Silent. Charged.

Like a fuse caught fire.

Eight

STEVIE

Four months Later

I'M CONFLICTED AS SHIT.

I glance out the window as steam coils off my coffee, fogging the chipped window above the sink.

Outside, Pullman's painted in grays and browns. Two students across the street are unloading lopsided pumpkins from the back of a rusted Dodge. One slips and splits open on the driveway. Seeds scatter. They howl laughing.

We're all finally waking up and it's not quite noon. Padraig's in the shower. I can hear Liam in the basement setting up for rehearsal. I'm not sure where Felicity is.

The house is thick with the aftershocks of last night's gig. Fireball played a packed-out frat house until nearly four a.m.

Bodies were pressed wall-to-wall, making the whole place heave like a living organism. After, Liam was buzzing so hard he practically vibrated. I've never seen him so happy. Padraig and Felicity beamed, basking in the glow of their biggest gig yet.

I was proud. Really, I was.

On the other hand, wedging myself between sticky couches and dodging grabby hands while the band shreds on stage isn't exactly my dream Friday night.

We didn't get home until nearly six. Padraig was keyed up. Erection pressed against my ass the second our bedroom door clicked shut behind us. He bent me over the bathroom sink, fucked me fast and deep with one hand around my throat and the other clamped over my mouth to muffle the sounds.

The man's a goddamn machine. Honestly, though? Even the most devoted girlfriend needs more than five hours of sleep. I'm wrecked.

At least we have our own place now, a lopsided off-campus rental untouched by contractors since the seventies. It's a disaster, honestly, with cracked drywall and slanted floors. The heater creaks and the carpet on the stairs downstairs to the basement crunches when you step on it. They've set up their rehearsal down there and it reeks of incense, sweat, and whatever body spray Liam's using this week.

The guys found the place right before the semester started. Felicity moved in next. Then, me.

When Padraig asked if I'd be okay with it, it wasn't really a question. "You'll love it," he cooed. "We'll make it ours."

I do. Mostly. He and I have the master bedroom, with an en suite bathroom and a door that locks, thank God. Making it "ours" means we splurged on a new king mattress which we keep on the floor. Books are stacked in uneven towers beside the bed and we have a thrifted IKEA desk where my laptop lives. Padraig's easel and paint are set up by the window.

Liam took the next-biggest room on the opposite side of the house. Felicity's room is across the hall from him.

I like her for the most part. Unlike her stage persona, she's quiet. Shy, almost to the point of invisible. Never in the way. Always humming. We haven't talked much, but she's easy enough to live with. Part of me is relieved to have another woman in the house.

I can't deny things are different than last year. Somehow the energy changed during the time I was back in Seattle with my family. I can't help but wonder if, in the space I left behind, Felicity's presence is propelling them into who they are meant to be and has reshaped itself without me.

Leaving me to figure out who I am outside the bubble of loving Padraig.

Fireball Isn't some scrappy project anymore. They've worked hard in a short period of time developing a distinct sound. Padraig is in a creative bloom, writing songs and creating potential logos. Liam's guitar and vocals are maturing. Felicity's haunting alto wraps around their Celtic rock-meets-grunge vibe like velvet over steel.

It's real and exciting and I've kept my promise to help. They're playing every weekend for the rest of the semester. Frat parties. Dive bars. Campus events. An upcoming wedding.

I do it because I love them.

No, because I love *him*.

The truth is, I'm good at it. Booking gigs, wrangling logistics, herding three creative minds, it comes easy to me.

So much so, I've locked in my major. I'm studying Hospitality Business Management. In two years, I'll be staging galas in five-star hotels, orchestrating destination weddings, and running fundraisers where everything sparkles. I sit in class envisioning soaring hotel lobbies and linen-draped banquet rooms. I map out timelines and venue layouts like I'm already orchestrating million-dollar events.

The problem is, instead of keeping up with my coursework, I find myself immersed in their band shit. Padraig behind his kit, drenched in sweat and joy, is more alive than I've ever seen him. Music softens Liam's edges…

They've had a rough few years and it's amazing to see them coming into their own.

"Babe?" Padraig steps into the kitchen, sleepy-eyed and barefoot. His jeans hang low, an old flannel is open over his lithe, bare chest. "You seen my new drum head?"

I nod toward the couch. "Leaning against the couch."

"You're a genius." He grins and leans down to kiss the top of my head. "I'm heading downstairs."

"I'll be down in a sec." I gesture to my coffee.

"Bring it with." He squeezes my shoulder and I dutifully follow him to the basement.

It's a mess of amps and cables and empty fast food containers. Felicity's perched on the stool in a track suit, her long black hair pulled into a high ponytail. She chews on her thumbnail, waiting for the guys to start.

Padraig replaces his drum head and sets the click track. Liam hits the first chord, nodding to Felicity. "Okay, from the top."

They launch into *Breakwater*, a new tune with soaring harmonies and a fiddle hook emanating from Padraig's Logic sampler he uses to recreate the instruments they don't actually have right now. Felicity's voice cuts straight through me. It's wild how fast she adapted her jazzy riffs to suit Fireball's Celtic sound.

The rehearsal continues in fits and starts. Felicity fiddles with her mic levels. Liam tries different iterations of a bridge he swore was final. Padraig moves through it all with a quiet intensity, knuckles tight around his sticks. Everyone's exhausted, but committed.

To finish the session, they run another new tune, *Tir na nÓg* and the whole garage vibrates with the thunderclap rhythm

Padraig and Liam built months ago. Felicity nails the final note, delicate, mournful, lingering, then it's done.

"Yeah." Padraig pulls off his headphones. "I think it'll be ready for the next gig."

I nod from my perch on the amp. "It sounds great. It'll even get better when you play it live a few times."

Truthfully, the song is more than great. It's haunting. Melancholy with an undercurrent of rage. It makes you stop midsentence, midstep, mid-anything, and when it's done, it lingers in your chest.

Rather than acknowledging me, though, Padraig glances at Liam and Felicity. Like he needs their opinion more than mine.

Going forward, this is how it's gonna be from now on, I realize as I trail behind him upstairs. My emotions are confusing. I've always rejected the idea of being their manager. I turned down the lead vocal position about a million times. The idea of touring has no appeal.

At the same time, in a few short months, Felicity's now their third. A true, permanent member of the band. She deserves to have more of an opinion in her role so it's probably as it should be, but it stings a bit.

Once upstairs, Liam wastes no time and takes off. Felicity disappears into her room. Padraig and I order a pizza and watch TV for a bit, then go to bed early.

We shower. Fuck lazily. Afterward, we lie tangled in our sheets, half-asleep.

"Something's different." I stroke little circles around his nipple.

His chest rises under my palm. "What d'you mean?"

"You." I flick my eyes up to his. "You're in it. Fully in it. With the band. With Liam. It's like I'm watching you blossom into a rockstar."

His silence isn't defensive. It's careful. Classic Padraig McGloughlin contemplation.

"Liam needs me right now, he was worried you and I were going to run off and get married and I'd quit."

I shift, pressing my cheek to his collarbone. "I'm not jealous or anything. It's an observation."

His hand slides up my back. "I'm enjoying myself."

"I'm trying to understand what's changed for you." I wind my finger around his long hair. "Other than the band logo, you haven't sketched or painted since we moved in here."

Another beat. He sighs. "When you were in Seattle, Liam and I spent nearly every night working on arrangements. New riffs. We'd fall asleep watching old Thin Lizzy live shows or arguing over drum fills. It was like when we were kids. Before everything went to hell."

I close my eyes thinking about how Rory turned into a monster and nearly killed Liam.

"Liam and I always dreamed we'd do this with Connor," he adds. "Be the next U2. The Irish answer to Zeppelin. It was dumb kid shit, but Connor had us convinced..."

"Babe. I was there. Up until recently, it seemed like you were living your brothers' dreams, though." I roll onto my back.

"Aye." Padraig flings his arm over his eyes. "I love to play, but I've never cared about being famous. Such a dumb thing to aspire to, right?"

"Is it?" I gently move his arm so I can see his eyes.

"Yes." He swallows. "It is. On the other hand, music changes lives. Either way, for Liam it's the only thing keeping him upright. I genuinely worry if we don't make it, he'll fall apart. Don't even get me started on Connor's disappointment."

Whoa.

I shift, prop myself up on one elbow and stare down at him. His chiseled features are soft in the low light. Lips parted. Brows furrowed.

"I know you love them," I whisper.

"I do, and you know how it is with Liam." He looks at me. His eyes darker than usual, serious. Emotional. "He's always on the brink of spiraling. Not like danger-danger, not yet. He's finally opened up a bit but I know there's a lot he's not saying. Or he doesn't know how to."

"I think it's hard for him to believe the life he wants is available to him in a small town like Pullman. Seattle? Maybe..."

"I agree. I can't imagine how it would feel to believe no one will ever want all of him." He winces. "He's truly convinced he'll never have what we have."

God. My heart aches. Not in a sharp, sad way. More like a steady dull pain in my ribcage.

"He's not wrong to worry." I take his hand and bring it to my lips.

Padraig looks horrified. "You don't believe that."

"I don't mean it's impossible. Let's get real, though. Most people aren't looking for what he wants." I massage his fingers, one by one. "I'd never be able to share you with anyone else."

"Well, I'd make room," he counters. "If it were you."

His truth settles over me like a blanket. "I know. I hope you won't be mad, but, it's wrong for Liam or Connor to put responsibility for their well-being on you. You deserve to be happy. Live the life you want. You shouldn't have to compromise."

He pulls me closer again, tucking me against him. His heart beats steady under my cheek.

"Life is always a compromise. I don't want you to worry. I'm never leaving you," he assures me unnecessarily. "Even if the band blows up. Even if we tour. Even if Liam needs me every fucking second."

"I know that too."

Padraig and I have found something most people spend their lives chasing. Our love is branded into my skin. It burrows so deep nothing else will ever feel this real.

Yet, sometimes, I lie awake terrified we found it too early. He doesn't realize we're shifting, slowly, gently, like two bodies drifting apart in warm water, reaching for each other but no longer securely anchored.

Regardless of his promise, I feel a crossroads looming.

One he doesn't see coming.

My fear is, whatever path he takes will leave someone devastated.

Nine

Six Months Later

THE FIRST NOTES OF *Tir na nÓg* chorus begin and the crowd
fucking ignites.

I don't even need to look at Liam to know.

We've got them.

This isn't some random frat basement or a Pullman dive.
We're playing The Bartlett in Spokane and it's packed.

Electricity zips through my chest when Felicity belts the
chorus. Half battle cry. Half blessing. I hammer the drums
so hard the sticks blur. Liam's beside me, possessed, guitar
snarling like it's alive. Sweat runs down his neck, his hair is
soaked, mouth open like the music's pulling breath straight
from his lungs.

We don't look at each other. We don't have to. By the time we crash out the last chord, the crowd's screaming like we're gods. Someone screams *"Fireball forever"* right before a bra sails onto the stage.

Felicity barely glances at it, instead smirks and boots it into the pit like a soccer ball. When the song ends, she bows deep. Graceful. Cocky. She owns every soul in the room, and knows it.

An hour later, we bolt offstage, lungs heaving, hearts pounding, laughing like we've pulled off a heist.

Drunk on a kind of adrenaline no drug could provide.

We're three shows deep this week. Thursday a Pullman bar set. Friday frat party. Tonight our first headlining gig in a half-decent city. Our official band email's blowing up with more and more offers.

Who knew I'd become addicted to the rush. There's literally nothing like the high of a crowd full of people rocking out to your band.

We file into the green room, which is really a storage closet with a busted door and a cooler of half-flat Red Bulls. Doesn't matter. I'd play a gas station parking lot if it meant chasing this feeling.

Exhausted, I drop onto an overturned gear crate. My tank is stuck to my back, lungs fighting for rhythm. Liam sprawls in a folding chair across from me, towel slung low over his neck, eyes shut, pulse visible in his throat.

Across the room, Felicity paces in slow circles, barefoot. Her heels dangle from one hand. She hums a piece of the chorus under her breath, glowing from the show. Until she glances over at Liam, who doesn't open his eyes. Doesn't move or acknowledge her whatsoever.

Her smile falters for a breath before she leaves abruptly. "I'll be back."

Lately, Felicity watches him all the time. Gives him yearning glances she tries to hide. Laughs at things he says a second too late. For some reason, he ignores her. He certainly doesn't encourage her attention.

In fact, he barely meets her gaze.

Neither of them have said anything in front of me but it's clear she's caught feelings and he's not cool with it. Whatever the hell passed between them, it's annoying. From the way she hangs on his every word, I can tell she hopes he'll throw her a bone.

She'll be waiting for a hundred years. I know my brother. If he's not interested, you don't exist. Which makes the situation uncomfortable.

"Fuck, that was good." Liam moans like he's having the orgasm of his life once she's gone.

My forearms are vibrating. "Yeah. I can't get over how many people knew the words to some of our songs. They love her."

"Nah." He opens one eye. "They love us."

What? He's delusional. Liam likes to be the center of attention for the most part. But, if you believe the hype, Felicity's the reason we're charting on half the college stations west of the Rockies.

"They love Fireball," I concede to keep the peace.

Technically, it's true. The live recording of *Tir na nÓg* made it onto some editor's playlist and now it's wildfire. Felicity's voice cracked something open creatively. Liam and I write the music and we may be the heart, but she's the vessel.

All of that being said, Liam's gotta keep his shit together or Felicity's gonna leave us and we'll be back to square one. He doesn't seem to notice she looks like a kicked puppy whenever he ignores her. We can't expect her to stay if she doesn't feel appreciated.

"Let's get outta here." Liam puts his guitar in its case.

The two of us pack and load the gear in a fog. Liam jumps in the driver's seat and I retrieve Felicity. She rides in the back, cheek pressed to the seat, earbuds in. Liam drives like he's chasing ghosts. His window is cracked barely enough to let the cold roll through.

Attempting to ignore the tension, I text Stevie. When she doesn't reply, I drum rhythms on my knees and count the minutes until I can climb into bed with her.

As usual, by the time we unload our equipment into the house, it's a disaster. Cables snake across the floor like vines. Instruments and amps line the hallway. Boxes of merch are stacked in the foyer.

Rather than help us hump everything to the basement, Felicity vanishes down the hall and into her room. Liam stares at the mess for a second, shakes his head and heads back out. I'm not about to finish the task myself, so I decide to leave it until morning.

I find Stevie curled up in bed, one of my old hoodies swallowing her whole. Laptop open. Sound asleep with papers scattered around her like autumn leaves.

I sit next to her, close her computer and kiss her temple. "We're home."

"Did it go well?" She blinks awake and smiles up at me.

"Amazing." I set her laptop on the nightstand. "We missed you."

She lifts her lips up to kiss me, but something seems off. Her lips part, warm and wanting, but her hand on my chest doesn't grip my shirt and pull me toward her.

I tuck her hair behind her ear, watching her eyes. "You okay?"

"Yeah, why?" She shifts in bed and looks down.

"No reason." I don't press. "I need a shower."

On my way to our bathroom, I strip out of my jeans and step under the scalding spray to try and recalibrate. The lights, the crowd, the crackle of adrenaline buzzes under my skin. Felicity's voice echoes somewhere in my skull.

Stevie's indifferent demeanor gnaws at me.

When I come back to bed, she's on her side. One arm tucked beneath her cheek, blonde hair tangled across the pillow. The curve of her ass catches the amber light from the bedside lamp, soft and familiar and fucking perfect.

I slide in behind her, my cock is thick with the kind of ache only she can ease. My hand trails down the slope of her waist to her thigh, then nudges her knees apart as I press close. Skin to skin. Heat meeting heat.

She doesn't say anything.

Just breathes.

Short, shallow.

I pull her panties to the side and guide myself between her legs, run the tip of my cock through her folds and ease into her pussy in one long, slow thrust. Tight. Wet. Fucking heaven. Her breath catches, and for a second I think I've got her.

She shifts her hips and rolls onto her stomach. Let's me climb over and fuck her.

Except she doesn't push back. Doesn't gasp or clench or beg me to go harder. Her body takes me like it always does, but it's quiet. Muted. Like she's offering herself without being in it fully.

I move slower, grip her thigh tighter. Kiss her shoulder. The base of her neck. Slide my hand under her breast, thrum her nipple and wait for her to arch into me.

She doesn't.

I keep going anyway, because I need her. After a show, this is how I reset. How I find my center. Buried in her. Breathing her in.

My hips roll in smooth, steady strokes. My orgasm builds fast, sharp and hot, cresting with a low groan into the hollow of her neck as I spurt inside her, every nerve fucking wrecked.

She doesn't come. Or make any sound of enjoyment.

Fuck. I'm a selfish bastard. I kiss her shoulder again, fingers drifting down to where we're joined. Try to stroke her the way she likes. Thumb circling her clit. Slow. Gentle.

"I don't think it's happening tonight," she says softly after a bit and moves my hand away.

I still. Rest my hand on her hip.

"Okay," I acknowledge, even though it's not.

Everything in me wants to fix whatever this is. I want my feisty Stevie. All of her. "Babe, are you even with me?"

Holy shit, I unlock the floodgates. She turns, buries her face in my chest and starts to cry. Not softly. Hard sobs shake her tiny frame. I have no idea what's wrong so I hold her tighter.

"I'm drowning," she bawls. "I'm such a fuckup. I forgot to return an email. A huge one. It would've paid the band enough to cover the studio time outright. I didn't even see it until tonight."

My stomach drops. "Shit."

"I'm so sorry, Padraig." Her voice cracks. "I'm doing everything I can, I swear. But school's hard this year. My classes are real. Demanding. I'm trying to be there for you and Liam. I can't keep up. I'm failing at life."

I stroke her cheek soothingly. "Stevie. Baby. You don't have to—"

"I do. Because if I don't, who will?" She sits up and wipes her eyes with the back of her hand. "You're so happy. I see it. I'm so proud. I've never seen you so alive. But you're gone most nights now. I miss you. I miss us. I don't want to be some girl you fuck at three a.m. because you're wired and horny."

I sit up beside her. Pull her into my lap.

"You are my everything. I miss us too, but I'm right here. I haven't gone anywhere." I thread my fingers through her hair.

"You haven't left *yet*." She leans her forehead against mine. "If I don't go with you to a gig, I'm all alone with so much time to think. Sometimes it feels like maybe we're not on the same path anymore and it scares the fuck out of me."

I swallow hard. The thing is, she has nothing to worry about. I'm not giving us up for anything and if she doesn't realize it, I'm the one who's failing. I want it all. I want the band. I want her. I believe we're strong enough to weather this. When we promised each other forever, I meant it.

"I'm not saying I'm gonna quit helping." She exhales. "At the same time, I can't keep up. I don't know how much longer I can pretend I've got it all handled."

Shutting off the lamp, I wrap her in my arms. "You never have to pretend. Not with me."

"Liam's gonna be furious." Her arms circle my neck.

"Shhhh." I feather kisses along her face. "We'll sort it out in the morning."

It's nearly noon. I can hear Liam in the kitchen before I open our bedroom door.

His voice carries over the hiss of the electric kettle. Assuming he's talking to Felicity, I tug on a clean t-shirt and pad barefoot into the hall toward the voices. Stevie trails behind me. No makeup, hair messy, one sleeve slipping off her shoulder. Her knuckles brush mine.

Immediately, I realize Liam isn't with our singer. The deep, musical laugh isn't one I recognize.

Stevie and I round the corner and stop short.

Liam's got some guy pressed against the kitchen counter, one arm braced beside his head, the other wrapped around his waist. Their mouths are fused together, and it's not some quick morning kiss. It's slow and full-bodied. A snog fitting only if you've fucked all night.

The guy is shorter and stockier than Liam with unkempt brown hair and a full beard. I'm not sure if they hear us, but neither seem to be in any rush to break away from each other.

I cough. Once. Twice.

Liam finally notices us and straightens, lips red, breath shallow. "Morning."

"Morning," I manage.

The guy shifts to lean against the counter. The rolled sleeves of his checkered shirt hug muscled forearms. He's got a pair of dark-framed glasses hooked into the collar of his tee. He exudes a calm, quiet energy and it feels like he already belongs here.

"This is Linus." Liam nods to the guy.

"Nice to meet you." His Irish accent is smooth and clipped.

Stevie's eyes widen. "Wait. Are you in Professor Madigan's event planning class? I think I worked with you on site maps during lab."

"Aye." He nods once, measured. "That'd be me."

I look at Liam, who shrugs like this isn't a huge deal, which we both know it is.

Before Stevie and I can say more, the front door creaks open and Felicity enters, thick braid tossed over one shoulder. She's holding a single iced coffee and her backpack. When she sees Liam and Linus side by side, her whole body goes still.

She looks them up and down before abruptly fucking off toward her bedroom.

Stevie holds up her hand. "Felicity. Hang on. Can you stay for a sec?"

Felicity stops but doesn't look back.

I take a step closer as Stevie wraps her arms around herself. She's strong enough to handle this, but I want to be close if she needs me.

"I owe all of you an apology." My girl looks down at the floor and back up again. "I completely spaced responding to the confirmation email for that big Eugene headlining festival gig. I tried to sort it out, but they gave the slot to someone else."

"Are you fucking serious?" Liam winces. "We lost a two thousand dollar guarantee. The band needed the money for the studio."

"I know. I'm truly sorry." Stevie doesn't break eye contact with my brother.

He shakes his head. "This sucks. You said you had it covered."

"I thought I did." She fusses with her hair. "I really fucked up."

Liam exhales through his teeth. "So. Not. Cool."

"Hold up, Dar. Stevie's been running point on every single thing for this band for years." I take her hand. "She won't take money, she does it because she loves us. And, she's been instrumental in getting us here. She made a mistake. Give her a fucking break and don't make her feel worse than she already does."

"I'm not trying to be a dick," Liam gripes. "I'm rightfully disappointed."

"I'll do my best to get you back on the roster." Stevie looks like she's about to cry. "Padraig's right. I love you guys. I love what you're building."

"We need to free you up." I turn to her. "Last night you told me you're drowning. You never promised to be our permanent manager. We can split up the duties and take some of it on."

Linus sets down his mug and wipes his hands on his jeans. "I could maybe help."

Everyone turns to look at Liam's lover.

"I've worked with an indie label in Dublin. Admin. Logistics. Helped book band tours. All of it." He shrugs. "I'd be happy to jump in."

Felicity turns and narrows her eyes at him, but says nothing. Stevie looks utterly relieved.

Liam tilts his head. "Seriously?"

"Aye." Linus meets Stevie's gaze. "I can assist you for a bit. Doesn't have to be permanent. That'd be up to you."

The offer hangs in the air like a lifeline.

It sounds good. *Too* good.

Linus seems competent. Has qualifications. Maybe he's the one person who could help Stevie wrangle our chaos. Did the universe drop the perfect partner for Liam into our lives?

Or, on the other hand, is it wise to allow one of Liam's random hookups to help manage the band? The idea seems...

Worrisome.

I mean, will Liam keep Linus around?

Doubtful.

On second thought, this could be a disaster.

STEVIE

Three Weeks Later

THE FRONT DOOR STICKS like always.

I jam it with my shoulder, bracing for the screech, and step into the usual band chaos.

Gone are the days when Felicity was a quiet mouse. Today, she's perched on the arm of the sunken couch, yammering on about the need for dressing rooms so she can do her makeup. Linus sits nearby, unbothered, a mug of black tea in one hand, the other absentmindedly circling Liam's thigh. Liam is buried in his phone, trying to ignore her.

Padraig glances up from the dining table, where the band's entire summer plans are stacked in chaotic piles of paper. Open spreadsheets. Wrinkled itineraries. Load in print-outs.

Burrito wrappers. He smiles when he sees me and takes a swig from the dented metal water bottle he never washes.

"Hey, babe." He waves me over.

"Stevie, I'm glad you're here," Linus drawls. Calm. Even though I'm twenty minutes late.

I don't bother to make an excuse. Instead, I take the last chair between Padraig and a half-eaten carton of pad Thai. Open my laptop. Nod to Linus and pretend to focus on my screen while I'm mentally questioning everything about the current state of affairs.

It's been a couple weeks since Linus moved in. Liam never asked us for permission, his stuff gradually migrated into the house and now he lives here. Neither Padraig nor I ever questioned it. We don't mind at all.

He's the best roommate. Courteous. Cleans up after himself. Doesn't raise his voice. Doesn't insert himself into anyone's business. He's like a walking exhale.

Felicity isn't quite as supportive.

In a fit of rage, she vented to Padraig about how she and Liam fucked and she doesn't deserve to be treated like a whore.

We asked Liam about it but he wouldn't give details. Typical. All he'd say was he told her it was a one-time thing and she didn't accept it so he cut off all non-band interaction. Unfortunately, his rejection has flipped an internal switch Felicity hasn't been able to shut off. She's borderline obsessed with, I dunno, getting him to change his mind?

It's been hard to ignore. Ever since she joined the band, she always angled to be close to him. Now, it's relentless. In the house, at rehearsals. Brushes past him in the kitchen like it's accidental. Watching him with wide, expectant eyes waiting for some acknowledgement that he never returns. Hangs off him like a blanket on stage when he can't do anything about it.

He never encourages her attention, so I was surprised he admitted fucking her. It makes sense why he hasn't engaged for so long. He'll be polite if she talks to him, but doesn't flirt. Or coddle. Never makes any small talk. He treats her politely, like a business colleague he's not friends with.

His attention is elsewhere now. Liam lights up around Linus. Laughs deeply, in a way I haven't heard since before Rory's accident. There's no second-guessing. No self-destruction. He's able to be himself and I, for one, am happy to see it.

I get why Felicity feels hurt. At the same time her diva-like behavior is becoming a distraction.

I'm snapped back to the band meeting when Liam tosses his phone on the couch. "Stevie. We're two weeks out. Have we received tech specs for the California dates?"

"Oh, aye. I've got San Francisco and Sacramento squared," Linus jumps in. "Waiting on the load-in time for LA and San Diego, though."

Padraig leans forward, forearms braced on the table. "What about confirmation in Seattle? That'll be the biggest local crowd we've had. Connor might play a couple of songs with us, so it's important."

"I'll email the manager again." Linus glances up.

Felicity studies her fingernails. "Stevie, did you confirm the radio appearances?"

The silence in the room is instant. All eyes are on me.

I blink. "What?"

"Remember? You're handling the radio." Liam glances between Linus and me, confusion giving way to quiet irritation.

"When did I say that?" I try to stay calm despite the oppressive weight of disappointing the twins again taking hold. "I remember telling you I didn't have time to make the calls. My midterm presentation is all-consuming."

Padraig sticks up for me, as always. "It's okay, babe. We'll figure it out."

"Well..." Felicity shrugs, tossing her hair over one shoulder. "I don't know why you're even coming to band meetings anymore. Linus handles everything and Padraig covers for you. If you're so busy, maybe you should step down."

Resisting the urge to get bitchy, I patiently remind her, "I'll do what I can but I don't need to step down from a job I don't have. I am *not* Fireball's manager. Besides, I won't be here for the tour anyway."

The entire room goes silent. In my state of shock, I realize I've blurted out some news I'd intended on sharing with only Padraig. Now I've blindsided him, and the rest of the band.

Liam tilts his head. "Wait. What?"

"Shit. I didn't mean to tell you guys this way." I inhale, slow. "So...I heard back from César Ritz."

A beat.

Then two.

Padraig's brows knit together. "As in...the school in Switzerland? You said they wait-listed you."

"Yeah." I look over at him sheepishly. "It was a nearly impossible long-shot, but a spot opened up and I'm in."

"For what?" Liam straightens like I've slapped him.

"An immersive internship for hospitality." I bite my lip and look down. "I can't say no. It's too prestigious. I'll be gone for about six months."

Padraig flinches but maintains his composure in front of the others. "When?"

"Two weeks. The session runs through the end of the year. It's the best program in Europe for hospitality leadership." I gulp down my excitement because I know this is a lot to take in and my delivery has been atrocious.

Out of the corner of my eye I notice Felicity doesn't even pretend to hide her smile. She's not sad about me not being around. That much is clear.

Linus closes his iPad and meets my eyes. "Stevie. How incredible. A great opportunity, so it is."

"Thanks," I murmur, though I can feel the vibes in the room aren't quite as supportive.

Liam doesn't bother to hide his irritation. "Fuck me. Were you going to tell Padraig before the van pulled out?"

"That's not fair. I got the email right before I got here." I slouch down in my chair a bit.

Liam presses his knuckles to his forehead, exasperated. "Well, as much as I hate to admit it, Felicity has a point. You're out, Stevie. No hard feelings, but Fireball needs stability."

I don't know what to say. He's right. And, other than my bad timing, I'm excited to do something else. Adulting sucks sometimes.

"You don't make the call for all of us, Dar," Padraig mumbles despondently. "Stevie's an important part of the band."

Liam looks between us.

"No, they're both right. You don't need to stick up for me. All of you are committed to Fireball, but I have my own career to think about." It comes sharper than I mean to, possibly because Padraig doesn't seem to hear me whenever we talk about it. "Managing Fireball isn't my dream. It doesn't fill me up the way it does all of you."

Hurt flashes in Padraig's eyes, but he masks it quickly. "So you decided, then. You *are* going?"

"Yes. I want this internship. As much as I love you guys, I don't want to spend the summer in a van eating string cheese and gas station burritos, pretending it's my passion." I try to take the sting out with a little humor.

It doesn't land.

Linus clears his throat gently. "Would you like me to take over officially?"

I turn to him, startled. "It's not my call."

"Just a thought." He shrugs, casual but not careless. He addresses the others. "She's done so much for youse but if she'll be gone for so long... Look. I know logistics. I'm happy to do it."

In an instant the vibes shift.

Probably from the weight of how things are changing, settling in.

Padraig stares at the floor. Felicity simmers. Liam nods slowly.

Not the ideal way to start a new job, but at least the band's in good hands.

An hour later after handing off everything to Linus, I close the bedroom door behind me, Padraig plunks down on the edge of the bed, elbows braced to his knees, phone in one hand, the other runs through his hair in slow drags.

He doesn't say anything right away. Neither do I.

After a quick trip to the bathroom, I peel off my clothes and climb into bed. The silence between us is loud.

"I'm so confused. You downplayed this thing," he accuses.

"No." I turn to face him. "It *was* a long shot. I was afraid to hope too hard."

He looks up then. Eyes sharp. "Really?"

I don't answer.

Padraig pushes to his feet. "You haven't mentioned it in weeks. How could you tell me like that? In front of everyone? This doesn't only affect the band, it affects *us*."

"I'm sorry. Really." I sit back against my pillow. "I was put on the spot out there and it slipped out."

"You couldn't tell me first? Privately?" He knots his eyebrows together.

I take a breath. "Obviously, I didn't mean for it to happen in front of the others."

"Are you sure?" He laughs under his breath. "Were you worried how I'd react, Stevie? I'm pissed. I thought we were in this together."

"You know we're in this together." I attempt to persuade him.

He paces a few steps, then turns back. "Do I?"

"Don't do that." I shake my head.

"Don't do what?" His voice rises, not loud, but tight. "Don't be upset you're bailing on me?"

"I'm not bailing on you. I'm bailing on managing the band." I wince at the implication.

He steps closer. "It's the same thing."

"No. This is called a once-in-a-lifetime opportunity. Something that makes sense for *my* future. I didn't think I'd get in, Padraig." I throw my hands in the air, frustrated. "I've supported you unconditionally for fucking years and for once I want to do something for me. Maybe extend me the same courtesy?"

The hurt flickers across his face too fast to catch fully, but it's there. A bruise blooming beneath the surface.

He nods, slow. "Is that why you let Linus take over booking the tour?"

"Yes."

Silence again. Jagged.

Padraig scrubs the stubble on his chin. "You could have gone later, though? Next semester?"

"Possibly," I say carefully. "But I don't want to. The timing on this makes sense for my big picture."

His head lifts and I can't bear the look of devastation in his eyes.

"Padraig. I've helped in every way I know how. I've kept it going when neither of you could be bothered. I've managed shows, schedules, equipment, media, drama." My voice trembles. "I'm proud of what I've helped you build. I really am. But lately..."

He shakes his head. "Spit it out. What?"

"I don't recognize it anymore."

He stiffens. "Because of your stupid beef with Felicity."

"I don't have a beef with her, for fuck's sake. I don't care enough. But, your comment about her is part of it," I admit. "I don't think she's a good fit. Neither does Liam. You and Linus are her cheerleaders and weirdly protect her. You've created a monster."

Padraig scoffs. "We wouldn't be anywhere without her."

His words are a dagger.

"She's a distraction," I shoot back. "You can't see the forest for the trees. Liam only tolerates her because of you. She's spiraling because he's with Linus. You're so scared she's gonna quit, you prop her up like the whole band hinges on her well-being. Don't be naive. With me out of the picture, you'll be her next obsession."

"You're wrong. She's crucial to the success of this band."

I grit my teeth. "For fuck's sake, she's not irreplaceable."

"She's fragile, Stevie." He sighs.

"She's manipulative."

He blinks. "That's not fair."

"She clings to some fantasy Liam will ditch Linus and suddenly give her what he never promised. The woman barely acknowledges I exist anymore." I point at him. "Even worse, she leans on you like you're her only friend. Why do you coddle her?"

He doesn't answer. Same argument. Different day.

I grab his hand and tug him down into bed. "Babe, you can't see what this is doing to you. You're emotionally carrying everything and everyone. For the longest time, the band was everything to Liam so you stuck with it. Now he has Linus. You're twenty-one. Is this really your dream too?"

"It is." He juts out his chin defiantly.

"Are you sure?" I gesture to a half-finished art piece taking up nearly an entire wall.

His shoulders sag, like I pulled the last string holding him up.

I don't want to hurt him. I love him. God, I love him so much it aches in my ribs. But I'm exhausted pretending I don't see what's happening.

"I'm going because it's what I want for my future career. Don't I deserve to pursue something too?" I nestle under his arm.

He doesn't speak for a long time.

"Okay."

I wait, but he doesn't say more.

"Okay?" I ask, wary.

"You want honesty?" he says, resigned. "I wish you'd stay. I wish we could spend the summer the way we planned. I'm not going to ask you to choose the band over your own career..." He pauses. "Even if I'm scared you'll come back and want to ditch me."

My throat goes tight. "You're nuts. I don't want a life without you. You're my beginning, middle, and end game."

"I'm only upset because you didn't have to keep it from me." He looks at me now. "I wish you'd have told me first, so I could have processed it."

My eyes sting because I've told him so many times and it's clear he hasn't listened. Now's not the time to get defensive. It's time to apologize and make up. "Babe, I'm so sorry. I fucked up. I never want to disappoint you."

"Stevie." His voice drops. "You could never."

I crawl into his lap, knees bracketing his hips. I press my forehead to his. "I'm not leaving you."

He swallows but doesn't speak.

"I love you," I whisper. "I want us. I want *all* of it."

He pulls in a shaky breath. "Why does this feel like the beginning of the end?"

"It's not," I promise, even though I worry too.

He exhales sharply. Then cups my face. "You're breaking my fucking heart."

Those eyes.

Everything I've ever wanted lives in them.

"I *love* you," I repeat.

"I love you too. Come here." He leans back onto the bed, dragging me with him.

I tug at his shirt, and he shrugs it off. His jeans go next. My panties follow. No words now. No space between us.

His gaze sweeps over me like he's starving. My knees straddle his hips and I feel the thick, hard press of his cock between us. He grips my thighs. Sits up to kiss me with his whole mouth. Hungry. Aching. Like he's imprinting me with every stroke of his tongue.

His hands roam everywhere. My shoulders. My back. The curve of my ass. He palms my tits, sucks a nipple into his mouth and groans like he's starving for it.

I reach between us and wrap my fingers around him. Guide him inside me with one hand, sinking down in a slow, aching slide.

We both gasp.

I plant my hands on his chest and push him back down. His fingers wrap tight around my hips. I start to move, slow at first, then faster as the tension builds.

He catalogues every inch of my body as I ride him. Palms my breasts. Skims the backs of my thighs. Trails up my arms. Cups my face.

I shudder. Rock harder. He meets every movement like he needs this to anchor him.

"I love you," he grits out. "Even when I don't understand."

"And I love you," I breathe back. "Even when I'm afraid I'm fucking everything up."

His eyes search mine. "You aren't."

I leaned down and kiss him. Open-mouthed. Desperate. He presses against my lower back so his pubic bone hits my clit and we move together in frantic rhythm. I come first, pulsing around him, mouth parted in a silent cry. He's not far behind, arms locked around me, hips grinding up deep as he spills inside me.

We stay connected. Sweaty. Shaking. Tangled together. Knowing the world's about to shift beneath us before we're ready.

Not a goodbye.

Not yet.

Eleven

PADRAIG

Three Months Later

THE ROAR OF THE crowd's rattling through my bones when the dressing room door clicks shut behind us.

All three of us are sweat-soaked, riding the afterglow.

It's our final show of the tour and we didn't simply survive it, we fucking crushed it. Seattle showed up big time. A packed house. Everyone chanting our name. I swear the floor shook during the finale of *Tir na nÓg*.

Connor follows us in from side stage, straight to the ice chest full of beverages. He digs through the cans before cracking open a root beer with a grin. "Proud of you both. Even prouder there's no booze."

Liam and I never second-guess our decision to tour dry. No beer, wine, or liquor in the dressing room. No drink tickets or after-show shots. No airline bottles or flasks tucked into duffels. It's our one nonnegotiable.

Not because of Da, though it's certainly a factor. We've seen too many bands use gigs as an excuse to party and it makes them lose focus.

Not us. We don't have the luxury.

Connor slumps into the sagging loveseat. He hasn't stopped grinning with pride since the encore where he joined us onstage. Liam paces, jittery from adrenaline, hair damp, cheeks flushed.

Felicity hovers near the makeup mirror, blotting her lipstick like she's prepping for paparazzi. She shoots me a look over her shoulder.

"C'mon. Can't we splurge on champagne for the last night?" She sticks out her lower lip.

I don't take the bait. "Felicity. If you want to get fucked up, we have the next few weeks off. Do it on your own time."

"For a bunch of Irish guys, you're no fun." She pouts. "Too fucking wholesome."

Connor's eyes pop out a bit. Liam acts like she doesn't exist. I shake my head.

She shrugs and resumes adjusting her eyeliner, like we're the ones being inappropriate.

"Hey, love, mind giving us a minute, yeah? Family stuff." Connor gives her a nod toward the door.

She looks up, feigning confusion. "Oh, don't worry about me. Go about your business."

"Jesus Christ. Take a fucking hint," Liam snarls, tossing a towel over his shoulder.

Her lips press tight. She stands, slow and dramatic. "For the record. This is *my* band too. I've been part of every show. Every mile on the road. Every song. I'm sick of being treated like an outsider."

"Felicity, c'mon." I try to soften the edge. "We haven't seen our brother in over a year. This isn't band shit, it's family, okay?"

She scoffs, yanks her bag off the floor, flips her hair over one shoulder and stalks out without another word.

The second the door closes, Liam flops into the chair across from Connor, exhaling hard.

"She's not happy," I sigh.

Liam raises an eyebrow. "She's never fucking happy."

Connor leans forward, forearms on his thighs. "So. Give me the download. Tour highs, tour lows, what the fuck happened in L.A."

Liam catches my eye and smirks. "What didn't?"

"Honestly?" I lean back and let my head hit the wall. "We made it through with minimal damage. Linus killed it as a manager. We had decent crowds. Alt Rock stations are spinning *Tir na nÓg* nonstop."

"And the band dynamic?" Connor's low voice is almost surgical.

Liam shifts. "There's no way around it. Felicity's...difficult. Intense. Great singer but, fuck me, she's unbearably entitled."

"You're too hard on her. She's a hard worker. Her bad attitude is because you shagged and dumped her." I toss a scrunched-up napkin at him.

He shrugs. "Dar. Let it fucking go. It was *months* ago. She slipped into my room night after night, wouldn't take no for an answer and I fucking regret giving in every day. Worst fuck of my life."

"Ah, well." Connor nods, unsurprised.

"She was heartbroken," I add. "Now, it's turning..."

Connor narrows his eyes. "Turning how?"

"I'm getting a vibe," I admit.

Liam clicks his teeth. "Vibe my ass. Call it like it is. She gets nowhere with me so she's now shifted to you."

"No." I blink. "She has *not*. She *knows* I'm essentially married to Stevie."

Connor sits back. "Actually, Liam, I see what you mean."

"What the fuck." I flush. "I haven't encouraged it."

"Don't act naive. You comfort her when she's spiraling." Liam flips me off. "You fawn all over her. Tell her she's amazing every show. When Stevie told us she wasn't coming on the tour, the woman lit up like a candle."

"Fuck you," I seethe. "You treat her like absolute shit. She's our *bandmate*. A singer who we can't get by without. I'm trying to hold it together. Because if she quits—"

Liam squares up to me. "You're an idiot. She'll *never* quit. We're the best thing she's got going and if you don't put her in her place she'll cling harder. Would you want Stevie to see how she 'accidentally' seems to always fall asleep on your shoulder in the van?"

"Whoa, that's not good." Connor looks between us. "And, she's not the reason Fireball works. You two are."

"She's got a great voice," I argue, annoyed that my brothers are ganging up on me. "The crowd loves her."

"Because her tits are hanging out. She's doesn't write. She doesn't manage. She contributes nothing but decent vocals." Connor leans forward. "In the five seconds I've known her, she seems like drama."

I glance at Liam. "Well, so is he."

Liam grins.

Connor nods curtly. "The difference is, you can trust him with your life."

I hang my head because I know he's right. Felicity has been a bit more clingy lately.

"Speaking of trusting with your life." Connor juts out his chin. "How's Stevie?"

The breath I take is a little too deep. "She's good. We're good. She loves her program. Switzerland's intense but she's thriving."

Liam quirks his lip.

"So, if I've got this right." Connor's gaze burrows into mine. "For the next few months, your girl lives in the Alps with some of the most eligible hospitality guys around the globe while you hole up in Pullman with a fame-obsessed vocalist who screwed your twin and probably is turning her attention to you?"

I tense. "I trust her."

"I'm not worried about Stevie." Connor crosses his arms.

Liam chuckles.

"Felicity has been part of Fireball all year," I protest. "Lay off."

"I'm not telling you to fire her, Padraig. I'm warning you to set your own boundaries. You're always the caregiver." Connor holds up his hand when I open my mouth to protest. "Say no to her. Don't indulge. Let her unravel without taking her side against your brother."

Shit. Is this what I've been doing?

Liam folds his arms. "Con, it's fine. Padraig has a kind heart and Linus keeps her in check."

"You sure?" Connor looks pointed. "Because she's still living with you. Holding on to whatever she can."

"Here's my take." Liam rubs the back of his neck. "She's not a long-term solution. Being Fireball's singer isn't going to be enough for her." He glances at me, then back at Connor. "When she joined the band, we were excited and invited her to live at our house, so we could write and practice. In hindsight, it was a huge mistake because we can't really kick her out." He huffs out a breath. "God, I hate my sex drive sometimes. It's created a dynamic we can't shake."

I shoot my twin a look. "Thank you for finally acknowledging it."

"Aye." Liam nods to me and continues for Connor's sake. "Look, I'm trying but I'm so uncomfortable around her."

My eyebrows raise in surprise. I didn't know.

"So, about Linus." Connor's gaze flickers. "It's real then?"

Liam pauses before grinning from ear to ear. "Aye, it's real."

"Good." Connor claps him on the shoulder. "You deserve it. You don't need to hide who you are."

Liam doesn't answer. We all know what he's thinking.

Connor's tone softens. "Well, maybe from Da. Thing's aren't great."

Instantly, a chill settles into our bones.

"How bad?" I brace for the update. It's been a blissful few months of ignoring the issues at home.

"He barely gets out of the chair." Connor wraps his hand around the root beer can, thumb tapping the rim. "Without the meds, pain's unmanageable. Ma's trying everything. Home physio. Massage. None of it's working. He's barely fighting anymore."

Liam's pacing slows. We both look at him.

Connor shakes his head sadly. "She doesn't say it of course, but she's scared. Really scared. I've hired someone to help me out so she can focus on getting him better."

The weight of what's happening in our family home lands heavy between us.

"She's excited to see youse," he reminds us. "We'll all have breakfast tomorrow so you can spend some time with her and the wee lads. We'll meet you at the restaurant."

My chest seizes as the reality of the situation sets in. Connor booked the band a couple of hotel rooms as a surprise. Obviously, he doesn't want Liam and Linus to stay at the house.

"We keep in regular touch with the boys. Tell the truth, how are they doing?" I tamp down the guilt I feel for leaving them behind.

"Coping." Connor considers his words. "Cillian's quiet. Apologetic for Da, for some reason. Always holed up in his room with headphones on, pretending he can't hear the yelling. Thinks if he ignores it, it won't touch him."

Liam snorts softly.

"Brennan's on his computer day and night. Also with headphones on. Hackathons, Discord. Reddit rabbit holes. None of it makes sense to anyone but him. He's coping the way he knows how, by zoning the fuck out."

I grimace. "And Seamus?"

"Ah, the wee one." Connor exhales through his nose. "Too perceptive for his own good. Keeps asking medical questions no one seems to be able to answer. Why Da drinks so much. If there's something wrong with his brain. I swear that boy is going to be a doctor or something."

Liam runs a hand over his mouth.

I close my eyes for a beat. Our childhood house used to be alive. Full of music and laughter and bad jokes. Ever since Da's accident, life as we knew it has imploded. It's hard to keep up hope we'll ever come back from this.

Connor stands. "You two staying away isn't a mistake. He's not even lucid enough to register any of us half the time. But Ma, she needs to see your faces. Even if it's only for breakfast and coffee."

"We'll be there," I promise.

Liam nods. "Aye, we'll be there."

"I'm proud of youse." Connor grips the door handle. "You've got this thing taking off but don't keep someone around who isn't worthy." He points at me. "Don't let Stevie get away." Points to Liam. "I'm glad you've found someone who sees you. He seems to be the real deal."

"He is," he murmurs.

"One last thing," Connor adds. "You're in the home stretch. Finish school. Don't roll your eyes, Liam. I'm serious. You've got momentum, but it's a fickle game. One viral hit doesn't mean stability. Get your degree. Music isn't going anywhere."

Liam stiffens, but nods in agreement.

"And, Padraig." His gaze lands on me. "You're allowed to want more than holding this together."

Then he's gone.

Silence creeps in as Liam and I exchange a glance. He gives me a two-finger salute and follows Connor. "I'm gonna find Linus."

I sit alone in the empty green room staring at my scuffed boots amongst the crushed water bottles littering the floor. The ghost of the crowd echoes in my ears.

Tonight was incredible. A high unlike no other.

Except for I miss Stevie.

Three months without her hasn't been easy. We have three months to go.

She asked me once, "Is this really what you want, or are you all-in because it's what Liam needs?"

I didn't have an answer then.

I don't now.

All I know is absence does make the heart grow fonder.

I can't live without my girl.

Twelve

Three Months Later

I'M IN THE MIDDLE of holiday chaos of SeaTac.

A toddler wails behind me in the long customs line while a woman in a red scarf shouts angrily into her phone. I'm being jostled and nudged nonstop. I may pee my pants if things don't get moving soon.

Doesn't matter. Nothing can dampen my mood.

I'm home.

When it's my turn, I dig out my passport and get it stamped, then everything moves in a blur. I grab my bags, coast through customs and head for the tram to the arrivals area.

As the train speeds toward my destination, I wrap the camel coat I bought in Switzerland snug over the blouse I steamed a million hours ago before I departed.

The girl who left Seattle wore t-shirts, denim, and ChapStick. This new version of me is polished. Professional. Certain. Like the woman I want to become.

Only, I'm quivering beneath it all.

Because I'm about to see him.

Padraig.

It's been months without his hands on my body, his mouth dragging over my skin and his breath heaving when I fall apart for him.

We may have spoken nearly every day, but a screen can't kiss you. Video sex kept us sane, but let's be real. A pixelated orgasm isn't the same as being split open by someone who knows your body like a prayer.

I've missed him every second with a deep, unwavering ache.

I loved Switzerland., but I love him more.

When I step off the escalator, my suitcases bump behind me as I weave past families holding signs and couples crashing into each other with duffel bags and wide-eyed grins. I scan the crowd, pulse in my ears, searching for the one person I've craved every single night since I left.

And then—

There he is.

Leaning against a column like the whole airport's background noise. Black jeans slung low on his hips. Boots beat to hell. Long charcoal hoodie layered under his ancient, cracked leather jacket. His hair is even longer than it was in June, brushing past the sharp lines of his cheekbones, over his shoulders.

Wild and stupidly perfect.

Padraig's fingers tug at his bottom lip until his eyes find mine. Everything in him stills as I approach. He lifts a white, crinkled paper bag. I recognize the logo. Café Besalu. I know what's inside. An almond croissant. My favorite since we were thirteen.

Everything inside me explodes.

For half a breath, I can't even move. He crosses the short distance between us in long, purposeful strides. Then he's in front of me and I'm enveloped in his arms. The croissant hits the floor. My arms wrap around his neck and I bury my face into his shoulder.

His arms cage me, one hand grips the back of my head, the other flattens against the small of my back.

"I missed you." I breathe in his scent. "*God*, I missed you."

His nose skims along my cheek. "I'm so happy you're home. You look and smell amazing."

"Oh." I laugh. "New clothes. Swiss shampoo."

His mouth finds mine. Hot. Desperate. Our lips smash together. His tongue slips in like he's starving and I'm the only thing he wants to taste. It's messy. Public.

I don't care.

He breaks away first. "Let's get the fuck outta here."

Ten minutes later, Padraig lugs my suitcases behind him and we weave past the crowds in record time. Outside, it's raining of course and colder than I expected. He yanks open the back of the band's van, sticker-bombed from the tour, and tosses my belongings inside. We get in and he peels out of the parking garage.

We don't talk much on the drive, not because there's nothing to say. We're too busy stealing glances. Caressing each other. His hand stays on my thigh the entire time, thumb tracing over the fabric of my slacks like he's relearning the shape of me.

I'm surprised when he steers downtown instead of taking the exit toward Capitol Hill toward our families' neighborhood. Seattle glows under the magic of a million holiday lights. Soft gold and silver strands strung from awnings and wrapped around trees.

When he pulls into valet at the W, I blink in happy surprise. "Seriously? You booked a hotel?"

"We've been apart six months. I'm not spending tonight sneaking into your childhood bedroom trying not to wake your parents when I fuck your brains out." He glances over and winks.

A beat passes. Electricity surges through my body. "Okay, then."

He hands the keys to the valet and leads me through the glass doors with unshakable purpose. Low ambient music pulses beneath the soft hush of voices in the lobby. Evergreen garlands drape the front desk, velvet ribbon threaded through golden pinecones. The scent of fir, leather, and something faintly spiced lingers in the air.

He checks us in. Confident. Calm. Focused.

Watching him, I burn. I want to crawl inside his coat, press my face to his chest, and revel in this moment. Strip away every polished piece of the woman I've become and return to the high-school girl who used to curl against him under the sheets as we learned how to please each other.

He palms the keycard, pulls me close and we're on the move. My cheek brushes his collar. Air stretches tight between us, thick with memory and need. Our time apart collapses into seconds.

The doors open to a long, muted hallway. Gold sconces flicker against dark walls. He finds our room and slides the key against the card reader. We step inside. Rain streaks the windows in silver ribbons. Exposed brick glows in the lamplight. A king bed waits in the center. Turned down. Untouched.

Not for long.

We stand there. Then I move. Or, maybe he does.

In any case, we collide. Mouths open, breath stolen. His hands grip my waist, then lift as his palms flatten over my ribs, my back, my hips. Each touch greedy and grounded, like he's desperate to confirm I'm real.

My fingers dig into his jaw, along his shoulders, then tangle in the long strands of the wavy hair I've dreamed about for months. Feeling him. Breathing him. Loving him.

The room tilts. We stumble toward the bed.

Padraig peels my coat down my arms. Tosses it. Unbuttons my shirt one button at a time, his mouth hovering, breath uneven. He doesn't rush. He maps me. His fingertips brush the swell of my breast above my bra, across the center of my sternum, against the mole below my collarbone he loves to kiss before we fall asleep every night.

Brown eyes find mine, misty with emotion. His lips part, like he might say something.

I shake my head. "No, let's talk later. I need you to keep touching me."

So, he does.

Both hands trail from my shoulders to my hips. No hesitation. Nothing held back. He drops to his knees and presses his mouth over the front of my slacks, inhaling deeply. Then he undoes the button, slides the zipper slow, and shucks them down my legs and I step out of them.

His mouth trails from my ankle up my shin, tongue tracing my inner knee. My thighs shake with anticipation. He groans and rises once again, sweeping me up in his arms. His lips slant over mine and our tongues dance to our favorite song.

I tear at his jacket. Yank it off. Then the hoodie. His shirt. He's thinner than when I left. Ripped, all sinew and definition from long hours onstage. My palms glide across his taut abs, nails raking lightly down his chest against his nipples and he gasps into my mouth.

We fall back onto the bed in a tangle of limbs and memories.

He kisses every inch of me. My throat, my sternum, the slope of my tits. He tugs down the cups of my bra and sucks on my nipples until I moan and I arch.

"I missed these." He licks the curve of my breast.

"You missed me."

"Every fucking day." His fingers hook the waistband of my panties and he pulls them down, lowering himself to kiss the inside of my thigh.

He moves lower and drags his tongue up my center with gusto. "Oh my God...*Padraig*—"

I barely get the words out when he wraps one arm under my thigh and pulls me closer. His tongue swirls, presses, plunges. I grab fistfuls of the duvet and clamp my thighs around his ears, but he doesn't stop. One finger slips inside. Then another. I lose track of words. Time. Space. Breaking apart in a rush, shaking and calling his name.

He doesn't stop until I tug his hair hard enough to make him growl.

Padraig looks up at me from between my legs, his eyes molten. "You're unreal. Fucking heaven."

"I want your cock." I reach for his jeans.

He helps, pulling them down and tossing them across the room. No boxers. No hesitation. Skin, heat, and his shaft heavy in my hand. Thick, hot, hard in a way that makes my mouth water. I stroke him once, twice, and he bites down on his bottom lip as his eyes flutter closed.

I guide him against me.

He pauses.

Then he slides into me slow, thick, and unforgiving. We lock eyes, my calves hooked around his waist, his palms braced beside my head, every inch of him buried inside me.

"Fuck, Stevie." His breath catches. "You're so fucking tight."

My back arches, heat blooms between my legs. "God, babe, don't stop."

His hips start to move, slow at first, then rougher, harder, until I can't think. Can't speak. I grip his biceps, my nails biting deep. Sweat glistens on his skin as he fucks me with an intensity I can't get enough of.

"You feel this?" His voice is shredded. "Am I fucking you good, Stevie?"

Every stroke hits exactly where I need it. Deep and deliberate. "Yes. God, yes."

He shifts, lifting my hips slightly so he can go harder and deeper. It steals the air from my lungs. My head falls back.

I can't hold still. Can't keep quiet. "I need you. I need you more than anything."

"I'm nothing without you." His mouth moves against mine, wet and bruising. His hips hammer until I break apart. My body locks and vision goes white-hot. Pleasure pulses through every nerve.

He flips me onto my stomach, palms dragging me back by the hips. "Again."

"Yes." I brace against the mattress. He drives into me in one brutal stroke. "Do not stop. I want you to be inside me all night."

The room fills with the sound of skin slapping, broken cries, the creak of the bed under every punishing thrust. One hand on my waist, the other between my legs, fingers rough and perfect until I'm coming again.

"Fuck, *Ohmygod*—"

Padraig grunts as he pulses deep inside me. When he finally collapses and rolls us to our sides, both of us are wrecked and breathless. His chest presses against my back and his arms wrap around me, locking me in tight.

We stay like that. Raw. Quiet.

His lips find my shoulder. My neck. My spine.

"I'm never letting you go again," he murmurs.

He turns me beneath him, cradles my face with both hands, and kisses me slow.

"And, don't fall asleep. We're not done," he whispers. "Not even close."

"I didn't know it would feel like this," I whisper against his lips.

"Like what?"

"Home is wherever you are."

He pulls me closer. "Thank God you feel the same way."

Thirteen

PADRAIG

Four Months Later

THE MORNING CRAWLS SLOW.

It always feels this way the night after a tough rehearsal.

I'm thankful for some alone time. It's rare. Light spills crooked through the bent blinds, slanting across the coffee table, which is littered with empty mugs and guitar picks. A couple of my cracked drumsticks poke out from underneath Liam's textbook.

I should clean up, it's probably my turn but I can't seem to move. My spine is sunk deep into the cushions, my legs stretched out in front of me. Some morning show's on mute and the remote is nowhere in sight.

I can't find it in me to care.

Class started thirty minutes ago. Doesn't matter. I'm not going.

I'm surprised when the door creaks behind me and Liam emerges from his room barefoot, tugging on a sweatshirt. His hair is wild from sleep. He squints when he sees me and smirks.

"Jesus, you look rough." He heads for the fridge.

I flip him off. "You're not so bad yourself."

He grabs a yogurt and a bottle of water, then flops into the armchair across from me. Rests his foot on the coffee table next to the mugs as he peels the foil off the container. "Where's everyone?"

"Linus must be in class, but you'd now more than me. Stevie's with her study group prepping for her marketing presentation. Felicity left early."

Liam snorts. "I thought it was too quiet."

"It's fucking heaven." I stretch out even longer and turn to my side.

His eyes narrow, but not at me. He been clocking it too. Felicity barely speaks to him anymore unless it's about a setlist or a rehearsal change. As he and Connor predicted, her sugary tone's reserved for me now.

Ever since Stevie left she's made it known I'm her new target. From the relentless hovering and trying to catch my eye to the suggestive text messages to the overt come-ons. It's uncomfortable.

Then, yesterday, she brought me a chai latte and dropped a hand on my shoulder when Stevie was packing up her laptop.

Let's just say, it didn't go unnoticed.

To make matters worse, Felicity pushed things too far during a band meeting.

Liam spoons a mouthful of yogurt. "So, now you have to avoid her too?"

"Yeah.." I palm my face in my hand.

He grimaces. "She's not subtle."

"No."

We sit in the silence except for the heater spluttering behind him. Something about the quiet makes me edgy.

I don't want to talk about Felicity. Not really. I have no choice after what happened.

Glancing at the clock, I realize Stevie should be halfway through her group session. She left this morning with her brow furrowed, no kiss or smile. She's upset and has every right.

"She pissed?" Liam juts his chin out.

I nod.

"She should be." He states the obvious.

I pull a throw pillow against my chest. "We never fight. It sucks."

"No relationship is perfect." Liam licks his spoon clean.

I glance at him. Raise an eyebrow.

Liam drops the yogurt container with a dull thud, eyes locked on the wall. "I'd be irate, Dar. Felicity humiliated her. All she did was clarify one historical detail Linus got wrong. Nothing dramatic. Felicity snapped. Told her unless she was strumming a guitar or shaking her tits onstage, she should shut her mouth about the band."

The memory hangs sour in the air.

"You didn't defend your girl, man," he adds. "You sat there. What the fuck?"

"What should I have done?" I sit up straighter, stomach twisting.

Liam doesn't flinch. "You should have put Felicity in her place."

I'm nearly able to conjure a smile at the memory of how composed Stevie was when she retorted, cool as glass, sharp as a knife.

"I was only clarifying the timeline." She lifted her glass with a serene smile she keeps in her back pocket for women who think

they're dangerous. "If you seriously feel the need to shake your tits onstage to get Padraig's attention, maybe the problem isn't me."

Then she stood, walked to our room and shut the door hard enough to rattle the frame.

In my defense, it all happened so fast I was stunned. For one, I had no idea what Liam's been dealing with and he actually fucked the girl. I also never thought I'd have to explain why I'm not interested. Do I really have to be an asshole? Stevie and I are a couple. She knows this.

"Stevie can take care of herself. She handled it like a pro. She'd never want me to fight her battles," I finally answer. It's not a lie. Not exactly.

Except, he knows how Felicity kept it going even after Stevie left. Tossing in snide comments about how hotel interns don't run bands and how band girlfriends are the worst.

While it was happening, Linus frowned down at his laptop. Liam didn't say anything right away, either.

Not until now.

Why? Because it wasn't their place. It was mine.

It all hits me at once. *Fuck.* I failed to stand up for my girlfriend.

"Shit. I fucked up," I admit.

Liam sucks in a deep breath. "Sometimes you are so fucking thick. Look, I love the girl. I'm not always the best at being sensitive to you and Stevie playing house, but she's like a sister to me. Dar, she looked gutted."

I know.

God, what's happened to me? I used to be the kind of guy who protected the people he loved. If something was wrong, I'd be the first to call it out.

For the past few years, I don't have the stomach for it. I've done everything in my power to keep things smooth. Calm.

Sometimes it feels like if I step wrong, everything will come apart again.

"I didn't mean to leave her hanging," I finally eek out a wimpy excuse. "She's mad, though."

Liam meets my gaze. "Remember. She doesn't need you perfect. She needs you in her corner."

"I get it. I didn't want any confrontations. We're weeks out from recording and the meeting was important to get through."

He clicks his tongue and paces toward the window. "So you decided it was okay for Felicity to piss on Stevie to keep the peace? How in fuck does your brain work? Who are you keeping the peace with?"

"It's not that simple."

"It fucking is." He points at me. "Miss Diva's got everyone walking on eggshells. Linus can barely wrangle her anymore, and he managed Alt-J during their UK Tour."

I laugh under my breath, more out of nerves than humor.

Liam doesn't mince words. "I think we should push the EP, fire Felicity and get a new singer."

"What?" I'm shocked because recording an EP is all he and Linus talk about. All day. Every day. "Are you serious?"

He turns, hands in his pockets. "Dead. I spoke with Linus last night and convinced him. We want to rethink the sound. Strip it down. Get it right."

"You and Linus are making creative decisions for the band now?" I'm genuinely unnerved by this entire discussion.

"Yeah. He's got great instincts and was trained by the best." Liam drops onto the couch beside me. "You'd know, Dar, if you ever actually looped in to a business conversation about Fireball."

I sit up straighter. "Don't start."

"Start what?" He leans back, one arm over the cushion, watching me like he's waiting to pounce.

"Acting like I'm not participating. You and Linus are always off scheming about what comes next, and I'm the one trying to hold things together while everything cracks."

His brow lifts. "I'm not scheming. I'm working hard on building something that'll outlast us if we do it right."

"So am I."

He doesn't blink. "Are you?"

The pause grows teeth. I glance at Liam's guitars leaning against the wall.

"You used to have a take on everything." Liam puts his hand on my leg. "You, me, Stevie. We made the early calls together. Every song, every gig, every post. Now she offers her opinion and Felicity slices her down midsentence. And you let it happen rather than standing your ground or offering your own thoughts."

His voice dips low. "It's gone on too long and I hate watching you fade out."

I shake my head. "You're not being fair."

"Maybe." He shrugs. "Maybe not. Convince me."

"I'm here." I slam my hand on the armrest. "Every fucking day. Sacrificing myself to keep the peace so we don't lose traction."

"Sacrificing my ass. Fireball is ours, no one else's." Liam snakes his arm around my shoulders.

I flinch, not meaning to.

"I know what it's like," Liam whispers into my ear. "Standing next to a couple, feeling out of place. For years, it was you and Stevie and I was always on the fringe. I used to pretend it didn't sting. Now Linus is in the thick of it with me, and I'm trying to make the band better. Future-proof. For us. For Connor."

"I'm not jealous."

"I didn't say you were." He releases me and leans forward. "My point is, as far as I'm concerned, Felicity doesn't speak for you. Or me. Or for this band. She's shifting the vibe and I don't like it."

I rub the back of my neck. "Her voice is second to none. She's...familiar. Predictable. At least we know how to work around her."

"Do we?" Liam asks. "I sure the fuck don't. Are you saying you'd rather keep spinning in circles with someone you don't even trust?"

My jaw drops. Is he right?

He nudges my knee. "You've always been the one who kept us steady. All I'm saying is, don't let her pull you under and wreck things with Stevie as you sink."

"What the fuck's that supposed to mean?" I shove the pillow aside.

"You've been all over the place lately. Checked out in rehearsal. Fumbling lyrics you wrote. Pretending Felicity's not a problem when she's tanking morale."

"I'm not pretending—"

Liam doesn't push right away. He lets me breathe, even though the long silence stretching between us causes the air to thicken with everything unspoken. Then he leans over and rests his arms on his knees.

"Dar," he says quietly. "You keep letting Felicity run the show because you think it's safer than starting over. I get it. You don't seem to realize it's killing the thing we built and now it's affecting your relationship."

"She's a pain in the hole." I scrub my palm down my face. "The thought of auditioning someone else and resetting makes me want to crawl out of my skin. I don't know if I've got it in me."

Liam squints. "Really?"

"She got a job offer in New York." I stare at my hands. My knuckles are pale from how tight they're clenched.

Liam's brow arches. "Stevie?"

"Yeah, a big hospitality group," I add. "Entry-level, but solid. Great pay. She hasn't accepted yet."

He whistles low. "Fuck."

"Yeah."

"She'd have to move?"

I nod again. "This summer."

"Ah, shit." He leans back, eyes narrowing. "What's she thinking?"

"She wants to go." I try to stop my eyes from filling with tears.

"And you?"

"I want her to have the world," I choke out. "I'd be lying if I said the thought of her leaving doesn't gut me."

He's quiet for a long beat. "Ah, well that explains your reaction last night. You're upset."

"Ah, fuck…" I shake my head. "My mind is everywhere."

Liam watches me, careful now. "You wanna go with her?"

"I've thought about it."

"Seriously?"

"It's just…" I pause. "I've always loved our music, yeah, but I'm not you. I don't need the spotlight. I've always needed her."

He exhales, rubbing his palm along his scruff. "I know."

"I'm not sure what to do." I gaze up at him. "I always thought Stevie would get her degree but tour with me. I've buried my head in the sand. She really *doesn't* want to do this with us."

"She loves you. Don't be mad at her for wanting her own career." Liam leans back and watches me carefully. "I understand how you feel, though. Linus' visa runs through school so there's a countdown with us too."

"At least he *wants* to manage the band and be with you. Stevie can't wait to leave," I admit. "I'd go with her in a heartbeat, but I don't want her to feel like I'm trying to cage her in."

"You would be, though," he says gently. "What's in it for you besides her? If you don't have your own plan it's not a partnership. It's pressure."

I lean back and stare at the ceiling. "I'm committed to Fireball, but I'm not sure I'm making the decision for myself or it's been made for me. I'm so focused on making sure you and me stick together and navigating Felicity's chaos, I don't even know what I want anymore."

"You're twenty-two. You're allowed to not know. You're allowed to change your mind."

I look over at him, the ache sharp and close to the surface. "I love her."

"I know you do. I'd fucking murder anyone who tried to come between you." He nudges my arm. "Don't let fear make your choices. Not about her. Not about the band. You've got more say than you think."

"My head is messed up." I'm utterly exhausted from the stress of all of it.

Once again, Liam doesn't press. He knows I need some space.

Eventually, he says, "Whatever comes next, I want you in it. I'm telling you, though, Felicity's not the answer. We started this thing because we believed in it. We believed in each other."

I nod, fighting tears.

"You're my anchor." He leans over and pecks my temple. "Always have been."

He doesn't say more. Doesn't need to.

I know what my future is.

Will Stevie be by my side?

Only time will tell.

Fourteen

STEVIE

The Next Morning

HE'S ALREADY INSIDE ME **when I open my eyes.**

Our bodies fit the way they always have. Perfect. Familiar. Everything I've ever needed.

Not enough to quiet the ache building in my chest.

Padraig's forehead is buried in my neck. His arms are braced on either side of my head like he's holding himself upright with muscle memory alone. We move in a rhythm so old it's tattooed into my spine. Slow. Deep. A little ragged. He kisses me mid-thrust, mouth hot and open, tongue sweeping mine like it's been six months since Switzerland and not six hours since the last time.

I squeeze my legs around his hips. "Harder."

He groans into my neck, shifts the angle and fucks me until my thighs burn.

I come with his name breaking from my lips. His breath catches in a suspended, sacred moment—then he's spilling inside me, chest crushed to mine, whispering 'love you, love you, love you,' like a vow.

We don't move for a long time.

My nails scrape lightly along his back. His hand drifts down my side, smoothing the sheet over my hip. He presses a kiss behind my ear, then my shoulder, then my collarbone like he's memorizing my body cell by cell.

"Good morning," I say softly.

He nods against my skin. "I wanted you to wake up full of me."

I press a hand to his chest. His heart pounds too fast. Mine echoes it.

There's no easy way to say what needs to be said.

Instead, I reach for his hand, lace our fingers, and pull it over my chest until he's cupping the swell of my breast like he always does when we're tangled in bed and avoiding the outside world.

"I booked my flight." I hold his gaze. "July first."

He winces.

I don't have to say where. We've gone over every piece of it already. He knows the start date, the program timeline, the salary, the apartment I'll be sharing in Hell's Kitchen with three other girls I haven't met.

What we haven't done is talk about what any of it actually means for us. Every time I try, he changes the subject.

Only now, we're nearly out of time.

Padraig rolls off me and stares at the ceiling. Doesn't say anything at first. His finger draw a slow, absent circle on my hip.

"I figured," he says after a long pause.

I comb my fingers through his hair. "I didn't want to spring it on you, but..."

"I didn't want to think it's real." He swallows hard. "I can't picture you leaving. It fucking kills me."

I know there's nothing I can do to soothe him. "I'm not trying to hurt you."

"I know." His hand slides to my waist and tightens slightly. "I *know*."

I shift up enough to see his face. His lashes are wet. "Babe, we have to talk about this."

"Okay." He jerks his head to stave off the tears. "Let's do it."

"Start with what you want." I kiss the stubble on his chin.

He turns to face me. "I want you. I want *this*. I want to wake up to you every fucking morning. I *want* you to stay."

"Padraig." I grip his arm. "I *need* to go, babe. I need to know I can make it on my own, outside of you. Outside of us."

His brows draw in, not angry. More...afraid. "We've *always* been us."

"We still are."

"Since we were kids." He turns his head to meet my eye.

"I'm aware."

"Then why—"

I cut him off. "If we don't stretch on our own, we'll shrink what we could be together."

My words sink in. Slowly. Like a tide rolling out and taking every bit of steadiness with it.

I sit up, drag the sheet around me, and rest my elbows on my knees. "We've been joined at the hip since we were kids. We fell in love and by seventeen we were as serious as a married couple. *Padraig*. This opportunity is important to me. For the first time in my life, I have something that's *mine*. I'm excited and I can't even talk to you about it because you brush it under the rug. Or change the subject. This isn't how we are or how I want us to be."

"*Fine*. It fucking scares me." Padraig raises his voice. "I can't live without you, don't you understand? When you were in Switzerland, it was the worst six months of my life. You have no idea what I had to—"

"I know you're angry." I interrupt by taking his hand. "You're disappointed I'm not helping with the band. We can talk about all of this."

He shakes his head. "What's the point? You've made the decision. You have no interest anymore."

"I do and we both know why I backed away." I squeeze his fingers. "I don't want to fight about Felicity and my thoughts about her because this is about us. I *want* us. But we're stuck in limbo and it's not healthy if we can't have a simple conversation about our future."

His voice cracks. "Fuck it. The band can go on without me. I'll move with you. We can figure it out together."

"Babe." I hold his gaze. "You don't even know what moving forward looks like right now other than Fireball."

He starts to object, but I shake my head. "Over the past couple of years, I'm watching you shrink. Where is the opinionated, take-no-prisoners boy who went after what he wanted? You've been going through the motions like you're waiting for permission to speak. With Fireball, everything you do is about appeasing Felicity. You're losing yourself."

He swallows hard.

"You used to have a strong point of view. You fought for songs, for the sound. Now you go along with this toxic situation the band finds itself in. Both Liam and Linus want to make a change and you're fighting it like you're afraid of blowing everything up. And now you say you'll leave it all behind to move with me to New York? Make it make sense."

I watch him wrestle with my words, but I keep going because this tough love is a long time coming. "I think you can't bear to disappoint the people who matter to you and it's preventing you from speaking your own truth It kills me. You're only disappointing yourself."

"No, you actually don't get it." He sucks in his lips. "The only thing I'm scared of losing is..."

My breath catches.

"You."

His fingers haven't let go of mine.

"We're *not* breaking up," I whisper.

Padraig glances out the window. "Except, it kinda feels like we are."

"You're not being fair," I protest. "Moving into a new phase and talking about how we navigate it is not breaking up."

His voice cracks. "Why can't you put it off for a year ? Or, say you're not going."

I don't.

I can't.

I shift to face him fully and grab his other hand. "It's not cool to make me feel bad for wanting something for myself. You have the band. You have Liam."

"Of course it's not cool. I'm being selfish. You don't think I get it?" He shakes his head glumly.

"No." I lean my head on his shoulder. "I think you do."

"No shit."

"I'm not going because I don't love you. I'm going because I do." I try to reassure him.

He grunts. "That makes no sense."

"It does. You aren't seeing it from my perspective."

His hand slips from mine and curls into the sheets. "No, how can I? It's not what I want and I'm not going to pretend I'm okay being without you. ."

"I don't want us to be apart either." I lean back against the wall. "At the same time, I've been telling you for years I don't want to be on the road and tour. It's not the life for me. Doesn't mean it's not the life for you."

"What about our promise to each other?" He punches the mattress. "Forever flames. Now you're taking it away."

"We're not kids anymore." I fold my arms across my chest. "You need to figure out what you want without me up in your grill every single day. For example, whatever happened to your art? You haven't picked up a brush in easily two years. If you were to say to me, 'Stevie, I want to leave Fireball because I miss art and I want to study in New York, here's where I plan to take classes.' Then I'd be psyched for you to come with me."

He exhales sharply. "Why does it seem like you're making the choice for me?"

"God. You're not listening." I squeeze my eyes shut in frustration. "I want you to figure out if you're staying in Fireball because it's your passion or because you're afraid to disappoint Liam. Because you have me as a safety net, you're no further along figuring it out than when we started college. What do *you* want to do with your future."

He says nothing.

"Figure out what your own goals are. For yourself. Without trying to appease me. Or him. Or anyone." I'm trying so hard to get through to the person I love most in the world and I'm watching him shut down.

"I told you." His voice is hoarse. "I want you."

"You have me. Me taking a dream job doesn't change anything other than we won't be in each other's pockets every minute of the day." I pull him into my arms.

He squeezes me closer.

I stroke his back. "Get it through your thick skull. We're not breaking up. We're changing the shape of what our relationship looks like. Give ourselves some time to grow up a little. We'll text. We'll visit. We'll have video sex. We're gonna keep loving each other through this transition."

He pulls back and studies me like he's memorizing the lines of my face. "Do you really believe we'll be okay?"

"I do." I nod, kissing his chin. "More than okay. We're gonna become who we're meant to be. And then we'll be together again—stronger, clearer."

Padraig closes his eyes. "I hate it."

"Don't. We'll come back together. Not as two kids trying to figure it out, but two adults choosing each other."

His eyes pop open. "Promise?"

"I swear."

He wraps his arms around me like he's never letting go.

And the truth is, he's not. Even if we're not under the same roof or sharing the same bed.

By taking time apart, our love isn't leaving.

It's becoming.

Fifteen

Six months Later

I KNOW THE RHYTHM of this block now.

The clang of delivery trucks, the morning rush of kids dragging backpacks too big for their shoulders.

It's mid-December in New York and the wind cuts sharp down these avenues, rattling scaffolding and carrying the burnt-nut smell from the food cart on the corner.

Stevie's ancient building's walk-up is always too warm. I've learned which stair creaks and how her lock needs a jiggle. Most nights, I get in before her.

She's working incredibly long days. Full of tours and walk-throughs and staying late for events nobody else wants to manage. As a junior event planner, she's understandably eager and determined to prove herself. Wears her blazer like armor. Swaps her sneakers for pointed flats like a true New Yorker.

When she's home, Stevie talks about floral arrangements and catering minimums like they're war stories. I listen, nod, try to follow. She rattles off the details like she's surprised she gets to be part of it. I love seeing her so excited about her career.

I'm proud. And gutted. At the same time.

She fits here.

Meanwhile, I've spent three straight days feeling like a loser, eating dollar pizza and scribbling unfinished lyrics on coffee shop napkins trying to get ready for the studio. Liam and Felicity are at each other's throats. Linus is trying to figure out how to stay in the country if we tour next summer.

A big fucking "if."

Don't get me started on Felicity's obsession with me. Fuck. I can't bear to even think about it.

Trudging up to Stevie's apartment, I hope none of her roommates are there. I could use some time to veg out until she gets home. I open the door. No such luck.

Rina, the nurse, is nowhere to be seen. Probably working the night shift at Mount Sinai. Mel, who does something with investments on Wall Street, is in the kitchen. Liv is filming herself doing an aggressive YouTube workout. Frankie's out on the fire escape smoking.

No one says hi. They don't exactly make me feel unwelcome. It's more like they don't clock me at all.

My phone buzzes:

> Stevie: Wanna meet me in midtown?
> Drinks w/ work friends. No pressure.

I read it twice before answering.

Of course I want to go. I came here after Thanksgiving to be with her for a month, not to sit on her lumpy futon eating bodega sandwiches and counting fire escape pigeons.

We've barely had a full night alone. Stevie's roommates are always buzzing through, the walls are paper-thin. She's either heading to work or dragging herself home from it, too tired to finish a sentence.

I don't blame her. Not really.

She's killing it.

My girl's amazing. But...I came here hoping for more. Reconnecting. Talking. Spending time together.

Fucking.

I tap out a reply.

> Me: *Yeah. Tell me where. I'll come find you.*

Three dots flicker, disappear. Then:

> Stevie: *You sure? It's just boring work people.*

I stare at the screen for a beat before sending back:

> Me: *I want to see you. Boring people and all.*

I pull on my jacket and grab my subway pass. Even if I'm the outsider now. The tagalong, long-distance boyfriend plopped into a world I don't understand—I want to be where she is.

For as long as she'll let me.

The bar has a kind of curated elegance you don't see on the West Coast. It smells like citrus peel, money, and whatever cologne the waiters are all wearing. Velvet bar stools. Gilt-edged menus. Voices kept to a murmur under the thump of slow jazz oozing from hidden speakers.

As usual, I'm out of place in my torn Levi's and beat-up leather jacket.

I catch sight of her near the back, tucked into a crescent-shaped booth with three others, framed by flickering candlelight and the blue glint of glass behind the bar.

Stevie doesn't look bored. Her head's thrown back in laughter, manicured hand resting flat on the table like she's trying to steady herself. She looks lit from inside. Confident. Polished. Entirely at home.

When she sees me, her smile blooms instantly, the one that's only mine. She waves me over and shifts sideways on the tufted velvet to make room. Her hand slides to my arm when I reach her, a quick squeeze on my jacket sleeve before her lips brush my cheek.

"You made it." She beams happily. Her hand stays on my thigh as I scoot into the booth beside her. "Everyone. This is my boyfriend, Padraig. Padraig, meet Rhea, Anthony, and Cooper."

Rhea's angular and sophisticated in a pressed navy pantsuit and sleek bob. "Ah, the famous drummer boyfriend."

Anthony's in sales. You can tell before he opens his mouth. Pink shirt, open collar, charm dialed up enough to make you wonder if he's ever actually off the clock. He gives me an easy grin and raises his glass.

Cooper's the last to look up. He's a normal dude in a white button-down, sleeves rolled halfway. Sharp jaw with dark curls smoothed back. Steel-blue eyes. Something unreadable sits behind them. He lifts his glass in a slow half toast but doesn't say anything.

His fingers tap the base of the glass once. Then again.

His elbow's hooked along the back of the booth, behind Stevie and I'm not proud of how fast I clock the distance. He's not touching her so it's not inappropriate. Too comfortable, though.

"Good to meet you all." I nod politely.

Stevie's hand shifts beneath the table. Finds mine. She laces our fingers together like it's the most natural thing in the world. She leans in, her shoulder against mine, warm and solid.

"Sorry we started without you," she whispers close to my ear.

"I don't mind."

She squeezes my hand again, and turns back toward the group, launching into some story about a vendor double-booking a ballroom. They laugh. I listen. Mostly to her voice. The way she's mastered the rhythm of this new world. She's light, witty and self-deprecating and sounds like she was born here.

I keep my eye on Cooper, though. He's not watching her constantly. That'd be obvious. He's aware of everything she does. He laughs when she laughs. His gaze drifts when she speaks. Every time she shifts, his posture adjusts by degrees. Always a few beats behind. Always tuned in.

It's not possessive. Not even flirtatious. It's worse.

It's familiar.

He looks at her how I look at her.

She turns to me when the server stops by. "You want a drink?"

"Sure."

"What do you feel like?"

"Root beer, if they've got it."

My order gets Cooper's approval, though I don't need it. "Good for you. Stevie said you never drink alcohol. I admire a musician with discipline."

I'm taken aback a bit. Has Stevie told him about my family? "Uh, thanks."

The drinks arrive and Stevie settles into my side. Her knee touches mine. She's warm. Engaged. Not hiding our relationship, in fact she gushes about how long we've been together. Part of me is surprised her coworkers know how important I am to her. The other part is proud.

We hold hands under the table and, once again, I realize I've never seen her this alive talking about anything that didn't involve both of us.

It makes me feel small, in a way. Which sucks and isn't fair. I haven't made any progress since she left. I'm living in Pullman. Fireball's on the brink of imploding due to tension with Felicity. Everything's up in the air because Linus confirmed he'd have to leave next year.

What the fuck am I doing?

I glance down at our joined hands. Then at Cooper. He's fully engaged in a discussion about some valet scandal with the others. He may look at her adoringly, but Stevie isn't interested. He also doesn't seem like the kind of guy who'd step in where he doesn't belong.

In an instant, I realize, he's not the threat.

As I predicted when she moved here, the distance between us is.

Stevie and her friends have everything in common, laughing at inside jokes I don't understand. They all know exactly which wine to order and what elevator is out of service and where to find the best five-dollar pizza in the city.

I don't fit here.

A couple hours later, we step out into the sharp chill of a December Manhattan night, the wind catches her blond waves as she listens intently at something Rhea says and pulls her coat tighter. Cooper says something low in her ear, harmless, probably, but her giggle stretches a little longer than I expect.

When she turns back to me, I tug her in close, and press a kiss to her lips in full view of the her friends. Not hard. Not claiming.

Well...maybe a little bit. "Let's get a hotel."

"Now?" She blinks, her breath frosting between us.

"Yeah. I want you. Alone. Without worrying about roommates hearing us." I don't lower my voice...much. "You've got tomorrow off, don't you?"

Her expression shifts as the others shuffle away and she turns her full attention on me. Not hesitation, curiosity. Mischief. Then she pulls out her phone, opens her company's hotel app with a few swipes of her thumb. "There's a suite open at the Astor. It's only a couple blocks from here. I've got an employee discount."

"Let's go."

We're checked in half hour later.

The room *smells* expensive. Fresh linens. Eucalyptus soap. A king-sized bed with million-count sheets and blackout curtains Stevie doesn't bother closing.

She tosses her coat on a chair and kicks off her boots. I press in from behind, palms sliding over her hips, lips tracing her neck. She leans back into me with the quiet whimper she always makes when it's me and her and nothing else.

Watching in the floor-to-ceiling window, I slip my hands beneath her blouse and drag it up over her head. Her bra goes next, dropped onto the plush carpet. Her nipples pucker.

I gently turn her and lean down. I cup her tits in my hands and lave every inch of them with my tongue. Her fingers thread through my hair like she'll never let go.

We scramble toward the bed, peeling off our remaining clothes, her hands shake with how fast she's trying to get me naked. She pushes me onto the mattress, climbs on and impales herself on my cock. She grinds down once, slow and teasing.

Then again. And again.

"Missed being able to do this," she says breathily. "Trying to stay quiet with all my roommates is such a buzzkill."

"Agreed, it's time for me to make you come so hard you scream." I flip her easily and pull out, kissing down her stomach.

Her thighs fall open. "Don't tease."

I don't.

I settle between her legs. Drag my tongue through her slowly. She gasps and bites her fist. Her back lifts off the bed when I fasten my lips around her clit and suck, rough and rhythmic, then dip my tongue lower and fuck her with it until she's squirming, her words wrecked and garbled.

"Oh God, don't stop—don't—"

I double down.

Stevie comes hard, hands fisting the sheets.

I kneel between her legs and hook her thighs over my arms and press them back so there's no space left between us. Sink in slow and deep. Her head drops back with a broken noise that shreds something inside me. I move in long strokes, grinding every time I bottom out. Watch my cock pump into her soaking pussy until the room's heavy with our sweat and skin and need.

Pulling her up into my lap, we fuck like we're chasing time. Like we may not know what comes next but our bodies fit together like a puzzle. She rides me, hair wild, hands on my shoulders, undulating in slow circles until she grimaces from coming so much.

When it's my turn, I flip her over so she's face down with her hips in my hands and her breath fogs the polished headboard. I rut into her and pull out, spraying her entire back with my come.

After we clean up in the shower, we collapse in the fine hotel sheets, laughing, wrecked and breathless.

She rolls over and grins up at me, wet hair plastered to her neck. "I think we broke the bed."

"Let's get some sleep and break it some more." I tug her to me.

Stevie drifts off curled into my side, one leg over mine, her body warm and damp against my chest. For a few minutes, it's quiet. Us. Like always.

And yet, she feels a world away.

In the week I've been here, it's obvious, She's thriving. Happy. Living her best life. Meanwhile, I'm scribbling lyrics in the margins of old notebooks, staring at empty canvasses, not any further ahead than when I started college. I thought we'd be able to talk more and I could share what's been going on with me.

Why bother, though. I'm chasing a dream I'm not sure I want.

I'm not even close to being on the same wavelength as Stevie. Maybe I never will be again.

I can't pretend I won't lose her anymore.

When I might've already.

Sixteen

Four Months Later

I can't seem to focus.

The floor plan in front of me blurs. Eight-top rounds. Stage risers. Buffet stations.

They all bleed together in one indecipherable mess. I blink, sit back in my chair, rub the base of my neck where a tension knot's been building since the catering team decided to overhaul the entire dessert menu. Again.

The office is chaos as usual. Landline phones ringing. Someone laughing near the Keurig. Muted clicks of heels on tile. I'm supposed to be finalizing VIP seating. Instead, I'm staring at a screen thinking about my man who's three thousand miles away.

Wondering why we don't talk every day anymore.

It's the first thing I can admit about our relationship.

We used to fall asleep with our phones on the pillow. Wake up to a good morning message, a voice note, a meme. Ever since Padraig went home after his visit, things have trickled off and I don't know why.

We never had a fight. Or disagreement. There's nothing I can pinpoint.

When he was here, things weren't perfect but I thought we made it work. Sure, my job is demanding. Between corporate Christmas galas, end-of-year banquets and a socialite's wedding with a cake shaped like the Chrysler building, my boss kept piling on events because I was "eager" and "sharp."

Let's be honest, it was more like I'm "low on the totem pole."

On the other hand, we snuck time wherever we could. I took long lunches. Pushed back meetings. He hung out with me and my work friends. Christmas was glorious, we took goofy selfies in front of the Rockefeller tree. Slept tangled up with fairy lights glowing from my roommates' fake pine garland. We rang in the new year with him inside me, orgasms substituting for champagne toasts.

When he left, he kissed me like I was his everything. Made me promise to call him every day. Everything felt okay. Good. Normal.

Once he was back in Pullman, I didn't expect it would mostly be me reaching out. His replies are short. Not unkind. Not cold. More like distracted. Indifferent. like he's pulling away.

Maybe he was right to worry about me moving so far away. I'm out of sight, out of mind.

Didn't his time in New York mean as much to him as it did to me?

I scroll through our text thread on my phone. The last message he sent was yesterday, a screenshot of some studio schedule from Linus. No "miss you." No "love you." No romantic words. A single photo with no explanation.

His behavior is so unusual, I'm worried. Is he okay? What's happening with the band? Does he love me anymore? I can't concentrate. My heart is in my throat.

Something's wrong. I need to know.

Closing my laptop, I rub the cracked corner of my phone. Should I text? Will he answer? Questions I never used to ask myself when it came to him.

Maybe he's giving me some tough love. I know how much he says he misses me. I've honestly been so busy, I didn't have much space to miss him.

Now all I think about is whether I fucked everything up with Padraig. My rock. My one true love. As much as I love it here, I'm drowning.

Fuck it. The banquet layout can wait. I type the words

> **Me:** *Want me to come out there for a few days? I miss you.*

I stare at the message. My finger hovers.

Then I hit send.

The text hangs in the thread like it's glowing. I set my phone face down on my desk. Pretend the pit in my stomach doesn't grow every second it stays unanswered.

"Hey," a deep voice startles me from behind.

I glance over my shoulder. Cooper's leaning against the cubicle wall, coffee in one hand. His tie's loosened, like it usually is after his second meeting of the day. His easy grin makes him look like trouble even though he's the most decent guy in New York.

"You okay?" His face contorts in concern.

"Eh." I shrug, shifting in my chair. "Logistics."

He raises a brow. "Hotel logistics or life logistics?"

"Both." I lean back in my chair. "Mostly the second one."

Cooper walks around to the chair across from mine and sits, balancing his coffee on the armrest. "Boyfriend troubles?"

I have no one to talk to about this, so I nod. "Yeah. Ever since he left here we've been off."

"I'm sorry to hear." He tilts his head. "Makes sense, though. You've been quiet for the last couple of months."

I rub my temples. "It's not like anything bad has happened. I thought we were solid. Now it's like. I don't know. He's pulling away. Or, maybe I'm imagining it. I feel crazy."

"What if..." Cooper pauses. "You're not imagining it?"

I study him. "I'd be devastated. We've been together for nearly seven years. Our future was all planned out but I wanted to see what life would be like if I took my dream job and we weren't tethered at the hip. I never thought we'd be here."

"Wow. Sounds familiar." He sighs heavily. There's a pause. "Angela and I broke up when I went home for Christmas."

"Oh, Coop. I'm sorry." His girlfriend is all he's talked about since I've known him.

"Well..." He shrugs. "The reality is, long-distance only works when both people make the effort. I've been so bogged down with work, I didn't notice until we were already over."

I hate how much his words land. "God. I'm afraid. When I took this job, he was devastated but I convinced him it would be good for us to grow individually before settling down for good. Now I'm scared I'm losing the person I love most in the world."

"For what it's worth? You're doing everything right. You're living your life. Killing it here." He takes a sip of coffee. "He has his own stuff going, anyway, right? It's not like you've done something wrong."

"No, he always knew I didn't want to go on tour." I swallow hard.

He nudges my knee with his. "Hey. You're not alone in this."

I manage to smile even as I keep listening for my phone to vibrate with his reply.

I rest my chin on my hand, eyes fixed on a crack in the corner of the desk. "It's weird, isn't it? How one minute everything's like a straight path you both agreed to and the next you're not even sure you're on the same planet."

"God, yeah." Cooper exhales through his nose. "Like you keep wanting to go back to the old version of things."

My eyes fill. "It's all I can think about."

"Ah, Stevie." He shifts in his chair. "Try not to be sad. You're out here building a whole new life. He's trying to find his footing in the old one without you. It must be tough for him too. Maybe he needs space to figure it out."

I nod, throat tight. It makes sense. "I tried to share this part of my life with him and he seemed to be so happy for me. If he needs space to figure his shit out, I'll support him because I want him to do something he loves. He's young, so there's no harm in following music where it leads him. He's never going to leave his brother hanging. And, I'd never ask him to."

"Are you worried he's pulling away from you?" Cooper says gently.

"I don't know." My voice cracks on the edges.

"Shit." Cooper taps a rhythm on his coffee lid with his finger. "Ever since Angela and I split, I've been wondering if we stayed together so long because we were terrified of the unknown."

The silence between us vibrates with understanding.

"I'm more terrified of losing him," I whisper as tears stream down my face.

"You won't," he assures me. "Not with your history. He'd be an idiot to let someone like you go."

My eyes sting, but I manage a small, grateful smile. "Thanks for not making this weird. Sometimes I feel like everyone else expects me to either be madly in love or completely over it. Like those are the only two settings."

"Yeah, well. Maybe we're both in the 'figuring it out and trying not to drown' camp." He smirks.

I nod. "Definitely."

My phone finally vibrates. I turn it face up to find a text from Padraig:

Padraig: *Yeah, come to Seattle.*

Four words. No fluff. No context.

My breath catches, and Cooper must notice something shift in my face. "Everything okay?"

"Uh…" I glance up. "Apparently, his ears were burning."

Cooper stands. "You want a second?"

I hesitate, then nod. "Please. Sorry."

"Don't be. Talk it out with your guy." He taps the top of the chair.

I smile gratefully. "You're a good friend, Cooper."

"Tell Padraig I said to get his act together." He mock punches the air.

Cooper leaves and another text appears, sending my heart into overdrive.

Padraig: *Can I call you?*

I don't text back. I call him instead.

He picks up instantly. "Hey."

"Hi," I say, quieter than I mean to.

"I miss you too, you know."

His voice makes me ache. It's deep and a little hoarse. Like he hasn't slept much.

"I didn't expect you to reply," I admit.

"I know," he sighs. "I've been weird lately."

I hit the video button and his beautiful face appears, chiseled cheekbones and soulful brown eyes. "You've been quiet."

"Ever since I left, everything's been off..." A pause. "The band's in shambles."

I lean against the desk, wrapping my arms tight around myself. "What's going on?"

"We're going into the studio to hear the final mix. It's real now. The album. And the gig at the Showbox in two weeks. Connor's new band, Less Than Zero, is opening. It's their first time playing live at a venue. The guitar player is some sort of musical savant and his dad is Carter Pope from Limelight. They haven't played a show yet, so it'll be kinda cool. They're so good..."

"Wow. That's huge." I'm genuinely thrilled for his older brother. Padraig doesn't talk about his family much these days so I'm glad to hear good news.

"Yeah. It is." Another beat. "At the same time, it doesn't feel that way."

He looks so lost, it breaks my heart. "Why not?"

"I want you to see it. To be there. You know?" He smiles weakly. "I hate bugging you when you're so busy with work."

"Um, okay." I close my eyes. "Padraig. You know I want to be there, it's just...."

"Then come."

I breathe out slowly. "I don't know if I can get time off so quickly."

"You told me you had some PTO." He cocks his head.

I laugh. "PTO? Since when do you speak in corporate terminology?"

"I've been googling."

A flicker of something warm lights in my chest. "You googled PTO?"

"Maybe. Right before I texted."

Instantly the mood shifts. I cross my eyes. "Nerd."

"*You're* a nerd." He sticks his tongue out.

Silence blooms, tender and full with all the things we haven't said. All the things we can't because of the miles stretched between us.

"I'm sorry for being a jackass," he says finally. "I miss you so fucking bad I've been avoiding you."

My throat squeezes and instantly I accept his explanation. "I've felt it."

"I didn't want to mess up your thing out there. You're killing it, Stevie. You've got friends. A life." He holds the phone away from his face. He's in our old living room.

Warmth fills my entire being. "You're the most important part of my life, Padraig. Truthfully, I thought something was wrong. I was worried about us."

He looks up at the ceiling and bites his lip.

"Is there something wrong?" Something close to gut instinct permeates my soul. "You can tell me."

He shakes his head. "It's nothing important."

I wait. He doesn't fill the silence. Doesn't meet my eyes.

"Padraig." A warning threads into my tone before I can stop myself. "We don't do secrets."

His jaw flexes. "We don't." A pause. "It's more the band, really. You were right about Felicity. Everyone was. Things are tense."

My spine goes rigid before I can stop it. He sees it. Tries to soften.

"Come see me. See the show. Stay the weekend. Hear the new tracks. We'll get a hotel and have an entire naked day together." Padraig's demeanor changes and he cheeses at me. "I'll tell you all about the mess when you get here."

Relieved, I'm already opening the flight website on my laptop. "Let me see what I can swing, I'll call you back in ten."

"No—" he says urgently. "Let me stay on. While you do it."

I rest the phone against my monitor. "Okay."

We don't talk while I scroll and click, but he's there. Breathing. Present. Real. I find a flight that lands Thursday at four. Decide to worry about telling work later. I click book. Screenshot it. Send it. "Got it. Now I gotta make up some excuse to my boss."

"Thank fuck." He exhales like he's been underwater.

"I'll stay until Monday morning." I can't believe how spontaneous I'm being. I hope I don't get in trouble.

"I'll pick you up."

"Okay."

Another pause.

"I love you," he says softly.

"I know. I love you too."

And I do.

I hate how our path is unclear. We've changed. Everything trembles with the weight of what's possibly been lost and what might be.

I'm going to see him. Be with him. Remind us both what it feels like to hold on, even when everything else is shifting.

I click open my intranet. There's a new DM.

Go get him. I'll cover for you. —C

My eyes sting all over again.

Next Thursday can't come fast enough.

Seventeen

A Few Days Later

The Showbox breathes, even in silence.

By late afternoon, the air throbs with a low electric current you only feel in rooms with history etched into every square inch. Scuffed floors. Freshly painted mushroom pillars. These walls have witnessed thousands of voices rise and fall.

I can almost hear the ghosts of a hundred bands tuning up and their amps crackling to life.

Liam crouches near the monitors, guitar tucked against his knee, his head bent over the strings while he tunes. Linus is beside him, talking low to the house sound tech. The two of them have developed an unspoken rhythm, threading between every look and nod.

Like Stevie and I used to have.

Felicity's planted at center stage, perched on a stool with the mic tilted toward her mouth, humming under her breath. Her heel taps a relentless beat against the stage, sharp enough to grate on my nerves before we've even started.

I sit behind the kit and tap the snare once. The crack echoes through the space. Felicity whips around and shoots me a dirty look. I've probably interfered with her "process."

Deliberately.

Same old. Same old.

A day after I got back from New York, we went straight into the studio. Convinced ourselves we weren't fraying at the seams. The entire album was tracked in two weeks because Liam, Linus, and I pushed through late nights and rewrites.

It's good.

Better than good, with the potential for a couple more crowd pleasers. It doesn't feel like it used to, though. Felicity fought Liam on everything from lyrics and melodies to entire arrangements. She rewrote vocal parts behind his back, then blew up when he called her out. Linus had to intervene more than once.

I stayed quiet. Didn't get too involved.

It's what I do now. Smooth it over. Keep the peace. Anything to keep things from blowing apart.

I'm not proud of it.

After a lot of self-reflection, I know when it started. The day Connor sent us off to college and told us not to look back. A big brother who meant well. Sacrificed his own happiness for ours without bothering to ask us what we wanted. To this day, I know I owe him everything.

At the same time, Liam and I are now completely disconnected from the family.

Sure, we do our best to call and text to keep our connection alive, but college life has a funny relationship with time. Suddenly, Cillian's learning the construction business. Seamus is a teenager and Brennan's a computer genius. Da's apparently working part-time and seems to be steadier. Ma wants us to come for Sunday dinner in a few days. I can't think of the last time I had a home-cooked meal. Or spoke with my father.

Without Stevie, I'm fucking adrift.

I hit the snare again. Louder this time. Felicity's head whips around. Liam cuts her a look sharp enough to silence her before she can open her mouth.

"Soundcheck." He points at her. "Not a fucking solo show."

She glares, turns to the mic and starts singing through half a verse like she's doing us a favor. The tension in the room doesn't break. It presses against the Showbox's walls. I look over at Liam and silently communicate to him how I feel.

I've had it. None of this is worth it. We need to let her go.

Doesn't mean the thought of starting over again exhausts me in a way I can't explain.

Finally, the thought of keeping her wrecks me even more.

I wonder if Connor's new band has these types of problems.

Doubt it.

With Da on the mend, Connor and his girlfriend's brother joined a band called Less Than Zero. They've only been jamming together a couple months and they're already electric. With a singer who commands a room, a guitar player who's rock star royalty, a drummer who's the coolest most even-keeled dude I've ever met and my talented brother, their sound is pure and raw and alive. I'd describe it as somewhere between grunge and gospel.

LTZ has an unexplainable magic. Something Fireball's been chasing for years but only managed to catch with our song,

Tir na nÓg . They're opening for us, but I have a feeling we'll be the opener for them next time.

On top of everything, Stevie's flying in tonight. I haven't seen her since I came home after New Years. We text. We call. We FaceTime. It's not the same.

Not enough.

She might deny it to me and to herself, but she's moved on from me and it's killing me from the inside out. She's thriving in New York. With a career she loves, friends, roommates. A whole new life in the Big Apple while I'm clinging to some dream of, what? Superstardom?

As if. My fucking band is hanging on by a thread and I'm sitting here, behind the kit Connor bought for me, gripping the sticks like they might keep me from unraveling.

Knowing the only thing keeping me upright is the thought of Stevie walking through those doors. I need her. Even if I'm not sure I deserve her anymore.

She doesn't know what I've been carrying. Felicity has tried to cross lines I've never blurred. The third time, I padlocked my own door. For protection.

I've kept this buried for almost a year. Not because I'd ever touch Felicity, I couldn't risk pushing Stevie further away while distance already stretched between us. Now the secret festers, chewing through whatever peace I pretend to have left.

Stevie shows up as we're finishing soundcheck, overnight bag hanging off her shoulder, blonde hair shining under the stage lights. I don't hold back.

"Stevie." I leap from the stage, scooping her up in my arms

I spin her in a circle right there in the middle of the Showbox floor, and kiss her like I'm starving. She tastes like mint and heaven. When it's gone on a beat too long, she laughs into my mouth, clutching my shoulders. I don't care who's watching. We've spent too many nights apart.

When I finally let her go, Liam's smirking behind me. Linus stands beside him with a quiet, welcoming smile.

"About fuckin' time you got here." Liam tugs her into a hug.

"Welcome home," Linus adds, kissing her cheek.

Felicity doesn't move from where she's sitting on the edge of the stage. She watches us like she's daring Stevie to get comfortable. The moment Stevie catches her eye, Felicity's mouth curves into a smile full of venom. Staking her territory. Letting my girlfriend know she's not welcome.

Stevie stiffens next to me, so I take her hand in mine and squeeze. "Come on, we've got dinner reservations."

We duck out the side door into the brisk night air and cross the street to Pike Place Market. Matt's glows with a soft light above the cobblestones, and I hold the door open for her.

"Matt's? Ohmygod." She squeezes my hand.

I press my hand on her back lightly as we're shown to a table by the window overlooking the Market and Puget Sound. "I figured you'd be starving."

By the time our food arrives, my stomach's too knotted to eat.

"You're not touching your food." She sets down her fork. "You don't go on for a couple hours, you should have time to digest."

I shake my head, staring at the untouched plate in front of me. "I know. It all hit me today. I've realized Felicity has to go."

"Wow." Her eyes widen, then she laughs. "You've always been the one who insisted on keeping her. If I didn't trust you so implicitly, I might have been worried about what it meant."

"I know." I rub the back of my neck with something resembling shame. "All this time, I thought I was protecting the band. Keeping it together. But I'm not. I'm holding it back."

She reaches for my hand across the table. "I'm glad you finally see it. You've carried too much on your shoulders, baby."

I swallow, which feels like dragging glass.

Stevie changes the subject to our plans for the weekend. She wants to see her parents, maybe visit my family if they're around. I want to disappear into a hotel room and make love to her and let the rest of the world fall away.

We settle on a combination of both.

By the time we get back to the Showbox, the venue is packed and buzzing. I lead her over to where Connor and the guys from Less Than Zero are setting up.

"Stevie." Connor's eyes light up as he bear hugs her. "Let me introduce you to the lads. Tyson, Zane, Jace—this is Stevie, Padraig's girlfriend...or should I say, wife? You've been together for, what? Eight years?"

Tyson, the frontman, is shy. He shakes her hand with a soft smile, blue eyes bright with a quiet charisma he can't turn off. Zane, full of bouncy energy and effortless swagger, waves as he tunes his guitar. Jace offers a nod from behind the kit, sticks tapping against his thigh.

I watch the easy way Connor laughs with his bandmates, and my chest aches with a mix of pride and something darker. Jealousy. They have a chemistry Fireball doesn't have anymore.

When LTZ takes the stage, the room filled with our fans erupts. Ty's voice is a force, deep and textured, pulling every person in the crowd closer. Zane's guitar weaves in and out of it like they're connected in some way. Connor's bassline is solid and sure, and Jace's drumming drives it all forward with precision.

It's tight. Polished. Pure magic in a bottle.

I glance at Stevie standing next to me. Her eyes glow, caught in the current. I feel a twist of bitterness again. Envy for what my brother has found.

When it's our turn, the difference is impossible to ignore.

Felicity steps up to the mic, tosses her hair and panders to the audience in the most inauthentic manner. Her voice is technically perfect, but her presence is all hype. Liam's playing is sharp but detached. And me? I'm phoning it in. Every beat I hit feels heavier than the last.

The difference between our bands is stark. I can't pretend we have a chance in hell. I've given up my life with Stevie for *this*. Fireball's nowhere near the standard it needs to be. A hollow shell compared to LTZ. All because I've been too afraid to listen to Stevie and my brother and make the hard call.

What has it gotten me? Fealty to a woman who's been trying to drive a wedge between me and Stevie for years. And I took her side.

My hands grip my sticks harder. I thrash and pound, trying to drown out the realization clawing at my chest.

I'm not the one holding it together, I'm the guy holding everything back.

My band. My relationship.

It's *devastating*.

We come offstage to applause, thin and distant, as if filtered through water. The hollow ache in my chest drowns everything else out. Liam drops his guitar onto its stand with a clang. Felicity is radiant in the corner, preening in the mirror, like she delivered the set of her life.

I can't breathe.

"Enough," I shout, cutting through the low buzz of crew and chatter.

Heads whip around.

"*Dar?*" Liam frowns.

I step forward, fists clenched. "I'm done. I'm not playing another fucking note with her."

Felicity turns slowly, like a queen interrupted. "Excuse me?"

"You heard me." My voice is steel. "This is over. You're toxic. You make every show, every rehearsal, about you. Fireball is bigger than your ego and I'm not letting it die because you can't do your part."

Her smile twists into something feral. "Oh, please. Spare me the holier-than-thou speech, Padraig. I'm the one who's been wronged here. You and Liam are fucking predators. First, he forced me into some fucked-up threesome with Linus and ever since Stevie went to Switzerland, you've used me as some sort of fuck toy then pretend it didn't happen so you can keep the façade of your perfect little relationship."

I go cold. "You're a pathological liar. You're the one who's thrown yourself at me time after time. I've tried to gracefully turn you down to no fucking avail"

"Don't act like you're innocent." She steps forward, voice rising. "Or did you forget the night in Boise? Or Portland? All those nights you told me I was the only one who understood you? How you were trapped because you didn't want to break her heart?"

"Jesus Christ," I seethe, shaking my head. "You're delusional."

"Am I?" Her voice cracks and tears glint under the harsh dressing-room lights. "You'd text me when she was asleep in your bed. You kissed me three nights ago and begged me to fuck you. Or maybe you've blocked that out, too?"

I can't find words.

Liam steps in, "Felicity, this has gone too far—"

"No!" she shouts, mascara streaking down her face. "I'm not going to let you or him throw me under the bus to save face. You both used me. Hid me. Let me think we had something and then shoved me aside, I'm not either of your dirty little secret anymore. You can't fire me, I quit. You'll be hearing from my lawyer."

The silence is deafening.

I'm in utter and total shock.

Then I feel it. A shift.

I turn and see her.

Stevie.

Standing frozen in the doorway. Her eyes wide, glassy, locked on mine.

I know without a shadow of doubt she heard every single word.

"Stevie—"

She takes a step back.

"It's not true," I blurt out, desperation scraping my throat raw. "None of it's true. She's twisting everything, you have to believe me—"

"Don't," she whispers, her voice breaking.

"You can't believe her." I step forward, pleading. "I would never cheat on you. I swear to God—"

Her eyes dart between me and Felicity, who's sobbing into her hands.

She walks out without a word.

I follow.

We pass the stage door, the ringing amps, a tangle of cords and backstage ghosts. I don't call her name. I can't. Not after what she heard. Not after what she saw in my face.

She stops near the loading dock. Faint orange streetlight spills through the cracked door. The air smells like ozone and dust. Her back's to me. Shoulders stiff.

When she speaks, her voice sounds like it's been clawed raw.

"I nearly sacrificed everything for *you*."

I reach for her but don't dare touch her. Not now. "Stevie—"

"For you. For Liam. For Fireball. Not because I wanted a front-row seat to every petty fight and ego storm, but because I loved you. I believed in what you were building." Her hand trembles as she holds herself upright against the wall. "I gave up classes. Pulled all-nighters so you could have press kits. Blew off interviews for my own major because you needed help booking a tour. You asked me to stay. So I did."

I don't breathe.

"Even after Linus took over, I ignored the times when Felicity treated me like I was nothing. When she made digs in every meeting. When she rolled her eyes every time I spoke." She turns. Slow. Deliberate. "You never once stepped in to take my side."

"I didn't know how to fix it."

"Bullshit." Her eyes narrow. "You didn't want to hurt her feelings because you were afraid she'd quit the band."

There's nothing I can say. She's right.

Her eyes are glassy, locked on mine. "And now the truth comes out. You've been lying to me for fucking *years*." She jabs her finger at me. "You knew she wanted to fuck you. I have no doubt she came on to you when I was in Switzerland. You never said a word. How many times has it been since I moved to New York? Yet you said nothing. You let me walk back into her web, over and over. Why? Were you mad when I decided to pursue my own career? Is this some grand 'fuck you, Stevie' sort of gesture?"

"It wasn't like that—"

"Oh, it is like that." Her voice hardens. "My gut told me I needed to find my own path. I wasn't sure why, exactly, because I've always believed in us. Our love."

Stevie is shaking so hard I have no idea what to do. I've never seen her like this.

Ever.

"I was so blind," she wails. "The reality is with you, everyone but me comes first. Always. You paint this pretty picture like you need me so badly you're going to give up everything, but you didn't, did you? Instead of figuring out what you want, you chose to stay in a college town in a band you're not sure about with a woman who was out to destroy us. I didn't have a fucking clue. Shame on me. It's all there in black and white now."

My mouth opens. I don't have an answer that doesn't make it worse.

"Congratulations. I'm *devastated*." She blinks hard, swallowing whatever new round of sorrow is rising in her throat. "I thought we were forever."

Here tears are now silent. Unstoppable. "I thought we were built on honesty. In the end, you chose her comfort over my safety."

"I didn't sleep with her," I blurt out, hoping it lands.

"I don't care if you fucked her." Her hands tremble at her sides. "You let her gaslight me for years. Lied by omission. Watched me shrink and blamed the schedule. Don't stand here and tell me you love me when you protected her more than you ever protected me."

"I was trying to hold it all together."

"No." She bites her lip. "You were trying not to lose her. And in the process, you've lost me."

My chest caves in. "Please—"

"Don't." She shakes her head.

A long beat. Then she adds, quieter now, as if it's breaking her to say it, "I know what forever means. You don't."

Then she turns.

And this time, I don't follow.

Because I don't deserve to.

Eighteen

One Year Later

IT'S BEEN NEARLY A year, and I feel the sting in my chest when I think about Seattle.

How the airport hotel room felt like a coffin.

I cried so hard I could barely breathe. My phone vibrated with calls from Padraig I couldn't bear to answer. I was too ashamed to tell my parents why we broke up and why we'd never get back together. Too gutted to move from the fetal position.

I can't make sense of how I kept breathing through all of it—the moment everything tilted sideways and never came back.

The worst part is, Felicity didn't need lies. She used truth. Twisted it. Dragged it into daylight and left it bleeding at my feet.

It's not her I blame. Not really.

I thought Padraig was mine. Knew it in my soul. Despite our challenges, I believed our kind of love was built to survive anything.

Instead, I found out how easy it was for him to hide things. Let them rot between us.

For years, Felicity was pressing closer. Testing boundaries. And he stayed quiet. Never said, "She's pushing too far and I don't know how to stop it."

Saying it out loud would've meant choosing.

So, he didn't. Not then. Not when it counted.

Every time anyone—me, Liam, Linus—said anything about replacing her, he refused. Didn't want to start over. Said it's better the devil you know. Thought she was why the band had any success.

I didn't let myself see it until he finally grew a pair of balls and fired her.

Once I knew the truth, I had no choice. I had to end it.

So I walked.

Not from love.

From the lie I would've had to live inside to stay.

It's taken months to feel halfway like myself again.

Cooper was the one who pulled me out of the wreckage. He'd gone through his own breakup and, among my friends in New York, was the only who understood the weight of waking up with an empty ache every day.

We made a pact to look out for each other. To call before any spiral started. Keep ourselves from wallowing.

He also encouraged me to keep the lines open with Padraig.

"You have such a long history and your families will always be tied together," he said one night over greasy diner fries. "You'll regret it if you shut him out completely."

So I didn't.

We talk. Not often.

Enough to remember what we were. What we can't be again.

At first, the texts and occasional calls with Padraig were excruciating. Being without him was like I'd lost a limb.

Talking about all of it, honestly, hasn't helped. His position remains, he would never cheat on me and he didn't want to upset me over something he considered a non-issue. I've tried to see his point of view, but deep in my soul I know we'll never be the same.

He begs me to come back. Sends half-finished songs, late-night voicemails, memories stitched into chords. He promises to leave the band if it means I'll give us another chance.

Sometimes I almost cave because I miss him so much. Of course I love him. Part of me always will. He was my first kiss, my first time, my first forever. We grew up wrapped around each other, too entangled to see where he ended and I began.

We were never fragile. We were flame.

Then I breathe. Remember.

Our unraveling started when I chose something of my own. A dream I didn't want to shrink to fit within the trajectory of the band.

The truth is, we built a life too soon. Played house and planned our future before we knew which direction we'd grow in. Our foundation cracked under years of mismatched priorities, unspoken fears, and diverging priorities.

What happened with Felicity brought it to light, but it was bound to happen eventually. Padraig and I are heading down different paths.

Doesn't mean I don't feel the burn.

It does mean I'm not willing to get scorched again. Both he and Liam are fully committed to Fireball. Even more so than before. Part of me thinks it's because Connor's band, LTZ is gaining momentum and they want to keep pace. Both of them are working harder than ever, and the effort shows even though he sounds exhausted whenever we talk.

Felicity's gone now, obviously. She didn't go quietly. There were ugly words, threats of lawsuits, a smear campaign on social media that fizzled when no one cared enough to listen. But the band survived.

A woman named Arleigh stepped in a few weeks later. She's talented, stable, and solid, which is exactly what Fireball needs right now. Padraig doesn't think she's their forever singer, but she's helping them get through a nationwide tour on the success of the album they finished before the implosion.

It's done better than they expected. Two songs charted on alternative radio, and Fireball's been headlining midsized venues all across the country. Unfortunately, Linus had to return to Dublin after graduation, which has left Liam as heartbroken as Padraig. The two of them have been forced to handle the band's direction on their own.

Last week he told me a big LA-based management company's circling, promising bigger opportunities. Hopefully, signing with them will relieve some of the pressure and allow him to enjoy the ride a bit more.

I won't be on it with him.

I won't go backward. My life is in New York now. I'm thriving through my heartbreak.

The hotel is more chaotic and consuming than ever, but I've also proved I can keep up. I'm not the tentative intern I was when I started. I'm a full-fledged event planner now, juggling corporate clients, weddings, and black-tie galas.

My reputation is finally starting to mean something in the company.

Besides, this city has a way of sweeping you up and making you believe you're part of something bigger. The constant bustle of activity. Late nights effortlessly bleed into early mornings. I love the thrill of knowing you can walk out your door and find anything from a pop-up concert in Central Park to a hole-in-the-wall restaurant with the best food you've ever eaten and a skyline so bright it erases the stars.

There's no shortage of people to meet or places to be and it's intoxicating. New York makes me feel limitless and I'm grateful to live in a place where I can get lost, build myself up, and become a better version of myself.

A year later and missing Padraig is quieter now, something I carry without letting it crush me.

He and I aren't the same people we were when we broke up.

Maybe that's the hardest part to admit. There's no going back, no rewinding time to what we used to be, so I've learned to lean into the present instead.

Saturday mornings with Cooper have become part of my present. He's already waiting outside my apartment when I come down the steps, scrolling his phone with one hand, a paper coffee cup warming the other.

"We're going uptown." He hands me my caramel latte, tucking his phone into his coat. "PB Brasserie in Harlem. Supposedly the best *croque madame* in Manhattan."

"Whoa, a big claim." I gratefully take my morning caffeine staple. "How long's the wait gonna be?"

He cocks his head. "What do you take me for? A chump? I reserved a table. Eleven-thirty. Which means if we don't leave now..."

"We'll be those people," I finish, falling into step beside him.

The subway is crowded but warm, a welcome change from the biting wind at street level. We grab seats across from each other, knees brushing as the train jolts forward. He fills me in on a disaster at work earlier in the week, his dry humor cutting through the monotony of the ride.

I can't help smiling; he's good at making everything sound less serious than it is.

By the time we surface in Harlem, the streets are alive with music and delicious smells. The windows of PB Brasserie's sleek exterior are fogged with the heat of a packed brunch crowd. Inside, the noise is almost lively and energized. I'm delighted when we're seated quickly near a window overlooking the sidewalk.

Cooper orders the steak frites. I go for the *croque madame*, naturally, and we add bottomless mimosas because, why not. The first sip has both of us sighing like we've won the lottery.

"This is dangerously good." I take another sip.

"You're the one who introduced me to bottomless drinks." He grins. "Now you're stuck with me enabling you."

Our food arrives and it's everything the reviews promised, cheesy, buttery perfection. We talk through every bite, about upcoming projects at work. Our coworkers' chaotic dating lives. My roommate's latest attempt to film workout content in our living room.

Cooper fills me in about his week at work. Accounting might not be glamorous, but he has a way of making me laugh about client meltdowns and spreadsheet disasters. I lament about a conference I'm organizing for a Fortune 50 company next month and how much pressure there is to get it right.

"You're gonna crush it," he states like a fact, not opinion.

When I'm with him, I feel a quiet confidence settle into me. It eases the knot of stress I carry all week. Cooper's steady and sure-footed, the kind of person who makes you believe things are going to be okay even when you're not sure. It's nice not to have to explain every little thing. He works there too, so it's easy. Comfortable.

By the time we split the bill, we're both a little tipsy, laughing harder than we should at nothing in particular. We step outside into the cold, breath clouding in front of us.

"Let's walk it off for awhile." He glances down the street. "I'm not ready to go underground yet."

"Sure." I slip my hands into my coat pockets and keep up with his brisk pace.

We stroll in silence for a few minutes, the sounds of the city filling the space between us as we head toward Central Park.

"So, I've been trying to figure out how to say this." He tugs his beanie down over his ears. "And I'm probably gonna screw it up, but, I'm gonna go for it. You've been the best part of this year for me, Stevie. After my breakup, I thought I'd be stuck in this weird limbo forever. But you made things easy again. You make me laugh. I like who I am when I'm around you."

I stop walking. "Coop…"

He shakes his head quickly. "I'm not trying to make this complicated. I like you. More than I probably should. And I know you've been through a lot. I know you're figuring things out with Padraig. But… I couldn't not tell you."

His words settle between us, the air sweet, sharp, electric.

I take him in for a second. Cooper's hard to miss. His dark hair never quite behaves, it's trimmed close at the sides and curls slightly on top. His broad shoulders fill out his jacket like he could walk into a rugby scrum and win. He's about Padraig's height, maybe an inch taller, but his frame's more muscled. His skin is more olive-toned, but he has blue eyes and features causing people turn when he walks into a room.

I'm attracted to him, it's not lost on me. I clearly have a type.

He catches me watching him, and grins, softening my heart a bit. He makes me want to stay in the moment. Take a chance.

Except...

"Cooper," I break eye contact and look off into the distance, "you've been there for me in ways I didn't even realize I needed. I care about you so much. But I'm not..." I trail off, struggling to put it into words. I look up at him, bracing for his reaction.

He nods, his expression steady. "I get it. I'm not asking for anything from you other than I wanted you to know where my head's at. You deserve someone who shows up for you. Every day, no matter what. If there's ever a chance, I want you to know I'm here."

The sincerity in his voice makes my throat ache.

"I don't even know what to say." I toe the ground. "You've become one of my best friends, Coop. Any girl would be lucky to be with you. I mean it."

"Well, one day you'll be the lucky girl. When you're ready," he says firmly.

I link my arm through his and lean into him as we start walking through the park. "You're good for my ego."

"Yeah?" He folds his hand over mine.

Squeezing his arm, I let out a breath. "Let's take this one step at a time, okay?"

We walk in quiet peace as the city bustles around us.

For the first time, maybe ever, I consider what it would be like to love someone other than Padraig.

I can't help but wonder if my heart has room for something new.

Nineteen

PADRAIG

Four Months Later

Fuck.

The Bitter End is smaller than I pictured. Dark-red brick walls. Decades of graffiti and band stickers layered over the old plaster. Why does every rock club seem to have low ceilings strung with twinkling lights? At least this place smells faintly of fresh paint and coffee from the café next door instead of the stale dive-bar stench at most venues.

We're in the middle of running *Sinners' Grace*, a song everyone's been playing on repeat for months. The one paying the rent right now. My sticks hit the snare sharp and clean in an attempt to keep pace with Liam's guitar.

Arleigh steps up to the mic with an effortless poise. She's small and pale as porcelain with a sharp, androgynous beauty. Black pixie cut with heavy liner smudged around piercing gray eyes. She doesn't bring the drama Felicity thrived on. Doesn't have a ton of complicated baggage. Arleigh shows up, does the work, and leaves us space to breathe.

She joined the band a few weeks after we moved back to Seattle. With Felicity, Stevie and Linus gone, Liam and I knew we couldn't stay in Pullman, not with the ghosts in the house and the band stuck in neutral. We found Arleigh a few weeks later and, for the first time in years, Fireball feels lighter. Cleaner. Fun.

We finish the last chorus. Liam bends over his pedalboard, letting the guitar wail one last time before cutting it off. He straightens, sweeps his hair out of his eyes, and shoots me a look.

"You're tight on the fills." He sets his guitar on its stand.

"Yeah, I know." I lay my sticks on the snare and join him at the front of the stage.

Arleigh stretches out her neck and steps off the riser, glancing at me as she passes. "Don't worry. Crowd's gonna love it tonight." She flashes a polite smile and disappears backstage, probably to warm up.

Liam sits on the edge of the stage and pats the space next to him, forearms braced on his knees. "Dar, I know you're wound up."

I plop down next to him. "I'm fine."

"You're not fine." He squints, reading me the way only he can. "She's coming tonight, yeah?"

I glance at the side door, where bartender guys are loading in kegs of beer. "Honestly? I don't know."

"You talk to her?"

"Aye." I nod. "Said I'd love to see her. Told her I'd put her plus one on the list. She didn't commit."

Liam doesn't have to say it out loud. I know she hangs out a lot with the guy from work. Cooper. She doesn't call him her boyfriend but, by the way she avoids talking about him, I can read between the lines.

"Rough." He leans back on his arms and stretches out his neck.

"Excruciating."

We sit in silence, the sounds of the staff getting ready for the evening fill the room.

Liam nudges my boot with his. "Kills you, doesn't it?"

"Fuck, yeah." I swallow hard. "Every day without her."

He exhales through his nose. "Linus and I..." He shakes his head. "It's the same. He's back in Dublin, I can feel him moving on. I hate it. I want him happy, but I wish it could be together. Honestly, what I want really doesn't exist."

"You mean bringing in a woman?" I ask tentatively because even though it's me, Liam doesn't open up on this topic much.

Liam restlessly drags a hand through his hair. "We've talked about it. I've never been into anyone as much as Linus, but both of us also love women. We talked a lot about how hard it would be to stay faithful. How, ideally, we would meet someone who wouldn't be scared off. And for the record? What Felicity said about us was absolute bullshit. She overheard us talking, twisted it and practically offered herself up."

My stomach knots. "Oh. You turned her down?"

"Of course we did. She wasn't what we wanted. She was looking for an in and when she didn't get it..." He shrugs, the bitterness in his voice obvious. "Well. You saw how it all went down. Thank God she's gone. I'm sorry you lost Stevie in the process."

I let out a slow breath, guilt and anger tangle up inside me.

Liam's quiet for a beat before he smirks without humor. "Two sad Irish bastards. Writing songs about heartbreak in our twenties. Very on brand."

"Jesus." I huff out a laugh, but it dies quick. "You think she'll come?"

"I think you should be ready either way. Whatever happens tonight, be kind to yourself." He stares at the ceiling.

The last time I saw Stevie in person was Seattle, and I'll never forget her look of hurt and betrayal. It rips me open in the middle of the night.

God, if only I'd told Stevie about Felicity coming on to me. Instead, I kept my mouth shut, convincing myself I was protecting her. Protecting us. Protecting the band. I see now how my silence made Stevie question everything we had.

How my cowardice and immaturity cost me the most important thing in my life.

I'm trying to make changes, even if it's too feckin' late for me and Stevie. Taking charge of Fireball has forced me to grow a backbone. To stand by decisions even when they blow up in my face. Thankfully, Stevie and I have stayed in touch even if she shuts down the possibility of a future together. She's given me grace, which I don't deserve. Her life is different now. She's happy with her job. Fiends. Maybe someone new.

"You're not holding out hope, are you?" Liam asks.

I hesitate. "I'm trying not to, but I won't love anyone the way I love her. I don't know how to move on."

"I know it seems futile." He claps a hand on my shoulder. "Perhaps it's time to figure out what's next, Dar. We both need to."

I nod, but as I climb down from the stage and glance at the venue doors, all I can think is whether Stevie will walk through them.

Will she be smiling at me or at someone else?

Could I survive if it's the latter?

A couple hours later, I'm checking my phone like it's a lifeline. Nothing. No Stevie. No text. No reply to the one I sent after soundcheck. We're minutes from stepping onstage and I have to accept she's not coming.

Liam slaps my shoulder as we line up side stage. "Head in the game. We go out there tight."

I nod and follow him out into the dark stage and can see the club is packed wall-to-wall. Two hundred bodies pressed shoulder-to-shoulder, voices lifting in a cheer so loud it rattles my ribs.

All for us.

Arleigh's first to the mic and the stage lights illuminate her form as Liam and I take our places. She's been a game-changer for our vibe. She's gorgeous and naturally magnetic, with a throaty rasp that threads through Liam's guitar perfectly. I settle behind my kit, sticks in hand, and the roar of the crowd drowns out the knot in my chest.

By the time we hit the opening chords of *Broken Compass*, the room explodes. Liam's solo blazes, Arleigh's voice a perfect counterpoint, and the crowd surges with us. Each song feels better than the last. By the time we hit the encore, *Ghosts on the Wire*, I almost forget she isn't here.

The energy in the room pulls me under and I'm lost in our music and the crowd who loves us. When the lights drop and the last chord rings out, I let it wash over me.

The three of us towel off backstage, Liam already grinning as he strips off his shirt for a clean one. "Good fucking show," he beams, sweat dripping off his nose. "Best in weeks."

Mitch, our one-person road crew, gestures toward the stage door. "Come on, guys. Fans are waiting. You know the drill."

We do. We've made a point of it since we started this tour. We talk to everyone who buys a ticket, sign whatever they hand us, and thank them for coming out. We're slowly but surely building enough loyalty to keep a place like this packed on a Tuesday.

At the merch table, we pose for selfies, sign our limited-edition vinyl, scrawl our names across shirts and setlists while Mitch sells t-shirts and snaps pictures for socials. Eventually, the crowd winds down and the energy softens as the line thins out.

Then I see her.

Tucked into the far corner, leaning against the brick wall, watching us. Her hands are shoved in the pockets of a dark-green trench coat. She's wearing black tights, ankle boots and a soft gray scarf looped around her neck. Her hair's a little longer than it was in Seattle. She's not wearing much makeup, but she doesn't need it. She never has.

Stevie Hayes is as breathtaking now as she was the first time I saw her.

Liam follows my gaze and his whole expression softens. He elbows me gently. "We'll take care of all this. Go get your girl."

I'm rooted for a second, stuck watching her like she's a mirage I'm afraid will vanish.

Our eyes meet.

It's all I need.

I cross the room like I'm walking through water, every step slow and heavy. Stevie doesn't move from the wall or break my gaze. When I'm close enough, her breath catches, and then I'm pulling her into me, arms locked tight around her shoulders.

She fits against my chest exactly how I remember.

Neither of us lets go. For seconds. Minutes. Hours.

I press my face into her hair and breathe her in. My whole body shakes with sobs. She's crying too. Our shoulders tremble as the noise of the club fades into nothing. A year of distance collapses in the space of a heartbeat.

I murmur against her temple, "Come with me. We can go to my hotel. We can just talk. Please."

"Padraig…" She stiffens a little in my arms and pulls back enough to search my face. Her eyes are red-rimmed, wet.

"Are you alone?"

Her breath hitches. "Yeah."

Relief washes over my entire body. This is my one shot, and I'm not going to miss. I cradle her face gently, thumb brushing away the tear clinging to her cheek. "Then let's get outta here."

She hesitates for a second. Then she nods.

I lace my fingers through hers. Afraid she'll disappear if I loosen my grip.

Liam catches my eye from across the room and gives me the smallest nod of approval.

We slip out into the cool New York night, hand in hand, the city's noise crashing around us.

I'm certain about one thing.

Stevie's mine and I'm never letting her go again.

Twenty

A Few Minutes Later

WE DON'T TALK IN the Uber.

Padraig's hand stays wrapped around mine, warm and unshakable, our fingers meshed together like muscle memory.

The driver whistles along to the radio, Manhattan's skyline streaks past in fractured neon. Every red light feels like it's dragging me forward and holding me hostage all at once.

I sneak a glance at him. His gaze is locked on the city rushing by, the muscles in his forearm shifting as his thumb moves slow, steady circles against my skin. It's a familiar motion he's always used to calm me down when life spins out of control. Exams. Family drama. Scary movies. Late-night fights about the future.

No matter what we've gone through, it means, "I've got you."

God, it's too easy to fall back into the gravity of this man.

The lobby of the Courtyard by Marriott bustles with a surprising number of late check-ins and elevators groaning their way up the shaft. Padraig doesn't release my hand as we cross the tile. Or in the elevator. Or when we step inside the standard room with beige curtains and a generic king bed tucked beneath a washed-out landscape print.

He drops the keycard onto the dresser with a soft clatter and turns toward me. He scans my body and gulps.

I drop his hand and shift back a step, the distance suddenly unbearable and necessary all at once. "Padraig…"

His eyes flicker over me. "I want to see you. To have five minutes without an audience. That's all."

"It isn't all."

He moves toward me, methodical and intense, until he's so close I have to tip my chin up to see him. My breath catches when I see the intention in his eyes.

"Stevie…" He sounds unsteady. "I had to bring you here. To see if we can…"

He trails off. I want to tell him I understand, but the words don't come. The walls I've spent over a year stacking brick by brick start to loosen.

I love him. I never stopped.

Will never stop.

But Cooper. Steady, patient Cooper. He shows up for me in the small ways. Gives me space without disappearing. He's steady and kind in a different way than Padraig. We have fun. Lots in common. I can see a future there, even if we're not officially a thing.

I edge back another step, though every cell in me wants to lean in. "Padraig, I don't even know what I'm doing here."

He studies me for a heartbeat, expression unraveling. Then reaches out, slow enough to let me stop him. His fingers brush mine with a familiarity making my knees feel weak. "Yes, you do. Stay with me tonight. *Please.*"

The air between us buzzes with everything we're not saying. My pulse trips hard in my throat. My soaked pussy clenches from wanting him inside me, where he belongs.

Padraig waits, letting me set the pace.

I step forward.

His breath catches when I curl my fingers into his shirt and pull, hard enough so the soft cotton stretches at the collar. His mouth crashes against mine with the force of something we're used to. Inherent desire. Deep love. Unwavering passion.

There's no talking. No hesitation.

We tear at each other, hands clumsy and hungry, pulling buttons apart, dragging layers over heads, tossing clothes where they land. My back hits the mattress as presses me into the sheets with the full weight of his body, like he's afraid I'll vanish if he doesn't pin me here.

"Stevie," he rasps against my throat, kissing me open-mouthed, down to the hollow between my breasts. His hands slide under my bra and yank it aside. His tongue circles a nipple and the sharp heat makes me arch into him. He growls when I do, the sound vibrating against my skin.

I push his jeans down, dragging at the waistband until they're gone. He's already hard, so thick and solid against my thigh it sends a spike of need straight through me. I palm him, desperate and shaking. He hisses, hips jerking into my hand.

"Touch me, God, touch me," he moans as his fingers hook my panties and rip them down in one motion, leaving me bare and aching.

Padraig's mouth finds its way back up to mine, kissing me until I can't breathe. He's inside me in a single, brutal thrust that makes me cry out. I clutch at his shoulders, my nails dig into his warm, flexing muscle as he sets a punishing, relentless pace. Every stroke lands in the precise spot inside me, pulling a whimper from my throat.

On each pass, he whispers my name like a prayer and a curse, forehead pressed to mine. "God, Stevie... I love you—"

"Fuck me," I demand to silence him, lifting my hips to meet every thrust. "Please, fuck me."

So he does. It's messy, sweat-slicked skin, tangled hair, lips swollen from too much kissing. Muscles straining from hard fucking. He grips my ass and pounds until I'm unraveling. My orgasm tears through me so violently I scream.

He follows almost instantly, flooding me with his release. Face buried against my neck, grunting and groaning until he's empty.

We collapse together. For a long time, there's nothing but the sound of our breathing. My fingers trace the edge of his shoulder, memorizing the shape even though I know I shouldn't.

Once isn't enough. It will never be enough.

Padraig's hands are already on me, greedy and rough, pulling me back into him. He sits up on his knees, flipping me effortlessly onto my stomach. My breath hitches when he spreads my legs wide and presses a knee between them, yanking my hips up until I'm arched and open for him.

"Jesus, look at you," he growls, running the blunt head of his cock through the wet heat along my slit. "My come is dripping out of your pussy. I'm not done with you. Not even close."

"Then don't be," I gasp, burying my face in the pillow, fingers curling hard into the sheets. "Keep fucking me, Padraig. Please."

He drives into me in one brutal thrust, knocking the air from my lungs. The slap of skin meeting skin fills the room as he pounds into me from behind, deep and hard, every stroke hitting my spot until my vision goes white.

I push back against him, wild and feral, wanting all of him, needing it. His grip on my hips tightens until it's almost painful. His rhythm so hard and fast I can barely keep my knees under me.

"Don't stop," I choke.

"I'm never stopping," he grinds out, leaning over me, his chest against my back, breath hot on my ear. "I want you to remember my cock inside you every time you close your eyes."

My orgasm rips through me with a scream as my body seizes around him. He pulls out with a strangled groan, rolls me onto my back, and doesn't give me a chance to catch my breath before he's between my thighs again, filling me in one raw, unrelenting thrust.

"God, you're so tight," he pants, hooking my legs over his shoulders to change the angle, and I arch off the mattress, clawing at his arms.

"Padraig!" I cry, tears slipping down my temples. "Oh my God—"

He kisses me punishingly, swallowing my sobs as his motion turns erratic. His face contorts into an ecstatic grimace when he comes with a guttural, broken sound. The entire experience tears something open inside me.

I cling to him through it, his body shuddering over mine.

When it's over, he doesn't move. He stays inside me, our ragged breaths filling the silence.

Finally, he pulls out slowly, still hard, still trembling, and slides down my body without a word.

"Oh, God..." My voice cracks, but he doesn't answer.

Instead, he pushes my knees apart and buries his face between my thighs, licking me with such desperate hunger it makes me squirm. The taste of us, of what we've just done, has him groaning low in his chest, his tongue fucking me deeper, lapping my pussy with an almost reverent need.

"Too much," I gasp, tangling my hands in his hair, but he doesn't stop. He sucks my clit into his mouth, drawing hard, like he's trying to drag my soul out through my skin.

Another orgasm rips through me again, harder than the others, leaving me thrashing against the mattress, my cries muffled by the back of my hand. He stays there licking and tasting every drop of our combined release until I'm shuddering uncontrollably,

When Padraig finally climbs back up my body, his face is wet with us. His eyes blaze and he kisses me so I can taste us too. I sip from him, desperate for the reminder of what we were and what we'll always be, no matter how much I try to forget.

He doesn't break the kiss when he slides back inside me, slowly until his hips are pressed flush against mine.

"Don't ask me to fuck you," he whispers against my mouth. "I'm making love to you, Stevie. Every inch of you. Every part I'll never get back if you walk away. Because I love you and I'll never love anyone else."

Tears sting my eyes as he starts to move, deliberate and tender, his cheek resting against mine.

"I love how you never give up on anyone." He cups my breast and thumbs my nipple. "I love how you see the world. How you see me, even when I can't see myself. I love the way you laugh, how you look at me like I'm worth something, like I matter, even after I made the biggest mistake of my life by keeping things from you."

He kisses my cheek, the corner of my mouth, whispering every word into my skin as his body rocks against mine.

"I love the girl who stayed up with me all night when things sucked at home. I love the woman you've become, even if it means you're going somewhere without me. I love you, Stevie Hayes. Always and forever."

My heart feels like it's splitting in two. This isn't possession. It's devotion. It's everything we are and everything we've ever been, laid bare.

We make love like it's the last time, because deep down, we both know it probably is. He finishes by flooding me, every muscle locked when he comes.

I wrap my arms around him and hold him, wishing I could stop time. My fingers trace the familiar slope of his spine, the ridges of muscle I've known since we were teenagers. It feels so achingly right, for a moment I almost forget why I can't let this continue.

Padraig presses a kiss to my temple. "I want to stay inside you forever."

Tears burn my eyes, heart hammering with the weight of everything I can't say. Then I ease back to meet his gaze.

His brown eyes search mine, unguarded. "Stevie..."

Shame washes over me. Tonight means something different to him and I didn't realize it. I cup his face, forcing myself to be steady. "We can't do this again."

"What?" His whole body tenses as he slips from my body. "No. Please don't say it. You know how good it is with us."

"It is," I whisper, agonized for leading him on like this. "Being with you like this feels incredible, but it pulls us backward. We've been broken up for over a year, Padraig. We can't fall into the past because it's easy."

He flinches like I've struck him. "Why not? We belong together. You're the only person I want. I've tried and I can't live without you. Don't you understand what this means?"

I thread our fingers together and squeeze gently to try to ease what I'm about to say. "You can and do live without me. We've built lives apart from each other and if you left Fireball and Liam right now what would you do? What would he do? You'd be in New York wondering why you didn't see it through. Besides, I'm happy here. I'm enjoying my life. There's no going back to how it used to be with us."

"You're wrong, we can figure it out. I'll leave Fireball tonight if you'd give us another shot." His desperation kills me. "You're more important to me than anything, baby. We belong together."

"I don't believe we do. At least for now." I shake my head, tears sliding down my cheeks. "Do you know what I think? You diminish how much the band means to you to try and appease me. The reason I didn't tell you whether I was coming tonight is so I could see you play when you didn't know I was watching. It told me everything. You belong on stage with Liam. Please don't try to make your own dreams smaller because they don't align with mine."

"I'm not." His hands tremble as he grips mine tighter. "You're my only dream."

My heart shatters hearing him say this, but I force out the words he needs to hear. "I love you. I always will. But, I don't want to get back together with you."

"Even after what we just did?" He stares at me, raw and disbelieving.

"Yes. I'm choosing to move forward without you," I sob. "You need to do the same. Even if it hurts."

His face contorts with sorrow. "I'll *never* be able to move forward without you. Or stop loving you."

"I'll never stop loving you either." I sit up and pull the sheets around me in a flood of tears. "You deserve to be with someone who can fully embrace your life. I wanted it to be me, but it's not. The perfect person is out there for you."

He blinks hard, tears brimming but refusing to fall. "Is this because of him?"

"Maybe. Cooper and I are only friends. He went through a bad breakup too. We're both processing our situations." I swallow, guilt slicing through me. "We're not official, but I want to be. Me being here with you, it's not fair to either you or him. Tonight I've been selfish. I'm so sorry for confusing things. I didn't mean to lead you on."

The hurt in his eyes nearly undoes me. "I can't believe this."

"Padraig, try to see it from my perspective." I try to soften the blow. "I want a life where I can put down roots. I want to have kids and make a family with a husband who's there doing it with me. For the next few years, you'll be gone most of the time touring, living a rockstar life with Liam. For the first time, neither of you are relying on me or Linus for the basics and it shows. Onstage, you're both more invested. Dedicated. Your new singer is a breath of fresh air. She's not dragging you down. Face it, you guys are going places and I won't be the person who keeps you from it."

He buries his face in his hands, shoulders shaking. "No. This can't be happening. I don't want to wake up without you. I don't want to go to bed knowing someone else might be holding you. I can't bear to think you'd marry someone other than me. We're supposed to be forever flames."

"We always will be. The time we've had together can never be repeated. We were each other's firsts on so many things. Nothing will change what we've meant to each other." I take a deep breath. "At the same time, we're not those kids anymore. We need to cut this off. Not talk for a while. Let ourselves heal." I lean forward and kiss his knuckles.

He searches my face. "You really believe that?"

"I do," I say, even though my trembling voice gives away my uncertainty.

I need to be strong for him. For us.

Padraig nods once, silent. The room feels impossibly small, filled with the weight of everything we can't change.

I brush his hair from his forehead, memorizing the way he looks in this moment. Wrecked and beautiful and mine, even as I let him go. "Goodbye, Padraig."

Tears fill his eyes, but no words come while I dress.

I need to get outta here before I lose my resolve.

I'll love him until the day I die.

I burst into tears when the door clicks closed behind me.

The end of our final chapter.

Twenty-One

Nearly Two Years Later

THE HOUSE SMELLS LIKE a childhood memory.

The table's full of platters of food. Three roast chickens. Fresh brown bread. Mounds of mashed potatoes. Carrots and parsnips.

Ma barks at Brennan and Seamus to set the table faster. The air is thick with chatter and nostalgia.

It's the first family dinner since Da's accident where every chair at the dining table will be filled. Liam and I have seen Connor, Ma, and the boys in spurts over the last year, but we've not spent any time here.

Coming home makes the ache for Stevie worse. Her parents still live next door and my memories of her are everywhere. I try not to picture her smile or the way she used to curl up on the couch while Liam and I rehearsed. Or how we'd ditch school early to sneak up to my bedroom and get lost in each other.

There's not a goddamn room in this house where I don't have a memory of the woman who smashed my heart to smithereens.

I try not to think about her in New York living the life we should have shared. Ma's best friends with Lucinda, so I know she married Cooper a year after we fucked each other raw. Since then I've banned her from sharing anything Stevie-related. If my brothers know anything, they respect me enough to STFU as well.

It's too fucking painful.

But, I'm here. Doing my best to move on. Sitting shoulder to shoulder with my family, even if the closeness we once shared is fractured.

Once the table is set, Ma calls us all in. Connor takes the head of the table where Da used to sit, broad shoulders squared. Our oldest brother carries the quiet authority he's earned with confidence. The rest of us join him as Cillian strolls in with a beer in hand.

Liam's eyes flick to mine. Neither of us say anything, but we're shocked. He and I stopped drinking after what happened with Da. Watching our twenty-year-old brother twist the cap off a Heineken like it's nothing twists my gut.

Not my place, though. Tonight's supposed to be a step toward reconciliation.

Despite the basic chatter, everything about this night feels off. It doesn't help I feel completely out of place in my own family, as does Liam. Connor's intentions of getting us the fuck away from Da may have come from a place of protectiveness, but it's clear we don't belong here anymore.

Looking over my shoulder at the shuffling noise behind me, I'm taken aback at the sight of Da. He's thinner and his face is hollow. Pain is carved into every line. The man isn't even fifty and he's using a cane like he's three decades older. His eyes are clear, though, and they sweep the table, landing on us.

"Good to see you, lads," he mumbles as he approaches.

I nod and force a small smile but Liam doesn't look up from his plate. Defiant in the way only he can pull off. Da lingers for a beat, waiting for an acknowledgment —which doesn't come—before he lowers himself into a chair with a sharp breath.

The atmosphere bristles until Ma waves her hands over the table.

"Now eat," she demands, spooning potatoes onto Seamus' plate. "You'll waste away if you don't."

We obey because it's what we've always done, and though Ma's food is delicious, it takes every ounce of effort for me not to bound out of here to a place where the air isn't so thick with sorrow.

Nothing about this family gathering feels normal. At least not for me. Connor, Brennan, Seamus, and Cillian have lived through it all. Every doctor's visit. Every night Da slipped too far into the painkillers. The verbal abuse. All the rest.

Liam and I have been spared, protected. The repercussions are obvious. We're visitors at our childhood home. Years and years of experiences we've never shared with our family and they've never shared with us.

They don't know us anymore.

Connor makes an effort to keep us engaged in the conversation. "The Mission tomorrow," he tilts his head toward me, "it's a big room. Sold out. Can't believe it."

"Yeah, it'll be a great show." I hover a bite of chicken in front of my mouth. "We haven't played Seattle since..."

He nods once. "You'll crush it. Appreciate you boys opening for us when you could be headlining. At least we'll have a crowd."

"Happy to." I shrug. Years ago, I predicted we'd shift slot positions and now it's happened. I try not to be too bitter.

After dinner, Connor leaves for band practice and Ma and I clear the table. As we stack plates on the counter, she presses a hand to my arm. "It's good you're home. We all miss you both."

"Yeah? It's not easy for me to be here," I admit as the sink fills with soapy water.

Ma dries her hands on a dish towel, hesitating like she's bracing herself. "I know and Padraig, I've respected your wishes not to bring up Stevie." She sighs. "There's something I need to tell you. I can't keep it from you anymore."

I go rigid. Every muscle tenses. "Ma—"

She reaches for my arm. "You know Stevie's married now, love. I don't think you heard she and her husband have a little girl—about a year old."

"Don't say another word." The air leaves my lungs in a sharp, unsteady rush.

Her eyes glisten, but her hand stays firm. "You deserve to move forward, my darling. I know how much you love her, I always thought the two of you would find your way back, but things moved quickly. Now there's a baby involved."

I look away, fighting the sting behind my eyes.

"Your first love is the hardest to let go." Ma cups my face like I'm a boy. "I don't want to see you stuck in the past while life passes you by. You and Liam both need more out of life than ghosts and heartache."

Her gaze shifts briefly toward the dining room where Liam's voice carries above the others, brittle and too loud. "He needs healing too. Your da's words and actions hang over this family like a shadow. It has to be faced someday."

I nod stiffly, but the oppressive ache in my chest makes it hard to breathe.

After the dishes are done, we cram into the living room. The TV's on but no one's watching.

Side by side on the couch, Seamus is curled up with his hoodie pulled tight, Brennan is hunched over his laptop, now working on some sort of artificial intelligence app, or something. Cillian's in the armchair with a second beer dangling loose between his fingers.

Once again, Liam and I clock it, but neither of us say anything. We're the long-lost brothers with no right to an opinion.

Da's cane taps against the hardwood. We all turn. He crosses the room, stopping in front of Liam. "Step out with me a minute, son. On the porch."

Liam doesn't move.

The impenetrable protective wall he's built since the incident is on full display. His jaw's set. Shoulders squared. Tension pools in the silence for so long I think he's going to tell Rory to fuck off in front of everyone. Surprisingly, he finally stands, and follows Da outside.

The front door clicks shut.

"What do you think they're talking about?" Seamus asks cautiously.

"Da's probably trying to apologize, I know he feels bad," Cillian reasons.

"Doesn't erase what he did." Brennan doesn't look up from the laptop.

I lean forward. "I wonder if he even remembers how bad it was. He was so far gone. The pills. The drink."

"We all remember." Seamus pulls at the cuff of his sleeve.

My mind whirls back to the day. Of course we do. The shouting. The reek of whiskey. Da snarling at Liam for being with a man, calling him a disgrace. Saying he wasn't his son. A slap so hard it sent me sideways. Liam's body tumbling down the stairs, limp and twisted, the sound of his head hitting each step.

None of us will ever be able to erase the memory.

"Yeah," I manage. "We all remember."

Brennan shuts his laptop with a sharp click. "He's ashamed. For weeks after, Da barely got out of bed. He never touched any of us, but he did turn the self-destruction on himself. Did Connor tell you he'd sneak out late at night to gamble in illegal poker games? He had to track Da down and bring him home. Lost so much money he nearly put the company out of business. Ma gave him an ultimatum, get help or she'd move us all back to Ireland. It's better now, but he's a mess."

"Da went cold turkey. He's making an effort and works a bit more these days. When I get my degree next year, I plan to take it over." Cillian hesitates, then shrugs. "Brennan's a genius programmer. He's gonna revolutionize the world. Seamus is going to heal us all. You and Liam are doing your thing. Don't worry about us. We're strong Irish stock."

"I know you don't feel like you're part of this anymore. Not like before. But, you're our brothers and you'll always be family," Seamus states matter-of-factly.

"Connor made us stay away. After what happened to Liam, he couldn't risk—"

"Look, odds are he's never going to forgive Da, and probably shouldn't," Brennan cuts in. "Liam didn't deserve what happened."

I don't argue. Because my astute, brainiac brother isn't wrong.

The violence goes without saying. His cruel slags can and will never be erased. It's taken years for my twin to accept who he is, and I'm not sure he's fully there yet.

Da made him feel like his desires were shameful. It's left him broken. Damaged. The repercussions resonate to this day.

"I don't blame him." Seamus shakes his head.

"Look, Da knows he made a mistake. If he apologizes, I think Liam should try to meet him halfway." Cillian sets his empty bottle down. "It's not who he is, you know. Everyone can hit rock bottom without their entire family shunning them."

"A mistake? The homophobia and misogyny came from somewhere." My hands curl into fists. "I wish..." My voice falters. "I wish Da had been the man we thought he was. Liam is the victim here and I'll take his side every fucking time."

Silence settles heavy over us, broken only by muffled voices on the porch.

Seamus shifts on the couch. "Do you think we'll ever feel like a family again?"

"Not if the two of youse stay away." Cillian juts his chin out at me.

I glance toward the door where the porch light glows through the window. "He's protecting himself. Always has. Hopefully Da's remorseful enough and they can figure it out. It's between them."

"I hope so too. Otherwise we'll end up being strangers who share blood." Brennan has a way of cutting straight to the point.

The thought saddens me to the core.

Both Liam and I know what it's like to lose someone you thought would always be there for you forever and the pain when it's ripped away.

Stevie is a ghost I carry everywhere. No matter how much time passes, nothing will ever fill the void.

I rub a hand over my face and stare at the door, willing Da to make things right. Whatever it takes.

This family needs to heal. One thing I've learned over the past few years is, when you stop trying, fractures widen. The people you love don't merely drift out of reach.

They leave.

Forever.

Looking around the living room at my brothers, all I feel is love.

My brothers are my lifeblood.

I'm going to do whatever it takes to make up for lost time.

Twenty-Two

STEVIE

Six Years Later

CHAOS FILLS OUR NEW Madison Park house.

Boxes crowd every corner in every room. The faint scent of fresh paint clings to the walls.

I weave through the mess slowly, one hand pressed to the hard curve of my belly. Jude shifts inside me with a kick sharp enough to knock the breath from my lungs and I stop, steadying myself against the doorframe waiting for it to pass.

Eight months pregnant and I can tell he already seems ready to break free. "Please." I rub him through my shirt. "Four more weeks, buddy. You can do this."

From somewhere upstairs, a shriek of laughter echoes down the stairwell.

"Mama!" Isla shrieks. "Lila took my bunny!"

"Did not!" my three-year-old yells back, the sound of her little feet pounding after her sister on the hardwood floors above.

"Girls," I call, more drained than stern. "Slow your roll. The hallways are not a racetrack!"

When Coop and I found out I was surprisingly pregnant again earlier this year, we decided to move to Seattle to be closer to family. He applied for and received a promotion to CFO for all of the hotel chain's West Coast operations. Three weeks later, we virtually toured and closed on this house close enough to my parents' house, but in an adjacent neighborhood. This way, we can lean on them when needed but are far enough away so Mom doesn't show up unannounced with casseroles.

Madison Valley is quiet and leafy, lined with beautifully crafted homes on large plots of land. There's a ton of space for the girls to run and play in our fenced backyard. The house itself is huge with a master and six bedrooms, enough for each of my children to have their own space.

I'm most excited about the detached guest house where I'll set up a home office to start my event planning business when the kids are older.

It's expensive, but exactly what we worked so hard for in New York.

As I plop onto the edge of the couch, I can't help an invasive thought from creeping in. If I'd stayed with Padraig, I'd probably be somewhere in Europe living adjacent to his rock star life instead of here with my babies.

Thank God I made the right choice. Nothing compares to listening to Isla and Lila tear through the house, feeling my unborn son roll inside me, and having the stability of Cooper, who is a steady and calming presence in all our lives.

"Need a hand?" My sister Joni's voice pulls me from my thoughts.

Dressed casually in a t-shirt and leggings with her brown hair pulled into a messy bun, she pushes through the front door with a bag of Dick's burgers in one hand and a six-pack of Gatorade in the other..

"Only if you plan to do *everything*." I wipe the sweat from my eyebrow.

"Absolutely not." She grins, dropping onto the couch beside me. "I'm here for moral support and lunch."

"You're the worst."

"I know." She pops open the top on the Gatorade and offers it to me. "Thirsty?"

"Parched." I take a long sip. The hydrating sweetness hits my tongue like heaven. Jude shifts inside me again, reminding me he's taking up every square inch of available space in my body.

"I take it Isla and Lila are upstairs?" Joni glances up the staircase at the sound of tiny elephant feet pounding the floor.

"Yeah. Running in circles." I shake my head. "I think I heard them say they're making a fort out of the empty boxes."

She laughs, then studies me for a beat. "It's weird seeing you pregnant in person. You're simultaneously glowing and menacing. You also look like you might murder someone if they look at you sideways."

"Accurate." I offer a weak smile. "Pregnancy is...a lot. My feet are the size of loaves of bread. Jude seems to think my bladder is his personal bouncy castle."

Joni smirks. "My glamorous big-city sister."

"One more month." I exhale and rub the top of my belly. "Then we're done. We'll have three under seven and I may insist Cooper gets snipped. The man has super sperm. I got pregnant with Isla the first time we had sex. The other two seemed to break through the birth control barrier as well."

"Now you have your family to help." She side hugs me. "I'm so happy you're home. I've missed you so much."

I don't answer right away. Because I've missed her too. I haven't returned to Washington since the night Padraig and I imploded. Even though I've moved on completely, he was such a huge part of my life here. It was too painful to revisit, especially with my husband and growing family.

It feels like the right time, though. Despite my earlier reminiscence, I barely think about Padraig at all anymore... Well, at least not until I moved back to Seattle.

Before I call the girls down for lunch, Joni and I wolf down our burger and fries. We chat about how, in a month, our lives will tilt again with a newborn.

Joni leans forward and nudges my knee. "You're thinking about him, aren't you?"

"No," I lie.

Her brow arches. "*Stevie.*"

I sigh and lean back. "I'm *not*. Well, I am, but not the way you think. It's been years since I've been in Seattle, so naturally I have thoughts about how different my life would have been if we'd worked through everything..."

She reaches for my hand, squeezing gently. "We all love Padraig and the entire McGloughlin clan. For you, though, Cooper is incredible. You've built a beautiful life and you're able to have everything you've ever wanted."

"We have," I admit.

Joni studies me for a beat. "Are you happy then?"

I smile at the sound of the girls' voices from upstairs. "Yeah. I am. Truthfully, I stopped mourning the part of my life I gave to Padraig after we hooked up the last time in New York. He and I had a good run. Our future goals were not aligned."

"You never told him, did you?" Joni reminds me of the one thing I never disclosed to my husband about Padraig and my relationship.

"No. He knew I went to the show. I never told him Padraig and I had sex and he never asked," I admit. "I stand behind the decision, too. Coop and I weren't officially together. We didn't make things official until about a month later. As you know, the condom slipped the first time we had sex and I got pregnant with Isla. By this point, we were fully committed to each other and the rest doesn't matter."

As we finish our lunch, I gush about how fundamentally terrific Cooper is. Steady, solid, dependable. Devoted dad. Easy on the eyes. All the things I love about him.

Coop's the kind of man who always picks up after himself, never forgets my birthday or our anniversary, gets home at six sharp unless something blows up at work. He devotes himself to making all of our lives easier. He's kind to everyone, whether they are high-end clients or cashiers at fast food restaurants.

Our sex is great too. He's caring and always puts me first. It's not the all-consuming frenzied fire I once knew with Padraig. It's a different kind of connection. We have the same hopes and dreams. We like the same things. Value our time at home. Never fight.

The two of us make a conscious effort to fill our house with love. For each other, our children and the little boy we haven't met who is currently trying to push his way through my ribs. The bottom line is I'm looking forward to a lifetime of making memories in this house together and my past with Padraig has no place here.

"In case you're worried about running in to him, Padraig and Liam are barely in Seattle. They're constantly on tour or winning Grammys," Joni reminds me. "You'll probably not even run into them."

"Whether I do or not, I'm indifferent," I insist. "He's bound to have moved on by now."

Truth is, the possibility of seeing Padraig is highly likely at some point. Our parents live next door to each other. Enough time has passed, though. If we crossed paths, I could absolutely handle it now.

As for him, who knows.

"Have you watched Ziggy's live streams from Europe?" Joni changes the subject. "I swear the kid's allergic to staying in one place for more than a week."

"I have. My prediction is he'll wander the entire world and somehow end up exactly where he started." I smile at the thought of my little brother who, unlike me, harbors a dose of the wanderlust.

"Yep. Back at Mom and Dad's house," Joni teases. "Speaking of, they're somewhere off the coast of Italy right now, living their best cruise life."

"God, they're obsessed." I laugh. "They've become the kind of people who plan their next cruise while they're on the current one."

"They're happy."

"They sure are," I agree.

"*Mommmmmy!*" Isla barrels into the living room, bunny in hand. "We made a fort!"

Lila follows, beaming. "Come see!"

"Let's have a look and then it's time for you to eat." I groan as I push to my feet. Carrying a boy is no joke. Jude makes everything about three times harder. "If I get stuck crawling in, you're responsible for getting me out."

Joni laughs and follows us up to the great room, where the girls have draped every blanket they could find over the unpacked boxes. It's crooked and lumpy and perfect.

"Do you like it, Mama?" Lila tugs at my shirt, her face glowing with pride.

"I love it." I crouch down with effort. "Can I see inside?"

"Yes!" Isla grabs my hand and pulls me toward the entrance.

Joni catches my eye as I lower myself carefully onto the floor. She doesn't say anything, but her smile says it all.

We both know I'm exactly where I'm meant to be.

Twenty-Three

PADRAIG

One week Later

Connor's Belfast estate is like something out of the movies.

A kind of place I doubt he ever dreamed he'd own one day.

Iron gates groan open ahead of me as my taxi drives through, tires crunching over the gravel covering the long lane up to the house, which is sprawling and elegant, made up of clean lines and weathered stone. To the side stands a detached triple garage with a loft perched above it like a watchtower. The whole property looks out over Belfast Lough. On a clear day you could probably see all the way to Scotland.

Today, however, it's a typical stormy autumn day in Ireland and the slate-gray expanse is speckled with whitecaps. Wind cuts across the open fields with enough bite to make me pull my collar up.

The front door swings open before I reach it. "Ach, there you are!" my aunt Saoirse calls, her Belfast accent wrapping around every syllable as warm as the tea I know she's going to force on me. She wears jeans and a sweatshirt with a scarf wrapped haphazardly around her hair.

"Aunt Saoirse." I can't help but smile as I step inside and stamp the chill off my boots.

"Come in, come in." She ushers me toward her with a brisk wave and pulls me in for a hug only an Irish auntie can get away with. It's comforting. She smells faintly of lavender soap and fresh paint. "We've got more to do than daylight for it. Connor wants the master suite ready for himself and Ronni when they arrive next week. Grab yourself a pair of gloves, lad. You're not here for decoration."

I laugh under my breath and hang my jacket by the door. Saoirse's always been direct, efficient, and not afraid to tell you exactly what needs doing. She's Da's older sister, and in a way she's become a second mother to Connor, Liam and me whenever we're touring Europe.

I follow her up the stairs. Connor's bedroom stretches out across the top floor, glass doors opening to a balcony overlooking the lough. "It's bloody huge."

"Apparently, Connor, the famous rockstar, doesn't do things by halves." She quirks a small smile. "He's worked hard for this. About time he has a place to call his own."

Internally, I wince at the inevitable comparison between LTZ's trajectory to Fireball's. In the music industry, even though we've been at it much longer, we're drastically less successful than Connor's band.

"Yeah, well, he can afford to hire professionals instead of roping in his relatives." I roll my shoulders and shake out my arms.

Saoirse snorts. "Aye, and give the neighbors more reason to talk? He's in love with a famous actress, Padraig. They're keeping it quiet. You know how the Irish love their gossip."

"Fair enough," I acknowledge.

Once we move the furniture out into the hallway, Saoirse hands me a roller and points to the far wall to prime over a dark-blue hue the previous owners painted the room. I set to work, muscles moving on autopilot. Throughout my teenage years, before Da's accident, Liam and I had no choice but to help out at McGloughlin Construction from time to time. I'm surprised at how good it feels to use my hands for something other than drumming.

Maybe I should take up art again.

Before long, the scent of fresh paint clings to the air as the walls change from outdated blue to soft white. Outside, the wind howls against the glass.

Saoirse breaks the silence first. "How's your band, then?"

"Still standing." I glance over my shoulder at her. "For now."

She's tilts her head like she's trying to delve through the words I'm saying, into the mess underneath. "For now? What do you mean?"

"Koko's leaving in a couple of months," I admit, turning back to the wall. "She's been offered a production deal in LA. Can't blame her for taking it, she's too talented not to. I'm so tired of the same pattern, though.. We find a singer, build momentum for a few years and then they're gone. Liam and I are holding it together with duct tape at this point. Each time, I don't know if I have it in me to start over, but I do it. Not sure if it's worth it, though. I'm getting sick of living on the road."

I dip the roller into the tray and pause, reflecting on the history of the band Liam and I have somehow been playing in for over a decade now.

Felicity's face flickers through my mind, with her sharp eyeliner and sharper tongue. Liam and I were sucked in because, when she put her mind to it, could command a crowd with one flick of her wrist. God, I was so naïve. She burned bright and burned me and Stevie to ashes.

Then came Arleigh. Polished. Precise. A professional to her core. She showed up on time, sang her parts, got along with everyone. No drama, but no fire either. We had a good run but ultimately, couldn't manufacture enough chemistry to take things to the next level.

And Koko. God, Koko has everything we thought we wanted. Seasoned, confident, capable of playing any room. A tiny dynamo who combined the best elements of Felicity and Arleigh in one package. In retrospect, she was never truly ours. She always had her own solo aspirations. Fireball was one stop on the way.

I push harder on the roller before the paint pools too thick at the edges.

Sometimes it's frustrating to be in the position we're in. Over the years, Liam and I have developed an incredibly strong work ethic. We're good songwriters and excellent musicians. I suppose we can chalk up our twin chemistry to the fact we've had a middling level of success. A few hit songs. A movie soundtrack here and there.

Of course, LTZ bringing us on their stadium tours as openers introduced us to a mainstream audience. On the other hand, it highlighted the glaring difference between our bands.

With LTZ, it's like witnessing magic every single time they're on stage. It's not merely talent propelling them success, it's something deeper. Authenticity. They're riddled with their own problems but they trust each other. Push each other to achieve excellence. They're aligned and committed to the same path.

They're so famous each of them has private security detail. A slew of PR representatives. A big New York management firm. Everything they do is in the public eye.

I don't envy Connor or his bandmates in that respect.

We only get recognized from time to time by our superfans because we're not on the cover of any big magazines. There aren't thousands of social media pages devoted to us. Even our Grammy is in an obscure category.

The best I can say is Liam and I get by. We make a good-enough living. In musician circles, we're respected and Liam's content to find a new singer and keep coasting. He loves everything about the lifestyle. The touring, the music, and the blur of faces every night.

I can't blame him. He's able to be exactly who he is, unapologetically. He has me, of course, for emotional and professional support.

As far as relationships go, he's given up and prefers to fuck groupies then send them on their way. I've walked in on him countless times with men, women, and every combination. He's embraced his true self and is unapologetic for what he wants.

I'm stuck in limbo. Unable to stop thinking about what I gave up and what I'm missing.

What I once had with Stevie.

I miss the way she looked at me, like I was hers and she was mine and nothing else mattered. I miss the sound of her laugh in my chest when she fell asleep in my arms.

Fucking random women on the road doesn't cut it anymore. It never has, truthfully, though I've indulged often to quiet the ache. Ultimately, when it's over, I'm reminded of how empty I am. I'm tired of pretending sex is enough for me.

Realizing I haven't answered my aunt, I rest the roller against the tray and drag a hand through my hair. "I think Liam's fine staying exactly where we are, as long as he can be on stage and play guitar, he's good. But me?" I shake my head. "Either we take the band to the next level or call it. I'm getting too old for this shit."

Saoirse studies me for a long beat. "You're lonely."

"Aye." I swallow hard, and admit, "I am."

Saoirse's brows knit together. "What would you do if you left the band?"

"I wish I knew. Fireball's not like LTZ. Connor makes stupid fuck-you money. Look at this house. It gives him freedom. We're slogging and I barely have enough to buy a decent car." I dip the roller back in the paint.

Her gaze fixes on mine. "Would walking away make you happy? How would Liam take it?"

The question hangs in the room like a challenge.

"I don't know," I admit. "I'm tired of replacing singers, tired of feeling like we're waiting for someone else to save us. Liam might be annoyed at losing another singer but he'll bounce back when we hire someone else. I think he'd go on forever this way while all I can focus on is what I gave up to pursue this with him. For what?"

Saoirse sets her roller down, crosses the room and rests a paint-stained hand on my arm. "Padraig, from what I've gleaned, you've always held everyone else together at the expense of yourself. I'm asking you again. What do *you* want?"

I can't help but remember Stevie asking me the same question so many years ago.

"I want a life. I want what I had." The ache in my chest is sharp. "Something solid. Didja know Da gifted us each a townhouse? At least I have my own place now but it's essentially empty. Sparse. It doesn't feel like home."

Her voice quiets. "You want love. A family."

I swallow hard and nod.

"Ach." Saoirse returns to her task and eases back on her heels to work on the baseboards. "Do you keep in touch with Stevie?"

I stop mid-stroke, my grip squeezing on the handle. "No. Ma does with her mom though. Apparently, she moved back to Seattle a few weeks ago." The words scrape out of my mouth harshly.

Saoirse watches me like she's afraid to push.

"So, I pick up bits and pieces. She and Cooper have two little girls now," I continue. "She's pregnant again. Due soon."

Fuck, the ache is a physical thing, hollowing me out from the inside. Every time I allow myself to think about her, I wish it was me with her every day. I *wish* those kids were mine.

I plunk down the roller hard in the tray, splattering paint across my hands.

Saoirse doesn't look away. "Ach, love. It can't be easy for you."

"I'm happy for her." I drag a hand through my newly shorn hair, not caring if I get paint all over it. "Really. But—" My voice falters. "She was *my* person, Saoirse. Even after all these years, I don't understand how she could have moved on so easily."

Saoirse's expression softens. "I'll be honest, Padraig. Love is a mystery to me and I can't say I've ever known what you felt for her. I scarcely understood how your ma stayed with Rory after the accident—the drinking, the pills—watching him fall apart. I thought she was mad for putting herself and all of youse through it."

I glance over, surprised. Saoirse never confides in me about Ma and Da like this.

"Seeing hows he's on the other side, doing better..." She shakes her head. "I suppose she and you are a lot alike. Rory's her person. Always has been from the day and hour she met him."

Huh. Frankly, I've never thought about my parents as two people in love, though I've often wondered how Ma chose to stick by Da when it nearly broke her.

"Their kind of love is rare," Saoirse adds, holding my gaze. "It can wreck you when it's gone."

"I had it and I let her down. When she left, I didn't fight for her." I choke up. "She walked away because I didn't give her a reason to stay after I fucked up so badly. Now I know, I'm never going to find what we had again."

"Padraig, you two were babies. I know it seems like you lost a future you thought you'd have, which is a grief all its own." She pats my cheek. "But, remember she never wanted to be part of the band lifestyle. You're a young man. Don't give up on having a family if it's what you want. Life doesn't wait. There's someone out there who'll want to be your true partner if you give it half a chance. Learn from your mistake."

"How?" I blink at her.

She leans forward slightly. "Don't stay stuck in this cycle forever. You've been carrying this melancholy boo-hoo shite around for years. You've distracted yourself by pouring yourself into the band and Liam to numb your pain. Now you're alone and you're hurting. That's no way to live."

"I can't seem to move past it." I stare at the wall, a half-painted stripe blurring in my vision.

"It's long past time for you to figure it out."

Her words settle deep in the part of me I keep locked away.

Because she's right.

The cost of stagnation is becoming unbearable.

We finish priming the room and spend the rest of the day moving furniture, clearing out the loft above the garage, and setting up guest rooms. Saoirse gives me space to think about everything we discussed and I'm grateful to have physical labor as a distraction to help me work through it.

I've spent years pretending I've gotten over Stevie. Pretending I've buried the grief. Though he remained notoriously tight-lipped, I'm pretty sure Liam's urgent need to visit Dublin was to look up Linus.

God willing, they'll reconnect and at least one of us will have a fulfilling relationship.

Then, maybe, he won't rely on me so much for emotional support and I'll be able to be fully honest with myself—and him.

I want something more than this life. I do want to meet someone. Build my own family.

Have something real again.

The question is, am I brave enough to go after it?

Twenty-Four

Eight Months Later

THE SUV DOOR SWINGS open. The five of us spill into the driveway, a tangle of limbs, bags, and leftover snack wrappers.

Isla hops out first, clutching the gift bag she decorated herself, peeking inside to make sure nothing moved during the drive.

"Careful," I warn, ducking into the car to unbuckle Jude from his seat. "No running up the steps, okay? We don't need another scraped knee."

She sticks her tongue through the space where her front tooth is missing. "It wasn't a big deal."

"I beg to differ. You screamed the whole way to urgent care." I lift Jude out and place him carefully onto my hip.

"I'm hot," Lila whines from the other side of the backseat.

"Me too," Isla adds, already bouncing on her toes.

"It's June," Coop says as he rounds the car, grabbing the diaper bag and handing Lila her sandals. "You'll live."

"Daddy, I don't wanna walk," Lila protests.

"Of course you don't." Cooper scoops her up and rests her on his shoulders as if she weighs nothing. He glances at me. "We're late."

"We're always late," I sigh, adjusting Jude's sun hat as he fusses.

"Well, we're wrangling three tiny demons. Your mom will understand." Cooper grins, steady as ever.

He picks up the cake box from the back and I glance up to the wide porch draped with hanging ferns and bright summer flowers. It never changes. It's exactly the way I remember it from my childhood.

We're about to head up when the hum of an engine makes us all stop and turn.

A black Jaguar F-Type pulls to the curb behind us. Low and sleek, but not flashy.

My breath catches as the driver's door opens.

Padraig.

He steps out, more handsome than I remember. Like he's grown into himself. His hair is shorter than the last time I saw him. Long enough to brush his collar, but neater now. He wears a white linen button-down with the sleeves rolled to his forearms, faded jeans, and worn-in boots. He moves with the same quiet confidence I remember.

He's not alone.

A gorgeous woman climbs out of the passenger seat, elegant in an effortless way. She's young. Much younger than me. Blonde hair pinned in a loose twist at the nape of her neck, not a strand out of place. A sleeveless cream silk blouse tucked into perfectly tailored navy capris. Nude leather sandals easily worth more than my entire Target outfit.

Despite her youth, she's the kind of woman who makes you straighten your posture without even realizing it.

I glance down at myself. Denim shorts, a tank top streaked with Jude's breakfast, sneakers I pulled on while wrangling three kids into the car. My hair's in a messy braid I started in the mirror and finished at a stoplight.

Not too long ago, I cared about lipstick, earrings, and polished hair. Now I consider it a win if I leave the house in clean clothes.

Standing here looking at the woman who must be Padraig's significant other, I feel every inch of the distance between the two versions of me.

Padraig closes the car door behind her and settles a hand at the small of her back as they walk toward us. The gesture is casual and intimate, the kind I used to know by heart.

His gaze lifts and locks on mine. For a fraction of a second, it's only us. The noise of the kids, the bright summer day, all of it fades. His expression shifts, almost imperceptibly. A flicker of something familiar and raw flashes behind his eyes before he blinks it away.

"Stevie," he greets me when they're closer, his voice steadier than mine could ever be in this moment.

"Hey," I chirp too brightly, adjusting Jude on my hip. "It's been a while."

"Yeah." He glances at Cooper and our kids before looking back at me. "It's good to see you."

"You too." I flick my eyes to the beauty next to him.

Padraig follows my gaze and smiles warmly. "This is Mara. Mara, this is Stevie."

"Hi." She offers her hand. "It's so nice to meet you."

"You too," I reply and take her hand briefly.

Padraig turns to Cooper, who's stepped beside me. "Coop." He clasps my husband's hand firmly. "How goes it? It's been a long time. Last time I saw you was drinks in New York."

I barely contain my wince. Unbeknownst to my children, the situation had been reversed back then. I'd been with Padraig and not their father.

"Good to see you." Unbothered, Cooper shifts Lila on his shoulders. "Busy with this lot, but good. You seem to be doing great."

"Aye, I'm touring most of the year so I'm not in Seattle often to have dinner with the family." Padraig glances toward my house before looking at me. "I heard your mom invited us all over later for cake. Are you're sure it's okay?"

"Of course," I say quickly, though this is the first I've heard of it. "Mom will be thrilled."

Padraig nods, but before he can speak, Isla—bold as ever at seven—steps right up to him and Mara.

"Who are you?" She tips her chin up, curiosity blazing in her eyes.

"Isla," I correct her gently, "manners, please."

She shoots me a quick glance before adding, "Who are you... *please*?"

Mara crouches slightly and offers a practiced, warm smile. "I'm Mara. This is Padraig."

There's nothing unkind in the way she says it, but by taking the lead in the interaction there's a quiet claim there too. So subtle I almost miss it. Mara isn't oblivious, my guess is she's heard about Padraig and me. How much, I can't begin to guess..

Isla nods, apparently satisfied and skips back toward me, clutching the gift bag she's giving to my mom.

Glancing up at Padraig, I catch something unreadable in his expression It's there for half a second before it's gone, replaced with polite neutrality.

Rather than second-guess, I gesture toward Lila perched high on Cooper's shoulders. "Our other daughter, Lila," I shift the baby slightly on my hip, "and our son, Jude."

Mara smiles at each of them in turn. "Your kids are beautiful."

"Thank you." I smooth a hand over Isla's shoulder.

Padraig's gaze catches mine for half a second longer than it should before he nods toward the McGloughlin house. "The troops are waiting so we're gonna head up."

"Yeah," I say quickly. "We're already late. We'll see you later for cake."

I watch Padraig and Mara walk up the steps to his family's house, her hand hooked familiarly at his arm. Jude shifts restlessly so I adjust him higher, glancing toward Cooper.

"Well," he raises his eyebrows as we turn toward my parents' house next door, "we knew we'd run into the rockstar eventually. It wasn't as awkward as I thought it'd be."

I exhale a short laugh. "No, it wasn't."

It was. It *totally* was.

"Girls." Cooper ruffles Isla's hair. "Did you know your mom, Aunt Joni, and Uncle Ziggy grew up right here next door to Padraig and his brothers? They all met when they were about your age."

Isla spins to face me, eyes wide. "Wait. You were kids?"

"Believe it or not," I adjust Jude's sunhat, "I was a little girl once."

"But, you're so old now." Isla stares in awe, completely serious.

"Thanks, honey," I deadpan.

Cooper chuckles. "Your mom, Padraig and his twin Liam used to run all over this neighborhood. Thick as thieves."

"Twins?" Lila tilts her head. "Wait, you knew that man when you were little?"

"I did," I say as we climb the short porch steps. "We were best friends."

"Weird." Isla wrinkles her nose, processing.

"Someday, you'll have your own stories about your friends. You'll see." Cooper winks at me.

Isla doesn't look convinced, but she's already distracted by my mom, who's waving at the front door.

"Grandma!" she squeals and races inside with Lila following close behind.

As always, the moment we step into my parents' house, warmth wraps around me. Dad's voice booms from the living room. Joni's laughter follows. The smell of Mom's marinara sauce fills every corner. This house hasn't changed since we moved in when I was Isla's age. It's the heart of our family.

Dinner is loud, comforting, and chaotic in the best way. Jude bounces happily on Coop's lap while Isla tells my mom about her upcoming horse camp. Joni teases Ziggy across the table. Dad presides over the entire affair by telling age-inappropriate jokes in front of his grandkids and getting chastised by both me and Mom.

Cooper fits seamlessly into the conversation, laughing at Dad's witticisms and nodding along when Ziggy goes off on a tangent about his latest social media project. Watching him now, it's hard to remember the overwhelming worry I felt about how my family would react when I got pregnant and married so soon after my breakup with Padraig.

The entire Mcloughlin family has been interconnected with my family from the time we moved in. Holiday dinners, birthdays, late-night card games at this very table, to the two of us christening every room in each other's houses when we started having sex. My mom used to be a shoulder he could rely on when things were bad at home with his parents.

Our families are permanently enmeshed, even if he and I aren't anymore.

Cooper isn't some stand-in for the boy who came before. Mom asks his opinion on the new landscaping like he's been part of things forever. Joni teases him the same way she teases Ziggy. Dad treats him like a son.

My husband is not only accepted, he's beloved for how he treats me and our children. The life we've built is real. Not some fantasy.

Everything feels easy between us.

After dinner, I'm bent over the changing table in the guest room, singing softly to keep Jude distracted as I wrestle him out of his onesie. He kicks happily, grabbing at the pack of wipes.

"Hang on, buddy. Almost done." I expertly wipe my fingers on the sheet to avoid getting diaper cream on my shirt.

There's a light knock on the door before Mom peeks her head in, dish towel in hand.

"Sweetheart," she starts carefully. "I invited the McGloughlins over for cake tonight. Maureen texted me a little while ago. Padraig's home and he's coming over with a girlfriend. I'm sorry if it'll make things awkward, but I couldn't exactly uninvite him."

I pause, holding Jude's legs with one hand as I secure the fresh diaper with the other. "Mom, you don't have to apologize. It's fine."

"I didn't want you or Cooper to feel blindsided." She steps inside. "I never know when her rockstar sons are in town, so I didn't think to ask. If it makes you uncomfortable—"

"It doesn't," I cut in, glancing up at her. "We actually ran into him and his girlfriend when we got here."

Her brows lift. "Oh?"

"Yeah." I lift Jude into my arms and fasten the snaps on his clean onesie, the faint smell of baby powder clinging to my hands. "He looked good. Different, but good. And she seems nice."

Mom sits on the edge of the bed, watching me gently bounce Jude to settle him. "How did it feel to see him after all these years?"

"I dunno." I let out a breath, my gaze fixed on Jude's tiny fist curled around my finger. "Strange, I guess. All the cells in my body remember when he was part of everything."

Mom takes my free hand. "You and Padraig shared a lot and now you've built a beautiful life with Cooper and your kids. You're happy, aren't you?"

"Of course I am." I nod, though it feels a little stiff. "Seeing him instantly brought a lot of our history back, both good and bad. We shared a special time, but it doesn't compare to what I have now."

She reaches over and squeezes my arm. "There's no need to compare. Those memories are a beautiful part of you. You don't need to discount the past to be grateful for the present. You have a good picker. Padraig was a wonderful first love and Cooper is your forever love."

My eyes sting, but I smile anyway, brushing a hand over Jude's soft hair. "Thanks, Mom."

"You're welcome." Mom stands. "Now let's get you both downstairs. I'd better cut extra big slices of cake. You know how those boys love dessert."

On the way down, the creak of the McGloughlins' gate carries through the open window, followed by the familiar rise of voices from next door. My pulse jumps, but I steady Jude on my hip and force a slow breath.

I have nothing to prove.

Padraig and I made promises to each other once, but we both made choices leading us to here.

Different lives. Different loves.

I won't apologize for the beautiful life I've built with Cooper. Not to Padraig. Not to his family.

I square my shoulders as footsteps approach the porch.

It's time for my past to collide with my present.

Twenty-Five

The Same Night

I'M STUFFED.

The kind of chockablock only a McGloughlin Sunday dinner can deliver.

Roast beef so tender it fell apart with a look. Ma's famous colcannon thick with butter and cabbage. Brown bread warm from the oven.

I lean against the doorframe, arms crossed, watching Ma herd Cillian and Seamus toward the front door like a general mobilizing troops. "Right, come on, we're heading next door."

"Next door" isn't part of the usual Sunday routine and had I known about it before inviting Mara to meet my family, I might have rescheduled. We can't get out of celebrating

Lucinda Hayes' birthday, even if the idea of stepping into Stevie's house again makes every muscle seize.

On our way over, Mara slides her hand into mine. She beams, cheeks flushed, polished as ever. I swear, the woman always looks like she's stepped off camera, which, I suppose, she has.

She's twenty-four. A broadcast anchor in LA with a solid social following and a real talent for making strangers feel like old friends. I met her on Raya six months ago. She thought it was a joke when she matched with me. Called me "the drummer with the poetry eyes." Told me she'd always wanted to date a rockstar.

I don't think she said it to make me feel important. She actually likes the idea of who I am and what I do for a living. I enjoy how easy it is to be with her. We've had a solid block of time to get to know each other, with Liam in Dublin with Linus.

Being out with Mara is electric. She slips her arm through mine like she owns the night. Loves the way people stare. Loves it even more when I lean down and remind her no one else gets this version of me.

When we get separated, she makes me wait. When I spot her across the room, she'll blow me a kiss like she knows exactly how hard I am under these jeans.

She's pure trouble. Conversation is top-notch. She's kind. Funny. Self-depreciating.

The sex is fantastic too.

So, yeah. I dig her. She's the first woman who's held my attention since...

Ugh. She knows about Stevie, but hasn't asked much. And, I haven't offered, to be fair.

Which means she has no idea how nervous I am about this birthday shindig.

"Does your family do this kind of thing every Sunday?" Mara adjusts her grip on my hand as we move down the walk.

"Family dinner, yeah. Cake with the neighbors? Not usually." I try to modulate my voice to something resembling normal.

"Oh." She smiles up at me. "Well, it'll be fun."

"Sure."

Seamus, who's now in medical school, helps Da down the steps with practiced ease. Cillian's behind them, carrying on a quiet conversation with Ma. They all look relaxed and content, like the tension coiling through the McGloughlin family has finally eased.

Cillian runs McGloughlin Construction on his own now, but Da's back working nearly full time. Mostly desk work as he continues to recover from his injuries. It's nice to see Ma relaxed. I guess she's not waiting for something to explode anymore.

It dawns on me. The dynamic is almost peaceful.

Glancing across the grass, past the flowerbeds separating our house from the Hayes', I catch a glimpse of movement inside.

Despite my blooming romance with Mara, deep down the situation with Stevie is an open wound. My stomach roils with nerves. Cake at the Hayes' used to be something I looked forward to because I'd get to hang out with Stevie.

Now I'm not sure how to act.

Their living room is buzzing when Mara and I step through the doorway. In some ways, nothing's changed. Laughter and voices overlap. Chairs scrape against hardwood. The smell of fresh coffee wafts through the air. Lucinda's giant birthday cake holds court at the table.

The Hayes' place is exactly as I remember. Wide front windows frame the yard, shelves are crowded with books and knickknacks Lucinda's collected over the years. The couch is where Stevie and I watched TV for hours when we were kids and where we lost our virginity together.

Everything's the same but so clearly different.

Lucinda stands at the head of the dining table. Ma joins her and soon, they're laughing like schoolgirls. Hank sits in the corner with Stevie's baby on his lap, making faces to coax out tiny giggles. As usual, Ziggy teases Joni over some silly thing.

And...there she is.

Stevie. Smoothing a loose strand of the younger daughter's hair back into its braid. She glances up as we enter. I catch the faintest flicker in her expression when her eyes meet mine before she quickly looks away.

Ah. So we *were* good and now we're gonna ignore each other.

Good to know.

Cooper, his hair graying slightly at the temples, comes in from the kitchen, cake knife in hand. "Let's get this party started!"

Mara's hand threads around mine, and I realize I've stopped in the doorway. "Should we sit?"

"Sure." I force my feet forward toward the empty side of the table.

"Padraig," Lucinda says warmly as we pass. "It's so good to see you home."

"You too." I step aside so Mara isn't blocked. "This is my girlfriend, Mara."

"Well, hello. How nice to meet you." Lucinda's eyes crinkle curiously.

"Thank you for having me." Mara offers her hand, which Lucinda ignores in favor of pulling her into a hug.

Without thinking, I glance across the room to find Stevie again. She's back on her feet next to her dad. Lila clutches her hand like a lifeline. Cooper moves to stand behind her, his easy smile never faltering as he drapes one arm casually around her shoulder, the other around the oldest girl.

The perfect family picture is almost too much for me to take.

I clear my throat and guide Mara toward the empty seats at the far end of the table. Everyone else also settles into their places. Ma and Da near Lucinda and Hank. Cillian, Seamus, Joni, and Ziggy leaning against the mantel as they chatter away.

Ma makes quick work of slicing the cake. Plates make their way around the table and I can't help but low-key stare at Stevie with her kids.

"Careful, Lila." Stevie steadies her daughter's plate as frosting threatens to slide off.

"Thanks, Mommy."

Cooper leans close to murmur something in Stevie's ear and she laughs quietly, shaking her head at him. The sound feels like a punch straight to the ribs.

Mara notices me watching and squeezes my knee under the table. "Is it tough seeing your ex?"

"It's fucking weird." I force a grin. "I haven't seen her since she had all these kids. It's a lot to process."

She smiles, but I can tell she's not convinced I'm being completely truthful.

Decidedly, I turn my chair to face her and the two of us join a conversation with Cillian and Da about construction site war stories. Mara asks a bunch of questions and charms both my brother and father with her insight. I sit quietly, thoroughly enjoying her using her reporting skills to ingratiate herself with my family.

Despite my efforts to focus on my girlfriend, every time I glance up, I find Stevie's eyes on me from where she sits on the couch eating cake. She doesn't hold my gaze for more than a second. Always looks away as soon as I catch her to focus on one of her kids or Cooper.

My God, even after all these years the pull between us is undeniable.

Sharp and familiar.

Wrong.

Does she also remember the last time we were in this house before everything went wrong? Before we started building lives that didn't include each other? We were shoulder-to-shoulder exactly where she's sitting when she discreetly jacked me off under a blanket with her entire family surrounding us watching a holiday movie.

Jesus. The memory makes my cock stir, which is wildly inappropriate.

I glance at Mara, who's asking Ma about her cooking. My girlfriend is making a huge effort, she's genuinely interested in me and I'm thinking about fucking my ex who's here with her small children.

For fuck's sake. I'm an asshole. The twilight zone of our two worlds colliding is too much.

So, I drift and tune out the conversation. Watch mouths move without registering words. My defense mechanism. I'm floating in my own world until I feel a presence beside me.

The older girl.

Isla stands close, silent, brown eyes locked on mine like she's trying to decide what to say. There's something careful in her stare. Like she's weighing me.

"I picked the cake." She points to the half-eaten piece on my plate. "Did you like it?"

I lean forward and shove a huge bite into my mouth. "Best I've had in years."

That earns me a small, triumphant smile.

She hesitates again. "Can I sit by you? Mommy says you're a rockstar and you used to be best friends."

"Course you can." I tap the cushion beside me as my heart simultaneously melts and then breaks.

She climbs into the chair next to me without a word and nestles in, her skinny shoulder pressing into my side. Doesn't speak. Or fidget. Just sits there. Solid and warm, eyes flicking between the other grown-ups and me with quiet interest.

I can't fucking breathe. The weight of her against me is nothing. And yet it stirs a longing inside me I don't comprehend.

I'm not her father. I'm nothing to her. She leans in trustfully, however, without hesitation. It levels me. I want to run. I want to hold perfectly still. I want to forget everything and I want to remember it all.

Not long after, Isla's breathing slows, her hand resting on my sleeve.

She's fallen asleep.

On me.

Across the room, Stevie's voice cuts through the conversations surrounding me. I look up, instinctively as her eyes survey the scene. Oldest daughter curled into me, my hand cradled awkwardly near her back. Something shifts in her expression. Then she turns away, moving toward Lucinda, who's started clearing plates.

Mara leans over. "Oh my God. How sweet," she whispers, grinning. "She must really like you."

I nod, unable to speak.

Stevie steps toward us a moment later, gaze pinned to her daughter.

"Isla," she commands, soft and sure. "C'mon, sweetheart. Wake up, we're gonna head home. It's past your bedtime."

The girl stirs. Blinks. Doesn't speak as she slides off the couch and pads silently toward her mother, taking Stevie's hand without looking back.

I force myself to appear unaffected. I stand and hold my hand out to Mara. "Ready to go?"

She nods. "Sure. I have to be up early tomorrow."

At the door, Lucinda folds both of us into another warm hug.

Hank claps my shoulder like no years have passed. "Glad you came, son."

"Me too," I lie, because tonight has been far too awkward and confusing for my liking.

Mara and I step into the night, the porch light flickers behind us. Stevie stands close to the doorway with her baby draped over her shoulder, his tiny fist curled into the strap of her sundress.

Her eyes find mine through the amber haze and hold for a single breath.

Neither of us say anything.

Then she looks away.

Damn. I guess she's someone I used to know now.

Mara's hand slides into mine.

I wrap my fingers around hers and hold tight, not for comfort. For clarity.

My feelings for Stevie? The longing and ache I thought I could keep at bay?

Nope. It's alive.

If I ever want a real future, with someone who sees me and chooses me, I can't do this.

Clarification. I *won't*.

From this day forward, I'll never allow myself to be in a room with Stevie Hayes again.

It's not worth it.

Our past is officially dead.

Twenty-Six

STEVIE

Three Years Later

It's too bright.

Not from sunlight. Not from warmth.

This light hurts. Fluorescent. Buzzing.

Artificial.

My body's here. Somewhere. A vague shape which doesn't belong to me. I can't feel anything.

Not really.

My mind and body are dull. Muted. Numb.

Something buzzes steadily near my head, layered over an occasional mechanical sigh. A breath. Not mine.

Or is it?

I try to turn toward the sound with no luck. I'm paralyzed. Or dreaming.

Maybe both.

Time is strange. Heavy. Thick. Wet.

A prickle runs across the base of my scalp. Something beeps. Once. Twice.

Then a voice. Low. Indistinct. Sliding through the static. *"...responsive..."*

Not familiar.

Another beep. A longer tone. Sharp. Urgent. The light above me flickers, or maybe my vision is stuttering in and out. I try to open my mouth, except it's too dry. Like sandpaper. My lips won't part. My tongue is stuck to my teeth.

Shadows float above me. Is someone here? Hovering. Watching.

Icy chills race down the side of my body. My nose itches but I can't scratch it. More shadows. Voices getting louder. The sensations are overwhelming. I blink. I think.

Slowly, the world rearranges itself in blurs. White walls. A ceiling grid. Tubes everywhere. Shapes. I chase them with my mind, try to name things. Words slide out of reach.

Is this real?

I don't know where I am.

I don't know who I am.

No—I do. I know...my name.

Stevie.

Stevie Hayes.

The recollection echoes strangely. Like I'm saying it underwater. Like the name belongs to someone else.

It's not enough. A name is a label on a box with nothing inside. I dig deeper, trying to follow the thread. The second I find a grip, pain comes roaring in behind it.

Sharp. Searing. A scream against bone.

My ribs clench. My thigh burns. My chest feels like it's caved in. The pain doesn't localize—it swells. Expands. Spreads to places I didn't know could hurt.

I gasp helplessly.

At least I think I do. My throat convulses, dry and raw, like it's been scraped clean. Nothing comes out but a rasp that doesn't sound human.

Suddenly, I'm aware every inch of my body has been ripped into jagged little pieces.

A weight against my left leg.

A tightness around my chest.

Something attached to my face.

Panic creeps in before the thoughts can keep up.

I try to move.

I can't.

I want to scream.

I can't.

My heart kicks, and the beeping beside me accelerates like it knows what I'm feeling. Another sound—closer now. Someone rushing in.

No lots of people surrounding me.

"Her pulse is up—she's agitated."

Agitated?

An understatement. I'm fucking trapped. Something is wrong and my brain is moving faster than my body can follow.

Another voice overlaps. Calmer. Familiar? Maybe not.

"Stevie. Can you hear me?"

I try to turn my head toward the voice. Nothing.

"Stevie, you're in the hospital."

Hospital.

What?

Hospital.

Why? Why am I here?

My mind reaches again, blindly, mentally, for something solid. A memory. A moment. Anything.

It hits me all at once. The sound. Metal on metal. Tires screeching. The crunch of impact. A scream—no, terrorized screams. Children. Crying. Then silence.

Then nothing.

I freeze. My body goes cold beneath whatever blankets are tucked around me.

Children.

There were children.

My children.

I don't know how I know, I just know. Like a string yanked from my soul. Recognition buried under pain and fog.

"Your vitals are stabilizing," the voice says. "We're going to keep monitoring you."

A hand touches my arm. Not comforting. Clinical. Measuring. I don't know who this is. I don't care.

I try to speak. Force something out of my throat. "My…" I rasp. "My…kids."

"You've been through a severe trauma, Ms. Hayes," the voice says slowly, carefully. "You're safe. We'll talk soon."

Safe.

The word breaks me open. Because I know something isn't right.

I blink again, harder now, like my life depends on it. The ceiling finally sharpens into focus. Too white. Too clean. A long, narrow light above me casts sharp shadows on the corners of the room. A hospital monitor sits at my left, numbers glowing. Another machine I don't recognize stands guard beside it, tubes leading into my arm and chest.

I try to sit up. My muscles won't respond.

Tears burn, pooling without falling. My throat swells with the effort to ask again.

"Kids…" I croak.

"We're going to have your family come in," the nurse—maybe a nurse—speaks. "You're not alone."

Not alone?

The word stings too. I need my children. Three beings I carried and fed and rocked to sleep. The three I buckled into car seats. The three people in the world I'd die for.

My heart. My soul.

The door opens. I see two shapes enter though I can't move my head. My vision adjusts slowly, like my brain doesn't want to believe what it's seeing.

My mom steps into frame first. She's pale. Hollow-eyed. Dressed in the same zip-up jacket I've seen a hundred times. She reaches for my hand like I'm five years old and I've skinned my knee. Her fingers are cold. Damp. She squeezes so tightly I think she might be holding herself together by my touch.

My father lingers behind her, a half step out of reach. His lips part, close again. He looks down, wipes his face. I don't think I've ever seen him cry.

I blink up at them. Words sit on my tongue, tangled and foreign.

My mother says my name softly, over and over, as though I might drift off again if she stops.

I swallow and manage to eek out, "Where are they?"

The room shifts. A crack runs down the center of my mother's expression.

She closes her eyes, then opens them. "They're okay," she says too quickly. "They're *going* to be okay."

A sob claws at my throat. "Tell me."

"Lila has a broken arm," she says. "The bone fractured clean, they did a pin surgery already. She was brave. She asked for you when she woke up."

My lungs fight for air.

"Jude's got a concussion. No bleeding, but they'll monitor him. He was...thrown." My mom looks back at my dad who nods.

Thrown? I can't bear to contemplate. My hands clutch weakly against the sheets. "Isla?"

Her face softens, then breaks all over again. "She...ah took the brunt of the glass. Has some deep cuts on both arms and hands. She's been stitched up. They think there may be some ligament damage in her right hand, but she'll recover. It'll be a while. Therapy."

Something deep inside me trembles. My kids are alive.

My kids are alive.

I whisper it to myself like a spell. Like maybe I can hold it in place, make it permanent.

Then I say his name.

"Cooper."

By the way they both flinch and go rigid—I know.

My mother's grip loosens. Dad sinks into the chair behind her, covering his face with both hands.

"No," I whisper.

Silence.

The machines beside me keep going. Steady, unbothered. Like this is just another shift.

"Mom." I'm panicked now. "Where is he?"

My mother can't look at me when she says it. "He uh. He didn't make it."

The words don't make sense. Didn't make what?

A flight?

A phone call?

"Stevie, Cooper died at the scene." My father looks me in the eye to deliver the news.

Something splinters behind my ribs.

"*No*," I say like somehow my words have time-reversing power. "No, no. He was driving. He always drives."

My voice gets louder. The monitor beside me spikes again. My leg tries to move and pain tears through it.

"He—he would've gotten them safe. He always checks the seats. He's—he's—" My eyes flick back and forth between them.

"He tried." My mom's now crying, a sound I haven't heard in years. "The paramedics said he shielded the kids. He turned into the slide. He saved them."

A howl tears through my throat, raw and animal.

Everything else stops.

My body, my breath—gone.

The only thing left is the image, painted across my mind in grotesque, cinematic horror. Cooper's hands on the wheel. The sudden lurch. The kids screaming. His instinct to protect. To save.

To take the impact.

Tears burn down the sides of my face and disappear into the bandages wrapping my face.

My mom leans over me, pressing her forehead to my shoulder like she can absorb the pain. I want to scream at her. I want to crawl out of my skin. I want to take it back. Rewind five minutes, five hours, five years.

He was my safe bet. The one who wouldn't leave me. We were supposed to grow old together. Fight about dumb shit and laugh about dumber shit and make it to gray hair and college graduations and grandbabies.

Instead, I'm lying in a hospital bed and he's—he's in a fucking morgue?

How is this possible?

I don't ask what hit us or how or who. It doesn't matter.

The father of my children is gone.

He didn't deserve this.

It should have been me.

Twenty-Seven

A Few Days Later

THE GLASS WALLS OF Isis Management gleam in the late-afternoon light.

Sun streaks across the polished floor like it's performing for us.

Liam lounges on the leather couch, boots kicked up, his usual restlessness surprisingly absent. Across from him, Linus paces in the steady, surgical way he does when he's building toward something. Even in a room full of noise, Linus commands it without ever raising his voice.

Even more so now than back when we were in college.

Our singer, Avonna Parilla, balances on the edge of the credenza with easy grace, until you remember she's the reason crowds go feral. Sandy-brown waves tumble past her shoulders, eyes sharp as knives even in her quiet observation. She looks deceptively sweet, but she's got a scorching internal fire.

Onstage, she's fucking immortal.

As for me, I'm going through a bit of a personal turmoil, so I stand near the window, arms folded, watching the skyline shift with the haze. Pretend I'm calm, when really I'm in a grown-up pickle.

Linus stops pacing. Smiles the way he does when he's won.

"Well?" Liam leans forward. "Why the fuck are you so smug?"

Linus doesn't drag it out. "Netflix. Ten-episode drama. Big budget. Think *Virgin River* meets *Derry Girls*. It's a remake of *The Kerry Line*, only this version's set in Appalachia."

"Jesus." Liam blinks. "They're using our track?"

Linus nods once. "They want *From the Ashes* as the official theme song."

A beat of silence, then—

"Fuck. Yeah." Liam jumps up and slaps Linus's shoulder, spinning toward Avonna. "We did it."

Avonna doesn't move, but her smile spreads slow and wide. "Of course we did."

I lean back into the glass and let the words settle.

Three years ago, we were a band people respected. Now, we're a band people *know*.

Linus opens his iPad. "They want press. A stripped acoustic performance. Ideally video. We're talking exposure in the millions, boys. This puts Fireball in living rooms across America."

"Fuck me." Liam whistles. "You know how long I've waited for something like this?"

"You earned it." I meet his gaze. "Every night on stage for nearly fifteen years."

He doesn't blink. "So did you."

Avonna's already halfway to the mini-fridge. "This calls for sparkling cider."

Linus cuts her a look. "We can celebrate, but you're on vocal rest after rehearsals. We can't cancel Saturday's show."

"You're the worst kind of manager." Liam flips him off with dramatic flair.

"Effective," Linus replies, not looking up from his notes.

It's easy between them. It has been ever since Linus came back. It sucked when he left the band and broke Liam's heart, even if it wasn't his fault. He's come back different. Calmer. Sharper. Not merely managing us, building something with us and the artist management company he founded.

And maybe with Liam again, but my brother's been tight-lipped, even if his actions give him away.

I glance over. Liam watches Linus now. His eyes are narrowed and his mouth twitches at the corners. Watching them is like watching a flame in the dark. Bright, volatile.

"Well, how about we celebrate a different way." Avonna hops off the cabinet and claps her hands once. "I want sushi and one of those gold-leaf dessert things costing more than a mortgage payment."

"Done." Liam grins. "Linus is buying."

"Aye, of course I am." Linus is already buried in his phone. "Let's be clear, I negotiated this deal. I get to expense the fish to the band account."

I hang back as they all gather their stuff. This is the dream, isn't it? Fame. Recognition. Hit songs synced to prestige shows. Fancy corporate dinners.

My phone buzzes in my pocket, and I don't have to look to know who it is.

Mara.

Her voice glides through the late-afternoon haze when I step out to take her call from the hallway.

"Hey...are you actually coming home at a reasonable hour today?"

I lean against the back of the door and press the phone to my ear. "I know I said I would, but we got some great news—"

"Padraig." She blows out a frustrated breath. Her tone isn't angry, exactly. More, weary. "You've been gone two nights in a row."

I turn my head to glance through the glass into the conference room where my band is planning which restaurant to dine at. The sleek lines and polished concrete of this office do nothing to soften the edge of a conversation like this.

"I know. But we found out our song's gonna be—" I decide not to finish. The band's success isn't an excuse to avoid being with my pregnant girlfriend. "Never mind. I'm sorry there's so much going on."

She exhales into the phone. "No, I'm sorry, babe. I know you have work to do. I'm not mad."

Silence.

"I um... I could use you here, Pads."

My spine prickles at the nickname she loves to call me but makes me cringe.

I shift away from the door and walk toward the side window overlooking Sunset. Her voice sounds soft now. Young.

I think of the way she looked when we first met on the rooftop bar on our first date in West Hollywood. Her hair in curls, heels kicked off, holding court in a silver cocktail dress and telling me she'd give anything to live a life with meaning. Not headlines. Not glamour. Meaning.

"You're nearly six months pregnant, you shouldn't be alone right now," I murmur. "I'll say my goodbyes. I know I'm fucking this up, it's taking a little getting used to but I've got you."

"Pads, really. Don't feel bad." Her voice cracks a bit. "I'm hormonal which makes me sad and scared. He's kicking like crazy. It makes all of this so real so I'm spiraling a bit on my own."

"I know, lovey." My soothing words are low, automatic. "I haven't been home much to take care of you."

Mara left the network eight months after we started dating, a decision she called "liberating" at the time. Said she wanted to travel with me and see the world. Told me the newsroom felt shallow. Convinced herself—and me—hanging out on the road would be interesting and fun.

I didn't ask her to quit.

I didn't stop her either.

Quite the opposite. Hell, I ate up her devoted attention and insatiable sex drive like a feast.

Of course, she didn't realize the grind of touring isn't the same as traveling on vacation. Long hours on buses. Band meetings. Rehearsing. Songwriting. Set lists. Technical problems. No privacy. Very little time to do touristy things. On days off, I'm so exhausted I have to catch up on sleep. There's not much downtime and very little time to spend together other than stealing back to the bus to fuck while the band and crew are eating.

So, we fought. A lot. Our dynamic disrupted the rhythm of the road to the point where Liam was barely speaking to me.

Somewhere in Europe, I realized I loved Mara but wasn't in love with her. I planned on breaking things off when our tour was over. Then she missed her period even though she had an IUD.

A dozen pregnancy tests later, here we are.

For some reason, Mara's insistent on going back out with us next month even though she'll be in her third trimester. I don't want her to go so every time she asks about the schedule, I deflect. Say we'll talk about it later.

What I'm really thinking is: no fucking way. I can't deal with her need for constant attention pressing into the one space where I feel somewhat like me.

"I'll be home in an hour," I promise. "We'll eat. Talk. Watch something dumb."

Her smile is audible through the line. "You mean it?"

I hesitate, because I really want to celebrate with my band. Responsibility wins over. "Yeah. I mean it."

Shit. I don't belong in a relationship with her or anyone else.

It's not Mara's fault she isn't Stevie. She's a good person who deserves to enjoy her first pregnancy. I truly care about her, I'm not an asshole. We're gonna be tied together forever and, despite my trepidation, I'm excited to be a father.

I won't abandon the mother of my son.

Why then, when I hang up and tuck my phone into my pocket, do I stay exactly where I am, forehead resting against the cool glass, eyes tracking the sprawl of LA as dusk creeps in.

The woman gave up everything for me. Exactly what I not-so-secretly hoped Stevie would do so many years ago. Now, I have exactly what I always thought I wanted and somehow feel more alone than I did before we met.

Goddammit.

Behind me, the office door opens. Liam's voice cuts through, low and amused, "So. Are you telling Mara she's not coming on tour, or you planning to ghost your convo till after the baby's born?"

I keep my mouth shut. Slipping back into my old habit of avoidance in this case is the easiest, least confrontational thing.

Liam doesn't wait for a response. "Ah, hell."

"What?"

"Spit it out." His ankle bounces as he scrolls through something on his phone, but his attention keeps drifting back to me. He waits.

"I haven't told her she's not coming," I admit eventually.

He raises a brow. "No shit."

"She's pregnant, Liam."

"She's not fragile glass. We leave soon. You know how I feel about it."

"Well, we're on the same page. Last tour was rough and this time it's not a healthy environment for her or the baby." I suck in a breath. "My challenge is, things between us are...strange. I don't want to be the bad guy. The way I figure it, Mara's doctor will never allow her to come. There's no reason to create tension between us when someone else will handle it. Alternatively, we can postpone some of the dates since we're already gonna have to reschedule the last part of the tour once he's born."

Liam whistles under his breath. "Well, shit. I'm not sure we can at this late date."

He doesn't say what he's really thinking. Fireball's on the edge of something huge. Our songs are finally charting, we're supposed to play to sold-out venues across Europe for six weeks. Now, with the Netflix deal, the last thing we need is for Mara to go into labor when we're onstage in Paris.

I rub the inside of my wrist. "Her latest idea is to bring along her doctor. He's gonna say no, so give it a few days and it should work out."

Liam doesn't look at me, but his expression says it all. It's a stupid, expensive, indulgent idea and I should handle my personal shit.

My phone rings again. Fuck. It's Ma. This is the third time she's called tonight.

I debate whether to answer it, but decide it'll be a distraction from the uncomfortable conversation with my brother.

"Hey, Ma," I answer.

Her voice is thin, like she's been crying. "Oh, God. Padraig."

I freeze.

"What's wrong?"

She exhales too fast. "Love. It's—Stevie. There's been an accident."

Everything inside me goes rigid. My body forgets how to move.

Liam, who must have overheard, takes the phone from me and puts it on speaker. "What kind of accident?"

"Her husband was driving them home from dinner. A drunk driver crossed the center line." Her voice cracks on the word drunk. "Cooper didn't make it."

I can't breathe. The world tilts sideways.

"What about Stevie? The kids?" Liam prompts.

"She's in surgery," Ma chokes out. "It's serious, love. Very serious. The wee ones are pretty banged up. Lucinda and Hank are with them at Swedish."

I'm already reaching for my keys. "I'll catch the next flight."

"Padraig—no."

"Ma. It's Stevie. I have to—"

"You can't." Her voice sharpens. "Listen to me. You showing up now, after all this time, when her husband's barely cold and she's in a hospital bed?" She pauses. "You don't get to make this about you."

I drop my keys on the table, heart thundering in my ears. This *isn't* about me, Stevie needs me. "I'm not—"

"You *are*. I know your heart's in the right place and you want to be there for her." Her voice wavers. "But our girl has a shattered family and her children to hold together. Don't make it harder by confusing things."

I don't answer. I'm too stunned.

Ma softens. "I called with the news because I thought you should hear it from me and not someone else. I'll be helping Lucinda, so if and when it seems okay, I'll let you know if it's appropriate to get in touch. Besides, you have other responsibilities now. Your focus must be on Mara. Your own family."

She hangs up. I nod into the silence, because she's right, obviously.

Liam watches me. "I get it. It's Stevie."

"Shit." I nod once. Sit down hard. "She's a widow."

Liam blinks. "Fuck."

"Yeah."

The moment expands. Delicate. Raw.

I think of Mara laughing in the kitchen this morning, her hands curved around the slope of her belly like it was the most natural thing in the world. She and my son are supposed to be my future.

And yet, Stevie will always be the one I can't stop loving, No one, including Mara, will ever compare.

Is it fair to stay in a relationship when I feel pulled toward the woman who'll always have my whole heart? The one who lives inside the quiet parts of me? Is it right for me to string Mara along when I'll *never* be able to give her close to the version Stevie had?

Liam speaks first. "You gonna tell her?"

"No. Not tonight."

I push back from the table and walk back to the window.

Conflicted.

Resolved.

Knowing I'm the biggest piece of shit on the planet.

Twenty-Eight

STEVIE

Three Months Later

My leg creaks in protest when I shift my weight on dining room chair.

I'm not used to the quiet.

I doubt I'll ever get used to it.

Stacks of paperwork clutter the table in front of me. Insurance forms. Medical bills. Letters from the funeral home. A claim for wrongful death I haven't opened sits, half-buried under a folder labeled *Final Estate Administration*. The words don't feel real.

None of this does.

My pen hovers over a section asking for "marital status." The question splits me wide open. I tick the box "widowed," hand trembling, then press my wrist against the edge of the table until pain distracts me.

Mom took the kids out for ice cream to give me a break. They earned a treat after yesterday's intense grief therapy session. I watched Isla fold her long sleeves over the fresh scars down her arms, trying not to meet her own gaze in the mirror. Jude covered his ears and cried when a car blared the horn. Lila didn't say much. She's not one for sharing her feelings.

Physically, we're slowly getting stitched back together. Emotionally, nothing's quite right.

Jude wakes screaming more nights than not. He doesn't remember much, but his body holds the trauma. Isla speaks only when there's no way around it. My once-sparkling girl fades behind a blank stare, her fingers trembling every time she tries to grip something. Lila's become the family clown, trying to keep everyone laughing to make everything better again.

I'm healing, technically. The bruised ribs have faded. My femur's held together with plates and screws. A thick scar trails the incision. PT's brutal. Step-ups, glute squeezes, balance drills. I walk with a cane, measuring progress in inches. It'll be months before I move normally again, but the doctors say it will happen eventually if I keep up the pace.

None of my physical or emotional pain compares to the moment I woke up in the hospital and realized Cooper was gone forever.

Cooper.

I try not to say his name out loud. It sends the kids spiraling which, once I've calmed them, makes me lock myself in the bathroom where I grip the counter and try not to scream into a hand towel. Losing my shit feels like a betrayal to whatever calm I've scraped together for the day.

He was everything steady. Everything solid. My husband. Their father.

The love I chose after my world fell apart when Padraig and I split.

There's a dent in the couch cushion where he used to fall asleep watching Mariners games. His mug sits in the drying rack because I can't bring myself to move it. I folded his t-shirts and packed them in a box. Opened it two hours later and put them back in his drawer. Not before pressing my face into the cotton like his oxygen might live in the threads.

The bedroom door squeaked last night. For half a second, I looked up because I forgot.

Lost him all over again when I realized he's never coming home.

Every mundane task provides more evidence of who he was to our family. The cable bill auto-pays from his account. His name's on every document. Every login code. Every emergency contact. His social media accounts live on, only now his feed is filled with sympathy posts from people he knew even if I have no clue who they are.

When his woodsy, warm scent started slowly fading from the closet, I bought a case of his favorite cedar-scented soap so I never forget how he smells.

I press my palms to my eyes.

Try not to cry. *Again*.

I can't afford to.

Three phone numbers are listed on the legal pad beside my laptop. The medical insurance adjuster wants updated injury reports. The life insurance company wants proof of everything from birth certificates to our marriage license to his death certificate in triplicate. My lawyer wants to discuss the estate.

Probate forms are half-filled, smeared with coffee and exhaustion. Isla's surgery triggered a lien I don't understand, attached to our house which I might not be able to keep. Warnings about interest. Penalties. Deadlines.

I haven't located the title to Cooper's car or figured out what to do about the shared bank account. His name is everywhere. On the mortgage, our car loan, the credit cards, the kids' schools.

Every form demands a different version of proving the same impossible thing: Cooper's dead.

I've checked the box "deceased" more times than I can count.

I have no idea what I'm going to do to support myself and the kids. I haven't worked since Jude was born.

Without his steady paycheck, we're cash poor. I can't reach out to my in-laws, Cooper's parents have gone radio silent, locked in their own grief. Thank God, I have so much help from my own family.

Joni moved into the guest room the day I was released from the hospital. She hasn't put a time limit on how long she'll stay, for which I'm eternally grateful.

Every night she and I cuddle on the couch and watch trashy reality TV to get my mind off things. She won't let me sleep alone, taking up the space where Cooper used to lie. Too often she holds me when I sob into the early morning hours.

With my leg fucked up, Ziggy is my official Uber driver, slipping into the rhythm of school, doctor and therapy drop-offs and pickups like it's always been his primary job. He texts me from waiting rooms, updates me on progress, and shields me from questions I'm not ready to answer.

My mom takes care of my kids and house like she's auditioning for sainthood. From folding laundry and cleaning toilets to cooking dinner the kids will actually eat. Working with Isla on her PT. Easing Lila into her sling without waking her. Rocking Jude through night terrors with a soft patience I can't summon anymore.

She makes it look easy. I know it's not.

And, Dad. He shows up with a toolbox and a quiet kind of devotion I didn't know I needed. He tightens wobbly doorknobs, replaces smoke detector batteries, fixes stuck kitchen drawers. Mows the lawn without being asked, then sits on the porch like he's guarding the whole house.

No one complains. No one asks how long they'll be needed.

They'd do anything for me.

Which makes it worse.

Because I don't know how to deserve it. Or, how I'll ever pay them back.

God, I hate requiring so much help. Hate I can't be a good mom. Hate the grief making everything thick and heavy. Hate waking up from dreams where Cooper's brushing his teeth, shirtless and smiling at me like nothing ever happened.

I fucking hate waking up. *Period*.

My fingers trace the stack of hospital invoices. The ER. The OR. The pediatric ICU. I memorize the acronyms because they're easier to face than the truth underneath.

We were driving home from dinner.

We didn't do anything out of the ordinary other than deciding to share a huge ice cream sundae knowing we'd get home a little later than the kids' bedtime. A treat for all of us. When we finished and buckled into the SUV, all of us sang along to the radio. I remember reaching back to hand Jude his stuffed elephant.

Then headlights. Metal. Screaming.

Silence.

I push the paperwork away and press my forehead to the table.

I can't do this.

How can I possibly live a life Cooper was supposed to be in? I don't know how to stop pretending I'm okay and actually *be* okay. Or how to stop resenting the fact I can't crawl into a hole and hibernate for a year. Or two. Or ten.

The front door opens, cheerful voices tumble in.

Jude's giggle. Mom's gentle reminder to take off their shoes. Lila singing like she's destined to be the next Taylor Swift.

I wipe the tears from my face. Force my spine straight. Close the folder.

Put on my metaphorical big girl panties.

For Cooper.

For our children.

I'm all they've got and I won't let them down.

Twenty-Nine

PADRAIG

A Few Days Later

My son cries so much, I almost don't register it anymore.

The sound is constant. Either high-pitched and piercing. Or whimpering and pathetically ragged. His agony scrapes the inside of my skull, disappears before I can catch my breath then repeats.

Rafferty McLoughlin is two months old with premature lungs, premature nerves, premature everything. His entire mind and body is tender and forming. He shrieks when the light shifts. Howls when I change his diaper. Whimpers when I rock him too slow or speak too loud or touch him with a shirt that's too scratchy.

I've never wanted to take care of anyone more in my life.

You'll often find me standing over his bassinet like a guard. Not a soldier, not a father.

Something in between. Something less heroic. Less sure.

Even when he's sleeping, my body braces for it.

Before he was born, Paula came in from North Carolina and temporarily moved into the guest room. With all of Rafferty's health issues, she's taken charge of our household, which is currently Mara's condo in Valley Village.

Everything about Mara's mom feels deliberate. Silk robes. Lipstick, even before sunrise. Hair always perfectly coiffed. She doesn't do sweatpants or chipped nail polish or vulnerability in front of strangers.

She was a news anchor once, too. Long before Mara followed in her footsteps. She's a big believer in keeping up appearances. I know this because she tells me how important it is about seven hundred times per day.

Rafferty makes a sound. Not a full wail... I hold my breath. My hand grips the bassinet frame, fingers curled where the wood's been worn smooth from use. We didn't buy it new. This crib's been in Mara's family since the nineties. Paula refinished the edges, stitched new lining—powder blue with silver stars—and shipped it to us.

I hadn't known how much Mara cared about tradition until she was put on bedrest and we had to postpone the European tour so I could stay with her.

Rafferty's eyelids flutter. He makes a tiny noise again, like a hiccup with a chaser of phlegm.

I slip one arm under his swaddle and lift him before it can turn into a scream. He's smaller than he should be. His whole head fits in the cradle of my palm, skin a perfect, pink-tinted map of veins and warmth and newness.

Walking him slowly over to the glider Paula ordered with rush shipping, I sit down and tuck him against my chest. He settles fast, which is a miracle. He smells like lanolin and baby soap. Breath coming out, thankfully, in little puffs. Before too long my shirt dampens at the collar.

I don't mind. I'd sit here for hours. The depth of love I have for my son is something I never knew was possible.

"You're a natural." Paula's quiet voice cuts through the tranquility like a blade.

I don't jump. Don't speak. She knows the drill.

Do. Not. Wake. The. Baby.

She stands in the doorway, arms crossed, designer glasses perched at the edge of her nose. "You should get some rest. I'll take him."

I glance down. Miraculously, he's sound asleep. My whole body revolts at the thought of letting him go.

"Nah, I'm good."

She hesitates, then nods. "I'll make you some coffee."

Paula disappears without another word. The kettle clicks on less than a minute later, followed by the telltale clink of ceramic. Even now, late into the evening, she makes herself useful. She brings order to this place, from rearranging the fridge to restocking the pantry. Last week, she located a bag of baby clothes I forgot we bought.

Even if I wish she didn't have to be here, Paula is the only reason I can function right now.

Out of the two of us, she knows how to reach Mara when I can't. Encourages her to get out of bed when the fog won't lift. Rubs her back when she won't eat, won't speak, and won't acknowledge Rafferty. When I need to shower or use the bathroom, she takes over without complaint even when he screams himself red.

Without her, I'd be failing both of them.

I know Paula judges me. Every time her gaze lands on me, I brace.

Not because she's cruel. She's not. She's measured. Deliberate. Always observing, never accusing. Paula never says it out loud, but her agenda is obvious. Bridal magazines are left open on the kitchen island, turned to pages filled with rings and white lace and words like healing and forever.

In her mind, Mara's not getting better because I haven't done the right thing. She assumes a proposal is the missing piece. Paula believes marriage would fix everything including her debilitating postpartum depression.

The thing is, I wasn't planning on asking Mara to marry me before Rafferty was born. Doing it now would be disingenuous.

An engagement won't pull her from bed or fill her mind with maternal instinct. It won't make Rafferty cry less or help me stop feeling like I'm flailing in a life I'm not sure I'm meant to lead.

Besides, while I love Mara as a person, she's not *my* person.

It's best to stay quiet and focus on my son. Kiss his soft forehead and sing old Irish lullabies I barely remember while the rest of my family is two-thousand miles away in Seattle looking after my da, who had a stroke not too long ago.

My place is here in Los Angeles, witnessing the woman I've tried to love disappear into shadows.

Tonight, at least, Mara's sound asleep in our master bedroom. Finally. After four straight nights of barely making it through pumping without bawling uncontrollably, she took two sleeping pills and went under like she hadn't slept in years.

None of what's happening to her now is her fault. I've read every article I could find. Postpartum depression's worse with prematurity. The NICU stay didn't help. Compounded by the stitches from giving birth naturally. Hormones. The fucking fear. We almost lost him before we met him.

So, I can't be angry and I'm not angry.

I'm something else.

Something more restrained.

Guilty.

God, the guilt I carry for not being the man who can give her what she wants.

Mara's smile used to be as bright as the sun. I've never met anyone who can make people feel more at ease. She quit her career to be with me and it wasn't enough. Right before I planned to end it, she got pregnant.

Now we have a premature baby and she flinches at her own reflection.

Yeah, I'm a real fuckin' prize.

Deciding to check on her, I carry Rafferty in, expecting the usual scenario. Shades drawn, air stale, Mara half-buried under quilts with her eyes closed, sleeping or pretending to sleep.

Instead, she's upright with her thin arms wrapped around her knees. Hair loose. Staring at the pale light from the lamp on the nightstand like she's forgotten what day it is.

"Mara?"

"Hi." She doesn't look at me or him. "It's okay. Come here."

I settle on the edge of the bed, sleeping Rafferty is pressed to my chest.

Her fingers twist the blanket until the fabric groans. "I need to tell you something."

My pulse kicks, but I nod. "Sure."

"I was finally able to sleep, and when I woke up, had some clarity." Her voice stays flat. "The thing is, ever since I got pregnant, my brain won't stop. It's been worse since he was born. It's not just the hormones. or the fact everything hurts. Not really."

She glances over, and her eyes are wide and wet. "It's all-consuming guilt."

Wait, *what*?

I stay quiet. Let her speak.

"I did something I never thought I would. Something I hate myself for. And it's eating me alive." The blanket bunches tighter in her fists. She breathes in once. Then out. "I overheard you. Last year on tour. You didn't know I was outside the stairwell. You were talking to Liam. You told him you didn't see a future with me."

My throat tightens, because I distinctly remember the conversation. It happened after Mara was so angry I couldn't walk the streets of Paris with her, she refused to come to our show.

"I felt it, even before. You pulling away," she continues. "The way you kissed me started changing. We didn't have sex very much. So I made a choice."

She pauses. Then—

"I had my IUD taken out."

All the air leaves the room.

"I didn't tell you because I didn't want to lose you. I thought if I got pregnant, maybe... I don't know. Maybe we'd make sense again. Maybe you'd remember how much fun we had together. Maybe you'd stay."

Rafferty shifts, letting out a quiet, warbling sigh. I rub his back slowly. Hold him a little tighter.

"I know what an awful person I am," she says. "I lied. I manipulated you. Justified it in my own mind and became someone I don't recognize. And now I'm stuck inside this body, this head, this haze. You're a father because I forced your hand." Her voice catches. "I don't want to be the reason you feel trapped here. I need to free you."

The silence between us grows heavier. I reach for her hand, and she lets me take it.

I want to say I'm fine. Tell her none of it matters. Promise her all is forgiven.

I don't.

Because it's not fine. And pretending it is would break something between us neither of us could ever fix.

I look at Rafferty's face, his mouth slack in a dream I hope is peaceful. None of this is his fault. He didn't ask to be born into uncertainty. He deserves better than a father stuck in his own head. And a mother who's guilt won't let her heal to be there for him.

Somehow, in this moment, I understand with perfect clarity Mara didn't do this out of malice. She's not cruel. She's not careless.

She was desperate.

I've breadcrumbed her for fucking years. Gave her pieces of myself but never the whole. I let her believe in a future when I didn't have the guts to tell her otherwise. I reassured her because I couldn't bear to be alone.

I fucked her and thought of someone else.

So no. I don't condone what she did. I'm no better, so there's no room to judge. There's no point. We're in this now.

"I'm not happy you lied," I murmur quietly. "It's not something I can pretend is okay."

Her breath catches. She nods, barely.

"What you overheard was really how I felt," I admit. "I'm not able to give you forever on a romantic level."

She doesn't speak. Doesn't look away.

"But, Rafferty's here. He's our son. And he's perfect." I choke back the tears.

She bites her lip and presses a hand over her stomach, like her body remembers carrying him.

"I'm not going anywhere," I add. "Not while you're healing. Not while we're figuring this out."

My fingers graze the soft skin of Rafferty's back. He shifts, lets out a squeaky sigh.

"We'll find a way forward. For him."

Her chin trembles, but she holds it together.

I lean in, press my lips to her temple.

"He's going to know love," I whisper. "Even if we're working out what our relationship looks like."

I mean it.

Somehow, despite this news, everything suddenly makes sense.

For better or worse, we're a family.

Thirty

STEVIE

Six Months Later

I DON'T CRY WHEN I open the envelope from the insurance company.

Instead, I read every line. Twice.

Then I slide it into the labeled folder with the others, which I've organized and color-coded. One for life insurance. One for the umbrella policy. One for the driver's criminal proceedings. I keep them in a portable file box now, tucked behind the staircase at my parents' house like a briefcase for a life I didn't ask for but don't flinch from anymore.

Jude stacks train tracks by the Christmas tree while I work at the kitchen table. My leg's elevated on a chair, iced and aching from the intense PT this morning. It's not unbearable anymore, though.

I can't kneel, run or walk down the steps normally, but I don't need help to get out of bed and can walk 5000 steps.

Progress.

Across from me, Joni scrolls her phone with her headphones in. She knows I'm in the zone and fueled by half coffee, half adrenaline. A version of me has emerged I didn't know existed.

The younger, take-charge version of myself is back. I track medical records, therapy schedules, legal correspondence, settlement timelines. Stevie 2.0 says no when doctors push too fast and yes when Isla cries in the middle of the night and needs to talk about her dad in heaven.

Somehow, old Stevie slowly disappeared once Jude came. Cooper began to handle everything. Bills. Finances. Home maintenance. Bedtime negotiations. It happened so gradually, I didn't realize how much space he filled until he was gone and I couldn't breathe under the weight of everything he left behind.

Now I'm doing it. *All* of it. For the girls. For Jude. For me.

"I haven't seen you much since I moved out. Wow, you've leveled up." Joni breaks the silence quietly, like she doesn't want to jinx it.

I glance up. "Well, I had no choice."

"I'm proud of you. You're a survivor," she says. "You're rebuilding."

I press my palm to the page and smooth it flat, like I can iron out the worry.

"Eh? I'm figuring it out," I say. "Some days feel steady. Some don't."

Joni doesn't push.

"Isla's afraid to get in the car," I admit. "She started talking to the school counselor. I gave her permission to go whenever she needs, even if it's in the middle of class.

She's painting and drawing a lot. Art therapy. It's helping strengthen all the muscles in her hand."

Joni tilts her head. "Amazing."

"She draws him." My voice trembles a bit. "What she remembers. What she misses. It guts me, but it's good she's letting it out."

"And Lila?"

"She won't talk about it. Not directly." I sigh. "I've been planting seeds like leaving coloring pages on her nightstand, which are grief worksheets in disguise. I also bought her storybooks about memory and healing. I never ask if she reads them but I notice she slips them back into the drawer when she's done."

"Smart."

I glance down to make sure Jude's occupied. "She opens up more when she thinks I'm not listening. Yesterday, she told Jude Daddy's in the clouds. He watches them when they sleep."

I can't help it, my eyes well up. Swallowing, I push past it.

"And Jude?"

"He doesn't seem to remember much anymore, so I'm grateful. The sounds, the fear, it's not stuck in his soul the way it is in theirs. He's resilient. He laughs with his whole body." I glance toward the living room at my precious boy, where his trains click together on the rug. "He talks to Cooper like he's here. Tells him about his day. About cereal flavors. His favorite truck. I don't correct him. I never will."

God, how I love him. He's exactly like his dad with his tousled dark curls, legs always in motion. He wears his joy in the bounce of his steps and the peanut butter on his shirt.

"I'm not trying to erase their grief," I add. "I'm trying to help them carry it so it doesn't break them. I want to give them tools I didn't have."

She reaches across the table and squeezes my hand. "You are."

"I'm trying." I squeeze back. "We talk about him all the time. I don't pretend he didn't exist. We say his name. Look at his pictures."

"I'm proud of you."

"Thanks."

While I appreciate my sister's support, this isn't about pride. Or accolades. It's about necessity. I'm standing at the edge of a cliff with three children behind me and I'm the only adult shielding them from falling over.

Even if we have the support of my family, which we do. I have to be the one who protects us all.

I turn the page in my notebook and circle the word business.

"I've been thinking." I glance at Joni. "Once the claims are settled, I'm paying off the house. Then I want to start an event planning business. Something small. Manageable. So I can work from home. I'll build something to fit into our life, not the other way around."

She arches a brow, "An event company?"

"I think so." I nod. "Local. Boutique. Family-first. Maybe daytime corporate events so I can work when they're at school. Nonprofits. I have the contacts and the experience. If this hadn't happened I'd probably never have the guts to do it solo."

Joni and I go back and forth about potential names for the business, and she's midsentence when the back door opens with a soft clatter of keys. I hear the rustle of grocery bags. Then my mom's familiar voice followed by Maureen's Irish lilt.

We both glance toward the kitchen, eyes wide.

Neither of us move. I haven't seen anyone in Padraig's family since my mom's birthday all those years ago.

Deliberately.

"Let me make you a sandwich," my mom offers. "I'll put a kettle on."

"You're an angel, so you are."

"Oh please." Mom snorts. "You've been running on fumes since Rory's stroke. He's doing better so take a load off."

Maureen laughs, but it's thin. "I've taken to pilfering biscuits from the rehab nurses' lounge. I'm afraid they'll catch me stealing their stash."

Their laughter quiets.

"He's making progress?" my mom asks gently.

"He's stable." Maureen exhales heavily. "Frustrated. In my mind he's recovering faster than I could have hoped for. He's nearly better than he was before. My boys have been incredible. I don't think I've had more than a day alone since it happened."

Joni shifts on the cushion, eyes flicking toward me.

I keep my gaze forward, locked on Jude, who's coloring at the coffee table.

"Connor and Liam flew up right away," Maureen continues. "Cillian and Seamus were already here. Brennan came up from the Valley a couple days later. They've all been committed to his recovery." She pauses. "It's meant everything."

There's silence. Mom prompts, "Padraig?"

My breath catches. Joni's hand clutches mine.

"He's in Los Angeles," Maureen explains. "Mara went into labor early. Little Rafferty came a few weeks too soon. He's doing well now but the NICU was touch-and-go at first."

I blink, stunned. Mom never mentioned Padraig and his girlfriend were having a baby. Then again, I've been pretty out of it for the past six months.

Wow. Rafferty.

I picture a tiny boy with wavy black hair and Padraig's quiet, brown eyes.

"Mara's been struggling," Maureen goes on. "Terrible postpartum depression. Bad enough her mum moved in to help."

"Oh, Maureen…"

"It gets worse. She confessed something to Padraig which changed everything." Maureen lowers her voice. "Apparently, she took her IUD out without letting him know. She got pregnant on purpose."

Joni covers her mouth, wide-eyed.

I'm sure my expression mirrors hers. My stomach flips.

"She was scared he'd leave." Heartbreak threads through every syllable Maureen utters. "He was going to break it off and she panicked."

I'm utterly mortified we're overhearing this conversation without them knowing we're here.

"Jesus, what a terrible thing to do to him." Mom sounds angry.

"He's forgiven her. For the time being he's staying for the wee lad, though they broke up," Maureen adds after a pause. "He adores his son. You can see it in his face. He's wrapped around that boy's finger. But Mara…" Her voice catches. "She won't be his wife."

Something long-dormant aches behind my ribs.

"They're coparenting," she finishes. "He's trying to convince her to move to Seattle. Her mom lives across the country and if they're close to us we can help when Fireball is on tour. Give Rafferty roots. Hopefully, she'll agree."

My ears burn. Joni's eyes flick toward mine, filled with concern about the thousand things I'm trying not to feel but are rushing through my body.

A thump breaks the silence. My head whips around toward the noise to find Jude splatted on the rug. His face scrunches up followed by a soft whimper. Then louder.

Now, full-blown crying.

Thankfully, he's not hurt, only startled. I scoop him into my arms, heart hammering. as my mom steps into view. Her smile fades when she sees us in the living room, obviously realizing we overheard the entire conversation.

"I'm sorry," I say quickly. "We didn't mean to eavesdrop—"

Maureen's eyes meet mine, her expression unreadable at first. I haven't seen her in years, but I feel it instantly. The love. The warmth. A knowing ache.

Suddenly, Maureen's arms are strong around me, the soft wool of her jacket brushing my cheek. I don't pull away.

When she finally steps back, she keeps her hands on my shoulders.

"How are you, love?" she asks gently. "Really."

I try to answer, but the words knot in my throat.

"You don't have to pretend. I've been through the kind of storm you can't explain to anyone else." She looks deep into my eyes so I'll understand what she's telling me.

I blink hard.

"I know Rory's still here," she continues. "But the man I married, he disappeared for a long time. Some days I look at him and wonder if he's ever fully coming back." She cups my cheek. "But I never had to bury him like you did, Stevie. Somehow, you're standing and fighting for your wee ones."

I swallow, the emotion catching at the base of my throat.

She leans in closer, her voice a whisper. "You would've been my daughter, had things gone differently. You always are, in my heart."

My chest cracks open.

Maureen smiles, soft and sure. "And you always will be."

I fall back into her arms without hesitation, letting the weight of everything settle between us.

It's muscle memory, this kind of love. Like I'm seven again, running across the street after school, slipping into her kitchen with Padraig and Liam while she stirred stew and sang along to the radio.

Everything's different now.

Except this.

The way she holds me. The way we understand each other without saying a word.

We've both been broken open. Reshaped by grief. Hardened by survival. Softened by love.
Mothers. Standing. Fighting.
Figuring it out one imperfect breath at a time.

Thirty-One

A Few Months Later

THE LOW HUM OF the monitors gives me a headache.

Maybe it's the smell of burnt coffee. Or the sharp clack of Liam's boots against the hardwood floor as he paces behind the mic.

In any case, everything's beginning to grind on me.

My brother is way, way off today. Has been all week.

For the past hour, Tyson Rainier, the lead singer of Connor's band who's making a name for himself as a Grammy-winning producer, has been trying to coax something real out of him. God bless the man's patience, but the rawness Liam usually pours into his vocals is missing. Flat. Disaffected.

He's holding back.

I'm sick of pretending I don't know why.

Ty waves a hand from the console. "Let's run it one more time, Liam. Drag the last line, yeah? Let it breathe."

Liam doesn't answer. He adjusts his headphones and closes his eyes. His jaw's clenched. Sweat clings to the collar of his tee. He looks like a coiled spring about to snap.

I slump farther into the studio couch, arms crossed. Why the fuck am I even here today?

Because it's what I do. Clock the hours. Play the part. Tell myself it's me holding together the band I've bled for. We've found success now, so they say.

Truthfully, I'm not needed anymore and my resentment's at an all-time high. I'm fucking sick of bending so Liam can keep doing whatever the fuck he wants while I'm filled with regret about most of my life choices.

I'm a single father. Living with the woman who trapped me. Pretending the silence between us isn't a vise around my throat. Years ago, I gave up on the one person who made me feel like I was worth anything. Leaving me here in a constant state of regret.

The thing is, I don't blame Stevie. I didn't deserve her. I didn't fight for us. Or find my own way outside of this band. I could've begged her to stay when she left for a life with Cooper, but I let her go and create a family without me. Now he's dead and I haven't even sent her a sympathy card.

Stevie is and will always be a ghost I carry through every hour of the day.

My one bright light is Rafferty. I swear I'm giving him everything I have. I've never gone all-in at this level before. Not with Stevie. Definitely not with Mara. Not the band. Maybe not even with Liam.

But, Rafferty? I'll never walk away. Never let him wonder if he's my first priority.

So I'm here. Fulfilling a commitment. Playing along for this album cycle. I'm gonna show up, smile for the press photos and nod along in the studio. When the royalties roll in, he and I will be set. Maybe not as financially secure as Connor, but I'll definitely be able to provide him with a comfortable life and my presence on a day-to-day basis.

Until then, if I stop moving, I'll fall apart.

Connor, misunderstanding my crabby mood, catches my eye from the opposite chair. "He'll get there."

I nod once. Then glance at the clock.

Two hours and I can get back to Rafferty.

Liam's voice crackles through the booth speakers. The chorus crashes in, but the edge is missing. Again.

Ty scrubs his hands down his face. "Break," he says into the mic. "Five minutes."

Liam doesn't argue. He sets the headphones down like they might shatter and steps out of the booth. Doesn't look at me as he passes.

Connor stands and watches him go, then gestures to me. "Let's take a walk."

Dutifully, I follow him out of the studio and up the narrow stairs into Ty's house. Everything smells like a fine hotel. His wife Zoey's yoga music pulses from a room down the hall. Somewhere in the backyard, someone's grilling. Likely their private chef.

Connor opens the fridge, grabs two bottles of Topo Chico, and hands me one. "Talk to me."

I unscrew the cap. Swig. "Not much to say."

"You sure?"

My hands curl around the bottle. I stare at the label like it might answer for me.

Connor leans against the counter. His tone stays neutral. "Liam's been off for days. You've barely said a word. Avonna keeps disappearing. Linus won't make eye contact. I'm not stupid. What the feck is happening? We can't waste Ty's time."

"I'm not wasting anyone's time. Sounds like you should be giving this little lecture to Liam." I cross my arms and stand my ground.

"Aye. Fair enough." He nods. "You and Liam always find a way. You've been through worse."

I meet his eyes. And in the moment, I nearly unload the storm I've swallowed since the day Liam decided rules didn't apply to him anymore. Since I found out about the situation he's kept hidden and I realized my brother is building on his own terms and I have no one.

For what? A bit of fame?

Instead, I say, "Well, this time it's more complicated."

Connor doesn't push.

I glance out the window toward the sun-drenched patio. "How's Ronni and the twins?"

"Great. You know how it is with newborns." He smiles softly at the thought of his own babies, Torin and Tristan, who are a couple months older than Rafferty.

I envy him more than I can admit. He has a partner to go through this parental journey with. The love of his life.

Mara and I are barely surviving. She's hurting. Hopeful in quiet ways that make me feel guilty, but not enough to give her faith in a future. She's through the worst of the depression. Her mother's gone home and we've figured out a rhythm, more or less.

But, I see it in her eyes. She wants more than I can give. Love. More kids. White picket fence. Blah. Blah. Blah.

It's never going to happen because every time I hold my son—my perfect, fragile boy who's clawed his way into this world and stayed—I experience it all over again.

Boiling anger.

Not at him. *Never* him.

At her. For her lie and the way she forced my hand. I'm trying to forgive her. Trying to move forward.

However, the truth festers.

I won't let it touch him, though. He'll never feel like a mistake. Never question if he's enough.

I'll make sure of it.

Which means I need to be more than a man who lives in regret and bitterness. It's up to me to be someone he can be proud of. I've finally stopped drifting and I'm looking toward a new chapter where I will stand all the way up and live to my full potential.

I drop my bottle in the recycling. "I'll go back down, I've gotta head out soon so if I can lay down some tracks or move this along in some way, I might as well make myself useful."

Connor watches me go, but he doesn't follow.

When I return to the studio, Liam and Ty are already reworking the bridge. Avonna's finally shown up, perched on the stool next to Liam. Linus is back too. Engrossed in his iPad, avoiding any eye contact with me.

I take my seat in the corner. Say nothing. Watch the three of them orbit each other like moons around a hidden sun.

I'm not part of their solar system.

I don't belong here.

Nah, I'm not gonna let myself spiral. Instead, I open the sketchbook I've been carrying since Rafferty was born. Flip to a half-finished idea for a collage I started last night. Scraps of lyrics, jagged brushstrokes, a torn picture of a fire escape. I've been expressing myself through art again and it's keeping me sane.

Soon, I'm immersed in my own inner world.

My pencil moves without direction, finding its way through memory. A curve mirroring the bend of her neck when she used to lean over her homework, ponytail loose. An outline of Capitol Hill rooftops, or maybe it's hope in the shape of home. I layer in textured slashes of crimson and bone-white. Sharp and fluid.

A burst of golden acrylic where our kids might play together in a backyard I've never seen. I picture Jude tracing dinosaurs in the dirt. Lila turning cartwheels. Isla teaching Rafferty to read.

I scrape back some color with the edge of a guitar pick and trace in more lyrics. Ones I haven't shared with anyone.

In this world, she never walked away. We never broke. The kids are ours and we are happy.

I'm not the outsider.

I'm enough even when it's messy and raw and impossible.

I press harder.

Let it bleed.

"Jesus, Padraig."

I jolt upright, graphite smearing the edge of my hand. Ty's standing behind me, eyes locked on my drawing like he's seen a ghost. Connor's next to him, holding a half-eaten protein bar, mouth slack.

The room's quiet. No more vocals bleed from the monitor. Everyone's focus is on my sketchbook laid open on the console, raw and exposed.

"Did you make this?" Ty crouches down, studying my drawing like it's sacred.

I flip the page halfway closed on instinct. "It's nothing. A sketch."

Connor grabs my wrist to stop me and steps closer. "This isn't nothing, Padraig. It's fucking——"

He doesn't finish. Stares.

Liam walks in from the vocal booth, towel around his neck. "What's going on?"

"Did you know about this?" Ty turns the sketch toward him. "Your twin's been holding out."

Liam comes over, and squints. "You back at it with the art?"

"Aye. To pass the time." I shrug, confused. "Started again to pass the time when Rafferty sleeps. I've been playing around on canvas, too. Mixed media. It keeps my head clear."

"You've been doing this for how long?" Ty asks. "Seriously?"

"Well, all through school. College. Gave it up until now." I rub the back of my neck, suddenly self-conscious. "I don't sleep much when I'm home. Once Mara and the baby are out, I let it out."

"Art therapy." Ty glances off into the distance. I know he's a man who struggles with many demons from his past.

Connor grins. "Christ, you've got talent, brother."

Liam doesn't speak. Instead, he sinks into the chair opposite me, staring at the notebook like I've been keeping a secret from him.

Which, I suppose I have, though not quite as big as the one he thinks he's been keeping from me.

We lock eyes.

It's all there.

The weight. The ache. The knowing.

We've spent our whole lives locked in orbit. Two halves of something fierce and fractured. Tonight, there's recognition.

Whatever's next, it won't be what came before.

We both feel it.

Our lives are about to change.

Thirty-Two

STEVIE

Four Months Later

THE SUN BLAZES UNSEASONABLY warm for June as we settle on the chipped wooden bench outside Molly Moon's.

Jude's already sticky, chocolate smeared along one cheek. Lila licks the edges of her cherry chunk cone like she intends to win a race. Isla sits beside me stoically staring at her mint brownie without taking a single bite.

We've just come from the cemetery.

I didn't know what to expect this morning. Whether they'd ask questions. Cry. Shut down completely. Jude is too young to remember much, thank God. Lila laid her hand on the marble plaque and whispered something I couldn't hear. Isla stood frozen beside me until I reached for her limp hand.

Now she stares straight ahead, melted ice cream dripping down her wrist. Of all my children, she's having the hardest time recovering. She was a daddy's girl through and through and can't comprehend the rest of her life without Coop.

"Want me to throw it away for you, love?" I offer, brushing a curl out of her face. She shakes her head, mute. Dumps it into the trash next to us and sits back down.

Lila, who's been adjusting surprisingly well, notices. "Isla's being weird again."

"*Lila*." My voice holds a warning.

She shrugs. "Well, she is."

"I'm not weird," Isla snaps. "I don't want to celebrate something sad."

"This isn't a celebration," I say tenderly. "It's remembrance. We're honoring your dad. It hasn't been easy and we all miss him terribly, but we have each other."

Jude tugs my sleeve. "I drew Daddy a picture and left it on the grass by his grave."

"It was beautiful." I lean down and kiss his sticky forehead. "He loves it. I know he's smiling down at you from heaven."

"I want to go home," Isla whispers.

She continues to unravel in her own quiet way.

I don't push her. I can't. Because my eldest won't confide in me, I've got her in more intensive therapy now, with someone who specializes in pre-teen grief. One thing has been working incredibly well—art therapy. She's constantly drawing in her notebook. It's her way of coping.

As for me, I'm taking it day by day. I've built a schedule, pay bills on time, cook meals and shuttle the kids around. Even when I don't want to I show up because I refuse to let the grief define us.

Some days, survival might be the only metric. On others, when the kids are settled and the house is quiet, I let myself dream again. Embers & Bloom Custom Events isn't real yet.

Not in the way it will be one day. I'm making progress, though.

I picked a name. Registered the business. Bought the domain. Locked down the social handles even though I haven't posted a thing. I made a rough logo on Canva and saved it to a folder I haven't opened since.

All of this preparation is kinda like laying out clothes for a life I'm not quite ready to live.

Every day, though, I move forward. Slow and steady. One step, then another. A list on the fridge. A spreadsheet on my laptop. Notes in my phone with color palettes and tagline ideas.

I'm not ready to launch, but I will be. When my heart stops feeling like a battlefield, I'll have something to step into. A business I own. I'll be able to show my kids how to survive the worst tragedy and move through it. Hopefully, I'll be an example they can look up to.

Until then, I do my best. I parent. I grieve. I breathe. I build.

Quietly. Carefully. For all of us.

Glancing, at Jude, I can't help but laugh. He's halfway through his cone, babbling to himself, "Yummy. Yummy. Yummy."

"You're a nutter," Lila tells him with a grin while Isla sits stoic with her arms crossed.

Something in the air transforms. Not suddenly. More like a tide rolling in, peaceful but unstoppable.

I feel it before I see it. A pull in my chest. A pause in the air.

My gaze lifts toward the door.

There he is.

Padraig. With baby Rafferty curled against his chest, snug in a sling-like carrier.

He doesn't see us. Not yet. He places an order with the girl behind the counter, rocking his son absently, a familiar rhythm in the sway of his hips. His hair's long again, pulled back into a knot at the nape. Chin dusted in scruff. He's thinner than I remember from the last time I saw him at my parents' house.

Today, every part of me always remembers every part of him.

Then I notice, Mara's beside him, clutching a small diaper bag.

I freeze.

Mom told me they moved up here a few months ago and Mara's living in Liam's townhouse—one of the matching units Rory built a few years ago for each of his sons as way to make amends for everything he put the family through. Apparently, Padraig's staying at his own place next door and they're coparenting. Nothing more.

By the way they interact, I'm not sure I believe it. She stands this close and gazes at him like he belongs to her. Old feelings bubble up unexpectedly. New ones too.

I don't understand how she can live with herself for trapping him and pushing him into a life he wasn't ready for. He deserved a real choice in the matter.

God, I'm judgmental. Like I'm one to talk. Cooper and I hadn't been together more than a couple of months when I realized I was pregnant and we had a happy life.

Mara gestures toward a painting on the wall. She leans in to say something to Padraig. They laugh, with her hand resting lightly on his arm. He doesn't seem to mind her touch. If anything, he looks comfortable with her.

My gaze drifts, almost without permission, to whatever she's pointing at.

The moment feels preordained. As if my eyes were always meant to see the painting, which pulls me in before I can think. Jagged textures clash and merge, layered scraps stitched together in deliberate chaos. The colors don't sit stagnant, they breathe, expand, and fold in on themselves like they're alive.

He's the artist. I'm sure of it. Every stroke feels like something I've known in my bones.

Padraig, pressed into canvas.

I can't look away. My pulse thrums loudly in my ears. The painting feels like a message I was supposed to find in this exact, perfect moment.

Then he turns.

Not toward the counter. Not toward Mara. Toward me.

The moment lands like a punch. His eyes lock on mine, and everything else dissolves. The whirr of the coffee maker. The chatter at the tables around us. The weight of this past year my kids and I have survived.

Time folds in on itself until it's only the two of us, suspended in a space we've always carried no matter how many years we've been apart and how much distance has been between us.

For a second, neither of us moves. The sounds of the shop fade. The kids, the chatter and the clatter of scoops in the metal bins all blur. We...stare.

He takes a single step. Then another. Like there's a string tied between us, pulling him across the room and suddenly he's in front of me, arms wrapping around me without a word. My body folds into his side like no time has passed.

The air between us is suspended with every word we've never said, every memory we've never let go of, and every loss we've carried alone. Grief lives here too. Threaded through the years, binding us as much as it's carved a canyon.

I inhale his scent. Clean cotton. Leather. Baby powder.

We don't speak. We just hold.

Until Isla tugs at my sleeve. "Mom? Who is this man?"

I pull back slowly, not ready, but knowing I have to for the sake of my kids.

"This is Padraig, Isla," I remind her. "He was my next door neighbor and best friend."

Padraig swallows hard. He looks down at her. "Hi, Isla. You're so grown up."

She blinks up at him, uncertain.

"You met him at Grandma Lucinda's birthday a few years ago, remember?" I prompt.

She scrunches her nose. "Um...sort of."

"This is Lila." I gesture to my youngest daughter, nodding to where she's now staring at Rafferty like he's a toy she wants to steal. "And Jude."

Padraig gives a small, awkward wave.

"Why is your baby in a backpack?" Jude points at Padraig's chest.

"It's a baby carrier." Padraig chuckles. "His name's Rafferty."

Lila peers up at him. "Raf-fer-tee. *Weird*."

"I know," Padraig says. "It's Irish. It means abundance and prosperity."

Behind him, I realize Mara is hanging back, watching the scene. She doesn't interrupt. Or insert herself. She politely stands to the side with a fixed, practiced smile pasted to her lips like she knows exactly where she fits in this moment.

Outside of it.

"Hi, Mara." I take a small step toward her, bridging the space.

Her smile brightens before she frowns. "Hi Stevie. I'm so sorry for your loss. I can't imagine what this year's been like for you."

I'm used to hearing this sentiment. A polite, measured thing people say when they don't know how to address such a devastating tragedy.

"Thank you, we're getting through," I reply on autopilot before switching subjects to her. "How are you doing?"

"Oh, better now. A change of scenery has helped a lot." She lets out a breath. "Still getting my bearings, but I like it up here." She glances toward Padraig, then back to me. "I recently started at KOMO. Field reporting for now. I hope to work toward an anchor spot once I rebuild my reel. I've had a few years off."

"Wow, how exciting." I try to exude positivity, though the words carry a strange weight.

A fleeting thought slips in before I can stop it. I chose not to follow Padraig and, as I understand it, Mara gave up her career to follow him. The irony isn't lost on me.

Now, here we are, all of us starting over.

Did I make the wrong call all those years ago? I glance over at Isla, her braid slipping over her shoulder. Then, Lila watching all of us with wide eyes and Jude's ice cream-sticky smile. Little Rafferty is strapped to Padraig's chest.

None of them would exist if we'd stayed the course.

Something akin to peace washes over me. Some things happen because they're meant to. Even if they break you first.

Padraig shifts Rafferty in the carrier, steadying him with one hand while the other brushes against Mara's back. The touch isn't romantic, it's stabilizing. Like he's bracing her the same way he's always steadied everyone else.

There's no spark in his eyes when he looks at her. No heat. No hunger. Mainly, duty. The same quiet loyalty he gives so freely, putting everyone's needs before his own without asking for anything in return.

Something twists deep inside me, sharp and not entirely unwelcome. For years I've buried the thing between us so deep it stopped breathing.

Rightfully so. I was married. I loved Cooper and my family. My loyalty was theirs and I never let myself wonder what if.

Yet, standing here after we've come from the gravesite and I've watched my kids trace their hands over Cooper's name in stone, I look at Padraig and feel an old current crackle to life.

It's wrong.

It's disorienting.

But, it's real.

I probably shouldn't be feeling this. Not here. Not now. Not with my children still

holding the weight of their father's death in their small, fragile hearts.

I do feel it, though. Grief and memory and whatever's always lived between me and Padraig collide in the same breath, and I don't know how to stop my heart from stumbling in my chest.

Everything disappears. The years. The almosts. The never-will-be's.

Padraig catches my gaze and something flickers behind his eyes.

Recognition.

Regret.

A love so old, so embedded, it can't help but show.

I swallow hard. "It's good to see you."

"You too," he grits out.

Then Rafferty whimpers, and the spell breaks.

He rocks his son soothingly. "We should—uh—get going."

I nod, stepping back, placing a hand on Jude's shoulder.

"Bye, Rafferty," Lila says.

Padraig meets my eyes one last time. "Maybe we could catch up soon?"

"I'd like to," I whisper.

He turns toward Mara, who adjusts the bag on her shoulder and follows him out.

Jude looks up at me. "He was nice."

"Yeah." I hold back tears. "He's very nice."

Lila tugs my sleeve. "He's your friend?"

God, he was so much more.

Some part of me will always ache for what we were and what we might have been. But not today.

Today belongs to my children and to the man who loved them.

To the life we had before it shattered.
Tomorrow, the ache for Padraig will be there.
Maybe then, I'll be ready to embrace it.

Thirty-Three

A Few Days Later, Present Day

I NEVER THOUGHT THESE pieces would see the light of day.

No one's ever known much about my art except Stevie. Well, and Liam.

Stevie used to love sitting cross-legged on the floor of my room while I worked, watching shapes and colors take form. She'd tell me I had something rare. Gushed about how I saw the world different from anyone else. I'd laugh it off, convinced the band was my real shot.

She'd shake her head, kiss me, and say I didn't have to choose. Back then, I believed I did.

During Rafferty's first fragile months and the hours spent holding him in the half-light, listening to his breath fight its way in and out, my hands itched for brushes, for paper, for color. Art didn't merely fill the silence, it kept me from falling into it.

Piece by piece, stroke by stroke, I immersed myself into something that made me feel more like myself than I ever had.

By the time we moved back to Seattle, I'd amassed quite the portfolio.

On a whim, I brought a few pieces into Molly Moon's, hanging them under a pseudonym—P. O'Malley, Ma's maiden name. Outside of my school exhibits, it's the only time I've ever put my work on a wall for strangers to see, and I didn't want the McGloughlin name anywhere near it.

A couple weeks later, Caden Price, owner of Ash & Iron Gallery, called me in. The second I stepped through his door, he pegged me from Fireball. I nearly bolted. He wouldn't let me. Said my work hit him harder than anything he'd seen in years. Practically begged me to join his inaugural "Masked" series, to highlight new artists.

No bios, no names, only art.

It was the perfect opportunity.

So here I am. My first real gallery show. Every mixed media piece I've made over the past year, plus a few collages from high school and some oversized acrylics I painted in college—all for sale.

I'd stored the older pieces in the old band rehearsal room at my parents' house. Sifted through the canvases leaning against the basement wall, edges wrapped in yellowed newsprint. Layers of dust dimming the colors. I peeled the paper away. Curated my favorites.

Now everything hangs under track lighting on whitewashed brick.

I move from piece to piece, half-listening to strangers' quiet reactions. People mill about and stop in front of each one, lean close, step back. They don't see me. Just the work. Exactly how Caden wanted it. An honest read.

I've kept this exhibit close to the chest. A quiet event no one can pick apart or twist into something else. Aside from Caden, Mara's the only person who knows about this event and only because I needed her to stay with our son tonight.

Being here's almost enough to drown out a memory looping since the day at the ice cream shop.

Stevie, her kids flanking her like they've learned to move as one. Isla's eyes locked in haunted stillness. Grief etched deep, years before her time. Seeing them hit me harder than anything in a long while. Split me open and left me raw.

Witnessing Stevie's strength and quiet resilience stirred something inside me. Fuck. I've been trying to figure out my future since the album wrapped. Liam's priorities pulling one way. My son's needs pulling another.

Things with Mara have been complicated. She's made no secret about her intention for the three of us to be a family, which we are and will be forever. I'm not getting back together with her, though, and it creates tension we both try to stuff down for the good of our son.

The day at the ice cream shop gave Mara and me a reason to finally strip every layer back and hopefully move forward on more stable ground. When we got home, she asked about Stevie and I told her everything I've been carrying for years.

How Stevie and I grew up side by side from the time we were seven. Lost our virginity on her living room couch and promised each other forever. How we lived every waking moment of high school and college inside each other's orbit, sure we were soulmates. How her leaving shattered me in ways I'll never recover from.

I also confessed the truth I've never spoken aloud. Music was Liam and Connor's dream, not mine. I followed them out of loyalty and family trauma.

In doing so, I lost the only woman I've ever loved.

Mara and I cried together. She finally understood why I couldn't give her more. Stevie's shadow has always been between us.

Then she asked me a question I've never allowed myself to consider:

What would I do if I got another chance?

I didn't have an answer. Still don't.

What I do know is I won't go back to being a man who puts himself last until there's nothing left. Rafferty deserves for me to be so much more.

I'm studying one of my newer pieces, a sharp-edged collage with colors so layered they look alive, when it happens.

A shift in the atmosphere.

I don't need to turn around to know.

She's here.

I pivot slowly, scanning the space until I find her near the entrance.

Stevie.

A black dress skims her curves, golden hair spilling over her shoulders. Her steady, unblinking gaze pins me in place.

She crosses the floor like she's walked into this gallery for me and no one else. Her faint scent of vanilla threads through the sharper scent of paint and varnish.

Stevie's eyes roam the walls before landing on me again, sharper now, alive with recognition. She's close enough I can see her pupils flare and feel the heat roll off her. Every nerve in my body wants to close the gap, but I hold before I take a tentative step toward her. She moves toward me too without looking away.

The crowd fades to nothing. Awareness turns into a throb low in my gut, matching the pulse at the base of my spine.

We stop with inches between us, her breath mingling with mine. She tilts her head, not backing down, as if daring me to remember every kiss, every gasp, every way we've come undone together. My fingers twitch, aching to touch her, to prove she's real.

"You did these?" Surprise, edged with a challenge. "They're...breathtaking." Her mouth curves into a smile. "So much for anonymity."

"Aye." I lean in, my voice low enough for her alone to hear. "Some things can't stay hidden."

Before she can answer, a hand claps my shoulder.

"Padraig, there you are." Caden steps between us, oblivious to the crackling current he's severed. "I want you to meet a few collectors. Looks like we're on track to sell out."

I force myself to step back and breathe. Stevie shifts, her attention sliding toward Caden. I catch the spark of recognition in his eyes as he greets her warmly, like they've spoken before.

Hmmm.

The next hour is a blur of introductions and champagne flutes, polite laughter and feigned interest in people who want to talk about technique.

Throughout, I know where she is at every moment. By the far wall studying my largest canvas, from our sophomore year in college. Lingering near the bar. Pausing in front of a piece I painted the week Rafferty came home from the hospital.

She's a magnet, pulling my eyes without effort.

As the crowd thins, she slips to my side again, empty glass dangling from her fingers. "Well..."

I tilt my head toward the door before she can say goodbye. "Want to grab a coffee?"

"Lead the way." A flicker of something unreadable sparks in her expression.

We find a quiet cafe shop a block from the gallery and take a booth in the corner, steam curling from our mugs. The shop's nearly empty with only the sound of the espresso machine filling the space between us.

She curls into her seat across from me and takes a sip of her hot chocolate.

"When I saw you at Molly Moon's," she glances up at me through her lashes, "I noticed the paintings on the wall with the placard—'P. O'Malley.'" Her lips curve. "I knew it was you. Using your ma's maiden name."

I can't help but let a small laugh slip out. "Guess I underestimated how easy it'd be for you to connect the dots."

"You forget how well I know you." Her tone isn't teasing. It's warm, threaded with something softer. "Once I realized it was you, I thought...wow. This is Padraig. Every brushstroke, every shadow."

I rest my forearms on the table. "God, it took everything I had to bring them in."

"Is that how tonight happened?" Stevie leans forward.

I take a bite of chocolate chip cookie. "Pretty much. Caden recognized me but wanted me in the show. Couldn't say no."

"How's Liam?" She takes another sip, eyes on me. "How's the band?"

I let out a slow breath. "We finished recording with Connor and Tyson Rainier of LTZ. The album's being mastered now. Liam's good. Linus is back managing us. He's got his head deep in planning what's next. We'll see where it goes."

Her expression shutters a bit. Understanding, but also inquisitive. "And you? Are you touring most of the time?"

"Jeez." I sigh. "It's complicated. You were right, you know. Music was always Liam's dream more than mine. I've stayed for him. But with Rafferty and this—" I motion toward nothing in particular, meaning the show, the paintings, all of it. "This feels like me in a way music never did. Sometimes I wish..."

I decide not to say it. Probably not appropriate. Or wanted.

She sets her mug down, tracing the rim with her finger. "You always had both in you. I told you over and over, recall?"

"Yeah," I acknowledge, thinking about how I was remembering her support when the doors opened tonight. Wondering if tonight is some sort of sign. "I didn't believe in myself. Thought the band was the only way forward."

Stevie reaches over and grips my wrist briefly. "I'm glad you figured it out."

"It was Rafferty." I glance at where she made contact. "He had a rough start. Mara wasn't well. He was so small and helpless. I started painting again to keep from unraveling. It anchored me."

She's quiet for a moment. "How is he?"

"Strong. Determined. Loves music already, God help us." A smile tugs at my mouth. "Mara's with him tonight. She's the reason I can even be here."

Her gaze softens. "Are things good with her?"

There's no edge to the question. No fishing. It seems like curiosity, which would naturally come from knowing my life is tied to someone else's.

"We're okay," I say carefully, because I'm not ready to talk about how my son came into this world with her yet. "Not together. Coparenting. She's staying at Liam's until we can find a permanent solution."

"Sounds like you're doing okay." She leans back, studying me. "You look lighter."

"Feels like it." I meet her eyes. "So, what about you? I'm sorry I didn't reach out when Cooper—I didn't think..."

I let the words trail away. Ma told me not to call, but I *should* have. Given her my support.

"It doesn't matter." Her smile turns wistful. "Honestly, with my injuries and the kids, it's all a blur."

"I followed what I could," I admit. "Didn't want to intrude. You lost the love of your life. The father of your kids."

Her gaze flickers up, something warm slipping past her guard. "I loved Cooper and I'll always be grateful for the life we built. He was a good man. An excellent father." She pauses, meeting my eyes. "You know as well as I do, love can look different, and some loves never really go away."

We both go quiet.

"How did you know to come tonight?" I decide to move away from a topic neither of us might be ready for.

"Well, it's a roundabout story. I stopped working after Jude was born and we moved to Seattle." Her fingers curl around her mug. "I wanted to be with the kids full-time while they were little. Then after Cooper...uh, I needed some time to figure it all out. I've decided to ease back in to event planning. I've started my own thing so I can work around their lives instead of the other way around." She makes a rolling motion with her hand. "Fast forward to yesterday, and I happened to meet with Caden when they were installing your exhibit. When I saw your work, I couldn't *not* come. The kids are having a sleepover at Mom's tonight."

"Why?" The word slips out before I can stop it.

She squeezes her eyes shut and takes a deep breath. Looks back at me. "Call it fate. Or maybe a sign. Something deep inside told me the gallery was where I was supposed to be."

Her words sit and I feel it too. We've both lived through hell and somehow ended up sitting here, ready to hear the other out. Looking at her, the years and the lives we lived without each other don't feel like they're in the way.

This thing between us is so familiar my chest aches.

"I'm glad you're doing something you love again." I can't bear to misread the situation so I try to navigate to safer topics. "You found your passion when you discovered event planning. You always could see every moving piece before anyone else did."

Her mouth curves. "I missed it. If I'm honest, I need to create stability for the kids. They need to see I'm steady and hard-working, even when I feel like an imposter."

"You've always been steady, Stevie." I swallow hard.

Her gaze drops to her hands. "Maybe. But sometimes...steady gets lonely."

The words sink deep. I'm not imagining what's happening here.

God, I want to tell her she doesn't have to be lonely. I've been waiting for her since the moment she left.

Instead, I watch her lift her mug, eyes flicking to mine over the rim.

Everything we were, everything we lost is all laid bare.

"You've got the kids covered tonight?" I finally ask.

A slow nod. "Like I said. They're with my mom. Overnight."

"Rafferty's at Mara's." My voice is rougher than I intend. "So... yeah."

Her lips part slightly, and the look in her eyes pulls the air from the room. "This is complicated."

"Fuck." I bury my face in my hands. "Is it wrong to want you so badly?"

For a moment, we breathe the same charged air.

Then she leans forward, elbows on the table, closing the space between us inch by inch. "No. It's the most natural thing in the world." There's a tremor in her voice, but her eyes are sure. "I want you to come over."

Hearing the words from her mouth hits like the lyrics of a song I've been waiting years to write.

I'm not going to second-guess.

This might be my only shot.

"Lead the way."

Thirty-Four

STEVIE

Present Day

THE SECOND THE DOOR swings open, it's all heat and motion. Padraig's mouth on mine, his hands on my body like he's been waiting a lifetime, and maybe he has. I don't even remember letting him in, only the jolt when my back hits the door and his body presses me into it.

My dress is bunched around my hips before I can blink. He's already inside me, raw, deep, the stretch pulling a cry from my throat before I can stop it. I cling to his shoulders, nails digging in, not to hurt but to hold on. Every thrust drives out the air in my lungs and drags a guttural sound from deep in my chest.

I've forced this fantasy out of my mind more times than I can count. Out of loyalty to Cooper. Out of sheer survival.

In this moment with his cock back where it belongs. Nothing comes close to the way we fit.

In the early days of my marriage to Coop, I'd find myself wondering if my connection to Padraig was merely sexual. We learned how to fuck together. Spent hours exploring each other's bodies in wonder, figuring out exactly how to get each other off. Did I mistake sexual connection for love?

One thrust of him inside me now obliterates my theory. On a molecular level, I know—have always known—Padraig and I are...

Fire. Need. *Soul.*

This isn't memory. It's a living, breathing truth I feel in my bones.

Dangerous and holy all at once.

God, he feels exactly the same. Better. Stronger. Our rhythm finds itself without thought, our bodies remembering what our minds tried to forget. Every push and pull is ingrained in our very being, no matter how many years or miles were between us.

We fuck like we're making up for lost time. Fast, fierce, no patience left in either of us. The slap of skin, his ragged breathing in my ear, the way his hands grip my ass to pull me onto him harder. His teeth graze my neck, dragging a whimper out of me I've never made for anyone else.

This is everything I've missed and swore I'd never have again.

I'm already close, the years of want condensed into every friction-slicked stroke. He knows my body better than I do and finds the exact angle to make my walls clamp down around him. Heat coils low and tight, and I cling harder, my breath ragged against his ear.

"Right there—" The words snap off into a gasp when he drives deeper, pinning me against the door like he'll fuse us into one. His hips grind into me, the rhythm rough and relentless until my vision shatters into white. My release rips through me, sharp and molten, pulling a roar from deep in his chest.

He's right behind me, his thrusts turning brutal, desperate, until he buries himself hard and holds there, every muscle locked. A guttural sound breaks free from him as he spills inside me, heat flooding deep, his forehead pressed hard to mine.

For a long moment, there's nothing but the sound of our breathing. His hands cradle my face, thumbs stroking my cheeks like he's grounding himself in proof I'm real.

I'm shaking, not from exhaustion, but from the weight of everything this means.

"Jesus, Stevie…" He's utterly wrecked. "I've missed you every second."

I kiss him. Slow. Searching. "Me too."

When he eases me down, I feel him slip from my body, leaving me empty and aching all over again. My skirt is bunched at my waist, my panties hang off one thigh. Neither of us moves to fix it.

I trace his scruff with my fingers. "It's still there."

"Never left." His gaze drops to my mouth, then back to my eyes.

We stand there, caught in the space between what we did and what comes next. Then he brushes his knuckles along my cheek, voice low. "Show me to your room."

I take his hand to lead him down the short hall. The air shifts as soon as we cross the threshold. Electric, but deeper now, slower. This isn't about erasing the years anymore. It's about claiming what's always been ours.

This time he doesn't yank my dress up in a frenzy. He takes his time, palms sliding down my sides, the heat of them soaking into my skin. His knuckles graze the backs of my thighs as he first slides down my panties and then gathers the fabric of my dress slowly, inch by inch, until it's bunched at my hips. Then he pauses, eyes locked on mine, before lifting it higher, over my stomach and my breasts until he draws it up and over my head in one unhurried sweep.

The air chills my bare skin for a heartbeat, goosebumps sweeping across my arms and down my spine. My nipples harden into little bullets. "Christ, Stevie. If you only knew how many times I've dreamed about these tits."

His hands come up, palms warm and broad, cupping the weight of my breasts. His thumbs brush over my nipples in slow, deliberate circles, sending heat ricocheting through my belly into my core. He bends, mouth closing around one tight peak, sucking until my knees threaten to give out. Then the other, lips and tongue working me into a state.

Padraig's hands skim down with deliberate pressure on my legs as we fall to the bed, the pads of his fingers trace over the softest parts before gripping tight to press my legs farther apart. Then he feels it. The long, pale scar carved into my right thigh, a raised ridge where they opened me up to piece my femur back together.

For a moment, neither of us moves.

Then he turns his attention from my nipple to study my leg, his finger stroking over the seam. He drops to his knees, not in hesitation, but with the gravity of a man paying tribute.

"Jesus, Stevie..." He chokes out. "What if you'd been taken from me?"

His words rip through me, sharp and hot.

He bends, pressing his mouth to the scar. The kiss is deep, deliberate, sealing something in place. Another follows, higher. Then another, until I'm trembling. "This—" his lips press to the mark "—means you're here. Alive. I will never forget what it's cost you."

The lump in my throat burns as his mouth trails higher, onto the soft skin of my inner thigh. His stubble scrapes and lips soothe, the mix of rough and tender making my pulse slam. The first stroke of his tongue over my pussy steals my breath. He groans into me, his hands gripping my ass and pulling me forward until my knees are over his shoulders.

"Fuck, we taste the same," he murmurs against my clit, before sucking it into his mouth and making me gasp.

I fist his hair. My hips jerk as his tongue works me. Broad, slow strokes giving way to quick, precise flicks. He knows exactly where to press, exactly when to slip lower and drive his tongue inside me, fucking me until I'm moaning his name.

His hands spread me wider. "I could spend the rest of my life between your legs," he growls, before sealing his mouth over my sensitive nub.

The orgasm hits hard, my thighs clamping around his head as I cry out. He drinks from me through it all, swallowing every sound until I'm shaking.

Then he stands, yanks his shirt over his head and shucks off his unbuckled jeans. His cock is flush against his abs, thick and long, the sight alone making me ache all over again.

"Against the headboard," he orders, and the demand vibrates through me.

I crawl back, settling on my elbows as he climbs over me, his weight pressing me into the mattress. The head of his cock slides against my soaking folds, teasing me, pushing enough to make my breath catch.

When he finally eases in, it's deep and deliberate, the slow, perfect slide sealing us together like two halves rejoined after years apart. He fills every space inside me, including the hollow places I've carried for so long, until there's no separation.

Only him. Only us. Finally whole again.

"God, you're perfect," he rasps as he starts to move.

It's not frantic. Not like at the door. This is a different way of reconnecting. Every grind of his hips makes me feel every ridge, every vein of his cock inside me. He kisses me like he's taking back every second we lost. His hands hold me in place so he can fuck into me at the exact angle that has me gasping into his mouth.

"I know this is completely inappropriate and the timing is probably shit, but I love you." He cup my cheeks. "I always have. We'll find a way. No matter how careful we need to be. No matter what it takes. Life is too short, baby. I don't want to spend our lives apart ever again."

"Yes." I grip his ass and pull him deeper. Tears roll down my cheeks because, despite my life with Cooper and my kids, I feel the same way. "I love you, too."

The heat between us builds fast, the slow burn turning sharp and urgent. I feel his cock swell as he gets closer, hips snapping harder, pounding into me until my orgasm tears through me again, He follows with a low, guttural sound, erupting until I'm flooded.

This time, he doesn't pull out. He stays inside, lowering his weight until his chest is pressed to mine, his mouth at my temple "We get this one life, and I'm not wasting another fucking second without you."

My thumb strokes the rough stubble on his face. The significance of everything we've been through sinks in. All the years of silence. All the nights spent living other lives pretending we'd moved on. We kiss languidly, like we're sealing a promise, and I feel him soften inside me before he finally eases out, his hand resting at my hip as if to say he's not letting me go far.

We lie together, limbs knotted, breath steadying by degrees. My fingers drift over the lines of his back, memorizing him all over again. When he shifts, it's not to leave but to roll me gently onto my side, fitting himself around me, his arm a solid band across my waist. He presses his lips to the curve where my neck meets my shoulder, and I swear I feel us slip right back into place as though no time has ever passed.

Except it has. I have three realities who have no clue I loved anyone but their father.

Neither of us speaks. It's not awkward but thick with everything we haven't begun to unpack.

He nuzzles into my hair. "I wasn't expecting to see you tonight, let alone…this."

"I wasn't expecting this either." I settle into his arms.

His palm spreads over my stomach. "Now all I can think about is how we make us work."

"We're not the same people we were." I turn my head toward him.

"No," he agrees. "We've both got our lives. Your kids, they're your whole world. I don't want to step wrong with them. And Rafferty—" He swallows. "He's a baby. I need to be careful for him too."

The mention of Rafferty softens something in me. "For this to work, I want them all to feel safe. My kids cannot ever think I'm replacing Cooper. Your son should never be confused about who's in his corner."

"We'll go slow." He studies me like he's searching for the map to whatever comes next.

"Get to know each other again," I agree. "Take our time."

Something in his eyes softens, but heat builds under the surface. He tips my chin and his lips brush mine before deepening the kiss until it pulls an ache low in my belly. His hand curves over my hip, urging me closer, his body molded to my back. The heft of his erection presses against the curve of my ass, hard and hot.

"Apparently, I need to be inside you." He kisses the side of my mouth.

His fingers slip between my thighs, coaxing me open as he shifts his hips, angling himself until the blunt head nudges where I'm drenched with his seed and my arousal. He pushes forward, slow enough for me to feel every inch fill me from behind until my breath catches and my hand grips his forearm.

By the time his hips meet mine, there's no space left between us. He's so deep I feel him in every breath. Every beat of my heart. We're locked together as though this is where we were always meant to end up.

We lie there, side to side, faces close enough for our cheeks to touch. His arm curls around me, his other hand cradles the back of my head. His hips move in the smallest, laziest rolls, more to keep us connected than to chase any ending.

"This," he whispers. "Is where I need to live."

The steady throb of his cock syncs with my heartbeat. My body answers without thought, clenching around him to keep him in place. Our tongues tangle until it's impossible to know where one of us ends.

Time blurs, each breath melting into the next. There's nowhere to be, nothing pulling us apart, only the heat of his body sealing to mine, the slow rhythm of him deep inside me keeping us fused in every way that matters.

Out there we'll move carefully, tread lightly. In here, there's no need. This is where we belong. Sleep claims us like this, connected and satiated.

When my eyes open, the room is washed in the pale light of dawn. He's by the bed, pulling on his jeans, hair mussed, eyes finding mine the moment he senses I'm awake. He leans down, brushing his lips over mine in a kiss more promise than goodbye.

"Call me later," he whispers.

"I will."

"I love you."

I comb my fingers through his hair. "I love you too."

Then he's gone.

The echo of him lingers long after the door closes.

Thirty-Five

A Few Days Later

I WAS SUPPOSED TO be there.

Had my jacket on, keys in hand. Then Rafferty started coughing. The wheezy sound wasn't normal. Mara didn't even have to ask me to stay, we took him straight in to urgent care.

Luckily, it was nothing. By the time we got back to the townhouse, I was two hours late.

I pulled up to the venue expecting a long line, lights, chaos. Instead, The Mission was dark. Not a soul in sight except a security guy who wouldn't tell me a thing.

I texted Connor.

Show's cancelled.

No explanation.

A couple days later, he's in my living room, looking like someone's taken a chisel to him and knocked pieces away. Liam's on the laptop screen between us, waiting as patiently as he's able, which isn't much. We've all seen the coverage. Salacious headlines, "unforeseen circumstances," the kind of wording indicating everything burned down without showing the charred remains.

"It's over." Connor shocks us. "LTZ is officially done. I can't get into the details, but we're clearing up our obligations through the rest of the year." His eyes flick between us. "I spoke to management this morning. They're going to offer Fireball every single one of our festival slots in Europe. All of them. Yours if you want them. Some of them at prime times."

Liam leans back like it's Christmas morning. "Holy fuck. Those are the biggest stages—"

"I know." I keep my voice even, but the knot's already forming. We can't turn this kind of offer down, not when a new album's ready to drop.

Connor watches me like he can already read the hesitation in my face. "You've earned this. Don't waste the opportunity."

I nod, but my heart's not in it. All I can picture is how much my son's face will change if I'm gone for months. Right now he needs me and his mother more than anyone else in the world.

Connor and Liam dive into dates, routing, production crew availability. Logistics, which should command my attention, but it all slides past in a blur. Rafferty's not the only thing I have on my mind. I think of Stevie. The feel her of her skin under my hands. The buzz in my body hasn't faded since I left her bed. Every nerve alive at the idea of our reconnection.

We didn't specifically talk about what comes next, not really. I know one thing. I want to be with her. Not in stolen nights between rehearsals and flights and tours. I want to start the slow process of merging our lives and blending our families without blowing them apart.

I can't say anything, though. No one knows what happened the other night but us, and we plan to keep it quiet way until we're ready.

Bottom line is, I don't want to be in Europe for months. No fucking way.

Leaning forward, I cut through their back-and-forth. "You're gonna have to find a fill-in drummer."

"What?" Liam's head snaps toward me.

"I can't do it. If you want Fireball to take the festivals, get someone else behind the kit. I'm not leaving Rafferty for three months."

Liam's brows draw tight, disbelief sharp in his eyes. "You'd walk away? From everything we've been building? We have a fucking album coming out."

"I'm saying figure it out without me." I can sense heat starting to rise. "My son comes first."

Connor's gaze flicks between us, reading the tension in the air. Liam paces, like he's got a hundred arguments lined up.

"Fine." Liam leans in, eyes lit with the challenge. "Bring Mara and Rafferty. We can make it work."

Connor nods. "It could. You'd have your own space on the bus."

"No. Being on the road at his age isn't cool," I counter. "I'm not compromising his health and I'm not leaving him."

Liam's tone softens, but the urgency stays. "We need you, Padraig."

"You don't." I shake my head. "Not for this. The three of you've got your groove. The album's tight. A fill-in could handle the festivals."

"Fuck this." Liam leans back, eyes narrowing. He jerks his chin toward Connor. "Talk some sense into our brother before he walks away from the biggest tour we've ever been offered."

When Liam's screen goes dark, Connor fixes me with a look only he's allowed to give. "Fer feck's sake. What's going on?"

I scrub my chin with my hand. "It's not one thing. Rafferty's fragile. Mara's been offered a weekend anchor slot. I brought her to Seattle with me so we could coparent. We may not be a couple, but my family is a priority. I'm not blowing up her shot because my plans changed. It's not fair."

"And?" Unconvinced, Connor makes a rolling motion with his hand.

"Stevie's back in the picture."

His brows lift. "Wait, Stevie Hayes?"

"Yeah. Ran into her at an art exhibit." I pause, knowing he has no idea what I'm talking about. "*My* art exhibit. I started painting again, showing my work. She showed up and..."

Connor shakes his head. "Ach, you've been busy."

"Busy figuring out where I belong. I'm not sure it's behind a drum kit anymore."

His mouth drops open. "You're telling me you want to walk away from Fireball for good? After nearly twenty years?"

"Don't tell me you haven't had the same thoughts." I meet his eyes. "You have babies too. I'm saying music isn't the only thing in my life anymore. My priorities have changed. For one, I'm not hauling Rafferty across Europe when he's this vulnerable. For another, I'm not disappearing on Stevie, not when we've finally found each other again."

Connor leans back, weighing it. "Liam's going to lose his mind."

"Nah. He'll be fine. I've sacrificed too much already to keep him happy. I'm putting myself first for once."

He stands. "Well, I'm gonna head home. All I'm asking is for you to think about it. Don't give Liam the satisfaction of calling you out for reacting out of emotion."

"Appreciate the pep talk." I huff out something that's not quite a laugh.

He claps my shoulder, squeezes once. "Look, you know opportunities like this don't happen often."

When the door shuts behind him, the quiet feels heavier than it should. My phone's already in my hand before I've decided what to do. One tap, and Stevie's face fills the screen.

She smiles, but it's quick, distracted. "Hang on." The picture shifts and blurs as she walks, a door clicking shut behind her. "Okay. I'm in the laundry room. Hi. You look stressed. What's going on?"

"Connor stopped by. LTZ can't do their European festival run. Some serious stuff went down and they're asking Fireball to fill in on their European festival tour."

Her brows lift. "How long?"

"Three months. A handful of big dates, plenty of downtime between. I don't want to do it."

The pause stretches. She tilts her head, studies me, making me feel both seen and exposed. "Because of Rafferty?"

"And because of us," I admit. "We're barely finding our way back to each other. I don't want to disappear before we've figured out what this is."

She moves closer to the camera. "Think about it."

Her words hit differently than I expect. There's no push or judgment. It feels like encouragement wrapped in something heavier.

I blink. "You'd be okay with me going on tour?"

Her shoulders rise and fall. "I'm saying I have regrets about how I handled things back then. I told myself I couldn't be with someone who lived on the road. I built a wall so high it blocked out everything we might've been had I been a little more mature. Yeah, it made things simpler, no false hope, no waiting around. But it also meant I jumped into a relationship with Cooper. Got pregnant. Took away our chance. I don't regret my marriage and my kids, but if we're going to be together, I *would* regret putting restrictions on what you can and cannot do. We're older, clearer about what matters and there's no rush. Besides, merging our families is going to take a lot of time."

The mix of hope and fear in her eyes twists in my chest. She's not pretending this would be easy. She's offering me something I never thought I'd get. A chance to do this with her, not in spite of her.

I search her face, trying to read between the lines. "I'm having a hard time believing you'd be okay."

"Padraig." Her smile turns wistful. "I never gave you the chance to see if we could make it work. Maybe this time, we bend. Test the communication skills we're supposed to have learned in the last decade."

Her words soothe places I didn't even know were raw. It wrecks me a little. Seems too good to be true.

I want to believe it's possible, of course. Navigating time zones and hotel rooms and weeks apart without losing what we've finally found again. It'd be amazing.

Performing on stage knowing she's not counting the days like a sentence she has to serve. Believing I'd be faithful to what we have.

I've also watched love fray under the weight of missed calls and seen trust dissolve in green rooms and afterparties. I've lived it. Hell, I've been part of it.

"I don't want to stand in your way," she says without hesitation. "Not ever."

"Huh." I tilt my head. "Didn't expect this reaction."

"I mean it," she says softly. "If you want to do these shows, do them. I'll be here."

I drag a hand over my face. "It's not so simple. Raff's so small—"

"I know." She nods. "This isn't about me deciding for you. You'll have to figure out what's best for him, and for you and Mara. All I'm saying is don't make your choice because you think I can't handle it. I can."

"The timing isn't bad," I admit. "We're not even close to blending our families yet. We haven't spent any time with each other's kids."

"Exactly." Her mouth tips into a faint smile. "We're building something between the two of us first. We don't need to rush anyone else into our day-to-day before we're ready. A few shows this summer won't change anything."

Her faith in me and us is nearly overwhelming.

"I'm going to really think about it." I pace back and forth. "I'll call Liam back and find out the logistics, figure out what it would mean for Raff and me. Then make the call."

She tilts her head. "Good. Then you've done all you can do."

"So...tomorrow good?" A smile pulls at my mouth. "Do you have a few hours free while the kids are at camp?"

"Yeah, I'll be counting down the minutes." The corners of her lips curve into a wicked grin.

"Me too." I linger a second longer. "I can't wait to be with you."

Her eyes warm. "Neither can I."

She hangs up and I can't help but cheese a little.

Marvel how, despite all these years, our flame was never gone.

Only waiting for the right moment to burn again.

Thirty-Six

STEVIE

Two Weeks Later

MAUREEN'S DOOR SWINGS WIDE before I can knock.

Ham and cloves roll out in a warm wave, honey and heat curling into the hall.

Voices I could recognize from three blocks away tumble over each other from deep in the McGloughlin house. Cillian's quick rhythm, Brennan's dry darts. Seamus steady and quiet. Liam low at the edges, Connor's laugh thudding under it all.

A baby squeals. Jude drops my hand and sprints toward the sound.

"Shoes," I yell after him.

He skids to a halt, kicks them into a corner heap, and bolts anyway, clutching the tiny gift bag with the lamb toy and board book Isla picked out. My mischievous, imaginative son has a knack for turning ordinary situations into epic adventures.

Isla hovers at my elbow, Lila at the other. Isla, at eleven, wears her wavy, honey-brown hair at shoulder length and always has a thoughtful, observant expression making her seem older than her years. Lila is seven, her slightly darker hair is in a ponytail. She sparkles with curiosity and mischief at all times.

I glance around the bustling living room, nerves fluttering under the swell of anticipation. Two weeks ago Padraig and I found our way back to each other. Every adult in both families knows. We're all quietly united in the plan to ease the kids into getting to know everyone before the shape of our worlds shifts for good.

Padraig enters from the hall with Rafferty on his shoulder, diaper bag slung cross   body, hair scraped into a low knot. He spots us, his smile slides across his face slowly. Seeing him makes the room seem softer at the edges for a minute, then snaps back into motion when Jude darts past yelling, "Mom, there's babies!" at a volume reserved for stadiums.

My mom emerges from the kitchen with three large bakery boxes balanced like trophies. "Pecan and cherry, and a tray of brownies," she announces, kisses my cheek, then sets them up on the side table.

Behind her, Joni breezes in with a bouquet of sunflowers and a grin bright enough to fight Seattle's gray skies for a month.

Rory and my dad follow with a stack of plates and a box of silverware. Padraig's da looks good. Sober eyes, steadier posture than last winter, and gait slow but sure. Dad hugs me and the two of them go off to accomplish their task of setting the table.

"Chaos. Pure chaos." Padraig smiles down at me.

Isla's gaze tracks Rafferty who's tiny fist is stuffed inside his father's collar, eyes alert. When he peeks over, my eldest daughter's expression rearranges itself into wonder and careful courage. "He's a lot smaller than the twins."

"Yeah, he was born a little early." Padraig crouches slightly to address her question. "He's catching up."

She nods, then edges closer. "Can I maybe hold him later? If he's in the mood?"

"Absolutely, let's make it happen." Padraig flicks his eyes to mine.

Mara tentatively walks over, polished even in a sweatshirt. She's stunning, with her hair in a low ponytail and makeup-free. When she catches my gaze, she gives me a small nod, and the mother in me immediately recognizes hours of post   partum nights, hard choices, private regrets, and edges smoothed by therapy and stubborn love. Respect rises in my chest without permission.

"Hi, Mara, you remember my daughters, Isla and Lila, from the ice cream shop." I gently urge them both forward and they stare wide-eyed at the woman who they've seen on TV.

Lila beams. "You're so bee-you-tiful."

"Ah, sweetheart." Mara caresses her hair. "Thank you, gorgeous girl."

We're interrupted by Maureen leading a food parade from the kitchen. She sets down the largest ham I've ever seen, glistening under a honeyed glaze. Liam follows with mashed potatoes, steam curling up in buttery waves. Cillian brings roasties, Seamus the caramelized carrots and parsnips, Connor and Ronni follow with soda bread, gravy, and a giant salad.

Maureen takes the knife, carving with swift, precise strokes while ordering everyone to sit, which we do in short order. We fall into the rhythm only a family this big can pull off. Passing, piling, swapping, without a word. Dad drops a slice of ham on each of my kids' plates, I follow with carrots, potatoes, and soda bread.

Rafferty sits in a high chair between Mara and Padraig, who spoons mashed potatoes and tiny bits of ham onto the tray. His small fingers prod, smear, then taste. His whole face lights up and Mara smiles proudly.

Talk swirls as we eat. Ziggy and Cillian joke around about a couple of women they met. Seamus, who's studying to be a neurosurgeon, describes a twelve hour surgical day as if it's nothing. Liam floats at the edge of every exchange infusing a sharp dose of humor, his gaze catching mine from time to time.

Rafferty starts to fuss, emitting a small warning peep. Padraig lifts him from the highchair and in one smooth arc he settles his son into the cradle of his forearm, rocking without thought.

Mara watches in awe. "He has a knack."

"You're both doing a beautiful job, you know," I assure her, and mean it without a single reservation in my bones.

Maureen jumps up and brings a small cupcake slathered in blue frosting over. "Padraig, let's sing Happy Birthday to wee Rafferty before he poops out." She sticks one fat candle in the center and waves her spoon. "Voices, let's hear them."

We sing. Loud. Off key. Perfect. Rafferty stares at the flame with holy focus.

Padraig gestures to Isla. "Help him?"

She meets my eyes. I nod. She leans in, cheeks puffed and blows it out. Applause crashes. Blue frosting meets small fists.

It doesn't take long before Raff's eyes slide heavy and his head tips into the space under Padraig's jaw, his frosting-coated hands flexing into little fists. It's adorable and makes me miss the days when my own kids were so small.

With his birthday celebration complete, the men clear the plates and Mara glances at her watch. "I've got an early call tomorrow. Why don't I take him to my place and get him settled so you can spend more time with your family."

"You sure?" Padraig studies her for a beat, then nods when he's satisfied she means it. "Alright. Let's get him in the carrier."

Together they ease him into car seat, Padraig guiding his feet through the openings while Mara steadies his head. Buckles click; straps tighten. Rafferty makes a soft noise, then settles.

Padraig grabs the diaper bag, slinging it over his shoulder as they move toward the door. He walks her out, his hand on the small of her back as they step into the cool night. Car doors open and close with the muffled finality of routines they know by heart.

I watch from the doorway, catching the way he bends to check the buckles one more time, then steps back so Mara can pull away. Headlights sweep the yard and vanish, leaving him in the quiet glow of the porch light. He shoves his hands into his pockets, then bounds up the steps, the door clicking shut behind him.

By the time he crosses the room, I'm seated on the couch between Isla and Lila, with Jude curled against my hip. My mom and dad anchor the other side, where he joins them.

I catch Isla eyeing him like she's not sure if it's okay to talk, so I give her a nudge. "Did you know Padraig's an artist too?"

"No, he's a rock star." Lila's head pops up.

Padraig grins. "Both can be true at the same time."

"What kind of art do you do?" Isla's curiosity wins over her shyness.

He leans forward on his knees. "Tell me about your project first."

She tucks her hair behind her ear. "We're doing paintings to look like they're moving. Mine's a soccer game. I'm trying to make it look like the ball's going fast without actually drawing it with speed lines."

"How?" Padraig encourages.

Isla blushes. "I'm putting all these blurry colors around it. Green for the field, white for the lines, a little bit of yellow so it looks sunny. Ms. G says it works better if I don't make the edges perfect."

His grin catches the light. "You'll have to come in my house sometime. I've converted my garage into a studio. Maybe we could draw together."

"Seriously?" Her eyes widen.

"Promise," he says, tipping his head toward me. "Your mom can vouch, I'm a pretty fun guy."

I nod. "He means it. And tell her about your gallery opening."

"I was scared." He gives a half shrug, half smile. "But I let a gallery display my paintings and sold every canvas."

"All of them?" Isla's voice jumps an octave.

"Every one."

She glows now, a kind of light no one can fake. "My friends don't believe me when I say I know people in Fireball and LTZ. Now I get to add 'sold-out artist.'"

"Wait. So you and Liam really are rock stars?" Lila looks impressed.

Padraig's mouth tugs sideways. "Connor too. Sometimes we play our instruments in front of very large crowds."

"My music teacher said one of your songs is in a TV show." Lila's giggle pops out before she can catch it. "She acted all funny when I told her you were Mommy's friend."

He winces, hand over his heart. "Maybe Liam and I can give her a signed poster or something."

"Can we go home, Mama?" Jude's thumb finds his mouth, his other hand curls into my hair.

It's the cue. Around us, the room shifts. Voices dip, chairs scrape, coats are fetched from the hook by the door. Lila disappears for a moment and returns with her boots half-laced. Isla stands with her hands in her pockets, sneaking glances at Padraig, who made a good impression.

Rory gets to his feet, slow from the long day, and kisses the top of my head before leaning in. "Good day, love. You did well."

My dad clasps Padraig's hand, firm and steady, before scooping Jude from my arms so I can get my shoes on. Across the room, my mom slips a container into my tote without a word, certain it'll be the kids' lunch tomorrow.

Maureen folds each of my kids into her arms, lingering a fraction longer with Isla, her gaze meeting mine in a quiet promise to keep this momentum. Joni and Ziggy corner Lila on the way to the door, teasing her about her Taylor Swift fixation until she dissolves into giggles.

Around us, the McGloughlin brothers juggle armfuls of leftovers, voices overlapping in the familiar tangle of a family trying to leave but never quite ready to say goodbye. The lot of us spill onto the front steps and depart. Car doors slam and engines turn over one by one.

Padraig waits as I get the kids settled. Isla climbs into the backseat, pressing herself to the window, Lila slides in beside her and immediately tells her about the fort she's planning for the living room. I strap Jude into his seat, and shut the door.

"Call when they're asleep." Padraig holds my door for me as I get in.

I smile up at him. "Will do."

We drive home with the windows cracked. By the time I park, Jude's out, a faint smile on his face. Inside, I move all of them through their bedtime routine on autopilot. Pajamas. Teeth. Stories. Lights out.

When the kids are asleep, I complete my own nighttime ritual, stretch out on the bed and call him.

"You cozy?" His handsome face fills the screen.

"Yeah. Everyone's out cold."

"Good day?"

"Better than I expected." I think of how much fun my kids had. "It felt easy. You really hit it off with Isla and she's the toughest nut to crack."

"Aye, though we were chums the first time I met her..." Padraig stops, realizing it was when Coop was alive. "Sorry, I never know where the line is. Ma was right, tiny steps."

My mind races back to the awkward dinner when Padraig showed up. "It's okay. I forgot, but you're right. She warmed up to you right away."

"Anyway, I'm glad we had today before I leave tomorrow. I feel good about how it went." He settles back against his pillows.

"I do too." I can't help it when a smile takes over my face.

He shuts his eyes and takes a breath. "I'll miss you."

"I'll miss you more," I tease.

He huffs a quiet laugh. "We'll see. I've gotta be up around four a.m. We may be filling in for LTZ, but we don't have the budget for a private jet."

"Liam seemed pretty contrite tonight. Are things better?" I know he and his brother are struggling. Liam's giving Padraig a guilt trip, which is more rooted in he doesn't want to lose his twin.

"It's fine." He sighs. "We'll hash it out on tour. I'm serious about coming up with an exit plan. I don't want to leave him high and dry but he doesn't really understand my perspective because he's not a father. His people travel with him. He's not like me."

I tilt my head and blow him a kiss. "You guys will be fine. I should let you get some sleep. Promise to reach out when you're settled in Paris?"

"The second I'm able." He kisses me back through the screen. "I love you. And, Stevie?"

"Yeah?"

"I'm glad we're doing this."

"Me too."
The silence lingers after he hangs up.
I hold the phone for a beat longer, already missing him.
We've only taken the first step and it might be a little messy.
This time I'll never let the flame go out.

Thirty-Seven

Six Weeks Later

THE HEAT HITS FIRST.

Not only from the sun, but from fifty thousand bodies pressed together in an open field, their roar building until it's a living thing.

The stage shakes under my kit, every kick drum thud shoots up through my legs. Liam's guitar wails to my left, Avonna prowls the front edge, hair whipping, her voice cutting sharp and clean through the chaos.

I lock into the bass loop I built for this song, feel it punch through the subs and into the crowd, shaking the barricades. Think about the years of dingy clubs, gear rattling in the back of borrowed vans, half-drunk sound guys. We climbed every rung to get here.

Almost twenty years of slogging to be what *Rolling Stone* calls "the longest overnight success."

Flags snap above the crush of people, pint cups lift in salute. When Avonna throws her mic toward them, they scream the chorus of *Tir na nÓg* back so loud my teeth buzz. Liam shoots me a sideways grin, sweat dripping, hair plastered to his face, and I answer with a hard crash on the cymbals to make him laugh.

Every song blurs into the next. Muscle memory takes over while my head rides the high. The view from behind the kit is all motion, lights sweeping in wide arcs, hands raised in unison, the shimmer of all the colors of fifty-thousand festival-goers.

It's beautiful, in its way. Wild. Free.

Even as I push into the last chorus, my mind drifts to home. Rafferty's lopsided grin when he sees me on FaceTime. Stevie's laugh when the girls argue over who gets to hold the phone. Jude waving a plastic drumstick like he's part of the band.

We hit the final note hard enough to shake the risers. Avonna throws her arms up and the roar doubles. Liam soaks it in, eyes closed, every bit the rock star he was born to be. I take it in too, pride swelling. Not for me. For us.

For every mile, every fight, every night we slept sitting up so the van's heater could keep the gear from freezing.

Then the crew is pulling us offstage to set up for the next act. Linus waits with fresh bottles of water and a grin indicating the set landed flawlessly. I nod, catching my breath. Rockstar adrenaline's a drug, but the first thing I want isn't another hit.

It's my people. The real ones. The ones not here.

I'm already calculating time zones, figuring out if I can catch the kids before they're off to school.

The stage manager waves us toward the wings. I'm soaked with sweat, my wrists buzz from the last cymbal crash and my heartbeat is synced to the crowd's chant. We spill into the tunnel under the stage, crew darting in every direction, cables coiled, amps rolling out to the trucks.

Liam hooks an arm over my shoulder. "Flawless."

"Thanks, Dar." I kiss his cheek and he's off, replaying riffs in his mind as if he's onstage. Linus flanks Avonna, whose talking to a notoriously demented radio host, her hair is dripping, eyeliner smudged to perfection.

I take in all of it, proud as hell as the clock in my head runs the numbers. Barcelona, 4:30 p.m. Seattle, 7:30 a.m. Perfect.

A quick shower later, I'm in our trailer wearing a fresh hoodie and jeans. My night's not over, it stretches on for a few more hours with interviews, meet-and-greets, and various sponsor crap.

Before any of it, I find a quiet corner behind the hospitality tent and hit Mara's number. She answers with Rafferty in her arms, the camera jostling as he reaches for the phone.

"Da-da-da-da," he babbles, cheeks flushed from breakfast.

"Hey, wee lad." I smile so hard it hurts.

He bangs a toy against the tray of his highchair, determined to be louder than the noise in my background. Mara rolls her eyes and adjusts him so I get a better view. Ten minutes of peekaboo, a blown kiss, and a promise to call tomorrow before she heads to the park.

Next, Stevie.

"Hold on," she says before I can speak, "they've been waiting."

She turns the camera, and Jude waves with half a waffle in his mouth, Lila blows kisses like she's on TV, Isla pretends not to be excited but her fidgeting gives her away. We talk about breakfast, school drop-off, and how the girls' fairy light fort is now a "permanent structure." They give me a full virtual tour, spinning the phone until I'm dizzy. It's chaotic and perfect.

By the time I hang up, I'm lighter. The noise of the festival fades under the sound of their voices in my head.

The next morning, I'm in my hotel room. It's dark except for the glow of the phone and the table lamp. I have the curtains drawn and the air is pretty stale and dry. I've been lying here since five, half-awake, waiting.

Stevie's call comes through, video immediately angled so I see her in bed, hair loose, voice low.

She's excited because her first event is booked. It's nothing huge, but a good way to get her feet wet. I tell her about all of the after-party shenanigans and how I've been hanging out mostly with my drum tech, Vince. Liam, Avonna, and Linus are in their own world, and I'm not part of it.

As usual, our conversation turns quiet, slower. We're able to stare at each other through the screen in the kind of space we only get when the kids are out cold and miles of ocean make the wanting sharper.

"God, I miss you. I wish you were here." She settles back against her pillows. Her tank strap slips halfway down her arm, showing me a slight bit of cleavage.

I smile into the dark. "I'm working on it."

"So…do you have something for me, drummer boy?" She bites her finger.

My eyes track the neckline of her tank, how it shifts with her breath. "Maybe. What're you wearing under there?"

"Guess." She doesn't hide the heat in her eyes.

"Nothing," I say as I yank the blankets down and expose my hardening cock.

She tips the camera down, angling it so I can see straight down her shirt. The neckline gapes enough to reveal the curve of her breasts, nipples peaked and straining against thin cotton. "You know me too well."

"Take it all off."

Her chin dips, eyes locked on mine through the screen. One hand slides under the hem of her shirt, peeling it up and over her head in one smooth lift. Her breasts sway free, full and perfect, nipples tight and flushed. Next, she grabs the elastic of her sleep shorts and slides them over her hips, baring the smooth swell of her belly, then lower, revealing the soft, tempting curve between her thighs covered in soft, blonde hair.

My cock thickens to full attention instantly.

"Christ, Stevie." My hand closes around the base, giving it one slow stroke. "Spread your legs for me."

She allows her knees to fall open and moves the camera down to catch every glint of wetness. My mouth waters and every muscle is tight with the need to taste her. To have her shuddering under my tongue.

"What're you thinking?" She cups her tit and pinches her nipple.

"I'd give anything to be there, tasting you." My hand moves over my cock again, slow enough to make my teeth clench. "Let me see you touch yourself."

Her fingers drag through her folds, unhurried, gathering every trace of moisture. She brings them to her mouth, lips parting as her tongue curls around the tips, sucking until her cheeks hollow. The wet sound punches straight through me, heat ripping down my spine. My hips twitch, cock straining for her, for the taste she's teasing me with from half a world away.

"Don't you dare come yet," she warns as her fingers circle lazily over her clit. "I want to see you."

I shift the phone, angling it down until the frame's full of my fist stroking my cock, thick, flushed, glistening at the head. Her eyes widen, lips parting on a quiet gasp.

"Jesus, babe…" she breathes, her hand faltering for half a second before she catches herself. "You're so hard for me."

"Keep going," I growl, my grip sliding from base to tip, slow enough to make my own stomach tighten.

Her gaze pins me, pupils blown so wide they swallow nearly every trace of color. Her chest heaves in quick, shallow bursts, breasts rising high, nipples tight and flushed, begging for my mouth.

She bites her lip, but her eyes stay fixed on the slow pull of my hand over my cock, watching every stroke, every bead of pre-come running down the length. Her breathing stutters when I squeeze at the base, dragging it out, and I swear I feel the heat of her stare through the screen.

She shifts, thighs flexing, pussy glistening in the light, and I know she's imagining me there. My mouth, my fingers, my cock filling her until she forgets her own name.

"Get your toy," I tell her, leaving no space for her to pretend she didn't hear.

Her hand dips out of frame. When it comes back, she holds the pale-pink vibrator which is about the size of my cock.

"Prop the phone up where I can see everything."

Stevie sets the phone on her stand and positions between her legs so the camera catches everything. Her spread thighs. Swollen pink pussy. Glistening and ready. She flicks the tip through her slit until it shines with her arousal.

"Now push it in," I beg. "I want you take all of it."

She's so wet, the head parts her folds easily, disappearing inch by inch into her tight heat. I can see her clench around it and the way her inner walls stretch and ripple as she works the length deeper until the curved handle rests flush against her.

"Oh, God," she moans.

"Now, pull it out. Slow until I can see you open."

She obeys, withdrawing until only the head is inside. A faint squelch comes through the speaker, obscene and perfect.

Then, she slides it back in with a wet glide so viscerally naughty, my balls tighten and I have to clench my base to avoid blowing my load too soon.

"Now turn it on and fuck yourself with it," I demand. "Hard. Make me hear how wet you are."

"Yeah, okay…" She flicks the switch and drives the toy in fast, hips rising to meet each thrust. Her clit catches against the curve every time, pulling gasps out of her throat. Her nipples stand tight and flushed as her breasts bounce with each movement.

The sound of her getting herself off fills my headphones, filthy and addictive.

"Eyes on me," I remind her when they flutter shut.

Her gaze locks with mine. "I'm trying, it feels so good."

"Tell me." My hand moves faster over my cock, lubricating myself with pre-come.

"It's…warm," she moans, "buzzing through my clit, right up into my belly." Her hips roll, pushing the toy higher. "It's thick. Stretching me. I feel every ridge." She rocks against it, eyes half-shut. "Fuck. I want it deeper. Where you'd be. Hitting my spot."

She drives it in to the base, her pussy gripping tight, wetness catching the light. Pulls it halfway out, then pushes it back in with a wet, filthy sound.

"How full are you?" I growl.

"Full enough I can feel my pulse in my pussy," she gasps, voice fraying at the edges.

My hand fists tighter. "Christ, Stevie. You're fucking gorgeous. You don't know what you do to me."

"I'm—oh, fuck—I'm right there—" She drives the toy harder, wetter, her thighs trembling.

Her back arches, hips jerking, a broken cry tears from her throat. The toy glistens as she fucks herself through it, juices dripping down her fingers. Her chest heaves and mouth falls open while her whole body ripples with aftershocks.

"God, yes, baby. Show me. Let me see you lose it for me." I stroke faster, watching every twitch of her clit against the toy.

Her moan shivers through the speaker, eyes glassy but locked on mine. "Your turn."

I pump like a goddamn madman, the sound of beating off fills the space between us. Her gaze flicks down my chest, over my abs, locking on the head as it glides through my fist.

"Oh, yeah." She licks her lips. "I want you to come all over yourself so I can lick you clean."

Holy. Fuck.

I brace one hand on the mattress, muscles tight, eyes never leaving hers as the heat pools, sharp and inevitable. "Fuck, Stevie... I'm—"

She leans in, her voice all silk and sin. "Give it to me."

My orgasm rips through me like wildfire. Thick ropes stripe my stomach, my chest, and my neck. I jerk myself until every drop is wrung out under her watchful eyes, groaning low. Riding it out until I'm a shuddering, breathless mess.

When I open my eyes again, she's smiling. Slow and knowing, flushed from her own high.

"God, I can't wait for you to be inside me for real." Stevie blinks sleepily.

"Counting the days," I agree. "Tonight will hold me over, but when I get home, we're gonna need a whole weekend of fucking. Maybe more like a year."

Her laugh is quiet but warm. "You always were stubborn."

"And you always were worth it."

Thirty-Eight

STEVIE

One Year Later

I PARK BESIDE CONNOR'S cedar-and-glass house and sit for one breath, watching wind skate ripples over the lake.

Even if it's in the most expensive neighborhood in Washington State, the place looks rooted, not flashy. A builder's home where every board knows why it's there.

I grab my tote, follow the flagstones, and knock.

Connor opens with a toothy grin. "Stevie." He steps aside. "Welcome."

He leads me back to where I hear the murmur of voices past a wall of windows overlooking the lake. Entering the kitchen, a gaggle of McGloughlin brothers, including Padraig, are waiting for me.

Ronni stands at the island, kettle in hand, wearing a sweater loose over a noticeable bump. "Herbal tea? I'm hydrating."

"Tea is perfect." I slide my tote onto a chair and flip my notebook open. "So, guys, today's going to be a fact   finding mission. I listen, you lot talk. We build a plan for Rory from there."

Cillian's on a stool in faded denim and steel   toe boots, phone facedown for once. Seamus wears a hoodie over scrubs, his hair flattened on one side. Padraig leans against the far counter, hair tied back, forearms crossed, mouth curved cheekily, indicating he's thinking about last night's grown-up activities.

I look away, hoping my blush doesn't give us away.

Connor claps once. "Let's start with venue."

"Shouldn't we host considering I'll be ready to pop?" Ronni offers before anyone else can answer. "It'll be winter, but we could use the patio if we set up a tent and heaters at the corners. String lights along the railings."

Connor shrugs, pleased. "Aye, sounds like a plan."

I glance around, this is a commercial kitchen times a million. "It'll be easy to prep the food here. Day of, staff can stage in the butler's pantry. What do you think the guest count is?"

"Family, close mates, a few old foremen, neighbors from the early years, your family of course," Connor says. "Fifty to sixty max. Ma will push for five more once she remembers someone she forgot. We can absorb it."

I scribble it down and look up. "Budget?"

The brothers look at each other and Cillian lifts a hand. "Let's go big. Da isn't fussy, but we should have good food and make it look awesome. Maybe some sort of party favor."

"Menu?" I ask.

"Ma will want to cook." Seamus shakes his head. "We won't stop her even if we try."

"We don't need to stop her." I tap my pen to my lip. "We support and supplement her. I'll hire staff for prep and service so she can supervise without hauling trays."

"Thank you," Padraig beams. "She'll appreciate it."

I draw a quick box for the patio and sketch zones. "I need to look around more, but after a quick glance I can see lounge pockets near windows, tall tables by heaters, stage at the far rail with a water station beside it, dessert station close to the kitchen. Flow in a loop so no bottlenecks. Do you want a bar, or are we going dry?"

Cillian leans in. "Da wouldn't care. He's exorcised his demons."

"*You* haven't," Seamus mutters under his breath.

"Well, you boys discuss amongst yourself and get back to me. We have a lot of time." I definitely don't want to be in the middle of the family dynamic on this decision. "Speeches?"

Seamus squints at the ceiling, "Short."

"Photos?" I ask.

Padraig speaks for the first real time. "We can sort through the albums and compile old site shots from the early days. Ask friends to contribute. Nothing to drag him into places he doesn't visit anymore."

We all hear what he isn't saying. Sobriety three years strong. Don't focus on the bad years.

"Let's ask Brennan to make a tight slide show," Connor says. "He'll deliver if we give him a drop   dead date."

"Done." I write a date, underline it.

Ronni nudges a mug of tea toward me. "Invites?"

"I think we go classy. Printed, hand   delivered where possible." I gesture with my hands. "No social media until after. Rory may not be online much, but everyone else is. The surprise will hold if we keep the circle tight."

Connor nods. "We're good at tight circles."

An understatement. The McGloughlins close rank with ferocity and humor.

The sound of the side door sliding open carries into the kitchen. Gigi, their middle-aged nanny steps in, flushed from the wind, with toddlers on each hip. Torin and Tristan, at two, are miniature versions of Connor. Dark ginger hair with wide grins already working an angle.

Connor's face lights. "There's my wee lads." He sweeps Torin into one arm and musses Tristan's hair before passing him to Cillian, who hoists him onto his shoulders. Padraig crouches down so Tristan can give him a kiss and Seamus holds out a fist for Torin, earning a solemn bump in return.

"All right, get outta here so I can feed the monsters." Ronni shoos the whole lot of them toward the living room. "Go figure out the bar situation."

The brothers depart, tossing Tristan between them in mock handoffs. Gigi sets the boys in their booster seats, and Ronni slides plates piled with turkey, strawberries, and buttered bread.

"You know," she glances at me as they dig in, "Sunday dinners feel strange when you're not there."

"It's been good for all of us." I lean on the counter next to her. "Jude loves being 'the older one' when he's with your boys and Rafferty. He takes it like a job. He was gutted when we couldn't come last Sunday, but I wasn't about to let any of you catch the bug we all had."

Ronni gives me a knowing look. "I appreciate it. But, now we're alone, so I need the goods. When are you and Padraig telling your kids?"

"Soon." My hand traces a pattern in the marble on the counter. "We're ready. It's been two years since Coop died. It's a long time, but when you've got kids, it's not. The grief shows up for them in different ways. I don't want to rush something and have it feel like another loss if things changed. They've been through enough."

Ronni nods, quiet.

"I've read enough to know you can't drop someone new into their lives at full volume. It has to be gradual. As much as Padraig and I want to shout it from the rooftops, I need to put them first. Give them space to process and let them have feelings about it without being told how to feel. Most of all, neither of us want them to think Padraig is trying to replace Cooper."

Ronni leans forward, lowering her voice. "Connor's always said it was tragic, you two splitting. He swears even back then, you belonged together."

"Yeah..." I let out a slow breath. "It's complicated. We were desperately in love, but life was happening fast. College, the band, my career. I made choices I thought were right at the time and now I have three beautiful kids. It turns out forever doesn't disappear, it waits."

Ronni smirks, handing half a cracker to Tristan before he can knock the whole plate to the floor. "You know, being with a guy in a band. People think it's all glamour. Truth is, you either learn to live with the absences or you lose your mind."

I laugh, because it's exactly what I've been thinking for months. What Ronni doesn't know is for us, the absences have an end date. "Exactly. The travel, the late nights, the last-minute changes. It's a lot. Padraig's heart is here, but the schedule pulls him away. It's not as bad as I imagined it back in college though. We're figuring out how to keep the connection without resenting the gaps."

"Connor and I had to learn how to balance too. Took a while. A lot of bumps." Her eyes soften with recognition.

It's true. The two of them have been through so much, it makes our situation look like child's play.

"In some ways, his obligations have been a blessing in disguise." I keep my expression even and my tone light.

The truth is, Padraig's leaving the band once this album cycle ends. It's been a runaway success, which has led to financial freedom and a ton of opportunities. The royalties alone from this run will set him up for life. He'll be able to paint full-time and be with his son.

For now, I let Ronni think this is our forever reality, because Connor doesn't know either. I'm not about to spill the beans.

"When he was on tour, he always made time to have long video chats with me and the kids, showing them where he was, letting them see the crowds," I continue. "When he's home, we've had a few casual outings where he can bring Raff. The zoo, a Mariners game, the Puyallup Fair. We've been careful not to blur the lines too fast. But the extended family dinners?" I smile as I bring the conversation back around. "The best. My family's always been close to the McGloughlins, so when we're all together for birthdays or holidays, there's no pressure. The kids get to see him in a big, loud mix without forcing us to define anything until we're ready."

Ronni smiles knowingly. "Sounds like you've been turning up the volume nice and slow."

"We're solid. Figuring out timing. It should be soon." A glance at the clock pulls me back to the rest of my day. "Speaking of timing, I need to grab Jude, then the girls."

Ronni waves me off. "Go. We'll keep the planning train moving."

I cross through the hall toward the living room, where the brothers are deep in conversation. Padraig spots me first, pushing to his feet. "Heading out?"

"School pickup."

"I'll walk you out."

We step into the warm June air, the lake glinting beyond Connor's walkway. The scent of fresh-cut grass carries on a light breeze. Padraig's hand settles at the small of my back, easy and familiar, as we follow the path to my car.

"Text when you're home." His voice dips into the private register meant only for me.

"I will."

He leans in, mouth meeting mine in a kiss starting off soft and turning certain. His fingers curve around my hip, holding me close until I pull back with a smile I can't quite hide.

I slide into the driver's seat, door open as he rests an arm on the roof. "Love you."

"Love you too." He keeps his eyes steady on mine until I turn the key.

I pull away with the image of him standing in the drive.

Sunlight catches on the edges of a life I'm ready to claim.

It can't come soon enough.

Thirty-Nine

Six Months Later

LIFE HAS A FUNNY way of kicking you in the ass.

I burst through the door of Cactus in Madison Park, late.

The restaurant's busy. Luckily no one's paying attention so I'm able to slide into the booth beside Stevie and kiss her without worrying about phones capturing our every move.

"You order?" I ask, glancing at the untouched basket of tortilla chips.

She smirks. "Nah, I was waiting for the rockstar."

"Jesus Christ." I groan. "Don't start."

"What? It's not every day my boyfriend gets four Grammy nominations." She bumps her shoulder into mine, eyes glittering. "I've heard of the Rock category, but the other three are pretty obscure. Is Linus losing it over your tour schedule?"

"Understatement." I shake my head. "He's got the next year mapped out in his usual color-coded hell. I went in fully ready to talk to everyone about taking a step back today, but…"

She raises an eyebrow. "But you didn't."

"But I didn't," I admit. "It's hard to tell them I'm done when the offers keep getting bigger. We've never had these kinds of opportunities before. I'm getting a taste of what it's been like for Connor."

"I bet." Her hand finds mine under the table.

We don't have to talk about the big-picture plan. The one where I hang up the sticks after this cycle and spend more time painting than sleeping in buses. The problem is this cycle doesn't seem to end.

"Mara texted me today." She dunks a chip in the salsa with her free hand. "A darling picture of Raff with Tanner at the park."

I suck my lips over my teeth at the mention of Mara's boyfriend. "Yeah. He's good with him. Still weird, though."

"You've been a good sport about it." She squeezes my fingers.

"Trying." I drag a finger over her knuckles. "I'm salty there are weeks Tanner sees him more than I do. I'm missing a lot. It makes me want this stuff with the band to end, but I'm also trying to enjoy the success. It's a mind fuck."

"You're a public commodity now." I swear I catch the shadow there. The truth beneath the tease.

I shake my head. "I'm not a commodity. I'm yours. I'd rather be here hanging at the climbing wall with the kids, or supporting Cillian when he gets out of rehab for fuck's sake."

"Climbing wall, huh?" She toys with the rim of her glass. "Is this a hint for our weekend outing?"

"Yeah. I think the rec center's perfect. Indoor. Big enough for them to run wild, no weather excuses. Isla can try the ropes course, Lila will love the crafts corner, and Jude—"

"—will follow Rafferty around until he begs for mercy." Her laugh is soft, a memory already forming in her eyes. "He really does take his older-kid status seriously."

"He's good with Raff," I say with pride, but also ache. "Wish they saw each other more."

"We have dinner Sunday."

"Not enough." I bring her hand to my lips and kiss it, grounding myself in the touch. "It's never enough."

Movement and chatter ripple throughout the room, but it all fades when our eyes meet.

"I know we said we'd wait until things settled to tell the kids," she says eventually, "but it's been two and a half years since Cooper passed. They've healed in ways I didn't think possible. I think they're ready."

"Are you?" I lean in and give her a peck.

"Yes. I'm ready for us to be in the same house." She kisses me back. "Only if you are too."

My gut squeezes. "I'm sure about you. About our kids. Always. The rest..." I blow out a breath. "It feels messy."

"Because of Cillian?"

"Yeah," I admit. "But he's in rehab now. It's more about Linus stacking the calendar. Another tour. More press. And this Grammy thing's lit a fire under everyone's arse. If I walk away now, I'm not only disappointing Liam. I'm turning down stupid money to keep us set for years."

Her smile tilts, equal parts love and frustration. "Then tell me your plan."

"We've got to be in the home stretch." I glance at the table, then back at her. "The cycle should be finished by the end of next year. I think I should bank what I can. Tell Liam I'm not going to be on the next album at some point so we can start looking for a drummer for when I'm done."

She doesn't blink. "You're sure?"

"Yes. More sure than I've been about anything except us," I assure her. "Fireball's survived four different singers, it'll survive losing a drummer."

The server appears with our plates, breaking the thread of the moment. We eat, talking about Isla's science project, Jude's latest Lego fortress, Lila's ballet recital. The ordinary things I miss when I'm gone too long.

"You're selling yourself short, you know. Fireball's always been about the twins more than anything." Stevie surprises me by bringing the band back up.

I lean back, brow lifting. "Here I thought people came for Avonna's voice."

"You're stupid." Stevie swats me. "No, seriously. Your music, your bond. It's what people gravitate to when they hear you. Without you, it's not the same."

"So what do I do?" I sigh heavily.

She fixes her gaze on me. "Despite everything, stop pretending you owe the whole world more than you owe yourself."

"I've got Grammy nominations, a sold-out tour and half the industry demanding we go back into the studio."

She leans in. "They're not the ones who have to live your life. You are. If you stay out there when your heart's in Seattle, you'll start resenting it and them. You already are and it's been this way every single cycle. When does it end?"

I drag a hand through my hair, the weight of it all pressing in. "I wish it were simple."

"Padraig. It can be." She strokes my cheek. "If you make it. Speak up."

I sit back, her words reverberate in my mind. Cycle after cycle.

She's right—I keep letting it happen. Every time an album wraps, I swear I'll slow down, and then the machine starts up again. I never hit the brakes, even when I could.

Connor didn't let LTZ burn him out. He pulled them back, made the shows rarer, more wanted. They didn't vanish, they became something you waited for. Maybe it's the answer.

"If we stopped chasing and played fewer shows, we could work around me." The words rush out as fast as I can think them. "Make it an event instead of a habit. Still write, release music, but on our terms."

Stevie's smile starts small, then warms all the way through. "You wouldn't have to walk away entirely."

"I wouldn't have to choose," I echo. "Could be here for the kids, for you, and keep the music alive."

"Don't forget you'll have time for your art. Sounds an awful lot like a win to me." She keeps her eyes steady on mine.

I grip her face between my palms and plant one on her for the books.

"You know what? I think we need to take our own advice for our family too. It's time to claim our own joy." Her eyes flash. "Let's do it now. I'll grab my kids from my mom's, you swing by Mara's for Rafferty."

I slide out of the booth excitedly. "I'll call Mara on the way, make sure he's ready."

We settle the bill and head for our respective cars, moving with urgency.

It feels like the first time in years I'm walking toward a real future.

Isla's on the bench in the kitchen when Rafferty and I get to Stevie's, legs folded under her, earbuds in, thumbs flying over her phone screen. Nearly thirteen and carrying herself like she's already seventeen. Her hair's darker now, waves pulled into a messy half knot, and she only looks up long enough to clock me before going back to whatever's on TikTok.

Lila's perched at the island, bare feet swinging against the stool. Nine, freckles scattered over her nose, flipping through one of Stevie's cookbooks like she's got something to prove.

Jude comes skidding in from the backyard, hair sticking up, cheeks flushed, always a ball of restless energy and big grins. Six years old and moving through life at full tilt.

Rafferty's warm and solid in my arms, no sign of those first months when I stressed about every sneeze and cough. He's a chunk in the best way, head against my shoulder, brown eyes scanning the room like he's sizing everyone up.

"Hey, Padraig." Jude's already trying to peek around me. "What's in the bag?"

"Fixings for ice cream sundaes." I set Raff next to Isla, who promptly snuggles him to her. "Figured we'd make them together."

Sweet treats get her attention. She takes one earbud out, slow like she's not sure she wants to commit. "What kind?"

"I brought a selection." I take the containers out of the bag while Lila digs for bowls. "Where's your mom?"

"Here, I heard there's ice cream." Stevie glides in, changed into her favorite athleisurewear.

We line up at the island, the kids crowding in, elbows bumping while I assemble the sundaes, squeezing chocolate sauce, whipped cream, sprinkles, cherries. Jude dumps half a bottle of rainbow sprinkles over his before I can stop him. Raff bangs his spoon on the tray, grinning like he knows he's in on something.

Once we're all at the table, Stevie gives me the look. It's time.

She sets her spoon down and puts on her mom voice. "So...we wanted to talk to you all about something important."

Four sets of eyes. Isla's guarded, Lila's curious, Jude's mouth already full. Rafferty points at me.

"I'm not sure if this is a surprise, but Padraig and I are more than friends." She glances at me. "We're actually boyfriend and girlfriend. I want to hear how you feel about it. Because it's important you know, he's not here to take your dad's place. No one could. This is about adding someone we care about to our family, not replacing anyone."

The words hang for a beat, and I watch their faces. Rafferty is too little to understand, so I focus on the other three. Lila tilts her head, bored. Jude licks ice cream off his spoon.

Isla taps her nail against the table like she's working through it. "We know."

Lila nods. "Yeah. You think we're babies?"

Jude grins. "Duh."

Stevie and I glance at each other and can't help but smile. Two years of taking it slow, letting them see me in small ways, and here they are. Unfazed, even a little smug about it.

"So," Stevie takes it a step further, "how would you feel if Padraig and Rafferty stayed over sometimes? Maybe, someday we'll all live together?"

Lila shrugs. "Fine with me."

"If you live here, can we have ice cream for breakfast?" Jude perks up.

"No," Stevie laughs.

Isla's quiet for a second, then sighs dramatically. "As long as you don't move my stuff." Which, from her, is basically a blessing.

"Sounds like we've got ourselves an agreement," I say.

Jude's eyes light up. "Tonight we should have a slumber party to celebrate. All of us. Even Raff."

Lila's already nodding.

Isla groans. "Seriously?"

"Great idea." Stevie stands and starts collecting bowls. "We'll pile on the comfy couch in the living room, jammies, a pile of blankets and YouTube DJ until we can't keep our eyes open."

An hour later, with Raff sacked out against my side, me, Stevie, Jude, and Isla pass popcorn and the remote. We take turns picking videos, the room lit only by the TV.

When it's Stevie's turn, she gives me a sly look. Suddenly, the screen's filled with grainy footage from a dingy college stage. Me, Liam, and Felicity in one of our first shows.

"Wait." Lila sits bolt upright. "That's you. And Liam. Who is the girl, it doesn't look like Avonna."

"She was Fireball's first singer, Felicity." I shake my head, remembering the drama she dragged along everywhere she went.

Jude practically climbs over my legs to get closer to the screen. "Wait, you were in a band then too?"

"Same band." I rub the back of my neck. "Fireball at the beginning."

Stevie appears off to the side, barely in the frame, but I remember the night like it was yesterday. She's nineteen or twenty, her hair long and loose, wearing jeans and a white tee. Watching me like there's no one else in the room.

Isla leans forward, eyes narrowed at the image. She doesn't say a word, but I catch the flicker of recognition like she knows exactly what the look means.

From his spot on the blanket, Rafferty stirs at the commotion, blinking awake. He squints at the TV, then points with one tiny finger. "Da-da."

"Wow. You really *have* been friends a long time," Lila squeals.

I glance at Stevie snuggled into my other side, she smiles up at me. "We have."

The kids start talking over each other. Lila firing questions, Jude wanting to see more videos, Isla leaning back like she's pretending not to care. Rafferty's conked out again.

Looking at Stevie, I realize her eyes are lit the same way they were in the old clip. Without thinking, I lean in and kiss her.

The kids shriek and throw popcorn.

I can't stop smiling as I kiss their mother.

Because if there was ever a sign we're going to be fine—it's this.

Forty

Six Months Later

THE KITCHEN'S QUIET IN a way it almost never is at my house.

I'm appreciating the quietness on a Saturday afternoon. It's unusual, to say the least.

Lila left for a sleepover a few minutes ago. Jude's off with my dad tonight for some "secret adventure" which probably involves sugar and some sort of *Star Wars* movie.

Out back, in the guest house Padraig converted into his studio, I see a flash of movement through the wide-open doors. Isla's ponytail swinging as she leans over a canvas. He's next to her, head bent, showing her something in the mess of paint between them.

They've been out there for hours.

It's one of the things I love most about him. How he gives his attention to my kids without making it feel like a performance.

Even with all the tension over Fireball, he's here. Really here. He's held his ground with Liam and Linus, trimming his commitment to the band without burning it down. June will pull him away for a few months on tour, but for now, his time is ours.

I finish slicing the apples, grab a box of crackers, and arrange them on a plate with cheese and peanut butter. My business calendar's open on the counter, reminders pinging for a client call and an event proposal, but I'm trying not to let my weekends be ruled by work. It's not easy when you plan events, but I do my best not to get dragged under.

Mara's wedding is circled in bright ink on the wall calendar. I've offered to take three-year-old Rafferty while she and Tanner are on their honeymoon, and while Padraig's on the road, so it'll be my first time with the little guy alone. I'm excited for him to fill the house with his soft toddler babble and gummy grins.

Balancing the plate in one hand, I cross the yard. The closer I get, the more I can hear Isla's insistent questions.

"So you and Mom always talk about how you were friends when you were my age. Did you ever kiss my mom?"

Padraig's paintbrush stops. "*Isla.*"

"What? I'm asking."

He sounds pained. "Uh, I'm not really—"

"Did you?" I'm close enough to see her poke him in the side with the handle of her brush.

He exhales. "We were close."

"What a stupid answer." Her chair squeaks as she turns. "Were you her boyfriend or not?"

"Ask your mom."

"That means yes," she squeals, triumphant. "How long? Did you write her songs? Did she have your hoodie?"

I step in. "Didn't realize I was the subject of an interrogation."

Isla swivels toward me. "I'm gathering intel. You always tell us to ask questions."

"Questions, sure. Fishing for gossip? No."

She grins. "So it's *gossip*? Were you in *love* with Padraig?"

I meet her eyes. There's no point pretending she hasn't already pieced together most of it. "Yes. We were friends as kids and then dated throughout high school and college."

Her eyes sharpen. "Like, before Dad?"

"Aye." Padraig nudges the plate of apples toward her like it's a barrier.

"Why'd you break up?" Isla sets her brush down.

"It's a long story," I say carefully. "Life took us in different directions."

"Was it because of Dad?" she presses. "Did he steal you away?"

Padraig blanches, but manages to keep his composure. We don't revisit this time in our lives often. It puts us in the uncomfortable category of "what if's" instead of enjoying where we are now.

"No. Your dad came later. He was a big, important part of my life. None of this takes away from the love I had for him. People's lives can have more than one chapter." I hope my explanation honors Cooper but also respects Padraig and my relationship with him now.

She tilts her head. "So, were you fucking each other back then?"

Padraig nearly chokes on his water. "Jesus, Isla."

"What? I'm not nine anymore. And it's not like I don't know about sex."

I pinch the bridge of my nose. "You're right, you're older now. But you will have a little respect for me and for Padraig. There's a difference between asking about things politely and trying to get a reaction by being crass."

God, teenagers. I swear.

Her eyes gleam. "You were fucking!"

Padraig shoots her a look. "Isla, lass. Some things are between your mum and me and are none of your business"

"It's a yes." She grins, victorious.

"Eat your apples." He taps the table.

"I knew it." She smirks at me. "They way you looked at him in the video like you wanted to—"

"Isla Mae." My voice carries a warning, but I keep it gentle. "I'll always be honest with you, but part of being honest is knowing when to keep out of things. We're changing the subject. *Immediately*."

She studies us both for a beat, then shrugs. "Fine. But if you two get married, I want to be a bridesmaid."

Padraig blinks. "Bridesmaid?"

"Duh. It's the least you can do for your favorite stepdaughter." She pops another apple slice in her mouth like she hasn't dropped a small grenade into the room.

Before either of us can respond, her phone pings. She glances down, then up again. "Emmy's outside. We're going to her place." She grabs her hoodie and skips toward the gate. "Don't do anything I wouldn't do."

It shuts behind her and the yard falls quiet.

Padraig exhales, leaning back. "Holy fuck. We've got years of this ahead of us, don't we?"

"At least a decade between the lot of them," I deadpan.

He rubs a hand over his face, then grins. "Wait, are we actually alone?"

I'm a little dazed from the conversation with Isla but more psyched at the prospect of some grownup time with my man. "Seems like it. Betcha can't beat me upstairs..."

I'm across the yard, through the kitchen and halfway to the stairs before I'm airborne. He hooks an arm around my waist, hauls me up against his chest, and takes the steps two at a time. I shriek-laugh, pounding at his back while he throws me over his shoulder. His palm smacks my ass as he clears the landing.

"You forget I'm faster." He kisses my thigh.

I shriek with laughter. "Gammy leg, don't forget."

Upstairs in our bedroom, he tosses me onto the bed. My shorts ride up and before I can breathe, he's over me. Mouth on mine, stealing the air from my lungs. His knee wedges between my thighs, spreading me while his hands tear at my clothes.

"You've been thinking about this all day." I giggle against his mouth.

"Yes," he growls, voice thick with need. He catches my wrists in one hand and presses them to the mattress, while his other shoves my shorts and panties down in one impatient pull.

Letting my wrists go, he strips in a rush. The sight of his cock, thick, hard, and flushed, makes me arch, wet and aching for him. "Padraig—"

He lines himself up and drives into me in one long, deep thrust causing me to gasp. The stretch makes my toes curl, my heels dig into the mattress. He grinds all the way in, holding there until I'm squirming.

"Christ, you're heaven," he rasps as he recaptures my arms. Then he's moving. Relentless, each thrust hits my spot as it always does.

"Yes," I gasp, rocking up to meet him. My wrists twist against his hold, wanting to touch him, but he keeps me pinned. His thumb finds my clit and circles.

"Come for me," he orders. "I want to feel it."

It's instant. My orgasm crashes through my entire body.

Padraig lets my wrists go and I grip his ass, pulling him closer as he pounds into me, chasing his own release. He follows with a low, guttural sound, grinding deep as he spills inside me. For a long beat, he stays there, our breath loud in the quiet room.

He finally lifts his head, mouth brushing my ear. "Guess I won."

"Guess you did." I smile against his skin, catching my breath.

He kisses me slow, lazy, still inside me. "We've got time before they're home," he says, flipping me over so I'm straddling him. "Round two?"

"Only if I win this time."

By the time Isla gets home, Padraig and I are curled together on the couch, hair damp, a movie running low in the background. The click of the front door pulls me upright.

She drifts in, hoodie sleeves pulled over her hands, cheeks flushed from the warm night air.

"Hey," she says quietly, dropping onto the other end of the couch with her knees pulled tight.

Padraig mutes the TV. "Didja have a good night?"

"Yeah. I, um…" She gives a little shrug, eyes fixed on the carpet. "I'm sorry for being an ass earlier."

I turn toward her. "Isla—"

"No, let me…" She pushes her hair back, but her fingers tremble. "I miss Dad." Her eyes fill. "A lot. It's weird, because I like you." She glances at Padraig, then away. "I really like you. Which makes me feel…messed up? Like I'm betraying him or something."

Padraig's eyes mist, but he lets her speak.

"I don't want you to replace him," she says in a rush, swiping at her cheeks. "I know you're not trying to. I guess when we're all together, part of me is happy, and then I feel guilty for being happy. I hate feeling so confused."

I know the shape of her feelings. The push and pull between grief and connection. I've lived my own version, and

I've read enough therapy notes to know there's no quick way through it.

"It makes sense," I say softly. "You can miss your dad and like Padraig. Those feelings can live in the same space."

She sniffles. "I don't even know what I'm supposed to feel."

"You're not *supposed* to feel anything in particular." Padraig leans forward. "You feel whatever you feel. I'm here no matter what. And, if you want me to say 'feel' again say the word."

This earns a smile through the tears.

I open my arms. "Come here, baby. Give me a snuggle."

She hesitates for half a second before sliding toward me. Padraig shifts closer, wrapping one arm around both of us until we're a giant tangle on the couch. Isla hides her face in my shoulder, breathing unevenly. I stroke her hair, and Padraig presses a kiss to the top of her head.

For a long moment, none of us move.

The air feels steadier, anchored. She leans back between us, her head between our shoulders. We hold her until the tremors fade, anchored together in the quiet.

"We'll figure it out together," I tell her.

She nods, tucking her legs up under her.

It's a solemn reminder.

My kids lost their father too young.

As much as I'd love to protect them.

His loss will remain an ache for the rest of their lives.

Forty-One

Six Months Later

The table's been cleared, but the chaos clings.

An empty trifle bowl streaked with berry and cream and a constellation of sticky handprints no one's owning up to.

Across the room, Stevie's corralled the girls helping with cleanup. Isla clears plates to load into the dishwasher with theatrical sighs while Lila sings into the silverware. From the kitchen, I see glimpses of Ronni and Stevie wrapping up leftovers, laughing about something I can't hear. Seamus's girlfriend hands plates to Ma like she's done it a hundred times.

The rest of the us are sprawled out in the living room with full bellies and unfinished stories. The whole house glows.

Rafferty's knocked out against my chest, limbs slack, cheek smushed to my collarbone. I shift him higher, as I brace myself on the arm of Da's chair.

Ma's pulled it off again. Over twenty-one people are stuffed to the brim, and I doubt she broke a sweat.

Connor's on the floor with the twins, baby Teagan in the crook of his arm, trying to keep them from launching half-eaten mince pies into the fire. Seamus leans back against the sofa next to Liam and Cillian, who looks lighter. Clear eyed. His laughter doesn't sound forced. In fact, his dry wit has kept Liam quiet for a full ten minutes.

Then he flicks his glance toward me.

Stevie and the girls emerge from the kitchen and plop down cross-legged in front of the hearth. Lila tucks into her side and Isla sits quiet beside her. Jude spins in a slow circle, making spaceship noises, oblivious to the tension climbing in my shoulders.

I already know what's coming.

Liam stands and crosses over toward me. Stands in my space, arms folded like he's holding himself together with nothing but spite and soda water.

I hand Raff to Stevie, kissing his hair before I turn. "You've been staring a hole in my head for the last hour."

My comment breaks the tension wide open.

Liam straightens. "We finally get *SNL*."

Here we go.

He says it like it's sacrilege. Like I've pissed on a cathedral.

"We've been clawing for this for going on two decades," he goes on. "We're coming off the best two years of our entire career. All the tours, all the bullshit, everything we gave up. You took half the year off. We waited around for you. And now you want to *breathe*?"

I cross the room slow, holding his gaze. "Yeah. I do."

A beat of silence.

I pour a splash of apple juice into one of the kids' glasses and take a sip.

"We've been pushing for years," I repeat for the umpteenth time, hoping he'll fucking hear me in front of our entire family. "Maybe now's the time to slow down before we burn out. Or our private lives get us dragged through the mud."

His eyes flash.

Seamus clocks it from the corner, but says nothing. He's learned.

We all have.

Connor leans forward, arms crossed, calm as you please in his attempt to settle us down like we're his wee brothers and not nearly forty-year-old men. "It's not about now, lads. LTZ hit our peak and we ran ourselves into the ground chasing every next big thing. You remember how it ended for us."

The whole room grinds to a halt. Even the fire.

Ronni's hand rests over his bicep. "He's not wrong."

"Some things are bigger than the next big gig." I nod to Ronni.

Liam doesn't move right away. He stares over the rim of his soda, the fire catching the edge of the glass, then says what he knows I'm thinking out loud. "You want out."

He turns partway toward the room. Not all the way. Enough to glance around without settling on anything. His gaze skips over Ronni with the baby, over the girls whispering on the rug. Over Stevie. Over Rafferty, curled asleep in the corner like he doesn't exist.

"You're chasing a dream, Dar. The whole family thing. The quiet life. Pretending it's enough." His voice stays rough. Tight across the vowels. "It isn't real."

The world slows to a stop as I stare at him, slack-jawed.

He doesn't say Stevie's name.

Doesn't look at her. Not directly.

Hasn't since we walked in.

He hasn't asked about the kids. Never even mentioned Rafferty's birthday he missed four months ago.

He stands here, shaking his head at me, pretending he knows what's real.

I'm watching him unravel and try to take me down with him.

This isn't about the band.

It's about me.

It's about the life I built while I was away from him. A *truly* fulfilling life.

Because all of our children—hers and mine—belong to me now. I'm part of their every morning, every scraped knee, every bedtime story whispered in the dark.

He doesn't have any comprehension of what it means. Doesn't know where he fits into my new life.

When, for years, there was no line between us.

I gave him everything. From the beginning. Every win, every failure, every damn chord, every fucking hour I didn't spend with her when she decided to pursue her own dreams. Every night I stayed on the road when I wanted to be with her. Every moment I told myself Fireball was my only future.

When it wasn't. Not necessarily.

I wouldn't trade the time my brother and I had together for the music, for the bond we've both bled for.

Now, my life's pulling me in a different direction and he doesn't want to let me go.

Last time it cost me the only person who ever made the rest of it mean something. I let it happen. I thought if I held it together—no—if I held *him* together, it would all be okay.

I'm not doing it anymore.

For the first time in my adult life, I'm where I belong. Over the past couple years with Stevie, we've slowly built our foundation back piece by piece. We've had the hard conversations. I've earned every bruise trying to be the kind of man who's worthy of this family.

Nothing can break us apart this time. We're solid now. Real.

I'm choosing what makes me happy.

What grounds me are the people who depend on me. They aren't asking me to be someone I'm not.

Possibly, it's what bugs Liam the most.

My brother can't face what he's avoiding. Doesn't understand the reason he runs. So he's turning it on me. Pointing the finger. Calling my life a fantasy.

As if loving someone fully is naïve.

And choosing to stay means I'm weak.

It makes me sad. All I see is fear, buried under everything he's trying not to say.

Without me by his side, he's gonna have to face what's been chasing him.

I wonder if he can.

My attention is pulled back into focus to the kids when I see how his words have affected them.

Isla shifts on the rug. Lila frowns. Jude stops spinning.

"Hey." My voice cuts across the room, sharper than I intend.

He lifts his chin, daring me.

"You don't get to talk about my life like it's a fucking prop." I square up to him.

Connor clears his throat. "Lads…"

I breathe once, hard. Then again. "I love the band. Always will. But I'm not measuring success by late-night shows and backstage passes anymore. I've got a family. I've got four kids who know when I'm gone too long."

Liam gestures to them. "They'll survive."

Stevie rises slowly and stands by my side. She doesn't interrupt. She doesn't have to.

The weight of her presence says everything.

I feel Isla looking at me. Her gaze burns more than Liam's.

"I'm not chasing the same things you are anymore." I jab my finger in his direction. "I know it's hard for you to understand."

Liam's jaw flexes. "You think I don't have a life?"

I don't answer.

Because it's not about what he has or doesn't have now. He's afraid his version of love won't ever lead here. To this.

He blinks once, then turns toward the door. "You're a fucking pussy."

It's cruel. Meant to cut.

"Better than hollow," I murmur.

He stops walking. Doesn't turn.

Then keeps going. The front door doesn't slam, but the silence it leaves behind does.

Stevie encircles my wrist, and leans her head on my shoulder.

"I didn't mean for the confrontation to happen in front of them," I say under my breath.

"I know." Her voice is soft. "But, *he* did."

The room feels warped, stretched too thin. No one moves. The fire crackles, almost too loud.

Ma puts away a serving bowl with more force than needed. Cillian stands by the biscuit tin, unmoving. Seamus's girlfriend clasps his hand. Connor exhales slowly, looking toward the front door Liam disappeared through.

I lean down and kiss Stevie's hair. "Let's get them."

She nods.

We don't make a show of it. No apology. No excuse. I reach for Jude first, and he wraps his arms around my neck. Lila looks up, worried, already reading the air. Isla won't meet my eyes, which makes my heart hurt more than anything Liam said.

Rafferty's asleep in the corner, mouth open, one sock missing. I scoop him up in my other arm. Stevie gestures to the girls, guiding them gently toward the hall.

Ronni gives my arm a quiet squeeze as I pass. Ma says nothing, but her chin dips, barely. Connor watches me go like he wants to step in and fix it, but knows he can't.

We slip down the hallway toward the small guest room behind the stairs. Used to be Da's recovery room, years ago, before he got sober. It's remodeled now, clean, dimly lit, a folded quilt at the foot of the twin bed.

I set Rafferty down and let him keep sleeping. Jude stays in my lap. Lila climbs up beside Stevie without hesitation. Isla hovers by the wall.

"Sit, sweetheart," Stevie says gently.

Isla slides down slow. Knees pulled to her chest.

I glance toward Stevie, and she nods.

"Listen," I start. "What happened out there wasn't okay. Not in front of you."

"Was Uncle Liam mad?" Jude gazes up at me.

"He's upset, yeah." I run a hand through his curls. "But not at you. Never at you."

Lila frowns. "At us?"

"No, love," Stevie says quickly. "None of this is about you. It's about grown-up stuff. Band stuff."

"You're not going back on tour?" Isla says flatly.

"I used to think being in a band was the most important thing in my life." I lean toward her. "For a long time, it was. I gave everything to it. To Uncle Liam."

Stevie's hand finds mine, grounding me.

"Over the past couple of years of getting to know all of you, I realized the most important thing in my life was already here." I kiss Stevie's temple. "With your mom. Rafferty. All of you."

Jude leans his forehead against mine.

Lila sniffles. "Is he gonna stay mad at you?"

"Probably for a little while." I shrug. "He always comes back. We're twins."

Isla picks at her nail. "He really doesn't like us."

My breath catches.

Stevie takes over. "Isla, he doesn't know you. Not really. He's figuring out what it means to have a family."

Isla doesn't reply. She gets up and gives me a huge hug. I pull her into my side, arms wide enough to gather her and Jude and Lila at once. Stevie leans into the tangle of limbs, her hand pressed against Raff's back, the whole bed full of kids and tired hearts and everything I never thought I'd get to have.

I don't know what Liam's future holds.

Mine is in this room.

Forty-Two

STEVIE

Eighteen Months Later

Our house is full in every way that matters.

Steady love with Padraig. Our kids are blended and thriving. I have more business than I can keep up with.

Baby Kellan.

The only thing left is the ring.

Tomorrow I try on wedding gowns with my two daughters by my side. We were supposed to get hitched last year, but my pregnancy surprised us. In a good way. Kellan is soft, sleepy, perfect.

A baby I never thought I'd have. Not with Padraig. Especially at close to forty. The little guy has bound our family together in a way nothing else ever could.

Suddenly, we weren't two halves of a combined family anymore. Kellen bridges the gap.

The whole gang is here for dinner tonight. Padraig is out grabbing takeout. Kellan's on my hip, gumming a teething ring while I try to straighten up.

For some reason, Rafferty's crouched under the dining table whispering into the bottom of a walkie-talkie without batteries.

"Raff," I lean over, "what are you doing under there?"

He looks up, serious. "Secret practice."

"For what?"

He whispers in my ear. "Missions."

Of course.

Kellan and I head back to the kitchen where Lila's planted at the island with her phone balanced against a jar of peanut butter, watching a red carpet breakdown on TikTok while thumbing through one of my bridal magazines. She's already got opinions locked and loaded.

"You can't wear anything with cap sleeves," she advises without looking up. "They'll age you."

"I'm not sure I asked."

"You don't have to. I'm here for your protection." She circles something with a sharpie. "This one's perfect if we put your hair up and do a deep part."

I raise an eyebrow. "Whose wedding is this again?"

"Ours." She scrolls to the next video. "We're a package deal."

I'm about to fire back when I hear the front door click open. Jude barrels past us in socks, nearly wipes out.

"Raff!" Jude tears through the kitchen into the living room at full speed, arms flailing. "Mission's starting!"

"Hey! Slow it down. This isn't a Marvel stunt reel!" I lean into the hallway.

He crashes into the doorframe and recovers instantly. "I'm not stunting! We're on a time crunch!"

"For what?"

"Secret ops! I told Raff to stay hidden!"

"He's under the table." I gesture toward the dining room.

"Perfect. Sector Safehouse secured." He crouches and clicks an invisible earpiece. "Raff, come in. We're go for extraction."

From beneath the table, Rafferty responds, deadly serious, "Copy that. Time for snacks."

Kellan coos in agreement, drool sliding down my arm.

"Padraig's bringing home dinner, boys." I catch Jude's arm as he rushes past. "One Go-gurt each and nothing more."

Somewhere above the chaos, the front door opens.

The door opens behind me. Isla steps inside, her boots landing soft against the tile. She hangs her backpack on the hook, peels off her hoodie, and walks past me to the counter without a word. Phone in one hand, eyes fixed on the floor.

Something's off.

I set Kellan gently in his rocker and move toward her.

She pulls open the fridge and stares into it without moving. Then the pantry. Then back to the fridge.

I lean on the opposite side of the counter. "Hey."

"Hey."

"Hungry?"

Shrug.

"Rough day?"

Shrug.

"Want to talk about it?"

She exhales through her nose, then opens the cereal cabinet and yanks out the Cinnamon Toast Crunch. Pours herself a bowl and eats it dry.

"No milk?" I raise an eyebrow.

"No mood."

I wait.

She cracks first. "Remember the blood type project?"

"The one for biology?" I nod. "You already turned it in."

"Yeah, well..." She shifts in her seat, eyes on the cereal box. "Mr. Kwan handed them back today, and I got an incomplete."

I'm confused. Isla, for whom anything less than an A feels like failure, doesn't bring home incompletes. Not ever. "Why?"

"He said one of my answers doesn't work with basic genetics, so I must've written something down wrong." She digs into her backpack and pulls out a crumpled results sheet and the folded poster board we made together at this same counter.

She flattens the paper against the wood and taps the top with her finger. "See? It says I'm O positive. But you're O negative, right?"

"Right..." My voice feels too careful.

"And Dad was AB negative?"

"Yes."

She flips the poster open, revealing the neat Punnett squares we'd worked on. Each box filled in, some marked with red Xs. She jabs her marker at the one labeled "O child" under "AB × O," the big red X slashing through it. "This square's supposed to be impossible. AB and O can't make O. And two negatives can't make a positive. Mr. Kwan double-checked the chart himself."

Her tone is even, but she's watching me now, like somehow I'll be able to tell her what the obvious mistake is.

I can't. These are our blood types. So I don't really know what she's talking about or why her teacher would say such a thing.

Unless...

Mentally I go back in time, calculate quickly and realize...

The floor creaks behind us.

Padraig is there with bags full of food, gaze locked on the poster in her hand. Then on her face. Then on me.

She glances between us, confusion knitting her brow. "What?"

Neither of us answers. And in the space where words should be, the truth is deafening.

At least for Padraig and me.

Now's not the time, though.

"Let's go over it later." I reach for the food. "We should eat while the food's hot."

We manage to get through dinner. The kids chatter over cartons of pad Thai and spring rolls while I focus on wiping sweet chili sauce off Rafferty's chin instead of the silent, seething current running from Padraig toward me.

Isla, thankfully oblivious, disappears upstairs the second she's finished. Jude insists on reading Raff his favorite dinosaur book before bed. Lila helps me bathe Kellan before heading to her room.

By the time the house is finally quiet, my nerves feel scraped raw.

His back is against the headboard, eyes fixed on me when I set Kellan in the bassinet next to my side of the bed.

I study my son to give me a second to gear up for the conversation I'm about to have with Padraig. His perfect bow of a mouth, the curve of his cheek, faint crease between his brows. His brown eyes. All traits he's inherited from Padraig.

The thought comes before I can stop it.

Did Isla's baby face hold the same features of Padraig too? At dinner, it's all I could think about. They have the same facial features, same demeanor, artistic talent. Isla's blonde, but there's no mistaking, her and Padraig have the same brown eyes.

Why didn't I consider the possibility back then? I've never doubted she was Cooper's. When I got pregnant, he and I were off to the races in creating a perfect family.

Now, with her science project fresh in my mind and Padraig's gaze burning into me, the question lodges somewhere I can't reach.

I tuck the blanket around Kellan and decide to face him.

"What's going on?" I decide to let him broach the subject. "You're acting strange."

The heat in his eyes makes me stop. Not desire, or danger. More like extreme, crushing disappointment.

"The chart," he forces the words out. "The blood type thing. I heard the entire thing and it doesn't add up, Stevie. If those blood types were correct, she's not Cooper's."

Hearing the words spoken out loud is too much, my instinct is to deflect. "She thinks she wrote it wrong. She said—"

"We both know she didn't," he cuts in, sharper now. He gets out of bed and paces a tight line across the room. "I've been doing the math all night. Counting back. Thinking about the last time we fucked in New York." He swallows hard. "I thought we were reuniting and you were breaking it off."

Memories flood my mind of how intense it was.

The heat of his hands on my skin and the way we'd clung to each other like we could fuse ourselves together if we tried hard enough. It had been desperate and consuming. The kind of night burned into your soul forever.

Walking away after felt like ripping out my own heart.

I'd told myself I was doing the right thing. For him. For me. For the future we both deserved but couldn't find common ground on back then. I buried my ache under reason, convinced letting him go would give us both a better life.

I married Cooper and forced myself to lock away the past. Bury it under vows I made and took seriously. Immerse myself into the life he and I built and the family we made together.

If Coop hadn't died, I'd be with him. Kellan wouldn't exist.

I press my palms to the edge of the bassinet, trying to find the right words amidst the heaviness of all of this. Reconcile how my prior marriage sometimes feels like a ghost, comparatively. Flimsy and fading as Padraig and I navigate toward the future.

Overwhelming.

Padraig takes a step closer, eyes locked on mine. "Tell me what happened after you broke up with me."

"Um…" My throat works around the truth. "I… I don't want to hurt you."

His teeth clench. "For fuck's sake, Stevie. Too late."

I close my eyes for a beat, then force it out. "It was four or five days later."

"Had you fucked him before you fucked me when I was in New York?"

"No!" I sob. "No. I'd never…"

His eyebrow quirks like he doesn't believe me.

His immediate silence is sharp enough to slice my skin wide open.

Finally, he drags a hand down his face, shaking his head like he can't resolve the timeline. "You went from what we did to him in less than a week?"

"I wasn't like… I didn't plan—"

"You didn't *plan*?" He laughs without humor.

I swallow hard. Over these past few years, Padraig and I have told each other everything about our lives without each other. Warts and all. Until tonight, I thought there was nothing we didn't know about each other.

Except this. I fudged the timeline to spare his feelings. Not because I was trying to hide Isla's paternity, though I can see how anyone with a brain would think so.

"I was young and confused, Padraig. When he found out we broke up, he shot his shot and it happened. Being without you wasn't easy for me. Coop was my friend. He felt safe.

Familiar. We had so much in common, but I never planned to jump into another serious relationship so soon."

Padraig's on the verge of tears. "Did you know you were pregnant when you fucked him?"

"What?"

"Did you know you were pregnant and deliberately not tell me?" His voice cracks, suspicion lacing through every word. "Because if you did—"

"No! I didn't," I cut in, firm. "You know my periods were always sporadic until I was on the pill. We broke up and I went off it for a while. I'd started again a few weeks before you and I... Anyway, I found out I was pregnant a couple of months after Coop and I started dating. I didn't even question whose baby it was. He said we should get married and I told myself it was the right way to move on. I didn't know, Padraig. I promise."

He stares at me for a long moment. "I don't want to say something I can't take back, Stevie. None of it makes sense."

"Okay." It scrapes out of me, thin and unsteady.

"When you didn't get your period, weren't you suspicious?" He folds his arms and stares me down.

I mentally think back to the time right before I found out. "I remember spotting. I used pads. I thought it was my body adjusting to the birth control again."

His gaze flicks to Kellan, then back to me, sharp and unrelenting. "We need to get a DNA test. No more guessing."

The air between us feels heavy. Every breath loud in my ears. I keep my grip on the edge of the bassinet, holding on like it might keep the ground from shifting beneath me. "Padraig—"

"What if she's mine?" The words are barely more than a breath, but they slam into me all the same. Splintering through everything I thought was settled, leaving nowhere to hide.

Confusion rattles through me. There was never, ever a question in my mind. Isla was Cooper's. The math never mattered, because the possibility didn't exist. Until now.

"Did you tell him?" He winces.

"What?"

"Did you tell him how hard I fucked you when I was in town?" Padraig snarls, sounding more like Liam than himself. "When he 'shot his shot' was it because he knew you were thinking how many times I'd made you come?"

"I didn't tell him. He never knew about our night together," I whisper.

He scoffs. "This timeline makes me physically sick."

"We weren't together," I bark, shame curling in my stomach. "I was trying to move on."

The muscle in his cheek ticks. "You realize, if she's mine, you've stolen nearly eleven years with my daughter. You allowed another man to raise my *kid*."

Something inside him seems to snap on the last word. I step toward him on instinct. "Padraig—"

"Don't." He steps back and holds up a hand. "Don't touch me right now."

The rejection cuts deep, but he's already turning away, crossing the room to the closet. I hear a sharp scrape of a hanger. The thump of a backpack hitting the floor. He yanks clothes from the rod without looking at me, shoving them inside with short, angry motions.

When the zipper rasps closed, the sound rips something open in my chest.

"Please." Panic tightens my throat. "Don't leave."

He whirls on me, eyes flashing. "Taking a night to catch my breath after potentially life-changing news is not fucking leaving, Stevie." His voice aches with fury and hurt. "No matter what happens with us, I will never abandon my kids. Or yours. They're mine now. Every damn one of them. Don't you ever think otherwise."

The certainty in his words hits as hard as the anger. He slings the strap of the backpack over his shoulder, strides past me down the stairs. I hear the front door close with an echoing click.

I stand frozen for a moment, my heart pounding in my ears. Kellan shifts in the bassinet, making a small, restless sound. I lift him into my arms, his warm weight pressing against my chest, and carry him into bed with me.

Curling around him, I press my face into his soft hair, letting the tears come hot and fast.

My hand strokes his tiny back in slow circles while the rest of me shakes.

I have no idea if Padraig will walk back through the door tonight.

No idea if the truth will tear us apart or bind us closer.

All I know is, in the span of four hours, my life might have imploded.

Forty-Three

PADRAIG

Later

THE DOOR SHUTS BEHIND me, soft as a breath, and the townhouse swallows it whole.

My bag slides off my shoulder and thuds to the floor.

I make it to the sofa on muscle memory, sit, fold forward, hands over my face.

The first sound surprises me. A dry hitch. Then another. I suck air, miss, and my insides break open. Deep and ugly. Ribs working like bellows, shoulders shaking until my muscles burn.

Tears push hot across my knuckles. I try to slow the flood. Useless. Every breath brings the scene in the kitchen back:

Isla with her poster. The way Stevie's mouth trembled when she looked at me.

Now I know the truth. She fucked Cooper *days* after I thought we were getting back together.

How. Could. She?

I couldn't get it up for another woman for *two fucking years*.

I press my palms into my eyes until stars burst. Doesn't help. Images keep coming. First days of school I didn't see. Loose teeth I didn't pull. Jokes I never heard, fights I never broke up, songs I never taught. Years stack in a crooked tower across the room and I can't reach any of them.

It ebbs only when my chest gives up. I fall back into the cushions, throat raw, shirt damp at the collar. Silence moves in again, heavy as wet wool.

I stare at the ceiling until it blurs.

I can't sit inside my head alone. Not tonight.

Unlocking my phone, I hover my thumb over his name.

We haven't spoken since the New Years Eve show with LTZ, what was supposed to be my last gig with the band. He was cold. Angry. It hurt, but I didn't change my mind.

Pride tries to pull my hand away. I hit call before it wins.

Two rings. Liam fills the screen, hair in his eyes, a square of dim kitchen behind him.

He blinks when he sees the state of me. Sits up fast. "Jesus. You alright?"

I shake my head. No sound comes.

"Okay." He focuses on me like he used to back in the days after Da's accident. Counts my breaths. "You with me?"

I nod, swallow. "Don't know where to start."

"Anywhere." He leans closer. "Start with the feeling."

"Empty." The word scrapes. "Torn open."

"Alright." He waits. Doesn't rush. "What happened?"

I comb through my hair, find a knot, pull until it hurts. "I keep seeing her face." I'm hoarse from crying. "Isla. Standing in our kitchen with questions Stevie can't answer."

"Okay. I'll admit. I'm lost."

"Dar." I look straight into the camera because I can't say it to a wall. "Tonight I found out she might be mine."

He doesn't speak. His eyes hold steady, like he heard me before I said it. "Come again?"

"Isla might be mine."

He exhales, slow and clean. "Alright. Well. Fuck." His gaze sharpens. "Why'd you think?"

"Some school project. A science blood-type thing." I can't get the visual out of my head. "She got an incomplete because Coop's type and Stevie's type don't make her type. One look at the results and it hit me square in the heart. No working it around, no easing into it. I *knew*."

Liam shuts his eyes, processing.

"I had it out with Stevie. We tore it apart, every angle. She swears she didn't know, but the timing..." I let the silence finish it for me. "She fucked Cooper four, maybe five days after she was with me in New York. It lines up."

"No shit?"

"In my head, she's mine. Has been since Stevie and I got back together. In my heart, too. Now, she's my actual blood. I've got no proof yet. I can feel it, though." Tears leak out of my eyes again. I'm so overwhelmed.

Liam sighs heavily. "Jesus, Dar."

I wipe at my face with the heel of my hand, but more tears slide out. "I don't even know what to do. I feel like my chest's split open."

"Breathe." He leans closer to the screen. "Try and breathe."

"That's all I've been doing since I left the house. Big, empty breaths." My voice cracks. "I keep thinking about the years. All the shit I missed. I don't know how to live with the loss if it's true."

"Then don't."

I frown. "Don't what?"

"Don't live with it like it's a punishment. You're already the father figure in her life. If she's officially yours, what's changed? You make the years you've got matter more than the ones you lost."

I look at him through the blur, trying to believe this woo-woo advice is actually coming from him. "You think it's simple?"

"It's not. It's worth it."

My eyebrows raise to the sky. Is this my brother?

He smirks faintly. "Don't look so shocked. Now, tell me exactly what went down with Stevie."

"What do you mean?"

"I mean, you said you had it out?" He leans back in his chair. "What was said and how did she say it? Did she freak out? Don't give me the shorthand."

I recount the story in as much detail as I can. "She swore she didn't know. And if I'm honest…" I exhale, eyes dropping for a second. "She seemed as shocked as I was."

"Then maybe she really didn't. You know Stevie, she's not a liar. If she looked blindsided, she probably was." Liam rubs his mouth, watching me through the screen.

I shake my head. "But she knew the timing. It had to cross her mind."

"Think about it, Dar. She'd been with you forever, then broke it off and suddenly found herself pregnant with a guy she'd barely started dating." Liam's arms are folded around his chest. "She was probably scared shitless he'd think she trapped him. It might never have crossed her mind to question it. Should it have? Maybe. But only she knows the answer."

I shake my head glumly. "Did I mean so little to her?"

"Get the fuck out of town. No woebegone bullshit. Look at the life you have now. The one you left our band for?" Liam shakes his head. "She did what people do when they're gutted. Grab what's right in front of them. I understand how it is. Besides, you've already lived with the hurt of her moving on for years. This doesn't make it new. You're over it."

I stare at him. "My first thought when I saw the paper was she knew I got her pregnant, told Cooper it was his and he swooped in to take my place."

"Jesus, Padraig." Liam sounds exasperated. "Does lying intentionally sound like our Stevie? *Nah*. If you stay locked in the 'how could she,' you'll eat yourself alive. You already replayed the movie on repeat. For fucking years."

My laugh comes out jagged. "What about Isla? She's sixteen. She knows pieces of who Stevie and I were back in the day. If she learns the man she's called Dad all her life isn't…" My voice trails off. "What will it do to her to find out it's me? She'll feel so betrayed by both of us."

"Isla already looks at you like you're her da. The ground might shake, sure, but it'll steady. You'll be the reason. Lila and Jude, they'll take their cues from her. It'll be a storm, but kids survive storms if love's holding the walls up. Look at our family, what happened to us was a hell of a lot more devastating." Liam takes a pull from his soda can.

I try to soften the bitter edge in my throat. "You sound like you've been taking night classes in therapy."

"Aye." He gives a half shrug. "Or maybe I'm watching my twin bleed out and trying to keep him upright for once."

The corner of my mouth twitches, but it's nowhere near a smile. "You're not wrong. Feels like I'm bleeding from the inside out."

"Then don't do it alone." He narrows his eyes. "You need to go back home."

I shake my head as I pace the length of the room. "I don't even know where to start. With her. With Isla. With myself."

"Start with the truth. Get the test done, face it head-on." He points at me. "Then you man up. Deal with whatever comes."

I scrub at my face, desperate to shift the focus. "What about you? How're you holding up?"

Liam shakes his head hard. "No. Don't."

"Don't what?"

"Turn it back on me." His voice firms, leaving no room for argument. "You've done this our whole lives, Dar. Looked after me, carried me, made my storms the bigger story. I've let you. Relied on you. Not tonight. I'm fine. This isn't about me." He leans closer to the screen, eyes cutting through me. "This is the first time I can remember you calling me in a crisis. The first time you've let me be the one to hold you up. So let me. Don't reach for my pain to take the weight off yours. Sit in it. I can handle mine. Tonight, I'm here to help with yours."

Tears stream down my face. I feel broken. Also, seen. I realize how much of my resentment toward my twin has stemmed from exactly what he's admitted.

"You fought me like hell to leave the band. You stood up to me and chose your family. Challenged me to rely on the people who love me." His emotions mirror mine, and I'm surprised to see his eyes well up with tears too. "Don't throw your family away now. Whatever's happened tonight, don't abandon them. Not after everything you sacrificed to be there."

The silence between us stretches, thick with everything we've said and everything we haven't. My chest heaves, tears sliding unchecked.

"I missed you," I choke out, the words foreign on my tongue after so long apart.

Liam blinks hard, a tear finally breaking loose down his cheek. "Christ, Dar. I missed you too. More than I'll ever admit to anyone else. You're my other half. Always have been."

My throat burns. "We've spent our whole lives side by side. From the worst nights at home to tour buses for twenty years. No one knows me better than you. Being estranged from you has gutted me."

"Same." He nods, tears streaking his face now. "I gave you shite for walking away, but truth is, I wasn't angry you left the band. I was angry you left me. Felt like I'd lost my twin for good."

The ache in my chest softens. "You never lost me. Not really."

"Good." He furiously wipes tears with the heel of his hand. "Because I couldn't survive it."

For a beat, we stare at each other across the screen. Two halves of the same whole. Cracked but never broken.

"I love you, Liam," I manage, voice splintering.

"I love you too, Padraig." He breathes it out like a vow. "No matter what."

We both hesitate, neither wanting to end the call. Finally, he nods. "Get some sleep. You'll need it."

"Yeah." I warble through emotion. "Talk tomorrow?"

"Aye. Give me the update."

The screen goes dark, leaving me in the quiet of my empty townhouse.

Lighter somehow.

The weight of what's in front of me shifted by knowing my brother's still with me.

Always.

Forty-Four

STEVIE

The Next Morning

I'M STIFF UNDER THE covers.

I haven't slept.

Kellan's curled against me, his little hand tangled in my shirt, while my brain runs jagged circles.

Every time my eyes close, the night replays. Isla's trauma at getting an incomplete. The way Padraig looked at me. The tension at dinner as we tried to act normal in front of all the kids.

The argument. Him walking out. Rightfully so.

God, the sound of the zipper on his bag.

I cry until my chest aches, then force myself into furious scrolling, phone lighting the dark room as I dig through articles and forums about paternity revelations, blended families, teens blindsided by truth.

None of it helps.

How do you protect a sixteen-year-old from having her entire foundation ripped out from under her? Every answer contradicts the last. Some parents recommend honesty at once. Others warn of devastation.

My thumb trembles as I swipe, because I already know in my heart. Isla is Padraig's. I don't need a DNA test to prove it.

Their similarities blaze like neon.

Isla's eyes *are* Padraig's. Not because they're the same shade of brown. Both of them carry more than they give away.

I never thought about her wavy strands of hair she fights with a straightener, same texture as Padraig's, even if the color's different.

The sketches crowding the margins of every notebook page, hours vanishing into creating art the way Padraig used to before the band consumed him.

They have the same drive, when they're focused. Unyielding and relentless once they take their sweet time deciding on a path. Until then, a bit flighty. Petulant.

God, her silences can sink a room. The way she shoulders responsibility no one asked her to—all Padraig. The instinct to protect and give herself away for the ones she loves.

All his pieces stitched into her.

How did I not see it before?

Cooper was thrilled when I told him I was pregnant. He pulled me close, called it fate. I let myself lean into his conviction, desperate to make the story true. She came out blonde and calm, the perfect blend of me and him, so it never occurred to me she wasn't his.

He died *believing* she was his. Gave up his life for her.

How do I reconcile the fact we created an entire family around a lie?

I robbed Padraig of his daughter.

I feel sick.

Clutching Kellan tighter, I press my lips to his head. Tears soak his baby hair. He stirs but doesn't wake.

Four kids plus Rafferty, who comes here so often I'm his second mother. We've built this amazing patchwork of children and family, entwined the Hayes with the McGloughlins into one sprawling mess of roots.

Somehow, I've shattered the ground beneath us.

At the end of the day, none of this isn't about me. Or Padraig.

Our hearts can break a thousand times over. We'll survive it. Maybe not together, but we'll persevere through the pain.

No, this is about Isla. My girl's already lost the father she thought was hers. I have to protect her when the truth she never asked for comes crashing in.

My phone slips from my hand to the mattress. I bury my face in Kellan's neck and sob again, because I don't know how to fix this. I don't even know if Padraig will stand beside me to try. Inadvertently, I may have pushed him right out of my life, this time for good.

The sky outside the window bleeds gray when the door opens. My whole body tenses.

Padraig slips into the room before dawn, quiet as though he doesn't want to wake me. My eyes are open anyway, raw from crying. Kellan shifts against my chest and I press my palm over his small back as if I can shield us both.

He stands there a moment, shoulders slumped, shadows carved into his face.

His eyes find mine in the half light. "What are we gonna do, Stevie?"

Tears rise again before I can stop them. "I don't know. I failed you. Both of you. I swear to God, I never knew. Now...it's all I see. Every expression, every silence, every bone in her body. It's you. It was *always* you."

Padraig stares at the floor like he's holding the weight of sixteen years on his back.

"I'm sorry," I whisper. "I don't know how I didn't see it. I don't know how I let you miss her whole life."

He exhales through his nose, slow and heavy. "What do we do now?"

"We have to put our own feelings aside, I think. Stop pretending we have a choice." I clutch our son tighter against me. "We put her first. No more secrets. No more protecting ourselves—well, me."

His gaze flicks to mine, torn.

"I can't go dress shopping today for a wedding we shouldn't have. Not when everything's broken open," I continue. "I want your opinion on this, but I think Isla deserves to know immediately. She's not a child anymore. We ask our moms to watch the kids and we sit down with her. Together. Before we do anything else. The three of us."

Padraig's shattered groan catches in his chest. "She's going to hate us."

"None of this is your fault. She'll hate me for a while, not you. You'll need to be there for her, whatever it takes." My voice wavers at the thought of hurting my eldest child but I push through. "She needs to know we didn't shut her out when we realized the situation. At the end of the day, she comes first."

The air thickens between us until he finally nods.

Not agreement, not forgiveness. The faintest thread of resolve.

He climbs into bed and takes Kellan. We lie beside each other until it's bright and then get up and start the day.

The morning crawls, thick with unspoken words. Padraig and I move through the usual motions using muscle memory to guide us through our mental and physical exhaustion. He cooks breakfast for Rafferty and Jude, I change and breast feed Kellan.

Every look between us feels like a deep, purple bruise.

By the time Maureen knocks softly on the front door, I'm strung out on nerves and no rest. She takes Kellan without asking, clucking over his chubby cheeks, promising she'll keep the little ones busy. Relief and guilt twist together in my chest.

Upstairs, Isla and Lila shuffle around, still in pajamas, hair wild. I call them into our room. Lila flops onto the bed with a dramatic sigh, Isla hovers in the doorway, wary.

"We're going to have to postpone the dress shopping today." I try to keep my voice upbeat. "Something's come up. Everything is fine, I promise, but we need to reschedule."

Lila groans loud enough to rattle the windows. "You've got to be kidding me." She stomps off, mumbling about wasted weekends. Slams her door for emphasis.

Isla stays rooted to the carpet, eyes sharp on me. "It's not fine. I heard you and Padraig last night."

"Sweetheart—" The bottom drops out of my stomach hoping she didn't hear the details.

Her chin lifts, defensive. "You were fighting."

"We were." I almost deny it but, what's the point.

"Hey, sweetheart." Padraig steps in from the hall to save me. "Everyone argues. None of it is cause for any concern. We do need to talk, Isla. The three of us without the other kids."

She looks between us, suspicion etched into every line of her face. "Talk about what?"

"Not here." I brush a strand of hair behind her ear. "We're going to go out for a bit. You and me and Padraig. We'll explain then."

Padraig drives, his knuckles white around the wheel. I sit in the passenger seat beside him, every nerve on fire, fighting the urge to reach for his hand when I'm not sure he'd take it. Isla sits in the back blasting something through her earphones, like a shield. The unease in her eyes says everything.

Neither of us speak until we pull up to his townhouse. It's early so the street is quiet. We decided to come here so there's no risk of someone recognizing him in a public place. The subject matter is too risky.

Isla eyes the townhouse like it's a test she hasn't studied for. "Why here?"

"Because we need privacy." Padraig cuts the engine and turns, finally meeting her eyes. "This isn't something we can talk about anywhere else."

She looks between us, searching, her brows knitting. "You're scaring me."

"We're not trying to." I twist in my seat to face her fully. "There's something you need to hear from us together. It's important."

We get out and Padraig unlocks the door to let us inside. Isla lingers in the entryway, backpack slung off her shoulder, waiting.

He gestures toward the couch. "Sit."

She doesn't move right away. She studies him. The same way I do when I'm trying to figure out what's up. She finally plows through the door and lowers herself onto the cushion. Arms crossed tight, phone clutched like a lifeline.

I sit beside her, Padraig across, so she has us both in her sightline. My heart drums so hard it's all I hear.

Steadying myself, I curl my fingers against my knee. "There's more to the story of me and Padraig than you know. You're old enough now to hear it and you deserve the truth."

Isla's chin tips up, cautious, but she doesn't look away.

Padraig leans forward. "The first time I saw your mom was when she moved in next door. We were seven. Even then I felt something I couldn't explain. She was my person before I had the words for it." His throat catches. "By the time we were your age, we already knew it was more than friendship. We were each other's firsts in every way. First love. First sexual experiences. We went to college together. Lived together. Your mom was the center of my world. Our bond was unbreakable, or so we thought."

Isla's mouth drops open with shock.

"For years we built our lives around each other." Padraig's eyes shadow over. "Until adulthood pulled us apart. I had the band, your mom moved away to New York to pursue her career. Neither of us knew how to close the distance without losing ourselves."

I exhale, taking over the story. "I met Cooper at work. We were in the same friend group. When Padraig and I broke up he'd already broken up with his girlfriend and we became good friends. It turned into more when I ended it with Padraig for good. He and I started dating and I got pregnant with you right away. We got married at the courthouse before I started showing and created an amazing life with you, your sister, and brother until..."

"He died." Isla crosses her arms, fingers absently tracing over the scars from the accident.

Her words cut through me, sharp.

"Yes. He died. It broke all of us."

Padraig shifts and braces his elbows on his knees, hands locked tight. "Isla, yesterday, when you came home from school and told us about the incomplete. Something happened for both your mum and me. We looked at each other and it clicked."

Her eyes narrow, arms crossed. "What clicked?"

"Um…" I swallow hard. "It made me consider something I'd never even thought about, but, it's possible—" my voice wavers "—Padraig might be your biological father."

Isla's mouth drops in horror. "*What*?"

"Isla." Padraig keeps his eyes steady on her. "From the time I came back into your mom's life, I've always thought of you as mine. *Always*. Yesterday it all shifted. It felt like the truth has been sitting there, waiting for us to face it."

"Wait." Isla blinks, color rising in her cheeks. "So you're saying my dad might not actually be my dad?"

I reach for her hand. "No, he'll always be your dad. He loved you with everything in him. This discussion isn't about taking him away. It's including you in a situation we find ourselves in and making sure you are part of deciding how we move forward. Whether you want to get a blood test to find out for sure. This is a lot of information. Shocking information and I can't promise your mother and me know what we're doing, but we didn't want to take further steps until we brought you into the decision making."

She turns to me, her eyes sharp, wet and furious. "How could you not know? How…gross!"

The words slice straight through me. "I *didn't* know. Cooper loved you from the second I told him I was pregnant but I would have never let Padraig be cut out of your life if I ever suspected he was your biological father."

"Bullshit." Her fists ball at her sides. "What kind of person are you?"

Tears blind me, and I shake my head. "I'm your mother."

Her face crumples through the fury, tears blurring her eyes. "I don't know who you are, but no mother would willingly put their kid through *this*."

Before I can reach for her, she turns, clutching at Padraig's shirt like he's the only solid thing left in the room. He pulls her in, arms closing around her as if he's been waiting her whole life to hold her this way.

She buries her face in his chest, sobs shaking her small frame.

"I've got you, *mo chroí*," he whispers into her hair. "No matter what. I've got you."

I press my hand to my mouth, grief and awe colliding.

Even in her rage and confusion, Isla went to Padraig. Straight to him.

How am I going to live with myself?

Forty-Five

Three Weeks Later - Christmas Day

CHRISTMAS SHOULD FEEL WARMER than this.

After all, the entire McGloughlin house is full of festivity.

Brennan and Cillian, arms around their wives, talk loudly about their plans for babies on the way. Seamus beams as he passes his baby son, Elias around.

Marcella, his wife, brought her entire family this year. For the first time ever, Ma has a rival in the kitchen. Marcella's chef sister, Rosa, has cooked every one of the Delgado Christmas delicacies. Da planted himself in the kitchen, tasting everything as it comes out of the oven while Marcella's father tells stories about their restaurant.

Liam's in the middle of the fray, laughing harder than I've seen in years at Torin, Tristan and Jude, who rip paper, shout over toys and spread the mess of joy across the floor. Lila helps Raff with his Lego tower while Teagan attempts to knock it over every time they make progress.

It should be everything I ever wanted.

Instead, I feel like crawling under a rock.

Stevie should be here.

I glance over at sullen Isla. Curled into the corner chair, eyes fixed on her phone, stubbornly pretending she doesn't notice her mother's absence. The test confirmed what I already knew in my bones. Isla is mine. She always was. Knowing it hasn't made any of this easier.

Instead, it led to a fight so brutal between the two of them, Stevie told me to take her to my townhouse for a while to cool off. "A while" has turned into three weeks where she refuses to be in the same house as her mother.

I tell myself time will help. Therapy gives us tools. Patience. The younger kids absorb more than I expect, but nothing soothes the fracture. I see Stevie's face every night, hear her voice every morning. She's in agony. I hate she's next door without her kids while I'm here pretending to celebrate with most of them.

Stevie and Kellan are spending his first Christmas at her parents' house. Isla refuses to speak to her, so this was the compromise. Split up the family when she should be here and we should be there. Every part of me aches for us to be together, messy or not, figuring it out in the open.

Instead, Isla's anger has stretched into something seemingly unfixable.

Dinner passes by as noise swells and laughter rises around us. During dessert, I watch Seamus and Marcella slip outside with Elias and wonder how long until I can get the fuck outta here.

The front door opens. I glance up, expecting Seamus and Marcella to come back inside.

Instead, my whole body stops.

Stevie.

She steps inside with her coat open, hair swept up, cheeks red from the cold. Too familiar in this family to feel like a guest.

My immediate reaction is to cross the room and invite her in. Get everything aired out in front of the entire family.

Then Isla shifts in the corner, shoulders stiff, eyes darting up for the first time all night.

I realize now's not the time. Not tonight. Not like this.

The words tear out of me before I can think. "You shouldn't be here."

Everyone in the room halts, shocked. Connor's glass hangs halfway to his mouth. Liam's brows lift, sharp and curious. I'd made a lame excuse about her spending the day with her own family and with all the chaos of the day, no one has said a word.

Now, all eyes are darting between the two of us, including all of our kids.

Yet, Stevie doesn't flinch. Her gaze finds mine, steady as ever. "I know."

It lands like a stone dropped in water, ripples spreading into every corner of the room. My feet carry me out before anyone speaks, the hall stretches long and dark. Behind me, I hear the whisper of her steps following.

I push through the door to the guest room and sink down onto the edge of the bed, staring at the floorboards like they might give me answers. Weeks of silence and slammed doors play back through my head. Enduring the near silence in the townhouse where I convinced myself I was protecting her. Holding the pieces together with patience and hope.

All its done is let the fissure in our family spread.

The door closes behind Stevie, shutting us away from the awkward laughter and clatter in the kitchen.

Her face is pale, eyes rimmed red, but there's steel in her spine. "This isn't working, Padraig. We can't go on like this."

"What could I do?" I press my palms to my knees. "She wouldn't look at you. Wouldn't even stay in the house. I thought giving her space might—"

"No. She needs us. Not space. Not silence," Stevie interrupts me. "Her world has been ripped apart. She's angry. Betrayed. All of the things. She's a teenager. She can't fix it alone. Isla needs *both* parents to show up. Even when it's brutal for one of us. Right now, we're letting her grief steer this family off a cliff."

The truth of it rips through me. I thought I was shielding Isla, but I've been hiding. Taking her pain onto my shoulders until it weighs on everyone else too.

"I don't want her to feel abandoned." I squeeze my eyes shut. "Not by me. Not ever."

"You did *not* abandon her." Stevie kneels in front of me, grounding me with her presence. "But you *are* abandoning yourself. And us. We have four other kids who need their dad. We can't keep living apart if we're going to get through this. If it takes counseling every single day, then we do it. But together. Not split down the middle."

Her hand slips into mine. "I love Isla more than life. This entire situation kills me. I can't stand by and watch you disappear into her pain. We have to lead as parents. United. Even if she hates us for a while. *Especially* then. I know all of this hurts you too. It's time to put it aside."

The words sting, but they lift something too. I squeeze her hand. "So what do we do?"

"If you love me and our family," her eyes shine with tears, "we face it. All of it. Together. *Now.*"

Her certainty pins me, and for a long moment I can't speak. Finally, I let the words out. "I know you didn't keep her from me on purpose. I see it in you, every time you look at us."

Her shoulders drop, relief cutting through her tension, but I don't let her exhale fully before I go on. "But, Stevie... I've had a daughter all these years and I didn't know. I've missed birthdays, first days of school, nights she cried herself to sleep, all of it. There's a hole I don't know how to fill. I can't pretend it doesn't hurt or sweep it aside because it's easier."

Tears slip over her cheeks. She doesn't try to defend herself, which almost breaks me more than if she'd fought. I take her in my arms and press a kiss to her temple. "I need you to let me work through this. I won't run from it, but it's not something I can fix with one promise. It's going to take time. For me, for Isla, for us."

Her breath shudders against my lips, but she nods. "Then we'll give it time, but can we do it together?"

"Aye, baby." I nod furiously. "Yes."

For the first time since everything came to light, I feel the ground steady under me. Not solid, not safe. Something squishy I can stand on while my core tightens. I let myself believe maybe we'll find our way back. Not only to Isla, but to all of us.

"Why don't you go get her," Stevie encourages.

I stand and make my way down the hall. The living room's bustling with activity. Isla's on the couch, legs pulled up, arms crossed tight. She looks up when she hears me, eyes full of suspicion.

"Let's go talk." I gesture for her to follow me. "It's time to clear the air."

She shakes her head. "No. I'm fine here."

"Aye, well." I gesture more forcefully. "Nevertheless, let's go. *Please.*"

For a beat, she studies me to see if I'm being serious. Which I am. Deadly. A moment later, she stands and shoves her phone into her hoodie pocket. Rather than following me, Isla pushes past me and heads for the bedroom. I follow, feeling every ounce of her stubbornness.

When we close the door behind us, Stevie stands. "Merry Christmas, sweetheart."

Isla doesn't answer. She hovers by the dresser, arms folded, chin tilted up like armor.

I take a breath. "We don't want to overwhelm you. The New Year is around the corner, and it's time to start finding a way through this, Together."

"Together?" she scoffs. "You didn't even know I was yours until a few weeks ago."

The words sting because they're meant to. "You're right. I didn't. We all found out the same moment you did. It's been tough for all of us to wrap our minds around for different reasons. We've spent the last couple of months focused on what it means for you. What it takes from you."

She doesn't look at me.

Stevie steps closer. "Honey, I swear to you. I never knew. If I had, everything would've been different. I would've told Cooper. I would've told Padraig."

"You expect me to believe you?" Isla snaps, tears flashing.

"Listen to me, Isla." I wrap my arm around her stiff shoulders. "Your mom didn't mean to keep this from you or from any of us. Cooper never knew either. He died believing he was your biological dad. This situation wasn't some scheme."

She shrugs me off her. "Wait, you're suddenly fine with all of this? She let another man raise me. You don't care you missed out on my whole life? She must have a golden pussy."

Stevie cries out in anguish.

"Isla Mae," I admonish, though the anger in her voice twists deep in my gut. "No, I'm not fine with it. I hate it. I wish more than anything I'd had those years with you. None of us can change the past. What I need you to know is this.

I've loved you as if you were mine from the second I met you. I never wanted to take Cooper's place. He was your dad, and I respected your relationship with him. Me being your biological dad doesn't erase him. It never could."

Her lip trembles, and for the first time she lets her arms fall.

"I get you're going through it." I turn her so she's facing me and tip her chin up to look me in the eyes. "Let me be clear about one thing. Do not speak to your mother disrespectfully ever again. What you said to her was abhorrent."

Stevie quietly sobs behind us. "I don't know how to fix this. I don't."

The room goes quiet as I release my daughter and turn to the woman I love. Isla drags her sleeve over her cheek, sniffing hard. I can see the storm in her. Anger, grief, confusion. She's sixteen, and the ground beneath her keeps shifting.

We all turn to the door when a soft, hesitant "tat tat tat" echoes in the room.

"Come in," I rasp.

The door cracks. Da peeks in first, Liam close behind him. Stevie starts to shake her head, but I hold my hand up. "Let them in."

My twin and father step inside carefully, as if approaching three wounded animals, which I suppose we are.

Rory's eyes land on Isla, and he softens in a way I rarely see. "Lass. I'm not here to meddle. I only want you to know something. I was a terrible father for a long time. Made mistakes that'll haunt me till the day I die. And the worst part of mistakes is how they fester, how they make everything rot from the inside. Don't let this do the same to you. Your mum—" he gestures at Stevie "—I've known her since she was a wee girl. She's kind, strong, fierce when it comes to protecting the ones she loves. She would never hurt you on purpose. Not ever."

Isla's eyes widen a fraction.

Liam steps forward then. "As for him," he gestures toward me, "Padraig's my twin. He's my soul. He's the best of us. Selfless to a fault. He'll give everything he has away and think nothing of it. But what he deserves, what he's *always* deserved, is for his family to be whole. All of it. Not just you, your brothers and sister too. You're what keeps him breathing. I hope you can forgive both of them, because I can't watch him break."

His voice cracks on the last word.

I'm speechless. Stevie and I aren't alone in helping to mend Isla's trust. The McGloughlins are stitching ourselves back together, too.

Isla swallows hard. "You make it sound so easy."

"No, love. It won't be easy." Stevie shakes her head. "It'll take time. Patience. Forgiveness. But we'll walk through it with you every step. You don't have to figure it out alone."

For the first time all night, Isla doesn't argue.

She sinks onto the bed between us, her body rigid but present. Da and Liam slip out, leaving the three of us alone.

I reach out, and after a long pause, she lets me take her hand.

A small step toward a new future.

STEVIE

Epilogue – Six Months Later

MY DRESS HANGS FROM the closet door.

I bought a simple silk sheath with a low back. No train. No corset. No lace shouting for attention. The skirt whispers when I move. The neckline sits where I can breathe.

Mom attached a thin ribbon from her own wedding dress as a belt, checking "old," "new," and "borrowed" off the list.

Joni pins a small sprig of a blue-violet delphinium into the low knot she coerced my hair into for the "blue" factor. "Hold still or I swear I'll hot-glue your head to this chair."

"So romantic." I smile at her through the mirror.

"She heard Grandpa tell the story about Grandma's veil catching fire on a candle." Lila slathers on lip gloss. "I think she's trying to create a TikTok moment."

Mom laughs from the cedar chest as I slip the dress over my head. "No, she's probably remembering the time I made red glitter hair bows for some school pageant. Those suckers shed for three entire Christmases."

Her fingers shake when she ties the ribbon around my waist. She looks so proud. Her eyes, rimmed pink already, feature lines I never noticed before. I glance at the bed where Padraig and I spent our teenage years exploring our sexuality. It's hard to believe it's over twenty years later. Back then we didn't have a clue the years to come would blow us sideways.

Joni squeezes my wrist. "How are you doing?"

"Good." I smooth my dress over my hips. "Better than I thought I would be."

Isla snorts with a snicker. "You look calm. Scary calm."

"Must be the therapy," I jest. "Progress *feels* real though."

Mom's mouth lifts. "Progress looks real too."

"Does progress mean not hiding in the pantry crying over a science chart," Joni deadpans, then flinches at her own joke. "God. Too far?"

"It's okay." Isla laughs with ease. "Not everyone gets two amazing dads."

Her hair falls in soft waves. A charcoal smear stains the side of her hand from last night's sketch. She's wearing a borrowed dress of mine after deeming the one she chose last week too "juvenile." She and I have come a long way. We're not perfect. We step on landmines occasionally, which is to be expected, considering.

Lila taps the gloss against her palm. "Iz, can I be nosey?"

"You always are." She quirks a brow.

"Are you meeting Kane after?" She tries for nonchalant and lands somewhere near flashing sign.

Isla shrugs. "Maybe. Depends on what we're all doing. A few friends have a bonfire planned, Kane said he might come if I go."

Joni waggles her brows. *"Might."*

Mom pretends to fuss with the ribbon so she doesn't grin. I keep my face calm on purpose. Pushing works like a broken clutch with Isla; everything lurches or burns out. It's hard to know if she returns Kane's interest. Lila, on the other hand, can't keep her infatuation with Isla's suitor under wraps to save her life.

"Well, maybe I'll tag along." Lila twirls in front of the mirror.

Footsteps thump in the hall. Dad's voice floats up the stairs, then a quick knock on the door. He leans in before he steps in, as if crossing thresholds requires permission in a house he paid for. His tie sits crooked like it always does, the man hates to dress up.

"You ready, kiddo?"

I cross the room and kiss his cheek. "Ask me in five minutes."

"Want a shot? I won't tell Padraig." He winks.

"Give me your arm instead."

Dad juts out his elbow with mock formality. Joni presses my bouquet into my palm. No roses. No peonies. More delphinium, a sprig or two of garden jasmine, some sweet peas all tied together with the other ribbon from Mom's dress.

We move toward the stairs in a cluster. Joni runs back to fetch shoes I forgot to put on in my haze. Lila and Isla fall in behind me as we go downstairs and through the kitchen to the backdoor.

Mom strung a length of muslin between the plum tree and the fence to soften the light near the arch Cillian built for us. Padraig's brothers wound cafe bulbs across the yard last night, and set up tables and chairs until midnight.

Voices drift over the hedge from next door where the McGloughlins must be in the middle of their own pre-ceremony circus. Seamus laughs at Marcella shushing Elias, who's singing some song at the top of his lungs. Brennan and Cillian argue over grill duties. Rory grumbles about needing an extension cord and Maureen tells him to hush before he trips over one.

I catch sight of Liam slipping through the opening with his guitar. He lifts his gaze long enough to meet mine, a flicker of a smile slides across his mouth. He looks happy, peaceful. Almost like the boy he once was before everything...

Isla leans in. "You look beautiful. I'm glad you two will finally make it official."

Tears threaten to spill so I look up and blink rapidly before kissing her hair. "Thanks, baby. I love you."

"I love you too."

"Everyone ready?" Dad asks.

"I think so. Where are Teagan, Torin, Tristan, and Raff?"

"Not a smudge between the four of them." Ronni and Mara guide the kids, who are tossing flowers and carrying rings.

We line up and the doors open. Conversation hushes into a tide that recedes and returns. Liam strums a melody he wrote at nineteen and pretends isn't about us even though everyone knows it is.

I spot him under the arch.

Padraig wears a suit in soft charcoal. White shirt open at the throat with no tie. His boots are polished and his hair is tucked behind his ears. He's the same boy on the school bus with drumsticks in his back pocket and charcoal under his nails because he sketched when he should have been in algebra.

When he sees me, he beams. Wipes his eyes on his sleeve.

Teagan sprinkles the path ahead with petals. Isla, Lila, Jude, and Seamus serve as our bridal party. Dad steps forward with measured care. I hold on to his arm, then let go when the path narrows and we stop beside Padraig and he hands me over to my man.

Liam switches keys without showmanship and folds his melody into silence. The officiant clears his throat, and we say our vows in front of our families. We exchange rings without fanfare. Our kiss isn't cinematic. No dip. Simple but passionate, we press our lips together while everyone cheers.

We turn toward our families as someone pops a cork on sparkling cider. Tables fill without drama. Maureen's feast is carried to the buffet by Padraig's brothers. Slow-roasted beef, salmon with dill, buttery new potatoes, and bright summer vegetables. At the center of it all waits our two-tiered wedding cake. One layer lemon cheesecake. The other chocolate fudge.

Our families fill their plates with food. Padraig carries Kellan to join us at the head of the table where he and I are sitting. Stories start without anyone having to ask for a prompt. Rory starts the toasts—or roasts, because all of the brothers slag Padraig and me to death. By the end of it, my stomach hurts from laughing so hard.

I'm surprised when Isla stands and grabs the mike.

"So, this isn't a speech, I'd call it a vow." Her gaze steadies on us. "The past will always be part of me, but it no longer holds me back. What matters now is the love I see between you, and the way it pulls us forward. I believe in it. I believe in us. I'll keep choosing this family, every day. I promise."

No one claps. Applause would flatten it. I lean on Padraig's shoulder, he wraps his arm around me. I'm overcome with emotion and gratitude. Rory bows his head over his water, he's a man who knows what vows mean when they're spoken for real. Ma presses the corner of a napkin to her eye. My mom blows me a kiss.

Dusk folds across the yard. Café bulbs spark to life, softening every face. Liam moves to the edge of the deck. Connor and Avonna join them and they play a medley of LTZ and Fireball songs with a sprinkling of other hits thrown in. Padraig's hand slips into mine beneath the table, his thumb traces the ridge where my wedding ring now sits, as if he's reminding himself this moment belongs to both of us.

It's not a dream anymore. We're finally married. It only took us twenty-plus years to get here.

"I love you." He nuzzles my neck. "Dance with me."

We stand and he holds his hand out. The air pulses with our love and all we've endured. From our youth and breakup. passionate nights to days where silence cut sharper than words, mornings when Kellan's laugh stitched me back together cell by cell, hours in quiet rooms where therapy gave us permission to speak and to heal.

It all lives in the fabric of our blended family, woven into the scent of roses. Illuminated by the glow of the bulbs strung overhead and the energy of our amazing extended family.

I lift my eyes. "I love you too. So much."

Evening light glances along his chiseled jawline, which softens into the smile I've known since we chased each through the hedge at seven.

The boy lives inside the man. The man holds the life we've built with stubborn, tender hands.

He leads me over stones my father set when I was ten.

Voices fade until only Liam's guitar remains, strumming our wedding song.

The only thing remaining is me and the man who is and always will be my forever flame.

Want one more moment with Padraig and Stevie? Read the bonus scene here.

Loved their story? A quick review goes a long way—thank you for supporting indie romance!

He'll never stop living for the band. But it's time Liam learns to live for love, too.
Preorder Hushed Harmony.

Behind the Scenes

If you've read any books in the *Charming Irish* series or *Fearless* in the *Less Than Zero* series, you've already met the McGloughlin brothers. Each with their own scars, secret and personalities. All of whom display fierce loyalty to the family that shaped them.

The twins, Padraig and Liam, have always stood a little apart. Talented. Aloof. Wildly successful. And maybe a little unreachable.

Until now.

Forever Flames is Padraig's story, but it's also the beating heart of the McGloughlin universe. This book peels back the layers—the music, the silence, the grief—to show how a boy thrown into family chaos finds his forever in the girl next door.

Stevie and Padraig's journey spans decades. Their bond was forged in fire, tested by time, and deepened by loss. They are each other's first love, first heartbreak, first everything. Their story is about finding your way back, even when everything has changed.

Forever Flames let me explore everything I love: complicated family dynamics, generational trauma, and the way love can hurt, heal, and reshape us. It was a chance to revisit the events of *Fearless* and the rest of the *Charming Irish* series through a new lens, showing the ripple effect of the choices we make in response to tragedy.

At the same time, I had to balance the emotional weight of *Forever Flames* with the secret scaffolding of *Hushed Harmony*, Liam's story (coming soon). It wasn't easy not to spoil you, but necessary. You'll get glimpses of Liam here, and when you do, I hope you feel the gravity of everything he's holding and get excited to read his journey to the type of love he never expected to experience.

In conclusion, this book gutted me in the best way. Writing it meant stripping Padraig down to his barest truth and letting him earn the love he never stopped chasing. And Stevie? She's everything. Strong, smart, heartbroken, resilient, hopeful. Helping them find their way back to each other reminded me why I write romance in the first place.

At its core, *Forever Flames* is about soulmates who never stopped burning. I hope it stays with you long after the final page.

With all my love,

Kaylene

Comforting Beef Barley Soup

INGREDIENTS

- 2 lbs beef chuck or stew meat, cut into small cubes
- 1 tbsp olive oil
- 1 large yellow onion, diced
- 2 carrots, peeled and sliced
- 2 celery stalks, sliced
- 3 garlic cloves, minced
- 2 tbsp tomato paste
- 8 cups beef broth (preferably homemade or low-sodium)
- 1 cup pearl barley, rinsed
- 2 tsp Worcestershire sauce
- 1 tsp dried thyme
- 1 bay leaf
- Salt and pepper to taste
- Fresh parsley, chopped (for garnish)

DIRECTIONS

Thick with tenderness. Tastes better the second day—if it lasts that long.

Sear the beef: In a heavy-bottomed soup pot or Dutch oven, heat olive oil over medium-high heat. Brown the beef in batches, seasoning with salt and pepper. Remove and set aside.

Build the base: Lower heat to medium. Add onion, carrots, and celery. Sauté for 5–7 minutes, scraping up any browned bits. Stir in garlic and tomato paste; cook until fragrant, about 1 minute.

Simmer it slow: Return beef to the pot. Add broth, barley, Worcestershire, thyme, and bay leaf. Bring to a boil, then reduce heat and simmer uncovered for 60–75 minutes, stirring occasionally, until beef is tender and barley is plump.

Taste and adjust: Discard the bay leaf. Taste and season with more salt and pepper as needed.

Serve hot: Ladle into deep bowls and top with chopped parsley. Serve with buttered soda bread or buttered brown bread.

Acknowledgments

COVER/GRAPHIC DESIGNER/FINDER OF HOTTIES: Regina Wamba
Editor: Grace Bradley Editing, LLC
Formatting: Willow Yanarella
PR: Dani Sanchez, Wildfire Marketing
Literary Agent: Stephanie Phillips, SBR Media
Website Maven: Sherri Kiarsis, Ruby Moon Designs
My Right Hand: Willow Yanarella
A special thank you the Kaylene's Backstage Krew!

Dedication

As always, to my husband and all to of our siblings.

About the Author

KAYLENE WINTER IS A best-selling author of steamy, contemporary romance.

Each character-driven novel is filled with snappy dialogue, pop-culture references and enough steam to make you fan yourself. Kaylene weaves authenticity, emotion and angst into a turbulent rollercoaster ride of love, passion and soul-searing romance always ending with a delicious HEA.

Kaylene lives in Seattle with her amazing Irish husband and her Pomsky, Phalen. She loves creating art of all kinds.

Other Titles